Robert A. Durant was born in 1936, number eight in a family of nine children. He saw the first of four older brothers leave for WWII in 1941. His dad was a share-crop farmer. Robert learned to plow at the age of 12. He worked as an Ad Composer in newspapers for 17 years. In 1974, he went to work for a chemical plant in Lufkin, Texas, producing Formaldehyde and Industrial resins. He retired in 1999 as a Lead Operator Technician. It was after he retired that he wrote *In the Shade of the Oaks*. He still loves to work in his garden, spend time with his wife of 60 years, and their four children and grandchildren.

Robert A. Durant

IN THE SHADE OF THE OAKS

AUSTIN MACAULEY PUBLISHERS™

LONDON * CAMBRIDGE * NEW YORK * SHARJAH

Ordering Information:
Quantity sales: special discounts are available on quantity purchases by corporations, associations, and others. For details, contact the publisher at the address below.

Publisher's Cataloguing-in-Publication data
Durant, Robert A.
In the Shade of the Oaks

ISBN 9781641823326 (Paperback)
ISBN 9781641823333 (Hardback)
ISBN 9781641823340 (E-Book)

The main category of the book — Fiction / Romance / Contemporary

www.austinmacauley.com/us

First Published (2019)
Austin Macauley Publishers LLC
40 Wall Street, 28th Floor
New York, NY 10005
USA

mail-usa@austinmacauley.com
+1 (646) 5125767

Introduction

First and foremost, this is a work of fiction. I do use the first names of my five brothers and three sisters. Using DuPree as a fictional last name. This book does not reflect where they live or what they do.

As a 15 year-old boy plowing in the fields or on the end of a cross-cut saw helping my Dad cut hardwood saw logs in 1951, I dreamed of becoming wealthy and owning a big cattle ranch, among other things.

I never became wealthy after paying into Social Security for almost 50 years, so I decided to write this book, give a fictional 15-year-old boy, in my family's circumstances in 1951, a way to obtain wealth, accomplish my dreams, and much more.

I used the names of actual Texas towns to bring attention to the area. Business places past or present are fictional. All names of characters presented are fictional. Fictional names of characters used are not meant to reflect on anyone living or deceased.

Political, sports, academic or any other accomplishments used are not true. The ownership of property in areas described is fictional. Rivers or areas of land may be moved, or not described correctly as a conduit to this fictional story.

What I do hope to accomplish is capture "The Flavor of East Texas and the Language of its People". And hopefully, to help educate young people about the transition from being normal teenagers to adults.

This you can believe as truth. Because of clear-cutting timber harvesting, I believe oak timber in Texas and the South Eastern United States has become an endangered species. Some species of wildlife are becoming endangered as well. I encourage readers to join the fight to prevent the destruction of a natural resource that is so vital to our lives.

If you read this book, it's like you shared part of your lifetime here with me. I greatly appreciate that. Thanks!

Robert Durant.

Chapter One
Life at Fifteen as a Plow-boy

Daddy told me the evening before that I needed to lay this field of corn by today. Our horse 'Old Dan' and I had been steadily doing our best to get it done since sun up. He told me to find what plow attachments I needed to do the job.

We normally laid cornby with a middle buster plow. All we had was a number two Kelly turning plow and a Georgia Stock. I selected a nine-inch shovel and an 18 inch heel sweep for the job.

"Just use your own judgement and get the job done," he said. Dad was good about telling me to use my own judgement!

The nine inch shovel was badly rusted. With a lot of work with water and a piece of red brick, I finally got it bright enough to plow with. By the time I got the Georgia Stock rigged, Old Dan harnessed and hitched and dragged the plow to the field, the cool of morning was gone.

It took some adjusting of the plow and harness to get it to plow the way I wanted. I thought I was doing about as well as possible with what I had to do with.

I stuck the hammer in my belt when I started to the field. First, I knocked the old iron plow stock forward on the wood beam so the shovel stood more on the tip. Plowed a short distance.

Forward too much, it would wear Old Dan out in a hurry. I knocked the plow stock back some and plowed a little further. *Looked good and better for Old Dan,* I thought.

Dad had taught me the adjustments on different plows and harness. He said there were more adjustments on harness and plows than mother's Singer Sewing Machine. *I could make adjustments on a plow and harness, make the plow kiss my behind,* I thought.

Well, maybe it was not actually kissing my behind this morning. But the sweat running down my bare back was about to. It was mid-June, the year of 1951. I had turned 15 the 24th day of March. I was a little old to be between the eighth and ninth grade in school.

Truth of the matter, I had flunked the first grade. I never went to school enough to pass. Mother said she never knew a boy could be so sick, and get well so quick after the school bus passed the house. After doing the first grade over, I managed to get on through the eighth grade.

The other thing about missing school; farm kids never started school in September. They started about the first of November, after all the crops were harvested. I was small, yet I could drive a wagon. Even drag a burlap bag with an old neck tie for a shoulder strap to pick dry peas or cotton. All farm kids worked.

The ninth grade held forth the only thing about that school that really interested me. I wanted to play football. All five of my older brothers had played as Buffalo Bison's. I did not intend to break the tradition. I was hell bent on making it six. Although I had not heard of Bob Lilly at the time, I wanted to be like him!

Truth of the matter, I thought teachers and students looked down on farm boys. Seemed to me the only way a farm boy could get any respect was to make that football team. My brothers had been coaching me since I was big enough to run with a corn cob. I was ready to prove to them and folks in Buffalo that I had what it took!

Well, there was one other thing about that school that did interest me now. She moved from Oakwood and started eighth grade with my class. Her name was Margaret Burkett. I never knew why she got behind in school, but she and I were the same age.

A couple of things I noticed about her right away; she was beautiful! Seemed the rest of the boys in the class never noticed that. I looked at the girl, not the wrapping. Her dresses were homemade. Her mother must have been great with a sewing machine. The intricate patterns of rick-rack on the dresses indicated that. But that rick-rack indicated homemade.

Margaret had warm brown eyes. The kind that could convey a message across a room. I sort of thought they conveyed the message that she liked me too. Some people with dark brown or black eyes, you can't read or trust. Hers were not like that.

She appeared to have a little Spanish or Indian blood in her background. Her skin was flawless, a little on the tan side. So beautiful I wanted to lick it!

She never wore make-up; I suspected she could not afford it. Her dresses were made from the same material my underwear was made from. Eighteen percent dairy feed printed sacks, or chicken feed sacks. But what stood out was that she was always clean and neat.

She never volunteered a lot in class, but when called on, she could answer the question. It became apparent she was the smartest kid in the class; her grade point average was higher than any of us. She never acted like she was aware of that. As a matter of fact, I got the feeling she never liked this school any better than I did.

Somehow, I always kept looking at her across the classroom, only to discover she was looking at me. Our eyes would meet, she would turn a little red, and quickly look away. If she did not catch me looking at her, I caught her looking at me. When that happened; we both looked quickly away.

After a few weeks of this at school, and always on my mind when away, I decided to try something different the next time our eyes met. It would require some cooperation from the teacher. She needed to turn her back side to the class.

The first time the teacher turned her back to the class, I looked at Margaret. Our eyes met. I stuck my tongue out at her!

At first, I thought I made the blunder of my lifetime. Her eyes registered shock, then anger. I quickly gave her my best smile. Her anger faded, her face relaxed, and I got the best smile I thought I ever had. We never looked away until the teacher turned around.

After that, when our eyes met, they locked together in longer sessions, and we both smiled. I managed to get behind her in the lunch line, and to my surprise, she started talking to me. That progressed to PE and we started spending time together.

Our time spent together at lunch time and PE became a regular occurrence. I never missed another day of school, the rest of the year. As a matter of fact, my grades improved. I was attracted to Margaret because she was so beautiful and intelligent. I would learn later, she was first attracted to me because of my last name. DuPree.

It was about mid-morning now. One thing about farm work is that you can think about other things. I admit Margaret was that 'other thing on my mind'. It was time to give Old Dan and myself a break. I had been stopping every now and then at the end of the row, to let him rest a little. A nine-inch shovel and 18-inch heel sweep is a chore, I knew.

One thing Dad believed in was taking care of his livestock. He often expressed the opinion that's the way people judged you; the condition you kept your livestock and fences in. Keep your livestock fat and your fence post straight and the wire tight.

It was the same with the crops in the field; they had to be cultivated to perfection. Dad did everything he did to the best of his ability and resources. I would have jumped in the middle of anyone that said he did not.

I turned Old Dan under the shade of a post oak tree, at the end of the rows and stuck the plow in the ground. I yelled "Whoa!" Old Dan was definitely ready to hear those words. He stopped in his tracks. I took the plow line rope from my shoulders and snubbed them up tight to the plow handles.

He had a muzzle on his nose, made from hog wire. He could not crop, corn, or graze. I knew he would not go anywhere while I was gone. He knew as well as I did, the only profitable thing for him to do was rest until I returned.

At the house, I stopped at the well, drew up a fresh bucket and took it into the kitchen to mother. She heard me at the well and had me a glass of ice ready.

This was the second house we lived in that had electricity. No running water, or indoor plumbing. But thank God, electricity! I sat down at the kitchen table to enjoy my cold glass of water. Mother was finishing shelling the last wash tub of cream peas. Dad and I had picked two tubs full yesterday afternoon. He and mother, Virginia, and I had shelled until bed time last night.

She had her pressure cooker going on the stove. Also, a pot of those peas and a pot of tomato vegetable soup which contained tomatoes, potatoes, okra, cut corn, and cabbage. The first thing I did coming in the kitchen was look in the pots to see what dinner would be. I knew it would be the same thing for supper as well.

About the only convenience she had in that kitchen was the refrigerator. Older sister Faye had got a new one and brought us her old. It was in good shape. I think sister Faye and husband wanted Mother to have a refrigerator.

Mother was cooking on a kerosene stove, which I thought was worse off than the wood stove she had until I was about ten. Sometimes you could actually taste the kerosene in the food.

When I got up to go, she said what I knew she was going to say. "Get a shirt on! It's too hot in that field to be without a shirt." So, I went and got a shirt. If one wanted to call it that. It was like a heavy t-shirt; one pocket and blue-gray in color.

Mother had ordered three from Sears, one blue-gray, one dark blue, and the other, green. Three for a dollar! The dark blue and green had worn out. I liked the blue and green better, suppose that's why I still had the blue-gray. It had stretched a lot but offered some protection from the sun and plow lines on my shoulders.

I stopped at the well and pulled up another bucket. Poured it in a five-gallon bucket I kept there. I took it back to the field and let Old Dan drink. It was not necessary to take the muzzle off. He could suck it all up through that wire. When he raised his head up, we hit that field again.

There's a few things I never mentioned about this field of corn. Dad had me plant a row and skip a row. He meant to plant the skipped row in speckled peas, but decided not to. Mother about had all her fruit jars full already.

So Old Dan and I were plowing two rounds to the middle. Or four trips to the middle. I meant to plow over the patch like this. Then adjust the plow and plow the middle out. Five trips to the middle. About an acre and a half of corn. But a lot of trips!

This corn was a little unique. It was brought to Texas in 1856 by my great-grandfather DuPree. Some ears were yellow, some pink. It had a very small diameter cob, and a very long grain. It cut off a lot for cooking and canning. And it was great for livestock feed. Dad fattened hogs on it. In the family, we called it the 'Dupree Corn'. But over the years, a lot of it had been given to Leon County Texas neighbors.

Dad had lost his seed for this corn. He made a special trip to visit his older brother Alex to get seed from him. This field was planted with that seed. Dad hoped to keep seed from this planting. Droughts, floods, other things can cause crop failures and loss of seed. One way or another, this corn had been kept in the Texas Dupree family for 95 years. I thought if I ever had children, I would pass on the DuPree name. And the DuPree corn!

The place we were living on now belonged to my dad's oldest sister. It was a small tract of land, only about 60 acres. My aunt's husband had died years ago with TB. Left her with four boys to raise. They grew up, married, scattered here and there. She lived alone for a number of years. But about two years ago, because of her age and health, she left to live with a son. Rather than rent the place, she asked Dad to move on the place. She knew he would keep the place up.

Dad had quit farming in 1948. We moved into town, he got a job night watching and clean-up duty at a handle factory sawmill using ash timber. When all the ash timber was cut in the surrounding area, the mill shutdown and moved.

Dad worked some cutting logs in the woods at a sawmill pallet manufacturing place, driving nails ten hours a day. Dad could drive nails with either arm. Yet his elbows swelled. Both jobs were part time, with periods of work or no work at all.

We moved on his sister's place, because the sawmill offered him a deal to buy a tract of hardwood timber adjoining her place. In short, the owner never trusted the sawmill owner. He would not sell to him. The sawmill put up the money for the board feet of timber. They paid Dad enough to give him a job, hire a helper, and pay for the timber. Dad had known the timber owner for years. He trusted Dad to buy it and handle the deal, which Dad explained to him.

Chapter Two
Family History and Love at Fifteen

This was the part of the county where my mother grew up. It was only about two miles to the place her parents owned. The place was still owned by Mother's brother; his daughter and husband lived there. He bought his three sisters share after Grandmother died. After her death, he moved to Houston to work.

A sister of Mother's and her husband owned the place next to Grandmother's. Her husband died and after her son went to Houston to work, she moved in with her daughter and son-in-law. He managed the place, she still had her cattle and a couple of horses. She let us keep Old Dan and a good Jersey milk cow. We would feed and pasture both, return any calf born to the cow.

Since we still had some chickens, two spotted Poland China sows with shoats, and Dad had a timber cutting job, we still existed in Leon County. Now you see why I was plowing this corn and farming about five other acres of assorted produce. Enough to help feed ourselves, and livestock.

Across the county road from the house was about a five-acre part of the place. About three acres were fenced for a hog pasture. She let a son build a house on two acres. Like a lot of married families in the county, they moved to Houston to find work. He rented his home out. We never knew who lived there when we moved.

It was late the next day we were there. Guess who came walking through the front yard gate. Margaret! Margaret Burkett. With her mother, a younger sister, and two younger brothers.

Mother and Dad were elated when her mom told them who she was. She was Sam Craig's younger sister. They had not seen her since she was a little girl, the same age as my oldest brother.

Her husband, Otis Ray Burkett was away at sea somewhere, he was a merchant seaman. He never came home very often. Last time he did, he rented my aunt's son's place, moved them, and left. She had four children to raise 12 miles from town and no transportation. We would find out more about her husband later. Let me explain about the Craig name and why it meant a lot to my family. Remember in your history books about the French-Huguenot wars? Old Bethel DuPree and Sam Craig left France to escape getting their heads removed.

They hired on as ship hands bound for Charleston, South Carolina. The ship captain opted to make slaves out of them. At gun point, when the ship docked at Charleston, they were locked up and not let off the ship. "Help sail this ship or drown," he said.

They were freed by another slave on the ship who the captain thought he could trust. They tied the captain up, located his stash of gold and silver, took that and loaded weapons and provisions in a small sail boat.

They set the ship on fire, went up river from Charleston. Bethel and Sam gave the slave that freed them a fair share of what they had in the boat. He parted ways from them.

They both settled on nearby land, both married a Cherokee Indian Woman. Their first sons were named after their father, Bethel Dupree and Sam Craig. Thus, it was my great-grandparent Bethel Dupree and Margaret's, Sam Craig came to Leon County Texas in 1856.

My grandfather was named William Bethel Dupree. William was added because his mother's father first name was William. Margaret's uncle was still Sam Craig. He and my dad spent a lot of time together in their growing up years.

Dad was named Benjamin Franklin Dupree. One brother was James Alexander, one Eugene Coley, the other William Bethel Dupree. His sisters were Jettie, Mary, and Annie.

When they arrived in Centerville, Texas, with their families, Bethel and Sam both needed land. Bethel to farm, grow cotton, corn, and other crops. Sam had a different interest. He needed land to raise horses, mules, cattle, and hogs. He brought a long-eared jack-ass with him for breeding purposes. Both could buy Long Horn Cattle, Mustang Wild Horses in Texas.

Each had three slaves to help on the long trip to Texas. Two big freight and four smaller covered wagons. Their families were in the big wagons. Sleeping and cooking was done in and from these big wagons. They fed the slaves, who did their sleeping in the small wagons.

Sam and Bethel both had two men slaves. One of the men slaves for each had a woman. These women helped their wives. On this long wagon trip, their wives and the slave women drove wagons. The oldest of Bethel's three children was six years old. Sam had a boy and girl, six and eight years old.

They had some Jersey milk cows and a couple of bulls. A couple of stud horses, and about 12 head of mares and geldings for riding, ten mules, and of course, Sam's Jack. They had to be herded behind the wagons, getting what grass they could as they walked. They soon learned not to try to stray, that they had a lot of walking to do.

Bethel had a half-brother already living in Centerville, Texas. He had visited Bethel, told him about a place called Washington on the Brazos, Texas and a steamboat line that maintained a warehouse there. They had a lot of their things shipped there. It was stored in the warehouse, for a fee of course.

So much of their personal furniture and things like dishes, silverware, and bedsteads had been shipped there. Most of their mattresses were on plank slats laying over a load in the covered wagons. All, except the one with the hogs and chickens! After they had built homes, they would go there for it.

Old Sam and Bethel were like brothers. Sam meant to only farm enough to feed his family and livestock. Bethel meant to farm and feed the family and livestock, ship cotton and corn north to be sold.

There were steam boat landings on both the Trinity and Brazos Rivers. The town of Houston was mostly where he shipped from. He could buy merchandise and transport back to the merchants in Centerville.

Story goes they rode out of Centerville to look at land they could homestead 160 acres on, buy adjoining land. They separated on the Centerville and Buffalo road at a community now called Social Grove.

Bethel rode east to the forks of Buffalo and Big Keechi creeks. In later years, the area would be called Beaver Lodge Marsh. He rode over a lot of it, killed a swamp rabbit for his supper and camped for the night. *This is perfect for Sam, not what I need*, he thought.

Old Sam rode west to land near and on Blitz creek. Hillside sandy soil, thin timber and easy to clear for farming. It was not far from the Buffalo community, although he never knew that at the time.

He camped for the night, roasted the breasts from a green head mallard duck he killed on a pond. *This land is perfect for Old Bethel*, he thought, *but not for me. I'll explore more in the morning.*

Old Sam was closer to where they separated, he rode around exploring some more. He found a five-acre lake which later became the DuPree Lake. On the way back to the separation point, he killed a big doe deer.

So many, no need to kill one until near where they parted. He field dressed the deer and tied it behind his saddle. At the separation point, he removed the inside tenderloins and started roasting it over a fire.

It was well after dark when his tied horse started pointing his ears and looking in the direction Old Bethel should come from. He grabbed his rifle, hid behind a tree away from the fire.

He never relaxed until he heard the sound of a Bob White Quail calling. He answered with the same call. He knew it was Old Bethel. They both knew nobody but them would use a Bob White Quail call after dark.

Old Bethel had a big ten-point buck deer behind his saddle. They ate the cooked meat, told each other what they had found. The opinion that each had found what the other needed.

Then they hit the road back to Centerville in the dark night with rifles across the saddle and hands on the pistol on their hips. This was a dangerous and vastly unsettled land. Outlaws and Indians were known to be about. Their families needed meat, they now had some.

Now maybe you know why Margaret had her eye on me. The DuPree name was one she recognized from way back. It sort of burst my bubble. I thought it had been my looks! But now it seemed to me it had been something between our families for a lot of years.

I plowed Old Dan out to the end of the corn rows next to the road. From here, I could see the front porch of the house she lived in. Hog wire had been stretched across the end of the porch, with honey suckle vines growing on it.

I knew Margaret was sitting behind those vines probably reading a book. I had caught a glimpse of movement a few times. I thought she was watching me when I plowed out to that end of the row. I had to get the grass roots out of the plow, spend a minute or two.

I was about ready to go back to my plowing. Then I saw the screen door open. I could see the top of her mother's head over the top of those honey suckle vines. I could tell she was talking to someone. Then a minute later, her mother went back inside, I saw the screen door close.

Minutes later Margaret came off the porch with the water bucket in her hand. She walked out to the well as cool as a cucumber, like she never knew I was watching her every move. I assure you, her every move was something to behold.

She started letting the bucket down in the well. Most people used a rope on their well pulley. This one had a chain, about the size people tie dogs with. A rope was much easier to handle, I hated that rough chain in her beautiful hands.

She had the bucket down now, I knew. Standing there listening for the gurgling sound when it filled up. She heard the sound. Both hands on the chain above her head, she began to pull down on the chain. She placed her bare foot on the chain to hold it and reached up for another pull. This is how she would get that heavy bucket of water up from 25 feet in the well.

Where there is a will, there is a way. She had the will and the way. When she pulled down on that chain, her behind pointed right at me. Doubt she realized that of course, but it excited me big time.

But as much as I was enjoying the view, it upset me as well. She had a younger, but much bigger and stronger brother than she was. Why, I wondered, did his mother not send him out for a bucket of water?

I wanted to run there and help her. But I knew she would finish and be in the house before I could get there.

With a dipper hanging there, she had a long drink of that cool water. Starting to the house with that heavy bucket, it had her leaning over. But she looked right at me with that beautiful smile and waved. Then she started laughing and up the porch steps and into the house she went!

I made about three more rounds and decided to call it dinner time. I was about two thirds of the way over the field now. In the shade of the post oak again, I laid the collar and harness back over the plow beam.

At the barn, I fed Old Dan five ears of corn. At the well, I drew up two buckets and poured in the five-gallon bucket. He could get to that and drink after he finished his corn, cob, shuck and all. The pasture gate was closed, no problem to catch him later.

Dinner that day might look like hard times to folks these days. But today, if I were the president of this country, I would eat what we had at least two days a week. But since I am not president, I may eat those things four days a week now.

To those fresh cream peas and the tomato soup that was cooking when I left; fried okra, squash and cornbread had been added, along with fresh tomatoes, onion shallots and sweet banana pepper!

Mother asked me if I had seen Margaret while I was up in the field. I told her I saw her come out to the well and draw a bucket of water. I never thought I needed to tell her anything else. Even that I wondered why her bigger and younger brother never did that.

But Mom knew. She was on to me about the way I felt about Margaret. After Mom's reunion with her mother, she asked what I thought about Margaret.

"Well she's in my class at school. Not only is she the prettiest girl in our class, she is the smartest! And she ain't a snob like some are."

When a mother digs that kind of reply out of a boy, she knows alright. But she seemed to be pleased about it.

There were things I never told her of course. It had happened back in April before school was out. Margaret and I now rode the school bus together. Sometimes we sat together on the bus. Sometimes another girl sat with her before I got on the bus.

Then there was her bigger (but younger) brother Harry. He was like stuff on a skunk's back. He was in the seat behind us, or the seat in front of us. He interrupted whatever we might be talking about. Margaret finally told me her dad told Harry to tell him everything she said or did. Harry got things and privileges from his dad for being a rat fink.

I never met her dad face to face. But I rode by there one day on Old Dan. He was standing in the yard looking right at me. I waved at the man. He never waved back. Just stood there, looking at me like I had some sort of venereal disease. He was still standing there when I rode back by. I resisted the urge to shoot him the bird, but never did. I just rode on by like I never saw him.

My peripheral vision has always been good. I could see I turned the worm. That I ignored his presence had angered him, I could tell. About 50 yards away, I glanced back. He was still standing there looking like he could cut my head off. *No telling what Harry had told him*, I thought.

Monday on the bus, Harry told me his dad had bought him a horse. Built a barb wire pen around some trees in the front yard to keep it in. His Dad had left to get a ship out of the Houston area somewhere.

Now, I may be a little dumb, but I ain't slow. If Margaret had a horse to ride, perhaps we could ride off somewhere together.

Back in those days, the first thing to do when you got home from school was change into work duds. I had three brothers in WWII.

A pair of army fatigue pants with the big pockets was what I had. Little big, but that was it. A pair of combat boots. The kind that laced half way up, the top part was held together with two buckles.

The old blue-gray T-shirt topped it off.

After changing, I saddled Old Dan and rode down there. I rode up to the pen the horse was in. I wondered what kind of fool would build a horse pen that small. But I kept that thought to myself.

Harry was in the pen trying to catch the horse. Not having a lot of luck. I knew where the mare came from. It was kept in a pasture place between us and the highway.

I was sitting there, my right leg over the saddle in front of me. Margaret was standing there by me, talking to me. She was amused at watching Harry trying to catch that horse in that little pen, as was I.

"Gotcha!"

I looked to see Margaret's mom, standing there with a camera. She had made mine and Margaret's picture together. I laughed. I should have worn a tie with this suit!

I got down, got in the pen with Harry and the horse. "Hand me the rope and bridle."

He did. I just threw the rope over the mare's neck. She stopped. I put the bridle on her and led her out of the pen. Really a good looking black horse. *For how long*, I wondered?

"There Harry," his Mother said. "That's the way it's done." Harry could not get on the bareback horse. She took the bridle reins, led the horse up by the porch. "Now you can get on, Harry."

Harry and I took a ride down the road together. When we got back, his mother was back in the house. I said: "Who's next?"

Harry never got down off his horse. I put little Kevin up in my saddle, let him and Harry take a ride. When they got back, Katrina got on Old Dan and she and Harry went for a ride.

While they were gone, Margaret told me her dad said that horse was Harry's. Nobody was to ride it but him.

"When we still lived on the Craig place, my Uncle Sam let me ride a horse he had. I rode with him often, in the woods checking on his hogs. Rounding up his cattle, horses and mules. I loved that horse so much." She sounded extremely bitter.

When they got back, she got on Old Dan. They were gone a good little bit before I saw her coming back. About 40 yards away, she put Old Dan in a run. Turned into the yard on the run. Swung one foot out of the saddle, stepped on the ground with that foot. Hand on horn, swung out of the saddle. Both feet were on the ground as Old Dan slid to a stop.

No doubt about it. She could ride and handle a horse.

Harry never came back with her. We stood there and talked. She commented she hoped the picture turned out well. She would get her mother to have a copy made for her. I told her she wanted it because I was dressed so well. But she kept looking down the road to see if Harry was coming back.

14

I knew she was worried about him. In spite of however her dad treated him and her, he was her brother. Being number eight in a family of nine, I understood that. I got on Old Dan, told her I would go look for him. He may have fell off the horse and can't get back on. I could tell that what I did pleased her. Pleasing Margaret had become the first ambition in my life.

Harry was a mile down the road when I caught up with him. He could not get the horse to turn around! The horse had been trained to neck rein like all riding horses are in our part of Texas. He did not know that. His horse knew he wanted to turn around. But horses, or mules, can sense fear or lack of experience in a person trying to handle them. The mare decided to just ignore Harry and keep on walking.

I grabbed her bridle bit and stopped her. Then showed him the technique of neck reining. Had him practice for a few minutes. The horse responded well. They left a lot of tracks in the road there, back and forth, but he got the technique down. Then we started back home.

I got to thinking about how Harry was his dad's pet fink. It was clear to me his biggest ambition right now was to master riding that horse and become a cowboy. I decided maybe I could offer him an opportunity to give him a feeling he was one. And give Margaret and I a chance to ride off together on old Dan without him following us.

"Harry, do you know James Brader that lives about half a mile past where we turned around?"

"Yeah, I think I do. He's the one with those chicken houses and lives in that brown house."

"That's him. He's my first cousin's old man. Wants me to come in a week or two and help move a bunch of cattle from one pasture to another. About two miles down the county road. Thought maybe you might want to come with us. Probably take all the help we can get. Lots of gates to open! He'll let me know when to come."

Don't think you could have driven a toothpick up his behind with a sledge hammer at the prospect of driving cattle. Yes, he wanted to help! "Then we'll leave shortly after dinner on a Saturday." We were back at their place now. I waved at Margaret sitting on the porch and went on home.

Sitting with Margaret on the bus, I asked her if she could get the horse so we could ride that afternoon. There was a place I wanted her to see.

"No, daddy said only Harry was to ride that horse. He would tell daddy and he would jump on my case. Which would upset mother. I don't want that to happen."

"We could ride Old Dan double. There is a place I want you to see."

"Harry would just follow us. And tell daddy."

"I think I know where to stop Harry from following us. And not tell his daddy. He wants to be a cowboy!"

"Alright, I'll go. He's been talking constantly about going with you on a cattle drive. Sounds like all the way to Dodge City! But Harry always goes straight to the outhouse when he gets off the bus. If we hurry, we can leave before he knows we are gone."

I never changed clothes. I had Old Dan saddled in minutes. She was standing by the road when I got there. I slipped behind the saddle, she got in the saddle. We were 40 yards down the yard when we heard Harry yell, "Wait for me!" We just went on.

At the end of their place, the county road made a 90 degree turn left. There a private road to the property Dad was cutting timber on that turned right. Had to open a big long plank gate to get in. I could open that gate wide enough for Old Dan without getting off. And push it shut. Harry would have to get off. And climb on the gate to get back on. *He would be there in a few minutes,* I thought.

As we started on from the gate, Margaret said, "He will be able to follow our tracks."

"Yes, he will. But I know where he can't follow any further." I spurred Old Dan, turned left about 200 yards down that private road. Rode through the woods another couple hundred yards to a hog wire fence. With only one barb wire on top.

I got off Old Dan. A post had rotted off at ground level. With my foot, I pushed the post, hog wire and all over. Stood on the post and said, "Come on, Dan!" He was careful about where he stepped and crossed over the wire. I stood the post, wire backup to look like a normal fence.

Margaret had slipped behind the saddle. "You can drive better up front. You know where we are going! Does this horse always do everything you tell it to?"

"No, not always. But remember, I told you I was taking you to a special place I often go to. Old Dan has crossed over that wire a number of times. I don't think Harry will follow us any further when he gets to that fence."

"I don't think he will, either," she said. Her arms were around my waist and I could feel her breasts against my back. Her touch was like a lightning bolt running through my body. Yet her words "you drive" were running through my mind.

"I can drive this horse, but I can't drive a car. I don't have a job. I want to take you on dates. Like the Saturday night picture show in Buffalo. The future seems so hopeless in this county to do anything after we graduate from high school."

"Robert, I know how you feel. But Mother says you work harder, know how to do so many things most boys your age can't do. I know you will leave this county, find a job and get out of this rut we live in. When you go, I want to go with you!" Her arms tightened around my waist, her body came closer to mine. Her face was against mine over my shoulder.

I never knew what to say, I put my hand over hers on my waist. Electricity was running through my body. Words would not come to me right now. My passion, the way I felt about her, was something I knew I never wanted to live without.

We rode on in silence now. We crossed a small, always running spring branch. What we called a myrtle head draw came into the branch there. Up the center was an open area covered with carpet grass about 30 feet wide. The edges were lined with a row of those myrtle bushes.

Beyond those bushes on each side, the land rose up on large post oak tree covered hillsides.

Margaret broke the silence. "This is so beautiful! There were so many places like this on the Craig place. So often, Uncle Sam and I would find his cattle grazing in places that looked just like this."

About 50 yards up the draw, I turned right up the wooded hillside. Before getting to the crest of the hill, I stopped Old Dan. Got off and tied the bridle reins to an overhead post oak limb. A horse could not rub his bridle off tied like this and leave you.

Margaret was already down. I put my fingers to my lips to indicate 'no talk' and led her to a clump of yaupon bushes at the top of the hill. We lay down on the dry leaves behind those bushes so that we could see a small man-made pond over a fence. Flag grass, or cattails grew on the far edge of the pond.

A female Wood Duck was out in the open water of the pond. The water out in the cattails was waving, so I knew the male was there. After a few minutes, he came out into the open water. His colors were the most beautiful of all ducks I thought. These Ducks were an endangered species. It was against the game laws to shoot Wood Ducks.

We watched them for a few minutes. Suddenly the female lifted herself out of the water and left. The male quickly followed. I knew where another pond was I thought they probably went to.

Margaret said, "Down at the Craig place, I sometimes sat and watched Wood Ducks for hours. They are so beautiful. We never killed Wood Ducks. Uncle Sam said they were not good ducks to eat anyway. He bought lumber and built nesting boxes. I helped him. We put nesting boxes in the marsh, up Buffalo and Keechi Creeks as well. We had to wait until the creeks were up, we could not get far up those creeks when the creeks were down."

"Did you hunt Ducks?" She had used the words 'We never killed Wood Ducks.'

"Yes. Uncle Sam bought me a 16 gage, Winchester pump shotgun. Squirrels, ducks, and deer. I loved to hunt with Uncle Sam. My gun and saddle, Uncle Sam bought me. We lived in the Old Craig log house up by the road. Uncle Sam lived just above Beaver Lodge Marsh, between Buffalo and Keechi Creeks. When the creeks were down normal, he could cross either at rocky places in both creeks. If the creeks were up, then he could cross by boat and walk to check on us. Or drive out to the Flo Highway."

"Uncle Sam fished and sold fish to a place over at Long Lake. I liked helping him run his fishing lines a lot. He never used traps or nets. Said that way was cheating, not fair to the fish.

"He talked about your Dad a lot. Seemed to think of him as the brother he never had. Sad thing for me, Uncle Sam is the last male member of the Craig family with the Craig name. He had no children before he left his wife."

"Dad talks about your Uncle Sam a lot and things they did in their younger days. Going to dances, week long church singing conventions your Uncle Sam beating up on some dude that shot his Dad's hog, staying with the Craig's because he and your Uncle Sam got a job splitting 500 fence rails."

Margaret was always surprising me. She knew as much about wildlife and the outdoors as I did. And I realized she loved it all the way I did. I just said, "I envy that male Wood Duck. When she flies away, all he has to do is follow her. If I go anywhere, I have to walk or ride Old Dan."

"It's not going to be that way for you always," she said. She was looking into my eyes when she said it. Suddenly, we crossed a bridge we had never crossed. We kissed, were in each other's arms, holding each other close. But we soon ended it. I think we both were a little breathless, maybe a little shocked it happened to us so quickly.

I decided to say something that had me bothered. "We think the world of your mother and your Uncle Sam. We don't understand why your Dad don't treat the rest of you like he does Harry."

"My dad was and is a merchant seaman. He stopped at the store Mom worked at, in Oakwood. He was between ships and on leave with the guy Uncle Sam whipped for killing Grand Pa's hog. My dad stayed with a friend of both over at Long Lake. He kept stopping until she trusted him. He can act decently if it serves his purpose. They dated a few times and married quickly. He only came home often enough for the four of us to happen. Never gave mother but very little money for support. Mother tried, but after we were all born, and no help from him, she started to hate him. Because of her religious beliefs, she never has divorced him.

"Uncle Sam married after his service in WW II. Got a job at the glass factory in Palestine. One night he went to work, the factory had a shutdown. He came home early, found her in bed with my dad. Mother never knew he was in the vicinity. Dad pulled a switch blade knife on Uncle Sam. Uncle Sam took it away from him, beat him near to death. And told him if he ever saw him near our mother or us kids again, he would kill him.

17

"Uncle Sam gave his wife the home he bought in Palestine. He never divorced her either. He built a home for himself between the creeks. Said he never expected to marry again. He took Mother to work at the store in Oakwood every day.

"After grandma and grandpa were gone, Mother took a job in Buffalo, running a laundry wash house for people she knew from Oakwood. She never wanted her brother to have to take care of us the rest of his life.

I know Uncle Sam could defend himself against my Dad in a face to face fight but my dad carries that switch blade knife. I don't doubt he would stab him in the back. Sooner or later he will try to kill Uncle Sam, Mother believes.

"My dad kept coming around the store at Oakwood, then at Buffalo. One night the wash house burned down. Mother thinks he did it. But Mother lost her job. Could not find another. Rent was due.

"He offered to buy her something to drive and rent the place we live at now and send her money. The car broke down in town the third time she drove it in. Man looked at it, said it had a blown-up motor. That he would give her 50 dollars for parts. He had a car like it. He could use the parts.

"This time, Dad came in after months of being away, bought Harry that horse. Left Mother only a little money. He was angry with me because Harry told him I was sitting with you on the school bus. He and Mother got into it about that.

"It upsets her because he seems to hate me. Everyone but Harry, who looks and acts like him. I pray that Harry will see the light someday, realize he is being used. Right now, I don't know what Mother is going do."

Margaret was crying. I took her in my arms, held her close. I never knew what to say. I just let her cry it out. She finally pushed back and said she was sorry for crying and telling me all that. "I just needed to tell someone. You are the only one I've ever told about this."

I took the tail of my old gray T-shirt and dried her tears. "I'm glad you trusted me enough to tell. Daddy and I are up the road. He and mother will do what they can to help your mother. If things get out of hand, call on us. We'll do what we can. And if needed, Dad could probably go find your Uncle Sam. I'm sure he would come and give you whatever help you need."

That's when she looked me in the eyes and said, "I love you, Robert. You're everything my Daddy never will be!"

I pulled her against my chest, buried my face in her hair and whispered, "I love you too Margaret!"

I started out gently kissing her ear and around her face, until our lips met. It was a gentle tender thing at first that quickly turned to passion. I don't know how to describe what was happening to us. We were like two starving people without food for much too long. Food was set between them and they could not get enough of it.

She lay back on the ground, pulling me down with her. Our lips were locked together, partly open in passion. I stuck the tip of my tongue to hers that caused her to try to raise up closer under me. I had just started fumbling with the buttons on her blouse when we heard it.

"MAR-GAR-REET!"

Margaret started trying to push her way up. Maybe she was relieved to find an excuse to halt where we were going. Maybe I was too. I never had been there before. And I doubted she had either. We both sat back up in the leaves.

"MAR-GAR-REET!"

"That's Harry over at that fence! We better get back over there before he kills himself trying to get over that fence."

I got back up, took her hand, pulled her up. Dusted leaves from her hair and clothes. She did the same for me as we walked back to Old Dan.

He kept hollering, "MAR-GAR-REET" until he saw us coming. I rode up to the fence and stopped. I could see horse tracks both ways looking for a way to get over that fence. He had come back to where he had followed Old Dan's tracks to. And started hollering.

He was angry that he had got fooled. And stopped from following us. He jumped on Margaret's case. "I'm going to tell Daddy you went off in the woods with Robert!"

My turn to talk I decided. "Margaret and I are tired of you telling your Daddy about everything we do. If you tell him about this or anything else we do, you are not going with me on a cattle drive or anywhere else on a horse."

"How did yall get over that fence?"

"Did you hear what I just said? Are you going to tell on us anymore?" I put my best leaked off sounding voice and attitude into that statement.

"Ok! I won't never tell again! But how do you get over that fence?"

"Get down off your horse and I'll show you." I got down off Old Dan.

"See this post here? Grab it at the top. Now put your foot on it. Push it over. That's it! Now stand on it!"

I led Old Dan over. Got on Old Dan. Looked at him. "Let the fence up." He did. "You sure you are not going to tell on us anymore?"

"Yeah. I'm sure."

I spurred Old Dan and we rode off. Left him standing there. I could feel Margaret laughing against my back. It was 50 yards to a log he could use to get back on that horse. We would probably be home before he found that log and a way to get on his horse.

We were nearly to the plank gate when I looked back, saw Dad and his hired hand coming out from work. Margaret and I both got down at the gate, she held Old Dan by the road. I opened the gate back for Dad to drive through in Old Ida Red. The 1941 Red Ford Pickup that belonged to an older brother in the service. As they drove through, I heard Dad say "How you, little Lady?"

I could tell by the horse tracks here Harry had a tough time getting on his horse after opening the gate and closing it. The horse evidently resisted being led up beside that gate for him to climb up on to get on.

I saw him coming, waited for him to get there. Let him through, locked the gate. Dad unlocked the gate in the morning, left it open for the log trucks to come and go. The land owner normally kept it locked.

I got behind the saddle and Margaret. Harry had gone on. He may have been a little perturbed about how things went for him today. I now had my arms around her waist. And I whispered, "How you, little lady?"

I expected that she would laugh, but she never did, and sounded completely serious when she said, "This little lady is happier than she's been in a long time!" I could say nothing, just hug her tighter.

Margaret's mother was sitting on the front porch when we got there. Said she hoped we enjoyed our ride. She was always so nice to me. She had the ability to make me comfortable about being around her. As I rode away, I definitely heard the words "Wood Ducks" as the two went in the front door.

That night at supper, Dad said: "That Margaret's a right pretty girl, ain't she?" He looked at Mother and they both smiled. Then they both looked at me like they expected some sort of response from me.

Truth is, the way I felt and what I thought about Margaret was no laughing matter. I simply said, "Yes, she is the best looking girl I know. And the nicest. I like her better than any of the other girls at school."

Mother looked a little grave when she said, "Yes, she is a nice girl. Her mother comes from good people." Dad looked a little grave also, but he said nothing.

Margaret and I finished the eighth grade. We only had seen each other on the school bus, lunch time and PE since our ride together. On a Saturday, I took Harry on that cattle drive I promised him. His dad had not been home, but he did stay away from us when we were together.

After school let out for the summer, my job was to stay home, do whatever farming work was required. So here I was, middle of the afternoon. Laying that corn by.

No longer could I see Margaret or their house for that matter. Bushes grown up on the road side fence made that impossible now. No need to tarry at that end of the rows any longer. I got over the patch, adjusted the plow and busted out the center middle. One trip to the middle, never took long to finish the job. I thought it looked good. I hoped dad would as well.

I fed Old Dan a little, left the lot gate open so he could get to pasture and water. I was sitting on the kitchen steps drinking a cold glass of tea when I saw Daddy coming in. He stopped Old Ida Red, he and his hired hand walked to the fence to look at what I had did to that field of corn. They both were talking and pointing this way and that. To this day, I still wonder if a farmer could talk if he could not gesture and point.

Dad had to take the helper all the way to Buffalo. He would milk the cow when he got home. Before we left the Old Place, he got a winter job in town. I was eight and brother, Regan H. was about 12. Dad never got home until after dark, he put us in charge of milking two cows, feeding the hogs, mules and horses.

Regan H. wanted to be a bull riding rodeo cowboy. We roped the milk cow's yearlings, he rode them and I tried. He rode both milk cows. One just ran, the other really bucked.

Invariably, we wound up in a fight, which progressed from bad to worse. He stuck a stick in a cow paddy and slung it on me. I got me a stick and I flung cow paddy at him. Slung and flung dung went on for about ten minutes before we heard Mother calling us. "Milk those cows and get on to this house!"

After about two weeks of fighting, riding rodeo cowboys and some milking, Dad had a Saturday off. "You boys go on, do whatever you want. I'll take care of the milking today."

I was in the kitchen when he brought the milk bucket in. It looked like it had about a pint in it. Nearest thing to profanity I ever heard him use was what he said to Mother. "Them God-durn boys has done dried both of them cows up!" It was also the end of our milking career.

But that night at supper, he allowed as how he and his helper both thought I did about the finest job they had ever seen of laying corn by.

In 1951, that was about the best wages a 15-year-old plow boy could expect to get.

Chapter Three
The Top of the Mountain and the
Bottom of the Pits

The old saying goes that "When the love bug bites you, you don't know where to scratch." I may not have known where to scratch, but I knew I loved Margaret. There was not a shred of doubt in my mind about that. She was the girl I wanted to share my life with. Grow old with. I had no doubts she felt the same about me.

She had looked me in the eyes and said: "I love you." To my way of thinking, that's why she told me of the predicament they were in. She trusted me more than anyone else.

Margaret had a lot of pride. She had been holding her head up and going to school. Acting like everything was fine and she had nothing to worry about.

In that sense, I suppose we were kindred spirits. That's what I had been doing. I knew that when Dad finished that timber contract, we were looking at a bleak future in Leon County.

Things now started to weigh on my mind that before, I had just tolerated. Sucked it up and went on. Like the second, third and fourth grades in school for instance. The teacher would call on Prissy Jane and Sissy Joe to draw a pig pen on the blackboard. With a rooter hog drawn in it and labeled in big letters "PIG PEN."

It was always the same two she called on. Go down the row and inspect each of us. "Stick out your hands! Any dirt under your finger nails? Open your mouth! Have your teeth been brushed? Has your hair been combed, ears washed, inside and behind?" If they found fault with any of that, your name was written in the pig-pen.

Like a few other farm boys and girls, I never stood a chance of getting out of that pig pen. I never knew what a toothbrush and Pepsodent tooth powder was until my older brothers returned from WWII. My older sisters probably had that, but kept it hid out. I can't say now I blame them!

Daddy would be doing something, like greasing the wagon wheels. "Here, hold this big two-inch nut that holds the wheel on. Be careful, don't drop it in the dirt! It's got grease on it!"

After four wheels and four greasy nuts, this might happen. "Get that five-gallon bucket. Your mother wants us to gravel a mess of new red potatoes. See where the ground is cracking. Dig there!" I don't know why Dad and Mother called it "gravel" potatoes. It was "dig there" with your bare hands.

Someone might say ignorance is bliss. My name stayed in the pig pen. Like other farm kids. With us, we may have been ignorant about some things. To Prissy Jane, Sissy Joe, and our teachers, their ignorance seemed to be bliss. To me personally, it was degrading, and probably to the other farm kids as well.

If the farming went well, mother ordered me two pairs of jeans and two shirts. The shirts were same pattern, but different colors. This was what I wore to school.

Mother made my underwear. Sometimes out of fertilizer sacks, which were rough as canvass. Don't worry about my size being 4-12-4. That old homemade lye soap in the wash pot would take the label off of anything. But I smelled like lye soap in the class room.

Trouble was, she never made a pee-hole in my underwear. It was bad enough to go in a stall, pull everything down to take a leak. What was worse, I imagined everyone thought I was a friggin queer to always hide in a stall to do what normal boys do standing up! I mean, I could not fart long and loud every time I went in there.

A brother-in-law left a pair of black swim trunks there at home. Mother cut the athletic supporter out. "Here, wear these for shorts." Nylon I suppose, felt less abrasive than the fertilizer sacks. But out playing football on the playground, they bloomed up over my belt and pants. A high school boy looked at me and said, "Boy, what the hell you got on?"

Then there was the matter of transportation. Up until the end of WWII, we went to town Saturday in the wagon. My two older sisters got out at the edge of town and walked on in. I wanted to follow, but that was not allowed. They never wanted me tagging along after them.

That Dad had Melton's 1941 Ford Pickup to drive made little difference to me. They had a week-long revival at the Baptist Church over on the highway. Mother, Dad and Virginia rode in the cab. I rode in the back with my Rose Hair Oil airing out in the breeze. Anywhere we went, that's the way it was.

Someone picked up the Burkett's every night and brought them to Church. Margaret and I sat together, along with Virginia, Katrina, Harry, and Kevin. The preaching and singing was good. I came under God's power. I know I was saved that night. I was about ready to get up, answer the preacher's calling.

But other kids sensed how I was feeling. They tried to get me up, drag me up front. Maybe the devil intervened, I don't know. But I decided I won't be dragged up front. I'll wait and one day I'll get up and go on my own power.

There never had been a time in my life when I did not believe in the Christian way. Mother and Dad lived by a rather simple philosophy. Work hard, do the best you could, put your trust in the Lord's hands. He would provide you with what you needed. If a crop failed, they just said the Good Lord never thought we needed it.

But back to the way I was feeling about the way things were. I went with James Brader over to the store on the highway one day. Mother had given me a dime for a dime box of Garret Snuff. After James paid for his gas, I plopped the dime on the counter and said: "I need a dime box of Garret Snuff."

The lady said, "I need two more cents. It's gone up to 12 cents a box!"

I took my dime back. My dad can get it later. The lady said, "you can pay me later." James offered to give me two cents. But I refused.

I felt I should have been given more than the normal purchase price to purchase anything. And I was never given any money. I felt I should have had some change in my pocket anyway. I resolved if I ever have kids, and send them for anything, I shall send them with more money than its normal cost.

When I got home, I gave the dime back to Mother. "It's gone up to 12 cents a box. I never had enough to pay for it!"

I guess all kids take things out on their Mother. I probably hurt her feelings about that snuff. But things like never having money, walking or riding Old Dan wherever I went, not being taught to drive, and not having decent clothes and shoes were hurting me. Mostly because there was nothing I could do about it!

A few days after I laid the corn by, I got the axe out of the wood pile. An old worn out cotton sack in the barn. A couple of two by four boards about two feet long. I headed for the woods to build a hide-a-way place in case Margaret and I got a chance to slip off again.

Mother and Virginia would not miss me, I knew. They were glued to the radio listening to "Stella Dallas." Stella had a daughter, named Lollie. Was it spelled Lolly? Or Lolley? I don't recall.

Anyway, the script went like this:

Lollie Baby: Oh Mother! He's breaking my heart!

Stella: Oh, Lollie Baby!

That was about it. Over and over. But Mother never missed the "Stella Dallas" radio show. I think it put her in the mood for her afternoon nap.

I went in the woods to about a hundred yards from the back side of the place. A clump of myrtle bushes grew there in about an 18 feet diameter circle. I crawled into the center with my axe. Which was not easy to do, it was so thick. I tried to look out in all directions. *Anyone could walk right past it and not see me*, I thought.

I cut bushes and threw them out of there. Made a six-foot diameter circle in the center of those myrtle bushes. Then with my pocket knife, I started cutting a few small limbs to make it easier to get in and out. I aimed for a huckleberry bush and wild blackberry vines on the outside. Where anyone was not likely to walk.

At the outside of my tunnel, I took limbs in both hands and bent them to cover the opening. I had to trim just a few blackberry vines to get to my way in and out.

Next was the hard part. It was a big open field on the place joining ours. Covered with sage grass. Out in the field was a deep gulley. I had never seen anyone in that field. I drug those cut bushes to our fence, threw them over. Then on to that gulley and threw them in! I doubted anyone would see them before they rotted.

I went back to my myrtle bush hideout. Took the cotton sack and the two boards in. Stretched out on the sack, laid the two boards under one end for a pillow. I lay on it to rest and cool off. It was hot! I lay there thinking for a good while before I realized it was getting late. *I better get that axe back to the wood pile.* If Dad saw me with that axe he might ask, "What have you been doing?"

Lying was not something I liked to do. But I decided on an answer. "There are bees watering over in that gully on this place. I've been trying to course those bees and find that tree."

Bee hunting was something Dad and my older brothers did before we moved from the old place. Regardless of whose land the bee tree was found on, bee hunters put a big X on the tree with an axe. That indicated it was a tree found by someone, that the honey in it belonged to them.

I lucked out. Dad was not home yet. No one had missed me. And no one knew what I had done. And the axe looked like it had never left the wood pile.

It was the middle of the next week. Dad's helper had to go in at noon for some reason. Dad took the afternoon off. I was sitting on the front porch when I saw Margaret's mother coming down the road. I got up, walked out, and opened the front yard gate for her. She smiled and thanked me for opening that gate. She acted like she never had a care in the world. "Is your mother and dad home? I need to talk to them."

I told her they were. I walked with her, opened the front door for her. Told Mom and Dad Mrs. Burkett is here. She went in and I went back outside. It seemed she had a personal reason for talking to Mom and Dad. I sensed my presence was not needed.

After about 20 minutes, I saw her going back home. I went in the house. They never told me anything, I never asked. I felt if they wanted me to know, I would not have to ask. Seemed Mom had an early supper, it must not have been 4 p.m. when we ate.

After supper, Dad got his hat. Said "I'm going down to Sam Craig's place." I asked if I could go with him.

"No son, you best stay here with your mother and Virginia. No telling what I'll get into down there. She gave me a key to a gate and drew me a map. It's been over 30 years since I was there. It's Sand Flat Country I have to go through." He got the shovel and axe and left.

That's the way it was back then. Parents never discussed private business with other adults with their kids. After he left, mother never volunteered any information and I never asked. That's another thing, if parents never volunteered to talk about such matters, kids knew better than to ask!

I took a glass of tea and went out to my chair on the front porch. Mother was listening to a private detective show on the radio. It was called "The Fat Man and the Swinging Door." That swinging door made a long screeching sound that was meant to make the hair stand up on the back of your neck!

Although I had been told nothing, I felt I knew what had happened. *Margaret's mom had done what she did not want to do*, I thought. She had asked Dad to go tell her brother she needed help. It was near midnight, I saw headlights turn in at the Burkett house.

Dad, I figured, to tell her he had found Sam. What else, I had no idea. In a few minutes, he came on to the house. I asked if he had any trouble with the roads down there.

"No, the roads were in good shape. I found Old Sam with no trouble. I just went down there to get some things Martha needed. We got to talking and I stayed longer than I meant to. Sam said he would be here tomorrow, bring us a mess of fish."

I went to bed, but sleep would not come. I was worried about Margaret, all of them for that matter. They were without food, I felt sure. Sam had probably sent what he had available by Dad. He would be here tomorrow, probably take his sister Martha to town for things needed. And bring us a mess of fish!

The next day was the first time I ever saw Sam Craig. He drove up in the front of the house with Margaret's mom in his pickup. Came walking in with a large card board box. Full of Blue and Channel Catfish. Covered with damp Spanish Moss. They were still alive and kicking. Shook hands with me. "You must be Robert? I hear you are quiet a farmer!"

Mother came out and they talked awhile. Back before Mother and Dad married, her family and the Craig family visited back and forth. It was about a half a day's journey by wagon between the two places. Before they left, Sam said, "Tell Ben I'll be over here Friday to get those three shoats he sold me. My side frames for my truck is over at the old place. I never took the time to go get them this morning." They left headed for town.

There was ten of those catfish in that box that must have averaged over three pounds each. I had to skin and get them ready for the skillet. One thing I knew for sure. If Old Sam Craig told you he would bring you a mess of fish, he did just that. When the older brothers came home from the service, they fished every weekend. I knew how to dress catfish. They had moved away and that ended the fishing.

Needless to say, I was impressed with Sam Craig. Keeping those catfish alive for 20 miles in that Spanish moss was an education for me. He seemed one of the most likeable, easy going men I ever met. He talked to me like I was a grown man, which I liked.

He must have been at least six feet four inches tall. He was built like a lean tight end football player. His arms looked like he could put a mule to sleep with one punch. My guess was he never dished out no stuff, he never took any either! No wonder Margaret's Daddy gave him a wide circle!

Dad told me to let Sam pick two females and one boar shoat when he came. A shoat is somewhere between a weaning size pig and a grown hog. We had Spotted Poland China crossed with Red Duroc hogs. Dad said Sam had the black woods hogs. He wanted a start of bigger hogs.

Friday morning, I took a little corn and pined the whole bunch. When Mr. Craig got there, he backed the pickup up to the pen. "You handle the tailgate," Ben said. "Take my pick. I'll get in there and catch 'em." Those shoats probably weighed 65 pounds. He grabbed hind legs and an ear. I opened the tailgate and he shoved them in like they were nothing.

One thing I noticed. What he took never averaged out to be the best we had. He just caught three good ones. That told me something about the man.

I remarked "Ain't that just like hogs. Mess as soon as they get in the pickup"

He laughed. "Never fails," he said. "When I get them unloaded, I'll back the truck off in the creek and wash it out!" He sat down on the running board of his truck. Took out his Prince Albert can and started rolling a cigarette. I just sat down on my corn bucket and waited.

Funny thing about a man that rolls his own smoke. He don't say anything while he's doing it. But you know it's coming!

"I met your dad at a dance when I was about your age. Your dad started riding into this neck of the woods and beyond to dances. We visited back and forth a good bit. He lived with his brother Alex between here and Jewett.

We landed a job splitting rails for a neighbor of ours. Your dad stayed with us for about three months until we finished that job. Ben could do more with an axe than any man I ever saw use one.

One night at a dance, big old red-faced boy pinched the girl Ben was dancing with on the behind. It was not your mother, but another girl. Ben told him he better apologize to the girl.

The old boy asked Ben what he would do about it if he never apologized. Ben hit him between the eyes. It sounded like two box cars ran together! They had to pour water on the old boy to wake him up!

That ended the dance. But that boy could not see to ride his horse home. His eyes were swelled shut. Ben and I led him home on his horse. Ben knew the boy's daddy. Thought well of him. He made that boy tell his daddy what he had done. And why his eyes were swelled shut!"

Abruptly, he stopped his story telling and asked "How you and Margaret getting along?"

"We get along just fine! We are in the same grade at school. She's the smartest girl in the class. She knew I was a Dupree, but I never knew she was part of your family until we moved down here."

"I miss Martha and those kids a lot. Margaret was the only one old enough to spend time with me fishing and tending to my stock on horseback. I wish Martha would come back and live with me. She still owns half of the place anyway. But Martha wants to paddle her own canoe without any help from me.

Robert, I told Ben the other night that husband of Martha's ain't nobody to trust. He said he would keep an eye on things down there. I would appreciate it if you would too."

"Margaret has told me about her Dad. We'll do the best we can for them."

He thanked me, shook my hand and started to get in his truck. But he turned to me and grinned. "Knowing Ben like I do, I bet he never has told you about hitting that old boy!"

"No sir. He never has. I'll just tell him you said the two of you danced a lot."

He laughed. "I'll see you," he said. And drove off.

Dad nab it all! I had forgot to thank him and tell him how much we enjoyed those fish. Margaret's favorite uncle!

I really had meant to say something. Those catfish had taken the ho-hum out of our existence. I had sneaked in the kitchen after midnight and ate cold leftover catfish! At the old place, we could walk to the upper reaches of Buffalo Creek and fish. As the crow flies, it was perhaps 20 miles or more to where Sam Craig lived. Where we lived now, there was no place we could go to fish.

That night at supper, Dad told me his helper had quit. Since the crops were laid by, I could help him. I started on one end of a cross cut saw when I was six years old. And I had been going with him and his helper when I had no farm work to do. Dad said I was a better saw hand than the helper that quit.

But using an axe, to try to help Dad was wasting his time! Whatever eye and muscle co-ordination Babe Ruth and Mickey Mantle had for hitting a baseball, Dad had for an axe.

We would work until noon. Sit down on a stump, each had a can of sardines in soybean oil. We split a can of pork & beans, a package of crackers, and shared the bottle of pepper sauce. Sardines need that pepper sauce! We now worked longer, about ten hours. He never had to take a helper home again.

Dad punched holes in the lid of a half-gallon washed out bleach jug. Before starting each morning, we sprinkled our shoes and lower pants legs with kerosene. That helped keep the ticks off. That jug was also used to put kerosene on the saw. Prevents tree sap build up and hardening on the saw. And makes the saw easier to pull.

Dad had a log scale with which he scaled each log we cut. Wrote it down in a small notebook. He knew what he and the land owner had coming in board feet.

Dad looked a tree over, determined which way he could make it fall. Then took the axe and cleared out around the tree. Vines growing up a tree were cut. They can knock you down when a tree falls. Badly leaning Oak Trees can split half way through and the tree fall. That split part can kick back and kill you. Dad cleared around the tree so you had a chance to escape all possibilities of getting hurt or killed. He did all that axe work, I watched. No need for me to waste his time!

One day about half way into a big oak, the saw pinched. We tried the wedges, could not make that saw move. He picked up the axe, chopped that saw out. It would have taken me half a day and I would have ruined the saw. It took him about ten minutes and he never touched the saw.

One day the owner of the log truck came to where we were. "Hey Ben, can you come help us figure a way to load a big log?" He had one helper, driving an old a-frame truck that had no doors on it. I've seen vehicles in wrecking yards not as beat up as that truck was. Logs were drug to the log truck and loaded with that truck.

Dad had one hand and arm leaning on the axe handle with the blade on the ground. With one arm, that axe came off the ground and he stuck the blade of that axe in a big oak tree about chest high. Said nothing, went with the man.

I knew Dad was leaked off about having to help them so much. I thought I could clear out around the tree while he was gone. That axe was decently stuck in that tree, not easy to get out. I tried doing what he did. No way Hosea! Realized I could hurt myself trying, that I never had his arm strength. Dad probably weighed 150 pounds.

He came back and had this to say: "All they needed to do was tie the front end of that loading truck to a tree to load that big log. I've helped them do that before! I told them not to be bothering us anymore. It was our job to cut 'em and their job to load 'em!"

It was the morning of July 19, 1951. Sort of a summer cool front had blown in. It was a slow drizzling rain. Dad said we were two weeks ahead of the log hauler, we would just take the day off. He went on the front porch to set and sharpen both saws. One was set to cut oak, the other sweet gum. I've seen that saw set for sweet gum drag out nine inch strings from a tree.

It quit raining about mid-morning. At dinner Dad said the rain would make that field of corn. "We'll get our seed back!" The sun came out, a light north wind was blowing. It was rather pleasant, a relief from the humidity and heat.

Margaret, Harry, and Kevin came up. I let the end-gate down on the back of old Ida Red. Margaret and I sat on the end-gate, both of us throwing a football to Harry and Kevin. They grew weary of that, walked up to us. Kevin had both arms around the football, holding it to his chest. His chin was resting on one end of the football.

I don't know if Kevin stuck out his tongue at Harry or what but Harry hit the bottom end of that football with an upper cut. Little Kevin was suddenly mad and crying. His tongue was bleeding, his teeth had cut it.

Margaret looked at the damage. Then she jumped on Harry's case. Mad she was. "You take him home. And tell Mother what you did. You better not lie to her. I'll find out if you do! Now take him home!"

We sat there for a few more minutes. I knew Mom and Dad were in the living room probably taking a nap. I took her hand and got up from the end-gate. "Come on! There is something I want to show you."

We headed towards the highway. Down a hill to a small creek bridge. About half way to the bridge, Margaret looked back. "If Harry sees us, he'll probably follow us."

"We'll lose him at the bridge," I said.

We walked out on the bridge. We jumped down about three feet to hard ground that would show no tracks. We crawled through a barb wire fence and into the woods. We were on the neighboring place to my aunt's now.

We ran a short distance, stopped to kiss long and with passion. Then we kept going until we crawled through barb wire fence back into my aunt's place. On our way to the hide-a-way I had made in the myrtle bushes, we stopped to kiss a number of times.

Once we were there, we crawled into the center. I spread the cotton sack out on the ground. It had dried out fairly well. We sat down on it. "How did you ever think of fixing a place like this?"

"So we could hide from Harry! I doubt he will find us here."

She laughed! "I love you Robert!"

I pulled off my old gray T-shirt and hung it on a limb. I looked into her eyes and suddenly we were kissing and locked together in passion. She had on shorts and a halter top. I started trying to get that halter top off. She saw I needed help. She stood up and took everything off. I kicked out of my jeans and underwear. I was seeing for the first time something more beautiful than I ever imagined.

I won't be all that explicit about all we did before it happened. We got to the place we had never been before. I was trying to get there and not having any success. "You'll have to do it hard," she whispered." I did like she said. We got there! She yelled out and grew tense. The she laughed and became passionate again. It was over for me quickly.

Too quick, I thought. But I tried to keep going. I did until she seemed to go somewhere only a woman knows where. When she came back from there, it was over and finished for both of us. We lay there in each other's arms to catch our breaths. After a little I said, "I'm sorry, if it hurt."

"It has to hurt some the first time. You must think I am a floozy pushover for doing it. I wanted it because I love you. I've never felt this way before about anyone else."

She was crying now. "I love you and respect you," I said. "I've never felt this way before either. The way I feel, we were just married. For the rest of our lives. We'll have to wait for a preacher, but we know we belong together."

She came into my arms. "That's the way I feel. Whatever happens, if we get separated, I'll wait for you. I love you."

We became passionate again. This time it was easier for us. I lasted a little longer before I heard thunder roll and saw lightening flash. She went to that place she went before at the same time I did.

Afterwards, we realized it was getting late. We got up to get dressed. We had passed being timid about being naked in front of each other. She had her panties nearly up when she said, "I'm bleeding a little. If I get blood on my undies, Mother may see it when she washes my clothes. Mother don't need to know what we've done."

"I'll fix something," I said. I had seen a box of women's things kept under a bed at our house. I pulled one out once to see what it looked like. I laid the tail of my gray shirt on the board, took my knife and cut off a two inch strip. Folded it in the shape I thought it needed to be and handed it to her.

She smiled and took it. Bent over and stuck her behind out and put it in place and quickly pulled up her panties. After dressing, we walked out to the county road at the backside of my aunt's place. We went to the 90-degree turn at the end of the place she lived on. She decided it was best she go on alone. Her mother might be upset that she was gone too long.

We agreed that whatever happened, we were married already. One way or another, we would be together. We kissed. I watched her until she turned into the yard at their place. I went back through the woods and home.

I must have gone to bed at 8 p.m. that night. My head hit the pillow and I was asleep. It must have been about 11 p.m. when I woke up. Always been that way for me. Seems if I am very tired, I sleep hard for a short time and wake up. Ready to get up and go.

No need to get up and go. But I knew sleep would not come soon. The GI cot I slept on never had a head board. The end was pushed against the wall. I put my pillow against the wall and sat up. To think.

About Margaret of course. It had surprised me when her nipples became erect at my touch. I never knew that could happen. You have to do it hard the first time! I never knew that. Must be girls where taught more about their own bodies and boy's ignorance by their mothers than men taught boys.

I thought women's hair down there spread out like a man's. It was narrow and curled over at the top. Somewhat like old Hitler's mustache. Maybe that was why Hitler was called a lunatic. He thought he had a woman's muff under his nose!

I thought girls being called a virgin just meant they had never did it. Now I knew it was more to it than just that. I heard older brothers and cousins talking about ringing a girl's bell. A cousin had said this: "If you don't ring a girl's bell the first time you do it, she won't let you have it no more!" I thought I knew what "ringing their bell" meant now.

Dad, I thought, *was too strict with my older sisters*. They had to walk the line. When they got out of high school and older, they married the first men they met. One was still married to the man. The other's marriage lasted two weeks. She later married a good man.

Margaret was in a predicament with her dad. Maybe that was why she let it happen with us. Perhaps in her mind, it was defiance against her dad! I wondered if today would have happened if her dad had treated her decently.

28

Maybe not. But I still believed she loved me. That there was a bond between the Craig and DuPree families that pulled us together. I knew what happened today was out of my love for her. I knew that I was willing to devote the rest of my life proving that to her. I had not lied to her. I felt we were married already.

Next day in the woods was a tough one for me. I had heard an older brother and a cousin talking about it. Likely, I would have been scared out of my gourd if I had not. They called the pain I was feeling in the center of my testicles the "Stone Ache." They indicated it afflicted almost all human males from teenage to early adult years. They agreed it hit them most often after being out with a girl. Whether they lucked out or just got aroused. My cousin said someone told him to get hold of his truck bumper and try lifting the truck. "I tried it, but that never helped me," he said.

Dad went to the truck for the other saw to cut a sweet gum. I tried lifting an 18 foot hardwood log and it never helped me either. I suddenly missed the pain about mid-afternoon, and what a relief.

The next day, my physical state was back to normal. My mental state was getting worse. We left early in the morning to work and got in late. There was not an opportunity to see Margaret and I needed to. Dad had told me to stay away from the Burketts. Sam Craig had told him that Burkett fellow is crazy. "No telling what he might do to you if he caught you with that girl."

I felt like Margaret was beating herself up about what we had done. I wanted to tell her I loved her. That I meant every word I said! We waved at one another sometimes when we passed by their place coming in from work. Margaret never came to our house except when I was in the woods on the end of that cross-cut saw. *I figured it out*, I thought. Margaret's mom had a talk with mine. They decided we never needed to be alone together again.

They did spend time with Mother during the day. Margaret's mom had a lot of empty fruit jars. Mother had filled her jars. We had produce that was going to waste. They picked it, prepared it for canning. Sweet corn, tomatoes, okra purple and cream peas. Carrots and onion. Bell pepper and crook neck squash. And we had fresh dug red potatoes. We would never use them all before they rotted.

Mother said this about Margaret. "She's a hard-working good girl. She knows how to do things and do it well. I don't doubt she's the smartest girl in your class at school, Robert. And she is the fastest pea sheller I have ever seen!" Mother had seen a lot of pea shellers in her time. She could out shell me so bad it made me want to give up! I never said anything. I never doubted what Mother said either!

On Saturdays, Dad and I went to the woods to cut firewood out of the tree tops we cut for logs. The landowner had told him to get all he wanted. "Sell it if you can. It ain't going to do nothing but lay there and rot!" We got what we needed and Dad did sell a few loads. Then there was the corn to gather, the dry peas to pick. My Saturday's were work details.

Dad let me start football practice the last two weeks in August. He got his first helper back, who was his nephew. His nephew was the best fiddle player I ever heard play in person. He played with a rather large band that performed over the state.

He would get tired of travel, come home for a spell. Maybe work some. Cutting logs with Dad was a job. He did not care much it seemed. Just enough money for cigarettes and fiddle strings! Dad knew he would go back to his music and the band. He just never knew when.

My oldest brother Franklin was a good singer, played standard and steel guitar. An injury in WWII to his chest ruined his ability to sing as well as he did before the war. Melton played some lead guitar. Regan H. was the better guitar player in our family. He played lead guitar some with a band at a club in Mexia, Texas. I was trying to play rhythm guitar and thump a stand-up bass some.

Thing about being a rhythm guitar player, to practice by yourself, you must try to sing. I was not very proud of my singing voice. Margaret's mom once wanted me to play and sing. She said I did great. But Margaret was there, it was right after we moved to my aunt's place. I never felt that great about my effort.

My brothers Lawrence and Elton never tried to play anything. Lawrence said he could whistle. But Elton could not even do that!

I never saw Margaret until the first day of school. When I got on the bus, she was sitting with another girl. During our second period class, she got up and whispered to the teacher, then left the room. You could not just get up and go to the rest room, you had to ask the teacher for permission with everyone in the class watching.

She never came back to class. If you got sick, did not have a way home, you were sent to a room reserved for that. You had to tough it out until school dismissed.

At lunch time, I checked in the lunch room to see if she was there. Then I went outside to look for her. I could see her sitting on the rock wall by the football field where we usually sat during lunch time. James Brader had paid me for helping him with his cattle. I got a Coke and Dr. Pepper out of the machine by the door.

I held out the Coke and Dr. Pepper when I got there. "Take your choice," I said. "I don't care what I drink!" She smiled and took the Dr. Pepper. And said, "You never ate lunch?"

"Well you never either," I said. "I wondered how you were doing."

"I was sick at my stomach this morning. This Dr. Pepper I think will help." I told her I had meant every word I said to her. That I loved her and that I thought our parents were trying to keep us apart.

Mom was upset that I was with you so long that day. I know she went and talked to your mother."

"We got four more years of school. That's a long time to wait. When we finish school, I'll find a job or go into the military. One way or the other, we can marry legally if you'll wait for me."

"I love you! For however long it takes, I'll wait! Do you realize you and I will be the first DuPree and Craig to ever marry?"

"Yes, Dad told me once it was a strange thing. Our families had been friends for generations, yet there had never been a marriage between the two." The bell rang, she said she felt like going back to class. I had two periods of FFA and PE. PE meant I got dressed for football practice, go on the field and start. The coach or someone would take me home after practice.

Margaret never came to school anymore that week. I asked Katrina about her and she said she was sick. I was concerned about that, but there was nothing I could do. But go to school and try to concentrate on my school work and football.

The school initiated a new system that year. No pass, no play. On Monday you took a card around to each class. The teacher marked the card with your grade average for a week. If failing, you would not play Friday night. Most of the boys in the upper grades were upset about that, threatening to quit football. They were told: "Quit if you want to. But if you want to play, make passing grades or you won't play!"

We would play our first game on a new field at home. Well, this was the second year. Our FFA class had went over there one day during the week. We were lined up at the goal line and given paper sacks. "Pick grass burrs and put in these sacks!" We made it about 15 yards in two class periods.

Friday came. Most of us rode a bus home. We had to stay at school and wait until game time. We all laid down on the front lawn of the high school building to wait. Until they fed us. Which would be one thin slice of baked smoked ham. One piece of dry toast with no butter on it. And a cup of hot tea! Hot tea I had never tried before.

Before they served us that pre-game supper, the senior boys decided to initiate the freshmen boys on the team. They cut a long stick out of the hedge bushes. Then split one end to make it hurt more. They tapped me about three light licks.

I had a friend that could run faster than anyone on the team. They hit him on the thigh as hard as they could. When we dressed for the game, I saw swollen bloody places on his thigh. *They did it,* I thought, *because he was a better athlete than they were!*

I realized something about bullies. They are not always completely stupid. I had older brothers and cousins around at the time. They knew they best not do that to me.

We were playing a school I had never heard of before. Someone said that the coach said they come from somewhere in East Texas, the other side of Crockett. The horseplay ceased when they started getting off their bus. Red headed, freckle faced, big old boys. They looked tough!

Turned out their uniforms were the same color and just like the new ones we had. So we dug out the worn, torn and tattered old solid color uniforms that were retired after a few years of wear. We were a ragged and tattered bunch.

But we won the game. I played left guard offense and defense the whole game. My friend with the bleeding thigh got loose and scored twice. The other team was upset about the grass burrs. We tried to act like they never bothered us!

Brother Melton had been discharged from the service. Regan H. was with him. Two cousins were there in another pickup. They were waiting for me after I got showered and dressed after the game. "Let's go to Centerville and get a hamburger Melton said!" I wondered why go to Centerville to get a hamburger? They had cafes in Buffalo.

When we got there, I discovered why. A beautiful young waitress worked there. They all wanted to date her. But that was my first hamburger. After tea and toast, I needed it. And it was so good!

At home, my cot felt good. Mother kept about three mattresses on each bed. When family came in, mattresses were put on the floor. Melton got the bed, Virginia got a mattress on the floor. Regan H. worked in Madisonville at the newspaper. He went home to his apartment.

I slept until eight the next morning. Mother had been through football seasons before. She left me a couple of buttered biscuits and fried eggs in the oven. With a pint of post oak grape jelly, it never mattered to me that it was a little cold.

Melton and Dad were gone already. Dad would go to the sawmill to get paid. He would get a few things Mother needed in the kitchen. We were about out of feed for the hogs and the milk cow. He would probably get a sack of corn and a sack of horse and mule feed. The hogs would get the corn. Old Dan and the cow both could eat the horse and mule feed. It was mostly oats with some crushed corn coated with molasses.

On the front porch, I leaned back against the wall in a straight back chair. It was probably 9 a.m. when I saw Margaret's dad pass. He looked at me, but never waved. I never waved at him either. Right behind him was a U-Haul truck. The man driving it waved. I waved back at him. *Good fellow*, I thought. I knew there was no chance to see Margaret today. Dad had told me to stay away from down there.

I watched that truck go down the road. My alarm went off when I saw that truck stop, back up to their front porch. I saw Margaret's mom bring the man a plate of food and a cup of coffee. When he was done, he went inside the truck, threw out some blankets then rolled out a two-wheeler. Damn it all to hell, they are moving!

31

The man folded a blanket and laid down on the porch. They had probably driven most of the night. They must be going to rest awhile before loading the truck.

After a little bit, I saw Harry coming up the road on his horse. With his dad right behind in his old car. Right in front of the house, he passed Harry and stopped. He got out and started chewing Harry out. "You got to hurry you idiot! Make that horse move! Now get going!" His Dad right behind him.

That's not Harry's horse anymore, I thought. Taking it back to the man they got it from. I bet his dad had never paid the man.

Melton and Dad came back. Unloaded the feed and the groceries. Melton parked the truck in front of the house. When I heard him playing the steel guitar rag on his old yellow Kamico guitar, I went out and let the tail gate down on the truck. Shortly, Harry and his dad came back by. Both in the car. Harry no longer had a horse. Sitting on the tailgate, I could see what was going on down there better.

I guess they rested up and had some dinner. Then they started loading the truck. The man and Margaret's mother were doing most of it appeared. By two o'clock, they were all loaded up and left down there. The truck following Margaret's dad. Her Mother and Kevin were in the front seat with him. Margaret, Katrina, and Harry in the back.

Margaret saw me sitting there. She looked back at me, put her hand to her lips and pressed her hand to the back window. I did likewise with my hand and waved at her. I saw her dad turn his head around shouting at her. Then I saw her mother shouting at him. Margaret held her hand to that glass until they were out of sight. The truck driver passed, waved at me. My hand was up anyway.

I put the tail gate up on the pickup. I knew Margaret was gone. To where, I knew not. *But she could let me know,* I thought. Even if she never remembered our box number. She could address a letter to Robert DuPree, Rt. 3, Buffalo, Texas. I would get it. I went through the yard, through the woods to our myrtle bush hide-a-way.

I cried some, I cursed her old bastard father some and I prayed some. I was not fit to be around anyone right now. I suspect Mom and Dad knew that. I stayed on that cotton sack until near dark. Then I sucked it up and went to the house.

I managed to make it through supper, no one seemed to have a lot to say. I got the old Kamico guitar, went out on the front porch. I took my feelings out on that old yellow guitar until my fingers hurt. There was nothing else to take it out on.

I went to my cot, took off those old combat boots. Put my pillow against the wall. Turned the light out. Never took off my clothes. Leaned back against my pillow on the wall. I knew I was not going to sleep anyway. Saturday nights were always miserable for me anyway. I never could go anywhere. That was nothing compared to tonight. This Saturday night, I knew what misery really was!

Sunday evening, I saddled Old Dan and rode over to the man's house that owned the horse. I saw the horse in his pasture as I rode by. He was sitting on the front porch when I got there.

No, he never knew where those people moved to. "That fellow paid me ten dollars and said he would pay me the rest later. He never did pay me anymore. Said yesterday he was not able to pay me, so he brought the horse back. But don't feel I lost anything. That woman and kids fed and took good care of the horse."

There was no escaping it. Margaret had vanished from my life. The only ray of hope I had was that she would write to me. Tell me where she was. One way or another, I had to find her. What was depressing, it would be a long time before I could look for her and finance the trip.

Monday morning, I got on the bus and went back to school. High school was somewhat better than the first eight grades. With the exception of FFA, {Future Farmers of America} we did stay in the same class room all day. But a different teacher came in to teach each class.

There was one teacher who gave a girl in the class and myself, a bad time. He made an issue out of how loud we talked. Pretended he could not hear us. And most of the questions he asked, he called on one or the other of us. I asked some of the other students if they had a problem hearing us.

"No problem," they said.

I talked to the girl about it. She knew as well as I, why he did it. Her family lived next door to my brother in town. This teacher lived across the street. He tried to run the neighborhood. Jumped my brother and told him that he needed to keep his dog tied. Her dad and my brother both told him that he best take his ass back across the street and mind his own business. They would tend to theirs!

I was taking FFA, the Green Hand Chapter. Officers were elected. I was elected Advisor. Parliamentary procedure was practiced at the start of the class almost daily. The President would call the list of class elected officers. Each would recite what his duties were. I only recall what I was required to say. It went like this:

"Mr. Advisor!"

"Here, by the Owl!"

"Why, by the Owl?"

"The Owl is the time-honored emblem of knowledge and wisdom. Being older than the rest of you, I am asked to advise you from time to time as the need arises."

Or something like that! I probably had done more plowing and farming than any other boy in the class. If it came down to questions about plowing and farming, I probably deserved being elected the advisor. But that plowing and farming had not been done sitting under a stuffed Hoot Owl!

I started out playing both offense and defense at left guard. Class 'B' School, I think there was 22 boys at start of season. A couple of boys flunked, which started a rebellion among the upper-class men. Some quit. I started getting put in at different positions. I played tackle, defensive end, and line-backer. Only 13 boys suited out for the last game of the season. That school had no lights on the field. On offense, I got put in at center.

Center, on a single wing formation team, is not that easy. I had to look between my legs to center that ball back ten yards. Hard to raise your head up before you got hit! Which is rough duty. We won but I still wonder how.

Mother was having health problems. Looking back, it was early treatment of her blood pressure. They knew not how to regulate the medication. She was getting too much and passing out. But medical expense added more to Dad's log cutting job salary than it would handle. There was no money to order new jeans and shirts this year.

James Brader was a good man. He helped people where he saw the need. He saw my need. He brought over a box of assorted shirts, overalls, and jeans. Said he had gained weight, got too big for it. Dad took some of it, I got a couple of pairs of jeans and shirts to start school in.

By the time football season ended, you could see daylight through the seat of my jeans. They had the football banquet; players took a date (if they could get one). They ate; players that lettered were advised that they did. All did, I heard. Twelve miles from town, I could not go. It was depressing. If I could drive and Margaret were here, I could have brought the most beautiful date there.

After that, one morning, the School Superintendent came to the class. He whispered to our teacher and left. Then the teacher announced that he told him our class could be proud. "Allen, you and Robert have been selected on the all-district football team!

Two girls jumped up. One, my friend, who had that hearing problem in another class. They got permission to take us to the other HS classes, tell them of our great accomplishments. We got in the hall. I said, "Let's talk about this before we do this. I don't know how Allen feels about this. But this is pure school politics. I feel about those that protested the no pass and no play rule. I don't want to do this. It would be embarrassing to stand in front of older guys that deserved this more than I."

Allen said, "That's how I feel." We spent 15 minutes outside the school front door and went back to class. My friend that had the hearing problem with a teacher in another class had an older brother that was a senior on the football team. She understood what I was saying. The teacher had said that Allen and I were the only two from our school on the all district team.

I hit the woods with the .22 rifle during the Thanksgiving holidays. With the nine hollow-point long rifle shells that we had left, I killed my first deer; a nubbin buck. Against the game laws, of course. Deer ate up pea fields in the neighborhood. We thought it fair to eat the deer! I never did anything others were not doing. And wardens were never seen in our area.

A nubbin buck is not very big; the family came in. Melton and Regan H. were still single. The rest of my older brothers and sisters were married and had children. Lots of mattresses on the floor for sleeping! But Mother killed a hen, between chicken and dressing, and the deer and things out of the fruit jars that we put up, we had a good Thanksgiving dinner.

I went back to school after Thanksgiving, but my mental attitude was at low tide. My clothes, no money, no way to go anywhere. About three .22 shells and five 16-gauge shotgun shells left to hunt with. The worst of it, Margaret had not written. No one I talked to knew where they went. Margaret's words to me was about all I had left to cling to. "I love you. I'll wait for as long as it takes!"

That one teacher seemed to increase his efforts to harass that girl and myself. Nearly every question was directed at one of us. As soon as we started to answer, he put his hand to his ear. "I can't hear you! I can't hear you!"

Dad had already left on Monday morning, after the Christmas holidays. Mother asked me why I was not getting dressed for school. "See these?" I said. I held up a pair of my jeans to the light. "See the light? I'm not going back to school anymore. I quit!"

The memory of the look in her eyes still haunts me today, one I can't forget. What I said, hurt her, I know. But she just said, "I don't blame you. I would not go in those ragged things either. I'm sorry. That's the way it is!"

I went out to the wood pile. With the one man saw and axe, I worked up the pile of limbs at the wood pile. That took until dinner time. After dinner, I took the .22 and three shells to my myrtle bush hideaway. If a deer came near, I could hopefully shoot it in the ear. I saw no deer, not even a rabbit or squirrel. Mostly, I just wanted to be gone, when dad came in.

I suppose Mother and he had talked it over before I came in. That night at supper, he told me that I could help him in the woods. He would just lay off his helper. I was a better saw hand than the one he had now. Maybe he thought that would change my mind and I would go back to school. At the time, anything seemed like a better alternative than going back to that school!

We finished that tract of timber, the second week in January. He looked for work, but found nothing. We did what we could, around the place, even cleaned up that fence row by the road and end of the corn rows. I kept looking at a now leafless honeysuckle vine and an empty house, down the road, and wondering why doesn't Margaret write to me!

Dad had sold the rest of his shoats after Sam Craig bought three. A neighbor's red boar came from a mile away, tore in the pasture and bred the two old sows he kept. Big hog, but he had a rooter nose on him that looked like he could eat corn out of the bottom of a half-gallon fruit jar!

Mid-January, it sleeted and snowed about seven inches on the ground. Took it a week to melt. Then it did it again. Another seven inches. Old Ida Red would not start. At the time, I never knew, and dad never knew, it just had a dead battery. But we were 12 miles from town, and no way to get there.

Mother used up most of things put up in fruit jars. We ate shelled dry purple hull peas. She made hominy out of dry corn. Put a little grease in a skillet, used cornmeal and water like making gravy. She called it corn meal mush, said it was something like eating grits. We still had a few red and sweet potatoes left.

Later in life, I ordered a pork chop with grits and gravy in a restaurant. I liked the pork chop, ok. Those grits, I never cared much for. I liked mother's corn meal mush, much better.

I got the notion that maybe I could track down a deer. Regan H. had bought a 16-gauge shotgun and left it there. We had one slug, two #1 buck shot and five #6 shots for it. I put on all the clothes I could get on.

Then I got the leather back-pack my grandfather, William Bethel DuPree had left Dad. It had leather loops in it. You could slide an axe handle through and carry an axe with you. Inside was a long-bladed knife that my brother Elton left us, some rope, and string. And a couple of rags, in case you washed your hands in a creek somewhere to get blood off.

I tied up Old Major, the red dog we had, with a piece of hay string. Never wanted him with me today. I meant to cross the road at the backside of the place, go into the place where we cut logs. Major soon trailed me up; he had chewed that string into. He ran a red squirrel into a dead hollow, small sassafras tree. I managed to shinny up the tree and stick my cap in the hole it went in.

I hit the dead tree a lick with the axe. Hard, like a flint rock. Had it been dark, I'm sure I could have seen sparks fly. I kept at it until I was finally able to push it over. Started chopping small holes, until I found that squirrel. I stabbed it in the ribs with my pocket knife. Kicking, I saw the tail of another. I chopped another hole and stabbed it.

Two big Boar Fox Squirrels. I was severely cold. I had some meat. I went home and laid the squirrels on top of the chicken house so the dog could not get them. I went in to warm up before I would skin those squirrels. After I told what happened, Dad went out and skinned the squirrels.

Mother boiled those squirrels tender, picked the meat off the bones. Found a half gallon jar of tomatoes, a quart of cut sweet corn. With a lot of chopped up red potatoes and a can of Wolf Chili, she made a squirrel stew that would feed us two days.

The next day, James Brader came by in his jeep. Said they were about out of a number of things as well. Dad went into town with him and brought home some things for the kitchen. I think he had to negotiate a little credit.

Brother Melton had served his time in the army, as a reservist called back to duty. He, my brother Elton & wife, and a cousin were all working at an aircraft factory in Ft. Worth. They wound up renting a house and living in Weatherford.

It was the first weekend in February of 1952, when my brother Franklin came with his family. They had recently moved to a place called Livingston. His wife's deceased Mother's family lived there. He worked at the local newspaper and Melton was working there with him. He had left the aircraft factory to train as a printer there under the GI bill. Melton had to work Saturday.

I saw Dad and Franklin, standing and talking, a lot. Somehow, I sensed my presence was not needed. After dinner on Saturday, he and his wife left the kids and went into town. Evidently, she knew what Mom needed in the kitchen in the way of things like baking powder, salt, sugar, cooking oil, etc. They also brought cabbage heads, spam, summer sausage, pork, beans, other canned goods, and oatmeal. We had things to eat for a while.

Sunday evening, when they started home, Dad got in the car with a change of clothing in a paper sack. He went home with them.

Virginia and I never knew he was going to do that. Virginia asked Mother "Why did Daddy go home with them?"

Mother's answer verified what I suspected. "Your daddy is going to look for a job. If he finds one, your brother will help move us to Livingston. Your brother has rented a big house, we would live in it with them for a while."

Monday night, James Brader came over. "Got a call from Franklin. Asked me to tell you this. Ben found a job, was at work by eight this morning. He wants you to pack up and move. Said for you to take the cow and horse back to your aunt's place, Robert. They'll be up here Friday night, to start moving Saturday."

Virginia and I got out a Texas road map. We found Livingston on the map. Franklin had told us it was 39 miles, east of Huntsville. Two ways to get there. Through Huntsville or Crockett. Suddenly, it seemed important for us to trace out every foot of the way there.

We packed up everything we could, in boxes, paper sacks, feed sacks, and tin wash tubs. I got everything together out at the barn, patched up a chicken coop to move the chickens in. Remembered the plow under that tree in the field. I toted it to the barn on my shoulders. The hogs, not anything I could do about them.

Thursday morning, I saddled Old Dan. Put a rope on the cow's horns and led her behind. The cow walked along behind like she was a dog following us. I think she knew she was going home. I wondered if she was thinking about that big red bull over there in that pasture.

My thoughts were on Margaret. No way I could let her know where we were moving to. The two of us ever finding one another was getting complicated. I wondered if her crazy dad did something to keep her from writing me.

I opened four hard to open gates before getting into my aunt's place. I opened another to turn the cow in the pasture where the cattle were. No cattle in sight. But that Old Jersey Milk Cow raised her tail and took off on the run to find them. She knew she was back home!

I unsaddled Old Dan, hung the saddle up in the barn where it came from. Led Old Dan out to the horse pasture. James' horse was in there I knew, but not in sight. I opened the gate, let him in. I patted his neck, took the bridle off. He just stood there. I took the bridle back to the barn and hung it on a nail where it came from.

Home was about a mile and a half through the woods. I walked by my aunt's house. Dad always said a house would fall down in a hurry if no one lived in it. It had been a neat house. A place on the front porch was buckled up and rotted. The screen on a window was loose and hanging somehow by only one corner.

When I crawled through the fence in the back of the house, I looked back.

Old Dan was still standing there looking at me. Then he turned and started walking away. That horse never belonged to me I knew. You may not understand this. But for the first time in my life, I felt I had something that was mine! That horse meant so much to me.

I turned and ran through the woods and brush until I could run no further. Then I walked on to the place Margaret and I had watched the wood ducks. I lay there and cried, cursed, and prayed. It was more than not knowing where Margaret was or giving up Old Dan. It was about leaving this county. My great-grandad Bethel Dupree came to Texas in 1856. He owned a lot of land, a cotton gin. His wife died and they said he gambled and stayed drunk until he lost most of it.

Dad's parents died when he was nine years old. His dad was a lawyer, County Attorney and State Representative. His land was sold by Dad's older brothers and sisters. Although we had nothing, leaving this county gave me the feeling I was being screwed out of my heritage. That we were leaving like a dog sneaking off with his tail between his legs.

I cried until I could cry no more. I got up and started home. I washed the dried tears and sand off my face in the branch. Went on, pushed that post in the fence over, and crossed it for the last time. A straight-line home took me behind the house Margaret lived in. I prayed to God to help me find her.

Franklin and Dad got there about nine Friday night. Franklin had rented a 16 foot trailer to pull behind his 1949 six-cylinder Plymouth car. Melton had to work until noon Saturday, he never came.

Dad seemed elated about his job. He rode with Franklin to his job Monday morning. Walked up to the Court House square. Asked a man sitting there on the railing next to the sidewalk where he might find work. The man directed him up the railroad to this wholesale place. They hired him, and he was at work by 8 a.m. "They handle everything from soup to hay," he said. We learned later the man sitting on the rail was a well-known lawyer.

Saturday morning, we loaded up the essential things. Like the refrigerator and the stove. We filled the box bed full then put half of Mother's mattresses on top of that and tied them down.

Franklin and Dad were in the front seat, Mother, Virginia and I in the back. We turned left on Highway Seven headed for Crockett. When we crossed the Trinity River at the Old Lock and Dam Bridge, I knew we were officially out of Leon County. This was as far as I had ever been in this direction.

Damn it to hell, I thought. *Margaret is gone. Now so am I!*

Chapter Four
The New Beginning

At Crockett, we left highway US 7 and turned on US 287. A few miles outside, the hub on one of the trailer tires was smoking. We had to unhitch from the trailer, take the tire and hub off. The wheel bearings were worn out.

Franklin, with Mom and Virginia, went back to Crockett for new wheel bearings and a can of grease. Dad and I stayed with the trailer. We were by a gate going into a pasture. By the gate, there was a huge pine tree. Nailed to that tree was a poster board with a poem written on it. It was about trees, written by Joyce Kilmer.

They returned, the new bearings with grease were installed, the trailer hitched back up and we were on the way again. At Corrigan, we turned south on US 59. We turned left about a mile north of Livingston. Went about half a mile, then turned left on another road. About 300 yards down that road on the right was the big old unpainted house he had rented.

We unloaded as quickly as possible. Franklin's wife had lunch ready, we ate. Melton and Regan H. were there. They returned with Franklin and Dad to finish getting the rest of our things.

Dad had me stay and gave me a work detail. There was a small fenced area that was once used for cows or horses. Inside was a small shed with a dirt floor. It was walled up with 12 inch boards about four feet high. The front had a door. Some of the boards were loose, or completely off. My job was to fix it so that our hogs could be unloaded into it.

That job never took me long, now I could check the place out. It had a butane tank, Franklin had a gas stove. The kerosene stove mother had would no longer be used. There was a wood burning fire place and it had electricity. It had a well with water that never tasted very good but was drinkable. The outhouse was out back.

The place must have been about ten acres. About two acres were fenced off for a garden area. Next to the garden area was a fair sized shed where we could store our plows and other things. There was a small pasture field, the rest was covered mostly with young pines, some hardwood. There were a few maple trees which never grew in Leon county.

Melton and Regan H. came in with a loaded Ida Red about 10 p.m. In Melton's words, "It ran like a spotted assed ape. Seventy miles an hour down US 75 to Huntsville!" All they had to do was jump it off! It started now, the battery had recharged on the way.

The side frames were on. Boards stuck between the slats. The chicken coop with the chickens on top of that. Along with the wash-pot, the corn, and dry peas I had sacked up. Boxed plow tools and assorted wrenches, wedges and the axe. A four-foot-long hog trough. Harness for horses or mules. Hoes, rakes, shovels, and axes were stuck in. The Georgia Stock and the No. 2 Kelly Turning Plow were wired to the side frames.

We unloaded the hogs first. They were under the boards stuck through the side frames. We had it all about unloaded by the time Franklin and Dad rolled in. They said that was it, they got it all. It could wait until morning to unload. We were a tired bunch after a long day.

Regan H. went back to Madisonville Sunday afternoon. Franklin, Dad, and Melton went back to work Monday morning. Virginia and Franklin's step daughter rode the bus to school. I was left with things to do.

Water had to be carried from the well for those hogs. Twice daily. The cow-pen had hog wire around it. I had to patch it up and put a few new posts in it. I never knew pine saplings used for post would rot in a year, I cut and used them! But the hogs had more room now. And the water-feed trough was a little closer to the well.

In a couple of weeks, dad bought a mule from someone he worked with. It was old, it had gray hair over brown. I had seen donkeys as big as it was. He also sold the hogs to the same fellow. The man told me "Them's the best hogs I ever seen!" Piney woods rooters were about it for this country, I decided.

I plowed around about two acres, burned it off for a garden. Flat broke it with the Kelley turning plow. Then rowed it up for planting. I had to stop often and let the mule rest. She was experienced, I could tell. But she was also old and small. The project took a full two weeks!

Mother went to town, she bought me a new pair of jeans, a couple of shirts and shoes. And a pair of overalls to work in. No longer did I have to wear the GI combat boots everywhere I went.

We were there two weeks before I actually saw the town. Melton took me in one Saturday night. Drove around until the midnight show. The theater was a Saturday evening, Saturday night and Wednesday night event. I thought the popcorn was the best I had ever eaten! He paid for it all. I never had a dime in my pockets, and I never felt good about that.

A young woman worked in the office where Franklin and Melton worked. She directed him to a place on the Trinity River where we could fish. He bought a couple of rods and reels. With minnow jars, we could go there after his work hours. Catch all the red horse minnows we needed in a few minutes. Mostly we caught drum, which I discovered people called gasper goo in this part of Texas.

Then there was a creek up near Onalaska we went to. We never caught a bass over a pound and a half. But with crawfish we caught a lot of them. Out of that creek they were good eating, unlike bass out of other places. The creek ran over limestone rock, then dropped off into holes at waterfalls. I loved the place, it was easy to imagine I was in Colorado! It was also easy to imagine myself there with Margaret. The creek was called "Big Rocky."

I was beginning to see that I should not have quit school. I had no money, nothing much to occupy my time. In short, I was making no progress in becoming able to search for Margaret. Margaret was never far out of my thoughts, even while fishing or eating popcorn at the mid-night show Saturday night.

Dad was liking his job, and his boss. Mr. John David Dobrinsky. He gave Dad a raise after the first week. Couple of weeks later, he promoted him to warehouse manager and gave him another raise. He also told me when I became 16, he would hire me.

There were both railcars and trucks to unload. Then trucks were loaded for shipment. Handled everything a grocery store might sell. Everything a horse, mule, donkey, cow, hog, chicken or other livestock might eat. Including hay. Then one warehouse was for hardware. That included cement, barb wire, and creosote posts.

I had really never worked for anyone but Dad in my life. I went in the Monday after my birthday. Needless to say, quite nervous and a little scared, I guess. Dad introduced me to Mr. Dobrinsky and went on to work.

Some people have the ability to put people at ease being in their presence, some don't! Mr. Dobrinsky quickly put me at ease in giving me an application form to fill out.

"When you are finished, just bring it into my office. I decide about people quickly." I liked this man.

The application was on a clipboard with pen. I sat down in the lobby outside his office to fill out the application. First Name. Middle name. Last name. I put my full name in the blanks. Robert Alton Dupree. We had sent for and I had my Social Security Card. I memorized my number. Age, address, and telephone number. We had no telephone. Place of last employment. Worked for my dad cutting hardwood timber. Salary? None!

I went in with the application. "Have a seat!" There were four chairs in front of his desk. I took one and watched as he read my application. Suddenly he looked up and said "Your name is Robert Alton?" And you were born March 24, 1936?"

"Yes sir! People call me Robert mostly."

"Well this all looks in order. I understand about family work and no salary. I've been there! Your dad has told me you always do the best you can on whatever he tells you to do. That included sawing logs or laying by corn! We'll start you at 0.75 cents an hour. Go on back there with your dad. He'll get you started. For now, you'll work under him."

My mind went back to Sam Craig, Margaret's uncle. Although he and Mr. Dobrinsky lived and worked in different walks of life, I believed they were made of the same stuff.

I found dad and a big Indian unloading a car load of horse and mule feed. I knew there was a reservation in the county. This was my first Indian to meet. Dad said this is "Big Jimbo" Jim Batise.

The Indian's face lit up in a smile! "Now we have "Little DuPree and "Big DuPree!""

They opened up that box car door and put a steel plate from the warehouse door into the boxcar. Five sacks of that horse and mule feed were put on a two-wheeler. It took me a few trips to learn, pushing a loaded two wheeler was a matter of balance on the wheels. Balanced right, they almost pushed themselves.

The feed sacks were being put in a five-way stack. Big Jimbo took one end of a sack, I the other. It was throw your end! The stack went up head high. Roll it over! Two people can pitch a hundred-pound sack of feed head high provided they learn that "roll over technique". "Throw your end" amounted to three sacks having to go end ways on a five-way stack. We unloaded a box car of carnation milk, another of sugar and one of sheet rock that week.

I learned after that first day, we loaded out trucks for shipment in the mornings. After the last load, we unloaded box cars or trucks in the evenings. I got sent to help the driver deliver the last load often. Sometimes 9 p.m. before getting back to the ware house and punching my time card. Sometimes we worked over unloading a late truck to get in or a box car on demerge. A penalty had to be paid if a box car was not ready for release in a certain length of time. I loved that overtime pay.

For the first time in my life I had money! With my first pay check, I ordered a 12-gauge single barrel Winchester shotgun. $19.95! Bought No. 4 and No. 6 shotgun shells. Opened a bank account. Tried to save most of what I earned. Never having money before, I hated turning it loose now that I had it! But I did buy more clothing, underwear, and dress shoes. And I paid my way into the midnight show and bought the popcorn! I also gave Virginia money to help some on her school wear needs.

It was mid-July when a woman in the office announced on the PA system "Robert DuPree, Mr. Dobrinsky needs to see you in his office!" *What have I done wrong*, I wondered all the way there.

"Have a seat. Robert. I have wondered if you plan on going back to school and getting your High School Diploma."

"Yes, Sir. I've been thinking about starting ninth grade over. And playing football!"

"I think it's important that you do. I got a proposition for you. Starting after the trucks are loaded today, I want you to work with the shipping clerk. You know in the evenings he works assembling on flats the small things for the next day's shipments. He needs help.

"I'll give you a key to the front door. After school hours, you can come in and work on that assembly job. I don't expect you to work all night. After football practice you might not feel like working at all! Just use your own judgement about the hours you work."

"Just use your own judgement" I heard often from Dad. I accepted his offer. I was now making a dollar an hour. I thought it would be easy to earn at least 15 bucks a week. I could get by without using what I had in my bank account.

He had another suggestion. The school offers a driver's education course. "You can get your driver's license. Next summer we may need you to make small deliveries in the pickup truck."

Brother Franklin and family moved to Longview. Dad rented a house in town. It had natural gas. Franklin had given Mother their gas stove. It had a fireplace, but Dad bought gas heaters. Mother had a kitchen sink and we had a bathroom. Hot and cold water! Dad thought it outrageous to have the outhouse inside the house. But he adapted quickly. He had no choice!

The school at Livingston was class 2-A in football. A big step up from class B in Buffalo. Virginia, who started school when we moved there had spread the word I was an all-district player. But because of eligibility requirements, I had to start football on the JV team.

The first day we had practice with the high school team, their coach moved me from left defensive guard to right guard. In front of last year's all state guard. I never knew if he was left handed or right handed. I never saw it coming. He knocked my front teeth up against the roof of my mouth.

The JV coach looked at it, told me to go to the shower room. I looked at my teeth in the mirror. My bottom and top lips were badly cut as well. I pulled my two front teeth back in position. Early the next day, the principal called me to his office. The high school coach was there. The principal asked "How did your injury happen?"

"I don't know. I never saw it coming."

The high school coach blurted out "What do you mean you never saw it coming."

"Like I thought, you pulled me from my regular position to put me in front of the guy, but you never watched what happened!"

My answer was the same. "I don't know. I never saw it coming."

The principal sent me to a dentist downtown. "Your teeth are broken off at the roots. But they'll tighten back up. You are too young now to do anything about it. Eventually you will have to."

I was back out for practice that afternoon. The high school team was practicing going down on punts. I was put in position to block for the punt receiver. I don't think the guy who knocked my teeth out thought I would hit him. I put my hip pads to his shins in a cross-body block that put him on his back six yards down the field. We practiced separately from the high school team the rest of the season.

Our first game was at Huntsville. Our JV coach called out his starting lineup. He put me at right guard! I had been practicing at left guard. It felt awkward being on the right side. We got beat, it was the roughest game I had played in. This class 2A football was a step up from class B! The JV team played on Thursday nights.

I got a surprise the next Friday night. Mr. Dobrinsky had driven to Huntsville to see the game. This is what he told Dad: "That boy of yours was the smallest boy out there.

But he was the best and toughest. If he weighed ten more pounds, he could play for the University of Texas!"

I learned later he never missed many games, that he was a member of the school board. And he had a keen interest in school activities and what went on. I thought in a matter of time, he was the reason that high school coach was not there the next year.

I worked at night after football practice with an elderly man who put the federal stamps on cigarette packages. Each case had to be opened, then each carton. The stamps were on a sheet of paper that appeared wet and slick. With three fingers on each hand, he slid those stamps off on each package of cigarettes in that carton.

I spoke to him a few times, and he just said "hum." But he got around to taking a break and buying me a coke. "I can't talk while stamping those cigarettes. If I do, I'll lose my concentration and mess up!" After that I never said anything to him until we took a break.

I soon learned that each store often got the same list of items I needed to assemble. I called these "Hot Items". As soon as I started work, I thumbed through the bill of ladings, made me a list of those "Hot Items." Before assembling for any customer, I brought them from the storage isles to the assembly point.

Mr. Dobrinsky often came back to his office at night and worked. One night he walked by and saw me writing in my notebook. He turned and came back to where I was.

"Robert, excuse my curiosity, but what are you doing in that notebook. I've seen you doing that a number of times."

I explained my system to him. "It's like this," I said. "If you need 15 small cases of penny matches to go on one shipment, only go down an aisle once to get them. It saves 14 trips! Most all stores get a certain number of things I list, which I call "Hot Items."

There is something else I've wondered why we don't do. Cut some assorted sizes of card board to separate each customer's order. They often fall together and get mixed up. Which slows our loading time down. We could get the cardboard out of rail cars."

"Robert, your dad has told me that when you do a job, you do it right and often find a better way to do it. These are the best ideas I've heard around here in years. I'll get the shipping clerk on it tomorrow!"

Dad told me the shipping clerk was finding errors on the items assembled, blaming it on me. "Better be prepared, I'm sure he's running to Mr. Dobrinsky with it. He'll probably be talking to you about it."

It happened, Mr. Dobrinsky asked me about it one night. I showed him the bill of lading I was working on. "I'm right handed. He's left handed. You can see that each item we check off is different. And if you will notice, I draw a small line where I start each night. If I have made mistakes, I'll try to be more careful!"

He went in his office. In a few minutes, he came out. "I went through the bill of lading copies we keep. Every error he complained about was what he assembled! I'll talk to him first thing in the morning!"

Dad said Mr. Dobrinsky came out on the loading dock the next morning. The clerk handed him four bills of lading. "The assembly was screwed up on these," he said.

"Show me which ones were screwed up," Mr. Dobrinsky said. The shipping clerk showed him.

"You did these," Mr. Dobrinsky said. "You got a left-handed check mark. Robert's is right handed. See this line. That's where he starts to finish the job you are supposed to be doing! I've looked at all the others you've complained about. Every one of these screw ups have been yours!"

Big Jimbo Batise told me later. "I've been working for Mr. Dobrinsky for over 20 years. That's the first time I ever saw him that pissed! That shipping clerk's afraid he's training you for his job!"

Virginia and I started 9th grade together. The first day, I signed up for the subjects I would take. That night she asked what I was taking. The next day she signed up for hers. We never had a class together. We took some of the same subjects, but at different periods. It would cramp our styles to be in the same class!

It must have happened during the move. Virginia had changed from a shy, quiet little girl to a beautiful young lady! Her eyes were blue, she had her hair cut short like a lot of girls wore after the movie "Roman Holiday." She tried out for cheerleader and got it. And she was elected 9th grade class girl favorite.

As for myself, I was taking driver's education as Mr. Dobrinsky had advised. Also, I was back by the owl. I was taking Greenhand FFA over again. And I was maintaining a sold "B" grade average. Part of it, I'm sure was my attitude of "I'm going to get it." I think part of it was the town and its people. It seemed this place was a little move advanced into the twenty first century than where I had been.

I had seen only one wagon in town. It had iron wheels, but they made no noise on concrete. They were covered with discarded automobile tires. I assumed the black man driving it broke up gardens for people. He had plows on the wagon.

The teachers all seemed to enjoy teaching. And they could smile! They made the subjects interesting and most of the students seemed to enjoy being in school. What a difference!

Virginia had made a friend in 8th grade she talked about a lot. In short, very intelligent, had the highest grades in the class. Her father was a Pentecostal Preacher at a small community church east of town.

They called our names the first day of school. When they called out my name, this girl turned to give me a quick look. She had blue eyes and blond hair. Platted and rolled up in a bun in back. Her dress was long and her white blouse was long sleeved and buttoned at the neck. *That's Virginia's friend, Mary Ellen Grimes*, I thought.

I knew I was right when her name was called. It turned out, our hall lockers were next to each other. She started the conversation. "You must be Virginia's brother. I'm Mary Ellen Grimes. Virginia talks about you a lot!"

"Yes I'm him! I've heard her mention your name quiet often. Glad to meet someone here I've heard about!"

"Well, Virginia and I are friends. I think it's commendable you are starting back to school. If I can help you in any way, let me know." With that, we headed for separate classes.

It never took long in my classes with her to realize Virginia was right. She was a very smart girl. Something else I decided. She tried to hide it by the way she dressed.

But with a little make up, let her hair down, and dress like other girls, she would be beyond the average beautiful. But perhaps because she was a preacher's daughter, Mary Ellen seemed to get left out of things. Like conversations, games, nominations for things. The smartest person in the class, I thought she should have been nominated for class president.

The year ended and I went back to five days a week. I never spent much time unloading trucks or rail cars. Mr. Dobrinsky told that shipping clerk to stay in the evening until the first two trucks out the next day were assembled. The next morning I would finish, he got on with truck loading duty. That afternoon, mostly I went with the last load out. If not, I worked with him on assembly.

One of the truck drivers was a man named Justin Wilson. Dad thought a lot of him. He mostly went to places like Houston, Beaumont, and New Orleans to pick up things. Lots of times he was late getting in. That truck had to be unloaded the next day. He just took another rig and left out again.

But on Thursday and Fridays, he took the last loads out. I went with him on those loads. Most other truck drivers rolled things to the back of the truck. I had to get it in the store. Once, I had to carry 40 sacks of four-bushel oats into a small feed storage building. Mr. Wilson, for the most part, had me rolling things to the back of the truck. He took it in the store!

He was drafted into the service and trained to operate heavy equipment in road building. On leave, he married. Then, he was shipped out to the South Pacific. Building airports, roads. On Iwo Jima with a dozer, he covered up the entrance to caves. Trapping those Japs inside. Sometimes they dug up inside their tents!

After the war, he got a job with a road building contractor in Lufkin. His wife had inherited the place where they lived at Livingston from her parents. He left his wife, daughter, and son for months sometimes to work. His daughter was 13 years older than his son Wade. About five years ago, he took this job. His daughter grew up without his being there. He would not let that happen with his son.

He inherited 360 acres from his parents up in Cherokee County where he grew up. His sister got 25 acres and the home across the road. She sold her part before he was discharged from the service. He had cattle on his place which was mostly in a creek bottom. He hoped to retire up there, but his land was not suitable to build on. For now, a black friend he grew up with helped tend to his cattle.

"Mr. Ben's the best man they ever had around that warehouse. He sees to it that my truck gets unloaded. Some before him never cared. Which caused me to wait around to leave and get in late."

That summer I bought my school clothes and gave Virginia money to buy hers. And a few things I wanted. A couple of Shakespeare Rods and Reels. A minnow seine and a minnow bucket. A box of no. 6 and no. 4 shotgun shells. Melton had located a lot of places on open timber company land we could hunt on. Mostly for ducks.

In August, it was back to two-a-day football work outs. With the heat and humidity of East Texas, it was enough to make you think about giving it up. Some did. It was a relief when school started. We only had to practice after school hours. We had a new coach and a new offense. Which he called a Split T formation. The backfield was like a regular T formation. It was the line that was split. We lined up with three feet between each position.

I played left guard on both offense and defense. Well it was mostly nose guard on defense. We ran a 5-3-2-1 on defense most of the time. Teams were lining up head to head on our offensive line. We won all our games but one.

Jasper had the answer for that Split T offense. They lined up in the gaps! Which screwed up our blocking assignments. Nobody was touching two linemen and a linebacker who were coming by me to my left and right. I could only block one. I told our coach I was looking at three people I needed to block at half time. His response was an angry one: "What do you mean? Just block somebody!"

I was trying to block the guy to my left, and hopefully get in the way of the linebacker that was right on his tail. I wondered about a coach that watched half of a football game and asked "What do you mean?" We got beat. That's what it meant!

I developed a friendship in 9th grade with a boy named Andre Batise. His father was Indian, his mother white. He was the 5th brother to play football at Livingston. He had a younger brother named Jason. Their dad worked for the Texas Highway Department.

44

Andre played middle linebacker on defense and left end on offense. On the 5-3-2-1, if he decided to rush, he would tap me on the butt right or left side, which indicated which side of their center I rushed on. If not, I had to hold that center up until I saw which way the ball was going, or if was a pass play.

Mr. Wilson told me his son, Wade and Jason Batise practiced football constantly. They lived and breathed football! They lived close together and spent time together almost daily.

At the start of 10th grade, I did something for Mary Ellen. I went to what was called our Study Hall period. It was in the library. Supposedly, you could do your class work assignments there, and have access to any reference books you might need. Mary Ellen was sitting at a table with one other girl. I took a seat next to her at that table. Andre and the girl he liked came and sat at the table with us. Being football players may have had something to do with it. Ten chairs around that table got filled shortly!

We could talk, but not loud. Mary Ellen got included! For her, it seemed to spread from there. She got elected class secretary. Then to head up our class in putting the yearly class annual book together. In this, she had to meet with students from all high school classes. It was also an advantage to me. I tried to get my assignments there because of football and work. If it was something I needed help with, she could and often did.

Andre was constantly on my case to date Mary Ellen. Because I sat with her in Study Hall, nominated her for class secretary, all the students seemed to think there was something going on between Mary Ellen and I. Virginia made a big deal out of it at home. "Robert got Mary Ellen elected class secretary! Mary Ellen talks about Robert all the time!"

One Saturday, I was in the kitchen lifting pot lids to see what was cooking. Mother asked me if I really was serious about Mary Ellen. "Virginia says she is such a nice girl!"

"Yeah, Mary Ellen is a nice girl! And she is the smartest person in our class. Because she is not Baptist or Methodist, I don't see why everyone is treating her like someone from outer space. That's why I nominate her for things, sit at the table with her in Study Hall. She's a friend of Virginia's and now mine as well. That's the way it is with Mary Ellen and I."

I don't know where the girl I care about is. That's Margaret! One way or another I'm going to find her. She promised to wait for me until I got out of Leon County, could support us and marry me! I'll be a junior next year. After football, I'll be able to work more. I hope to save enough to get a car. Then I can start looking for Margaret! Mary Ellen is a friend and that's all it's ever going to amount to!

I think mother was happier here than she had been anywhere else in her life. A doctor got her blood pressure under control. She had electricity, indoor plumbing, a telephone, a gas cook stove, automatic washing machine, and neighbors to visit and talk to. Dad had a steady income now, farming had been nothing but a gamble for most of their married life.

Mom's sister's husband passed on. Staying with a son's family in Ft. Worth, she came to visit. A wealthy neighbor friend of mother's offered her room and board, some pay to live in the house with her. She accepted. Mother and her started making patch work quilts. The wealthy old lady came and helped. Even Virginia and I helped stitch those quilts together. We learned to love an aunt we had only seen a few times before in our life.

My aunt had a daughter that must have been like Mary Ellen. Brilliant! She got a scholarship to college. Then during WWII, she went to Washington to work in the Pentagon. They never knew what happened to her. Perhaps jilted by some high ranking married official. Or dealing with the records of all those killed in the war. Mostly they believed she was put on experimental drugs. She had a mental breakdown.

The Pentagon notified the family they could come after her, or she would be put in a mental institution. Two of her brothers drove to Washington to get her. They tried to get an answer about what happened to her. They could find out nothing. The only answer was "You can take her home or she'll be kept in a mental institution." They brought her home.

After about five years at home with her mother, she became violent. She attacked her mother with scissors once. They had to put her in a state supported mental institution. Still there, it was a depressing thing for my aunt. My aunt stayed there at Livingston about a year. Her daughter-in-law from Ft. Worth came and got her. Her death came about a year later.

As soon as football season was over, I went back to work. Dad told me Mr. Dobrinsky had talked to him about his plans for me. That he meant to train me in every aspect of his business. Said he was not getting any younger. That he could foresee needing someone he could trust to help run the place. He thought by the time I graduated from high school, I would be ready.

We learned a lot about the man little by little. He lived in a hotel downtown. The owner was a woman who owned half interest with him in the big sawmill at the edge of town. She fixed his breakfast every morning. Other meals he ate in restaurants in town, or where ever he happened to be.

He was out of town a good bit, he had a lot of real estate interests in other counties. He owned a half interest of the local Ford dealership and also a Redi-Mix concrete business north of town. He was also president of the local school board and a Deacon at the Baptist Church downtown.

That summer he called me into his office the first day. "Robert, I'm not getting any younger. If you are willing, I want to start training you to run this business. That means you'll work in the office. Go with me to my places of other business interests. To my land holdings, which are mostly timberlands. But some of it, I've bought for future development in Lufkin, Diboll, Cleveland, and Crockett. Especially my private ranch, up in Cherokee County!" He laughed. "I don't have a cow on it yet, but I want your opinions on how to develop it into a working ranch."

"Now then, I know you and your dad walk a mile to work and back home each day. You walk a mile to school each day, and you walk a mile here to work during the school year. Your family needs transportation! I can get you a good used car. Since I own half interest in the Ford Place, I can discount my share of the profit. We can hold $10 per week out of your check to pay for it.

And before you ask, you only have two more years of school left. We'll find something here to work at after school. But we won't hold out $10 bucks from your check while you are in school. How about it? Are you interested in my offer? If not, you can still work here as you've been doing."

Was I interested? "Yes, Sir!"

It was a full summer. He put me in a 1953 V8 Ford with only 22,000 miles on it. For $10 bucks a week! But I was into work I had never dreamed of doing. Like working with his office manager. Reviewing receipts. Costs. Payroll. Retirement plan. Health care insurance. Often, he called me into his office to ask me my opinion of what his options were on certain aspects of running the business. If he agreed that I was right, he told me so. If he thought I was wrong, he explained why he thought so.

I took a general business course the year before. To be honest about it, I was actually beginning to be glad I took that course. I also took typing. I was not very good at it, but it now helped. Mary Ellen would throw that then manual carriage before I could type the words "All good men" in a words per minute speed drill!

He asked me to go with him to his ranch one Saturday. The first surprise was that he had a home there. One of those order the logs cut and ready to put up homes. It was three bedrooms and two baths. He showed me through the house, the bed room he slept in when he spent the weekend there. The kitchen was well stocked with cooking utensils, with a gas stove. A refrigerator which had nothing in it. "I just bring what I want when I come," he said.

Outside, he showed me the artesian well he had drilled. Three-inch pipe elbowed over and full flow. The water line with a shutoff valve was welded into that three-inch line to supply the house and outside faucets. The water flow had enough pressure to accomplish that. Most of the water flowed off downhill to what he called Devils Hurricane Creek. "It don't run all year," he said. "But a lot of water comes down it when it rains."

He opened up a two-door garage attached to the house. Inside was a four-wheel drive Dodge Power Wagon and a rather plain looking but well-kept International Pickup. He backed the Power Wagon out, I got in. He seemed to love driving that wagon, I could tell. He put that thing through places a piney woods rooter hog would not go.

But he showed me most of 3600 acres. Some hardwood had been left along that Devil's Creek, and up some draws and one spring branch that came into the creek. The place had been mostly clear cut over by the timber company before he bought it he said.

Next to the creek, about half a mile from the house, was a field that must have covered 75 acres. Once pasture, I suppose, it looked like bottom land that would grow anything.

Near the house was about two acres surrounded by large cedar trees. It was easy to tell they had been planted there. They were all the same distance apart and in straight rows. A chain link fence surrounded the area just outside the cedars. There was a double gate up by the black top FM we got there on. Near his log house was a walkthrough gate.

"Is that a cemetery," I asked?

"Yes, it's an old one. I had the fence put around it. There is a few old grave stones up near the front. Some are marked with just red rocks. See that concrete pen right in the center. My wife and infant son are buried there. I've had a marker made, they'll put it up after I'm put here. The funeral home at Livingston has directions for my funeral and burial here."

He never elaborated any further and I sensed I should not ask. That's the first I ever knew he once had a wife and a son. My guess was his wife died in childbirth.

I went back to school for my junior class year. It was now just Virginia and I at home with Mother and Dad. Melton had married the girl in the newspaper office he worked with. He took a job in a town south of Houston. They lived there now, but came up about every weekend. They managed to attend most of my Friday night football games at home; a few that were sort of on the way.

On Saturdays, Melton and I continued to duck hunt. Mr. Dobrinsky had shown me land he owned across the Trinity River. He said there were hogs, deer, squirrels, and ducks. We hunted there some, killed a couple of hogs. I knocked a buck down with buckshot, but never could find it. But if it rained much, we knew better than trying to get to the place.

With the car, Virginia and I could go fishing up at that creek near Onalaska. Virginia invited her friend Mary Ellen to go with us. We seined crawfish, took sandwiches, and cold drinks. Mary Ellen loved it, she had never did anything like it before. I dressed the fish to take them home with her. We met her dad and mother, they seemed glad that we took Mary Ellen with us.

Things happened in our junior year that kept getting me into deeper water with Mary Ellen. We still sat at the same table in study hall. She talked about us fishing together. I think that sort of deepened the water! Then I nominated her for football sweet heart. She never won, but that seemed to deepen the water more. But one way or another, she was a decent person, a friend as far as I was concerned. To heck with what people thought. She deserved to be involved in school activities.

I got involved with two boys in FFA. One played steel guitar. The other played standard guitar and could sing. I thumped the standup bass to try to make us a three-man band. And I tried to sing as well. We met at our homes a lot, it was just fun and something to do.

Then a girl friend of the steel player invited us to play at her house. Next a classmate wanted us to play at his birthday party. Half the school was there it seemed. An older man from Lufkin joined us there with a fiddle. We set up on the front porch, the kids danced in a hard packed dirt yard.

Our FFA teacher heard we had a band going! "You boys come with me Friday. Bring your instruments. I'm entertainment chairman at Rotary Club. Come play and you'll get your dinner free!"

"We just try to play for fun. We are not good enough to entertain the Rotary Club."

"You boys want to pass this class, don't you?"

We played about three times at the Rotary Club. Also the FFA Father and Son Banquet. And older brother had given dad a suit. He came to the banquet in a suit and tie. The first time I ever saw him dressed like that.

I decided I was not taking FFA my senior year. The steel player would graduate this year. So next year, I thought I would end my musical career. But looking back, I think that FFA teacher saw a ray of hope for the three of us boys in music.

One Friday night at work, Mr. Dobrinsky was there. "I need to go out to the rifle range to sight in a rifle tomorrow. I'd like for you to come with me. If you do, I'll pick you up about nine in the morning." I told him I would be ready.

The rifle was a 243 Winchester. A heavy barrel and no sights. It had a Redfield scope on it. I knew that was an expensive combination.

"You ever shot a gun with a scope before," he asked?

"No, sir. All I've ever shot is a shotgun and a .22 rifle with iron sights."

"I can't hit a bull in the butt with a bass fiddle with iron sights," he said. "But I'm a fair shot with a scope."

He put the gun in a vise thing there to hold it. Took out the bolt. Started looking through the barrel at a target a hundred yards away. And adjusting on that scope until he finally said, "I think I'm about as close as I can get by bore sighting."

He put the bolt back in. Loaded it. Took it out of that vice thing. Laid it on sand bags and fired it at that target 100 yards away. Looked at the target through his binoculars.

"A little high and to the left he said." He did some adjusting, then fired three rounds. Looked through his binoculars. "That's about it he said. I'll put up another target."

"I'll go put up the target," I said." I found three holes in the target center not an inch apart.

When I got back, he said "Now you shoot three rounds."

He was looking through the binoculars. "You must have learned a lot shooting that .22. That's meat on the table shooting!"

He put the gun back in the hard box like case he brought it in. Handed it to me. "That's your gun now! You are doing a good job for me, I want you to have it. Let's get back to town and eat a burger!" We had a burger at a place on US 59 about a block away from where his warehouses were. When he let me out at home, he handed me a full box and the partial box of ammunition we shot out of at the range.

I wondered long and often why he was taking such a special interest in me. Some might think of him as being a gay bird with boy interests. He never acted like that. When I showed Dad the gun he gave me he said what I had come to expect. "Yes, he asked me yesterday if I had any objections to giving you a gun. He said you had earned it." The man always got Dad's approval before he did anything for me.

I learned that morning he was very much into hunting. He and friends went to Colorado for elk and mule deer. To the Gulf Coast for ducks and geese. And Southwest Texas for deer, turkey, and quail. He also said this: "I have a closet full of guns. Owning guns is like having money in the bank!"

Football my junior year was the same old Split T. We lost one game. Our coach still had no answer for Jasper's defense. On Mondays, we met in a classroom before practice to hear scouting reports about the team we would play next. Andre, I suppose got on the coach's black list with me. Before the Jasper game, he asked "What are our blocking assignments going to be if they line up in the gaps like last year?"

His answer was an angry one. "Just block somebody like you are supposed to!"

The all-district player awards came out in the local newspaper. Two players from our team were on it. Our right half back and our quarterback. Both deserving players and another reason I believed we got out coached at Jasper.

Mr. Dobrinsky read it and had this to say: "That coach should have put you and Andre Batise in for all-state awards! He never even put you in for all-district awards! He won't be coaching here next year!"

"Football is over for me. I'm too small to play college football anyway. I know I played the best I could! What matters to me is Andre is big enough to play college football. I doubt he will get a scholarship, because like me, he will be too old to play our senior year."

"If that coach had put him in for awards like he should have, colleges would have come knocking on his front door! Yours as well! That coach won't be here next year!"

I asked Mary Ellen to attend the football banquet with me. She accepted my invitation. Which was all over school in a short time. It was announced at home by Virginia as well! I was supposed to take someone, and I thought Mary Ellen deserved to go! To heck with what everyone wanted to believe!

To be honest about it, I was somewhat surprised when I picked her up. She had on an evening gown that showed her flawless white shoulders! She had let her hair down. Which hung down to her mid back. Her lips were lightly red. I knew she would be the most beautiful girl there!

Members of the team had to stand up, tell who they were, what position they played, and introduce their date. The girl introduced would stand which always got applause. When I introduced Mary Ellen Grimes, everyone in the room stood up to applaud long and loud! No doubt about it, I was not the only one that noticed how beautiful she was!

That summer, it was back to office work and training. Mr. Dobrinsky belonged to the Lions Club. He took me with him when they met. We looked at property in Diboll, Cleveland, Lufkin and Crockett. "You need to know where it's at! When these towns grow, we'll cash in!" Back at the office it was "Look in the land files. I need a report on the taxes we paid last year on every tract of land we own!"

That was not a 15 minute task! It took me almost two days! All the time wondering, why does he keep saying "WE" so much! But I knew why he had me do the report. I now knew he had a special bank account he deposited money into that was used for nothing but tax payments! Like trucking and fuel costs. Kept under a separate office file and a separate bank account. Every aspect of his business was set up that way! By doing reports on all those separate files, I got a handle on everything he owned.

By the time my senior year in high school started, I had a fair handle on the business, I thought. I knew where his land holdings were, about his different business partnerships. The amount of cash in the general fund was beyond my imagination. He called that the "Growth and Unexpected File!" Something else I knew. There was half a million bucks in his Ranch Fund at the Wells Texas bank. But when school started, my office job reverted back to my old assembly job.

I got to work longer that summer. No before school started football practice. There was a new head high school coach. He asked Andre and I both if we wanted to help coach the JV team. We both declined because we both worked after school. Shortly after school started, he called me into his office one day. "I'm not running a "Split T" line this year. It'll be a toe to toe regular "T" formation. What's your advice about handling a defense that lines up in the gaps, like they tell me Jasper does?"

"Lining up toe to toe will help a lot. But it will, I think, create some confusion in blocking assignments. They rush linebackers on almost every play. To start a game against them I would throw quickly left and quickly right passes until they backed those linebackers up. On all plays, have all your linemen block in towards the center."

"Now this is what I think needs be done. You got four men in the backfield. The fullback and a halfback needs to each double team block with two of your offensive linemen to open a hole. With all your linemen blocking in to the center, your center should be free to go after a linebacker."

"Have you ever considered being a football coach," he asked?

"It has crossed my mind a few times. My guess is you have plays designed to run against teams that line up head on defense. It should be easy to convert a few of those to everyone blocking towards the center. Jasper evidently has some great scouts! I don't think you should use anything but your plays until you run up against a split the gaps defense."

Two things I gave Mr. Dobrinsky credit for after that conversation. Last year's coach was not there anymore! And he advised the new coach to talk to me about Jasper's defense!

Mary Ellen could draw anything. A lot of the time it was just black pencil. The brown paper book covers they gave us seemed a favorite place for her to draw. Sometimes she oil painted her drawings on those book covers. One day I walked by her desk in classroom before the teacher came in. A book on her desk had a red rose painted on it. It looked so real you could almost smell it.

I stopped, put my elbow down on her desk. With chin in hand, I just stared at that rose. All chatter ceased in that class room. Mary Ellen looked around, turned red, then back at me. Finally, she said: "Robert, is there something wrong?"

I stood up. "No, nothing is wrong. I was just trying to decide if that was a rose or a petunia on your book cover!" Everyone in the class laughed!

Mary Ellen grew redder. But she said "Robert, if you can't tell the difference between a rose and a petunia, I'm not going to tell you!" Then she laughed with everyone else!

I went on to my desk. A few of the girls were looking at me. Like are you Dr. Strange Love, or what?

I sat down at my desk. My mind went back to Margaret. Sticking my tongue out at her to get her attention. *Why had I pulled such a bonehead stunt today?* I got Mary Ellen's attention and about 20 other classmates! Andre gave me a thumb's up sign. They all thought I was putting a move on Mary Ellen!

I only went to one football game that year. I had to drive to Jasper, but I wanted to see what happened. Livingston got the ball first. They hit them with quickly left and right passes down to the 20 yard line before they quit rushing those linebackers. Then the line blocked to the center. The fullback and the right halfback led the left halfback around right end. The center got a linebacker trying to head them off. The ball carrier scored without being touched! They went on to win the game. District champs!

They lost in bi-district play by one point. Eight guys on that team were classmates. Four made all district, two others received honorable mention. All six got a scholarship to a different college in Texas. My friend Andre Batise was a player forgotten. Football was over for him as I was afraid it would be.

Mr. Justin Wilson invited me to go up to his place during late November. His black friend had called he said. Two dead pines had fell on his fence. He sort of brushed it in hopefully to keep the cows in until it could be fixed. "Wade wants to hunt. I can put the two of you on a stand in a good place. I got corn out. Wade is only seven years old, but I've taught him to shoot. Bring yourself a lunch, his mother will fix him one."

It was bitter cold that Saturday morning. Eighteen degrees in Lufkin, the radio weatherman reported. I noticed after we got to Lufkin, we headed out the same way Mr. Dobrinsky had took to his ranch. *We were getting near it,* I thought. He turned off the highway to a plank gate. Just across that FM blacktop, from Mr. Dobrinsky's place.

"That's Mr. Dobrinsky's place across the road?"

"Yeah, I see him up here every now and then. When I was growing up, I hunted all over it. He's got a lot of work to do to make it into a cattle ranch."

I got out and opened that gate. He drove through. "Just leave it open," he said. "I'll close it when I come out. Them cows is over yonder waiting to be fed I imagine!"

We went through places down through that open pasture bottom that we probably could not have made had the ground not been frozen. "See that fence yonder ahead of us? That's the back side of my place. If you shoot something and it goes over that fence, go get it! Wade knows the man that owns that place. He's a good neighbor."

He turned right suddenly and brought it to a halt. Right in front of a red bluff iron ore hill. He got out. We got our guns and lunches. I had a small ice chest with a 6 pack of Dr. Peppers in it.

He had a seat about as wide as a porch swing on the edge of that bluff. It was roofed over, walled up in back and both ends. "It's about a hundred yards to that corn. Wade will show you where it's at when it gets daylight. Behind this stand, is a gulley. We got wood down there for a fire. Building a fire down there won't hurt a thing. You got matches?"

"Yes, sir."

"Ok then! If you kill something, just field dress it. A hog ain't going to ruin today! It may be dark when I get back. We got a lot of work to do!" With that he left us there. I had a flashlight. "Wade, I think we might as well go ahead and build that fire." I figured they might have some brush for the fire. He had seasoned and near green split red oak down there. With pine heart kindling. It was dry down there and we had no problem getting a fire going that would last awhile.

Day light finally got there. The stand blocked the wind fairly well. The pasture had narrowed down where we were. There was perhaps a 25-yard open space across the creek bottom. The corn is just across the creek. See that fence over yonder past the corn. That's the other side of our place.

51

Wade picked up a 12-inch pine board leaning against one wall. On each side wall, a two by four had been nailed. He laid that board across in front of us, ends resting on those two by fours. He picked up sandbags from the floor, two for each of us. "If I have to get out of here, I just duck under," he said. I laid my gun on those sandbags. It felt just right to shoot from.

The sun was up bright and clear. It was about mid-morning when two big sows and about a dozen other hogs came out on that corn. I estimated they averaged about 125 pounds each. Four had their tails cut off. Wild hogs, they had been trapped and surgery performed. Those four were barrows.

Wade you sight in on that red barrow with the black spots. I'll aim at that black one. When you are ready, shoot!

I had my cross hairs just above that corn eating black hogs head. I knew when he shot, that hog would raise his head up, freeze for a second before the bunch hit the woods. It worked, and we each got a hog. Wade hit his in the ribs behind the shoulders.

One at the time, we drug both down into the bottom of the creek bed. There we field dressed both. Now considerable lighter, one at the time we drug them to the foot of that bluff bank where the stand was. It had not warmed up any it seemed.

We went to the fire, put a little more wood on. We ate our lunches, washed it down with a Dr. Pepper. No need to get back on the stand for a while now after killing those hogs. We stayed with that fire about two hours, I think. We had us another Dr. Pepper and Butter Finger. Then went back to the stand. I thought it was getting colder.

It seemed nothing, not even a bird or a squirrel was moving. We sat there until I told Wade "In about 30 more minutes, it's going to be dark!" Two minutes later, I caught movement of a deer coming down the creek bottom. It was on our side of the creek. "Wade I see a deer headed for that opening. It most likely will stop to look when it gets to the edge of it. If it's got horns, let it have it!"

Wade was shooting a 308, he got that hog right behind the shoulders. I was not going to shoot unless the deer tried to get up and run. It was a big 8-point buck and it never got up! No need for silence now. "You got him Wade! You got him!''

We field dressed the deer and drug it to where the now stiff hogs were. We could hear Mr. Wilson coming! When he got there, he was elated. "You boys got the meat! I heard three shots down here and by doggies, they all got meat!"

When he let me out at my house it was "I'll back this pickup in the garage where dogs can't get to it. Cold as it is, we can wait until morning to work up this meat. I'll probably start about nine. Bring Mr. Ben with you if he wants to help us!"

He had a meat grinder. We made steaks out of the back straps of the deer. Chopped up the hog ribs for frying. Made chops out of one of the hog loins or back straps. He and Dad agreed we best grind up the rest for sausage making. He had a different way of seasoning than we did. He normally bought casings to smoke his in. Dad had Mother make cheese cloth bags about four inches wide and 20 inches long. Mr. Wilson wanted to try that with his. He would have his wife buy cheese cloth Monday and make bags for all of us.

He insisted we take half of everything home with us. Mother seasoned our sausage the way she always did. Sprinkle sage, salt and red pepper on it and hand mix. Then fry one! Taste it. She kept mixing and frying one until she got the taste she wanted.

We took that seasoned sausage back over to the Wilson's place Monday afternoon. We bagged it all up. Flattened them to about an inch thick. Then he hung half of his in one place. Half of ours went with that. His and our half left was hung sort of apart.

"That looks about right he said. I'll put the hickory smoke to it. I'll bring yours to you in about a month."

His was I suppose sort of Italian in taste. Ours was like a breakfast sausage. Recipes were traded. "From now on, I'm smoking sausage seasoned both ways Mr. Wilson said." I loved sandwiches made from his way of seasonings. It was easy to split a sandwich length piece and make two sandwiches for a lunch that would hold you until supper time!

The reason most of that meat was ground into sausage, not a lot of people had home freezers then. It could have been salt cured, but we just preferred smoked sausage which would keep. I might add here, a few people had television. Those I had seen were like watching it snow!

Mary Ellen was elected class president. Virginia got All School Favorite Girl. Nominated for Senior Class most beautiful. She never won that. But in four years, she received a lot of awards. Class Favorite Girl three years in a row. Homecoming Queen. Football Sweetheart. Duchess to the Woodville Dogwood Festival. Head Cheerleader.

In my senior year, I was elected Senior Class favorite boy. I think my classmates decided Virginia had received so many awards, her brother deserved something!

Mary Ellen, to raise funds for the Class trip to New Orleans organized a car wash. It was at a service station owned by a man that attended her church. I volunteered that Saturday along with a number of our classmates. Virginia for some reason was not there. Mary Ellen painted a sign which read:

Get Your Car Washed!

$1.50

Help the Senior Class of 1955-56 Get to New Orleans!

We had a blast that day! She had a girl collecting money, lining the cars up for a wash job. One thing about the town, folks pitched in to help school kids. But lunch time came. "Mary Ellen, why don't you and I slip across the street to the Greasy Spoon and eat lunch?"

"Greasy Spoon! Why do you call it that?"

"My friend Big Jimbo Batise calls it that. Dad and I eat lunch there often during the summer with him. They make a great hot roast beef sandwich. Trust me! It's good."

"I'm hungry enough to eat anything," she said.

I ordered two. When they brought those steaming plates out she said "You call this a sandwich?"

"That's what they call it." It was thin sliced beef brisket, over mashed potatoes with gravy. With green beans and two pieces of thick Texas toast and ice tea. For $1 you would not leave hungry!

I never had wanted to rain on her parade. But I felt I needed to tell her about Margaret. I thought this was the best opportunity yet. I did not tell her everything, but that we loved one another. That we made a commitment to marry. As soon as we graduated, I meant to try to find her.

Mary Ellen looked on the verge of tears. But she said this: "Virginia told me once she thought you still cared for a girl where you once lived. I believe people should keep the commitments they make."

That was that. It hurt to see her hurt. But I had to do it.

We took in over $250 dollars for the class that day. Not that we washed all that many cars. People were giving us $5 to $10. I heard that girl collecting the money say "That Dude gave us $20!"

I asked Mary Ellen to the Junior-Senior Class Prom. She accepted. She seemed to be going along with this friendship thing between us. Everyone else thought it amounted to more than that. I think we both liked that, no one would bother either of us. Virginia just laughed about it when I told her I was going broke buying corsages for Mary Ellen!

I could have just got a plain carnation corsage for $5. I got one all right! With blue violets in the center to match Mary Ellen's blue eyes. Which cost $8.50!

Getting dressed in a dark blue suit, white shirt, cuff links, and maroon colored knit tie, I wondered what my life would be like now if I were still in Leon County. I doubted I would have any of what I was wearing tonight, including black dress shoes. Or the black trousers with the buckle in back hanging in the closet. The light pink shirt to wear with those! The black loafer shoes with the quarters stuck in each that was the style all boys wore! How "Hep to the Jive" would I be now if we had not moved to a place where I could work?

I suppose it was an evening dress Mary Ellen had on. Knee length but a not so dark blue. Bare shoulders showing her flawless white skin. Her Mother pinned the corsage on, I think she saw I was a little reluctant about trying to do that on an almost low-cut neck line. Her Dad had a camera, he took a number of pictures of us standing together. "Now you kids go enjoy that prom!" he said.

Mary Ellen is the most beautiful girl here, I thought. Well, sisters don't fit in the equation when boys think about girls being beautiful!

On the way taking her home, she said, "This is the most beautiful corsage I've ever seen! I'm going to paint it before I dry it to keep!"

"You can draw and paint better than anyone I've ever knew," I said.

After a moments' silence she asked, "Robert do you think that girl is going to wait for you like she promised? It would be a miracle if she did, it seems to me. It's been so long!"

"Mary Ellen, that's the opinion everyone else has. They don't know Margaret the way I do. I do believe she is waiting for me. I could not live with myself if I broke my promise to her. I know in my heart she feels the same way."

It seemed they let up on us in our senior year. There were a lot of activities going on. I suppose that's one reason we had so little homework. We were near the end of high school for us. The trip to New Orleans was the next week. I gave Virginia 50 bucks to make the trip. I well knew what it would be like to go without money! Mary Ellen asked me if I intended to go.

"No. I think I'll go up to the creek fishing. I can work some. And I need the money."

"I'm not going either. I don't think Mother wants me to go. And I just don't care about it anyway." She smiled, then said: "I'd rather go fishing with you!"

I was somewhat shocked! But how could I say no to Mary Ellen!"

"Let's go Saturday then. They leave Thursday, will come back Saturday. I don't work on Saturday nights. I'll pick you up about eight."

"I'll fix us lunch she said. You can get the drinks!"

I bought a couple packages of bait shrimp at a place in town. As I expected, we only got a few crawfish at a place we seined on the way there. The place was almost dried up, we never got our feet wet.

Mary Ellen had on tight jeans, a long sleeve shirt, sun shades and a big hat! Seeing her in those jeans I admit was a strain on my resistance. I knew if I touched her, knowing how she felt what would happen! I could not let that happen!

Those bass were getting after those shrimps. So were channel catfish. I had never caught a catfish here before. I never had fished with the bait they wanted! I cut a couple of willow poles, rigged them out to fish using a cork. We started fishing with them, casting out a shrimp with our rod and reels.

The fishing got fast and furious! Never had I seen anyone enjoy catching fish like Mary Ellen was. I was stringing up fish more than I was fishing! I finally said "Let's Eat!"

She had fried chicken and potato salad in the little ice chest she brought. Inside was a couple of paper plates and forks. It was so good up there on that creek under the shade of a big red oak leaning out over the creek bed.

We called it quits on the fishing about 3 p.m. We had three stringers of fish, those catfish weighed up to three pounds. I had a big ice chest with ice in the car. We took it down to the creek. I skinned and dressed them all.

"That's enough for both our families! I'll get my ice chest and take some for us she said. I put about a third of the fish in her ice chest and she said that's enough. There are only three of us."

When we got to her home, before getting out of the car, she said this." Robert, this has been a day I want ever forget! Thank you so much for taking me. I love that Creek up there. I think I can paint it from memory." I helped her get her fish to the door. Went home. And that was a day I would never forget either!

Virginia got home late Saturday evening. We sat in the kitchen Saturday night. She was so excited about the trip. Telling about a tour of New Orleans. The Morning Call Cafe. The French Quarters. And a boat ride on the Mississippi River on a paddle wheeler boat called "The President." Staying in the Jung Hotel with boys from a school in Arkansas in their room! But she finally wound down. It was "Well Robert what did you do?"

"I worked about five hours both Thursday and Friday. Today Mary Ellen and I went up to Big Rocky Creek fishing. That's why we had fish for supper!"

"You and Mary Ellen went fishing together? That's why you both never went to New Orleans! Yall had this planed! I should have known!"

Graduation came in late May 1956. Girls and boys were paired up to walk the isle together, then separate and sit on separate sides of the auditorium stage. I got paired with Mary Ellen. I also got paired with our Class Valedictorian!

The Principal made a speech. "This Class was special to me, not just because my son is one of the students. One reason is two of these students left school, started over and are on this stage tonight! Few that quit school have what it takes to do that." He went on to list other things, wound up introducing Mary Ellen to speak as the valedictorian of our class.

She got up with a confidence she may not have had when I first met her. She never stuttered and she never stumbled. Her speech was about the world beyond tonight. It would be a challenge, but we must dedicate ourselves to working to accomplish whatever our dreams might be. In the end, she said she would pray that God be with each of us to achieve whatever goals we hoped for in this life.

We got our diplomas and that was it. It meant a lot to me that the principal had said he was proud of Andre Batise and Myself. He never called our names but we both knew he meant us. Also the end of Mary Ellen's speech. She said she would pray to God that all of us achieve our goals in life. She knew finding Margaret was my goal.

My sister and family that lived in Wichita Falls were there for our graduation. Sunday afternoon Virginia went home with them. I went to work full time Monday morning. I was about two months passed my 20th birthday. But I got it! That High School Diploma!

Chapter Five
Moving Up and Being Alone!

Monday morning, I dressed for the middle of the road. I had no idea what I would be doing. I put on my best jeans, a new shirt, and wellington type boots that shined up good. After shaving, I dabbed on a little Old Spice after-shave lotion.

Mr. Dobrinsky was waiting for me in his office. When I asked him where he wanted me to start work, he laughed. "Your days of working in the warehouse are over. I've added another desk to this office. That's where you will work from. Let's go to the break room for coffee before we get started!"

In the break room, he continued to talk. "I'm not getting any younger. You got a good handle on our different business files and accounts last summer. One of the things I need help on now is purchasing. I'll help you get started. Any questions you have, don't hesitate to ask."

That turned out to be easier than I thought. Salesmen from different companies came in, checked their inventory. Came into the office, we agreed on how much they would ship us. "They try to overstock us," Mr. Dobrinsky warned. "Over stocking ties up space, increases labor costs. But if they find their product out of date, or gone bad, they will remove it and refund us."

Dad did one of the inventory reports each morning. The other departments also did so each morning. It was easy to determine what was needed, and order it. It took about two weeks, and a lot of questions, but I decided this job would be easier than I thought.

He belonged to the Lions Club, which met once a month. He had me go with him as guest. I bought a couple of sports jackets and dress pants to wear daily. Those sports jackets hung over the back of my desk chair most of the time. I never knew when he would say we needed to go somewhere. School board meetings were at night, he asked me to go with him to those as well.

He had a retirement plan for his employees that was a number of years ahead of any I knew of. Up to 10% could be withheld from your pay check. He matched each dollar withheld with 50 cents. The bank was paying compound interest on your account. If you retired or quit, you withdrew what you had accumulated. In case of your death, you designated who would receive your fund.

My dad's sister that lived in Jewett passed on. Her husband had passed on years before. Having no children, she left Dad her home on an acre and a half of land. Mother and Dad wanted to retire there. The house needed a lot of work. It had city water. The water meter was outside the front yard fence next to the street. Inside the fence, was a faucet. His sister used a bucket to carry water in the house for years.

It had electricity. There were ceiling lights in each room. But not a wall plug in the house! The house was like so many in Texas. Her husband ordered it. Dad said every pre-cut piece came in on the train. He got a carpenter to put it together. The walls were 12 feet high, constructed with one by 12-inch pine lumber.

A bathroom, kitchen cabinet and sink were needed. A septic tank system installed. The place rewired with wall plugs. Get a propane tank delivered. An eight-foot ceiling put under the 12 feet one in the living room. Paneling in the living room, sheet rock in the other rooms.

My brother Lawrence brought a pipe threader, cutter, vice, and pipe wrenches. I did the under-house work, he did the engineering. We got water and gas lines put where needed. Melton and I rewired the place. Sister Annie's husband put ceramic tile in the bathroom and kitchen. But we got the place ready by Thanksgiving that year.

Virginia got a job in the dentist office on the airbase near Wichita Falls. Her brother-in-law was a Civil Service Instructor there. He was able to help her get the job. She met an Air Force trainee there and in September, a wedding date was set.

I told Mr. Dobrinsky it would be on Saturday night. I needed to take Mom and Dad. "Wichita Falls! That's up yonder. You and your dad take Friday and Monday off."

We left Thursday evening. Stayed all night at the house in Jewett. Friday, we stopped for about an hour with brother Elton and family at Weatherford. We got to Sister Faye's house at Burkburnett about mid-afternoon. Saturday night, I stood up with a brother-in-law to be in a Baptist Church there in Burkburnett.

Sunday morning, we headed home. Stopped again in Weatherford. Spent the night in Jewett and back home Monday. Three months later, Virginia and her Air Force husband were stationed in Turkey!

It did not take long to realize that office work was not a bed of roses. I went home some days as beat as I would have been unloading box cars all day. The office manager was Mrs. Elizabeth Ivers. I now knew that she and the three other women in the office worked harder than I had imagined.

Mrs. Ivers husband was wounded on Iwo Jima. They had a place out near the Indian Reservation. He got hit with shrapnel in a hip. He could get around with a walking stick, run his tractor, see after his cattle. He did some gardening, and did most of the cooking. But since WWII, she had worked in the office for Mr. Dobrinsky. She was the bread winner in the family.

Dad retired early the next year. He had accumulated some retirement. Mr. Dobrinsky also gave him a $2500 bonus check for a "job well done." He also told me I could use one of the trucks if we moved on a weekend.

Melton and Lawrence came to help on a Saturday morning. I took the biggest delivery van on the lot. Along with a two-wheeler for loading appliances. A couple of 2x12's out of the hardware warehouse that had somehow got beat up too bad to ship. But they were strong enough to roll a loaded two-wheeler up.

The van held it all. Everything they owned. Lawrence and his wife took Mom and Dad on to Jewett. After we unloaded, Melton came back with me. He had left his car at a now vacant house in Livingston. I parked the truck on the lot where I got it and unloaded the two-wheeler and the two by twelves. Got in my car and went home to my apartment.

It was a garage apartment actually. A small kitchen, a bathroom, and one large room that had a bed and two straight back chairs in it. It had an automatic washing machine in the garage which I could use. The people I rented from used it as well. They lived in a big house in front of the apartment. They told me no pets, no drinking, or loud parties!

Mother gave me a cast iron skillet, a few pots, and pans. And a patchwork quilt. I bought a coffee pot, sheets, and pillows. Pillow cases and two alarm clocks. An electric radio which had a clock and alarm. Mother had always got me up and going. I wanted to be certain I got to work on time.

I had a telephone installed. I was subject now to being called out after regular working hours. A truck might break down somewhere. Or run out of fuel. And of course, mostly for use with family. I was now alone. And it was lonely!

There was a closet in the bathroom. The fellow that lived there before me left a stack of assorted girly magazines on a shelf. In a playboy magazine, was a girl that looked like and reminded me of Mary Ellen. The blue eyes and blonde hair did it. I wondered how she was doing.

I took those magazines, drove thru an alley downtown. Threw them in an open top dumpster there. Went on to work. That evening, I passed back by that alley. Bicycles were parked or laying all around. Teenage boys were all around and over in that dumpster!

Mr. Dobrinsky had given Mary Ellen a $5000 check for being class valedictorian so that she might attend college. She also told me her father was giving up the church. They would move back to a home and place they owned near Tyler. She planned to attend college in Tyler.

But one thing about being alone was that I could now go on weekends and start trying to find Margaret. I had to help Mother and Dad get that house ready at Jewett. That had delayed me a year almost.

One thing I had found out at Jewett. One of Dad's nephews told us Sam Craig was dead. His house burned down on his body. Lots of folks thought he was murdered, and the house set on fire. "That Sheriff we got now ain't gonna do nothing!"

Dad said "I expect not. I was with Sam long before that fellow was Sheriff. Sam beat him up for killing one of his Daddy's hogs!"

Margaret's Daddy killed him was my guess.

The weekend after the move, I went to Oakwood. Margaret had told me where the old home place was and cemetery. I found the cemetery with no trouble. A fairly fresh grave. No headstone, but a funeral home marker had Sam Craig's name written on it.

I went back to town. Pulled into a service station for gas. I asked the service station attendant if he knew Sam Craig.

"Shore do. Knowed him always. Finest fellow I ever knew! I believe somebody kilt him. Then burnt the house down on him!"

"I'm Robert DuPree. I've been trying to locate Sam's sister Martha and her kids. I wonder if you know anything about where they might be?"

"I've heerd Sam talk about you DuPree's. Martha air none of her kids were at Sam's funeral. I was there. I knowd 'em all! Jim Williams owned the place this side of Sam. Like brothers they wuz. Jim got up, saw smoke where Sam lived. *Too much smoke*, he thought. He saddled his horse and rid over there. Shore nuff, the house was dang near burnt up. He told me he could see Sam's remains smoking just inside whar the front door wuz. He got our worthless Sheriff out there. Late that evening!"

"Can you tell me where I can find Mr. Jim Williams? I drove out there to the cemetery. I stopped at what was probably his place. It appeared the house was vacant."

"He lives in Palestine now I hear. I don't know where. I know where that ex-wife of Sam's lives. I wuz there with Sam years ago."

I wrote my name and phone number down and handed it to him. "If Mr. Williams stops here, would you ask him to call me collect? If you learn anything about where Martha and her kids are, call me collect."

He gave me directions to Sam's ex-wife's place. "The street is Pine Burr Drive jist past a Texaco Station on yore left. It makes a moon shaped circle back in there and comes back on 79 about a half mile from whar you left it. I don't remember the house number, but az's a big holly tree in the front yard."

I found that holly tree! Knocked on the door. The woman cracked the door open.

"What are you selling?"

"I'm not selling anything! I was wondering if you knew where Sam Craig's sister Martha lives. I need to find her."

"You a lawyer?"

"No. I'm not a lawyer. I'm a friend of her daughter Margaret."

"I don't know, and I don't care!" Then slammed the door shut!

I stopped at a pay phone. There was not a Jim Williams listed in the Palestine phone book.

I turned west on US 79 to Jewett. It was mid-afternoon. I had supper with Mom and Dad. They seemed about settled. It was after 6 p.m. when I got home Sunday. I knew I had accomplished very little. But that old neighbor Jim Williams. I would go back and take another shot at trying to find him.

The next weekend, Mr. Dobrinsky asked me to go with him up to his ranch on Saturday. We drove around in the power wagon again. He had a blueprint of the place which he laid out on the dining room table along with field notes, everything that goes with the deeds to land.

"Robert, you've progressed greatly learning the business. It's time we got to work on this place. I want you to come back up here Monday. I'll leave the key in the power wagon. You can use it. I'll give you money for eats, gas, whatever you need. I want you to make a study of this place. Don't do it on this map, you'll need to get drawing poster paper, pens, rulers, whatever. Just use your own judgement!

"Now there are about three things I need to tell you. I want a lake built down there on that creek. Ten acres at least. And I want this artesian well water that's going to waste running into it. The next thing I need to tell you, we're going to need heavy equipment to develop this place. I know it's going to cost! Don't worry about that."

"What I want you to do is make a study and give me a detailed drawing of just how you would want this place developed if it were yours! Again, don't worry about the cost. We will dip into the unexpected fund if we need to!"

I packed my bags and went by the office Monday morning. He gave me $250 bucks for expenses. I brought my ice chest, a five gallon can for gas. Filled up my car and the five-gallon can. I felt I really did not want to drive that power wagon into Wells to get gas. I went to Perry's, got poster board, a three foot ruler, a couple of 12 inch ones also. A big eraser! Pens and black pencils. A box of colored pencils.

I also bought a card table with four chairs. I would use it to work from. He had a nice dining table I did not want to risk messing up.

At the grocery store, I got things to make out on for two weeks. Potatoes and a family pack of pork chops topped my list. Vegetable soup, pork and beans, sardines, crackers, and a loaf of bread. An assortment of canned goods. Eggs and pork sausage, and canned biscuits. I stopped for a bag of ice, put it and the things that needed to be kept cold in my ice chest. It was after ten before I left Livingston.

I stopped in Lufkin at a place and had a chicken fried steak for lunch. With gravy, mashed potatoes, and green beans. It was good. Next door was a convenience store. I remembered what I forgot! I picked up a 12 can box of Dr. Pepper and one of RC Cola. I was loyal to RC Cola. They gave you more for a nickel than any other soft drink. The bottle was bigger!

Owning a ranch, having the money to develop it for cattle, horses, and mules, hogs is a dream I think I must have been born with. The dream involved doing enough farming to support the livestock. Also, a lake to fish in. Woods to hunt deer, squirrels and wild hogs.

In recent years, that dream included the conservation of what I believed to be an endangered species. Because of timber company practices to cut everything. Make chips out of it! Then replant the land in pine plantations. Oak and other hardwood timber was disappearing rapidly.

The place had to have access roads to the different parts of it. A fence had to be built around it, as well as internal separation fencing. The cost of everything that needed to be done would stagger a mule. But he said not to worry about that. Lay this place out like you would want it if were yours. That's what I meant to do! If he carried out my game plan for his ranch or not, was his choice. I had nothing to lose. I was getting paid to do as he asked.

A county road split the place. Twenty-four hundred acres were on the side the house was on. Twelve hundred acres were across a county road from that. That I decided was where I would put the cattle ranch. Divided into four approximately three hundred acre pastures. With a road centering each 300 acres, two separate 150 acre pastures created.

I laid that out in four parts. Numbered them 1, 2, 3, 4. Number one pasture started at the FM road we got to the place on. I was three days on 1, 2, 3, and 4. In the center of each, a road would be constructed. An all-weather gravel road. Between 1, 2, and 3, and 3 and 4, steel cattle guards would be installed. A gate installed by both cattle guards in case cattle had to be moved from one pasture to another. In pasture one, a locked gate would allow access to the FM road.

I had to get back to the 2400-acre tract now before I could finish the cattle ranch part. The county road that split the place ran north and south. On the south end was the FM road that we got to the place on. On the north end was a FM road that went into Wells. The back side of the 2400 acres was that FM road. Devils Hurricane Creek came under a bridge into the 2400 acres. What I wanted was a road that crossed the property east and west. Also, one that crossed it north and south.

Just past the cemetery, I wanted an access gate. I drew the road roughly through the center of the place which came to a gate on the FM road to Wells. About a hundred yards from Devils Hurricane Creek.

I started a road on the east side of the place, crossed the creek and on by the north edge of the 75-acre field. It crossed the north & south road about 200 yards past the field. It came out about center of the number 3 pasture across the road. That's what I needed to determine. We could install a gate on each side of the road, cross the road into the cow pasture. My drawing on the 2400 acres now looked like a big plus sign!

Now I could get on with the cow pastures. Fencing was now another expensive step. Both sides of the center road would be fenced. Gates facing each other on each side going into roughly 150 acre pastures. My idea for that was you could graze one pasture, let the other rest.

The other plan was, you could put cattle in the road from any pasture, drive them to the single corral cattle working and loading facility in pasture 3 to be built. This place would be fenced with 4-point barb wire. Outside and internally.

A 75-foot square concrete slab would be poured separate from the corral. A barn with 12 feet high walls built. Drive through garage like doors front and back. Hay and bulk cattle feed would be stored here. Sheds were built on each side of this barn with feed troughs along the walls. A 150 by 150 foot corral was built out back of the barn. The fenced roads from 1, 2, and 4 had gates on each side opening into the corral. The corral had a separation pen with a loading shoot.

I had already penciled in cattle guards in the connecting pasture road. To drive into any 150-acre pasture however, you would need to go thru a gate. Whoa now! Erase those gates going into those 150-acre pastures. Both sides of the road!

Back those road fence end posts back ten feet. Then angle back 20 yards to the gate posts and gate. Now there was the space needed to drive a truck, trailer and loaded bull dozer into any pasture. Costs just went up!

A cattle shed 50 feet long and 20 feet wide facing south would built be in pastures 1-2 & 4. Extended from each shed would be a 10x20 hay and feed storage room. Both 150 acre pastures could be opened up in winter. So only three of these needed to be built.

I penciled in a water well near the barn in pasture three. I labeled it artesian, windmill or pump with timer. From the top of the hill it could serve 2-3 & 4. I drew in a big pond serving pasture one. I was able to locate potential places and draw in small ponds on each 150-acre tract.

Also, water from the well would be piped to the barn and corral. Inside the corral a float controlled water trough would be installed. And a water faucet and water hose would be by the barn. Provided we got a well that produced enough water, it could be directed to some of the ponds.

Last thing to complete the cattle ranch 1200 acres was next to the county road. I drew in green next to the fence 50 yards wide completely across the place next to the county road. I labeled that green streak "Long Leaf Pines". Which would be a long-term income project. And those old cows could lay in the shade of those pines!

I penciled in these words next to the drawing and circled it. "When properly seeded with pasture grasses, each 300-acre tract should support 45 head of cattle easily."

Now I was down to completing the 2400-acre tract. I drew in a dam, a lake in blue. Estimated 15 acres. The blue showed water backed up Hurricane Creek almost to the north end of the place. I drew in a bridge on the creek where the east-west road crossed it.

Next, I drew in a building to be developed into a fruit canning, vegetable shipping center. An electricity supply line was drawn in from the north side FM road and power line. It looked to be closer. And irrigation supply pump at the creek. And a well put down to supply the produce building. This would all be at the big creek bottom field.

In the center of the field, I put this note: "It will take a few years to get fruit trees, berries, grapes etc. going. Pecan and other nut bearing trees years! But farm crops can be started soon. The field must be fenced hog and deer proof.

The irrigation system must be installed. Electricity obtained. We will need at least two good sized tractors with disks, bush hogs and breaking plows. A hay cutter, baler and rake. We will be able to cut hay in the Pecan Orchard for a number of years.

On what appeared to be good soil, I penciled in food plots for wildlife and humans! There were five that ranged from two to ten acres. I noted they would be fenced hog and deer proof. But they were scattered in different areas of the place so deer and hogs would not travel far to find a food plot. Food plots had to be kept closed until whatever planted matured.

I started at the southwest corner of the place by the county road. I penciled in green to the northwest corner by the county road. Then green by the FM road to the northeast corner. There, I stopped the green, because the east side fence got close to the hardwoods left by the creek. I labeled this green streak 'Long leaf Pines' and a hundred yards wide.

Next to the pines and inside the place, I drew in and labeled 'Gravel Road'. I stopped this road at the north-south road. Up by the gate, I put the road next to the fence to the northeast corner. I labeled 'Low Water Crossing' at the creek. Up near the northeast corner, I put in a gate to enter or leave the place on the FM road.

From the northeast corner, I penciled in the road, down to the east to west road. Below that was a boggy marsh area. Which was colored blue. It would become part of the lake. The fence would only be a short distance from the lake. A road here was questionable.

You might wonder about these pines and roads next to them. Long Leaf Pines were also disappearing. They would be a long-term, selective cutting income source. The ground they stood on had to be burned off after a few years so that their seed would reproduce. That was one reason for the road. It would make it easier to control a burn off.

It was important for two other reasons. It gave access to different areas of the place. For years, the place had been Timber Company owned. They allowed people to hunt on it. They did so because they felt that people hunting on it would not set it on fire. If it were my place, I wanted it to be a family and friends hunting place only. I thought people would be reluctant to cross a road where they might be seen. You might call it a patrol road.

The next thing was about a 20-acre horse and mule pasture. I put it across the north-south road, across from the cemetery. Young hardwood timber, about 200 yards wide, had been left up to the southwest corner by the FM road. The pasture started at the edge of those woods and bordered the north-south road.

Holes could be dug in the small spring branch that crossed the pasture to hold more water. A small barn to hold feed and hay. A shed on one side to hang saddles and harness. And store plows and plow attachments.

This shed would be boxed in with a door that locked. On the other side of the barn, a shed would be built to protect the horses. Also, to be fed under. An oak lumber fence would enclose this shed and extend out 50 feet to create a horse corral. A gate placed in front of the shed and one at the back side of the corral.

Next, in the back of his log home yard, a shed would be built to keep heavy equipment, tractors, and tractor attachments in. My estimate was we needed a big size bulldozer, a big track back hoe, a dump truck, a truck fitted out with winch and 'A' frame, a truck and low boy trailer to transport any heavy equipment we purchased, and a cattle trailer; big enough to haul 15 head of cattle.

Included in this shed, I wanted a kitchen built in the center, a room, front to back, doors on each side. It shall include a refrigerator and kitchen sink, with counter top and shelves above. It shall include a wood burning heater and a box air conditioner in a wall. It will need a table and chairs. Electrical wall plugs. A bathroom with just a shower stall, lavatory, and potty.

Another smaller room would be built to house a meat freezer, meat cutting and grinding, and sawing equipment. It shall have a heavy-duty meat cutting table. And a separate table for wrapping meat for freezer storage. It shall have a concrete floor, designed to wash down and drain across the road. Water faucets with hoses shall be installed. This room will take up most of the width of the building. The door needs to be wide and in front of the room.

Between the front door of the room and front wall of the shed, shall be left an area equipped with two overhead chain drive hoists, large enough to hang two steers, hogs or deer. It needs a concrete floor, wash down hose, and drain across the road. The road in front of the shed would continue down to the lake dam.

Across the road, in a rather wide area in front of the shed, will be the hog pasture. The fence would go up the north-south road to the big field. It would be a hundred yards wide against that field fence. Corner and back to the road in front of the equipment shed. The front of a feed barn would be built into the front fence facing the equipment shed. A door front and back and a large hog pen with a gated loading shoot built into the fence, would be built. A shed over a farrowing pen would be on one side of the barn. An access aluminum gate is needed in the front fence, near the barn.

The spring branch, which crosses under the north-south road, runs into the pasture. It spreads out into a marshy area in the hog pasture. Since the pasture will have a gated cross fence, some work with a back-hoe may need to be done to get water to both parts of the pasture.

Since the complete 2400 acres would be fenced hog proof, I knew we would fence in a lot of wild hogs. My plan was to raise good bloodline, big hogs in the front pasture. A few male, barrows, and female shoats would be placed in the back part of the pasture. Corn would be thrown over the fence, along with water melons, other farm produce to keep them alive until they were grown and the females bred.

A small gate would be installed out into the creek bottom. Inside and outside that gate, corn would be placed to get wild hogs and good hogs in the same area. The good hogs in our pasture would become semi wild in the process. Then, the gate would be left open and they would join the wild hogs. In a matter of a few years, the wild hogs in the 2400 acres should be greatly improved.

Most of the hogs produced, however, would be sold. Some we would butcher, salt and sugar cure, and hickory smoke for home use. That would include bagged sausage with two different flavors!

The south fence of the 2400-acre place cornered on the FM road we came in on. The FM road turned left down that fence north, for about 250 yards. The fence cornered here and then back to near the creek. It cornered there and ran straight to the northeast corner of the place. I shaded this 250-yard wide area yellow, to cross the creek and almost up to the driveway to Mr. Dobrinsky' s log house.

I labeled it 20 to 25 acres. It was colored bright yellow with no explanation about what it was for. I wanted Mr. Dobrinsky to ask! I might add here, most of the explanation I've did in this book would be verbal to him.

In case you are wondering, the rest of the 2400 acres were not designated for something specifically. It would be planted in oak and hard wood trees of different kinds. That would be most of it. I was finished with my blueprint of what I wanted 3600 acres to be developed into. Like I said, the cost would stagger a mule! This I knew. Mr. Dobrinsky was not a mule!

I was finished Tuesday noon of the second week. I called Mr. Dobrinsky. I'm finished with the 'Dream What I Want' project. I wonder if you want me to bring it to the office, or if you want to come up here?"

"Just stay put," he said. "I'll be up there later this afternoon."

I went ahead and packed up my things. Put it in the trunk of my car. One way or another, I'm through up here, I felt sure. *Why was he,* I wondered, *coming up here?* I could have brought my posters to the office. I did two, one on the cattle ranch and the other on the home place.

Three hours later he was there. "You got this did sooner than I expected," he said. "I left everything in the hands of Mrs. Ivers. I've been so anxious to see what you have come up with!"

"It's here on the card table," I said. "It's going to be costly. You may not want it the way I've laid it out!"

"Don't worry about that. Let's look at it!"

His eyes fell on the blue part at first glance. "That's my lake?"

"Yes, Sir! My guess is, it will cover at least 15 acres."

"I see, you put in a lot of roads. No doubt, this place needs roads!"

"Yes, Sir. I never made a note of it, but the creek, tributary branches, and ravines have a lot of sand and gravel in them. If we could get it out of there, we could put it on the roads."

"We'll see, he said. "One way or another, we need all weather roads. What's this building, you've put up there in that field, about?"

"The place must have sources of income, it seems to me. My idea there is to put the field in fruit trees, black berries, and grapes. Grow a number of produce crops. I think we might even grow asparagus there. Long term, put out pecan, black walnut trees. The building is a place to process what we grow there. We'll need electricity there. Also for irrigation."

"I see a note here; it's closer to the other road to run a line from. You are probably right. I also see you want everything on this place fenced hog proof?"

"Yes, Sir. And that will be costly!"

"Well, don't forget. I run a wholesale hardware business. I can get things cheaper than most folks. I suppose these long leaf pines are long term income."

"Yes, Sir. There's not a lot of those left. I think we can get seedlings from the Texas Forest Service. You might note the road next to them. One purpose is, long leaf pine needles and underbrush needs to be burned off after they start producing seed. The Long Leaf seed won't reproduce unless you do. Another reason, people have been hunting on this place for years. I think that road will help stop them from sneaking in here. And you may notice that this road goes on to almost surround the place. Fences must be maintained; the road allows access for that."

He next started asking about the cattle ranch. I explained every detail of that as best I could.

Finally, he said "Looks like you know what a ranch needs. Looks good to me! But I need to know about one more thing. What's this yellow here that you have not designated for anything?"

"Well, we need heavy equipment. Seems to me we also need a heavy equipment operator. Also, one that can weld. Mr. Justin Wilson was trained in both during WWII. He also worked highway construction for a number of years. He owns the place across the road from you. He wants to retire up here. But his land is all in creek bottom. He has no place to build a home."

"What if you offered to buy his place at Livingston? Put it in the deal to trade or sell him what I've marked in yellow. Give him a place to build a home. And work up here for you until he retires. A place this size is going to require a lot of help."

"He's my best truck driver. I hate to give him up. His place in Livingston would be a super investment! There is a proposed loop that will cross part of it. Sounds like he plans to sell the place anyway. I'll think about it."

"There's a couple of things we have not talked about," I pointed to the shed. "I've listed what equipment is needed, you might notice. I've also made notes of what I want in the shed other than equipment storage. Truth is, I have no idea about how big it needs to be, until we get the equipment."

"I see. You want a meat cutting facility and a break room?"

"Yes, sir. If I owned this place, I don't think I would ever go to a meat market. And as I said before, this place will require help. They'll come and go from this shed. Even work in it. That's the reason for a break room."

"I never noticed this hog pasture before. What's your plans for it?"

I explained that to him, "Sell hogs. Release some to the wild. There is also one other thing." I pointed to the horse pasture and explained that.

"Well, thanks to you, I think we got a game plan for this place. Good job! I better get going."

"Well, I guess I'll see you in the morning at the office then?"

"Just stay up here," he said. "I'll be back up here in the morning. I need you to go with me to the bank in Wells tomorrow. We'll add to the ranch account there. And maybe we can find out where to go to get a telephone put in this house. We're going to need one." With that, he left.

I went out and got the things I needed to put back in the refrigerator. Also, a decent shirt and pants that I had brought, in case I needed such. Then, to heck with it! I put it all back in the house.

Then, I sat on the back-porch steps with a cold RC. He never seemed to disagree with anything I proposed. Which I knew was bound to cost a million bucks! My proposals were my dreams. He did not seem to care about anything but the lake! Why so much interest in the lake? He could fish about anywhere he wanted to.

I decided to give up wondering about it. Put my empty RC can in the trash bag I meant to return home and let the City of Livingston pick it up! There's something else about up here that I had not thought of. Perhaps, if we got heavy equipment up here, we could dig a trash landfill!

I never wanted to cook, or anything that I had brought. I went in to Wells to a fast food place. Had myself a double meat hamburger with everything on it. Fries and a strawberry milk shake.

The next morning, Mr. Dobrinsky was there by nine. We went in to the Wells Bank. He put $500,000 more bucks in his ranch account there. Papers were drawn up for me to write checks. I had to sign with the name I would write checks with. I put Robert A. Dupree. He ordered checks for both of us.

They told us at the bank where to go for telephone service. We drove to Rusk for that. He got that took care of. They would probably be there on Friday, to hook it up. On the way back he said, "I guess we'll have to go all the way to Lufkin to eat."

They make a good burger and milk shake at Wells. We had a burger and milk shake at Wells.

On the way home, he told me, "The bank account up here is primarily for buying every day needs as they come up. I still have a Ranch Account in the bank at Livingston. The expenses like heavy equipment, big costs, I will pay for out of that account. Of course wire and building materials, I'll have delivered up here. One thing we got to have is diesel and gasoline tanks. I'll take care of that. You stay up here and wait for that telephone man tomorrow. Call me to see if it works!"

The telephone man was there by 8:30 a.m. It had not been discussed where the line would run. He had a long ladder, he tacked it up high on the electrical poles to the house. I can only leave you one phone. However, I can run jacks to other rooms if you want. I had him put the phone in the living room, jacks in the kitchen and Mr. Dobrinsky's bedroom. The man tested it, assigned us a number. He was there about an hour.

I called Mr. Dobrinsky. That was quick he said. Took us longer yesterday to order it! Let me have that number!

Is that all I need to do up here?

You need to get on down here before 3 p.m. You have two pay checks you need to pick up. And I need to talk to you.

I lit a shuck getting my things together and on my way. He had given me $250 bucks cash for expenses before I came up here. I had $175 left that I needed to return to him. I stopped in Corrigan at a Burger place. Tomorrow I'm eating something besides a burger! But I was there by 1:30 p.m.

He handed me my checks. "You probably need to get to the bank before three. If you do, why don't you go take care of that. Then come back if you will. We need to decide on a few things about that ranch project."

I reached in my pocket, pulled out $175 bucks. My expenses were not all that much. I stuck it out to him.

"No, keep it! Not telling what it would have cost me to hire some so-called expert to do it! I like your plans for that place. It suits me fine!"

I went to the bank and deposited both checks. I had $150 in cash more than I normally carried around!

When I got back, he got down to it. "Robert, I want you to move up to the ranch. I'm talking about maybe two or three years up there. We have a game plan and I want you in charge up there. I also know we are going to need six or eight more people up there once we get that heavy equipment. Mr. Wilson left out early this morning. He has about three different stops to pick up things in Houston. So, likely, it will be Monday before I see him. Have you talked to him about this?"

"No Sir. I won't say anything to him about it unless he tells me he's talked to you."

"Well, I plan to try to buy his place. Give him that 25 acres we discussed. If he accepts my offer, I'll tell him he works there until he retires or quits. Also, I'll give him check writing and purchasing power at that Wells Bank. I said I wanted you in charge up there. I want you and him to be in co-in-charge up there!"

"It's like this Robert. You've been trained to run this business if my health fails, or it gets too much for me. I might have to call you back here. If that should happen, then Mr. Wilson I have confidence in to keep it going up there."

"I hope we get him up there. He knows a lot more about how to get it done, than I do. I've spent a lot of time with him making deliveries. He's talked about his love for his place and moving back up there. His wife grew up in that neighborhood as well."

"Well, what do you think Robert? How do you feel about working up there?"

"My rents about due in another week. I want to work up there. But if you think it's going be long term up there, I don't need an apartment here."

"No, you don't. Just move your things up there this next week. Weather Mr. Wilson accepts or not, we're going to move on that project! I've been talking to a salesman about an auction down at Austin. They sell all manners of army surplus. That includes bull dozers, back hoes, trucks, you name it. He's going to let me know when the sale takes place. I hope we can get the equipment we need."

"Mr. Wilson is the man you need with you! He's had a lot of experience with GI equipment. He told me once he covered up cave entrances on Iwo Jima with a bull dozer. He was there to help build an airplane landing strip!"

I asked him if he wanted me back in the office Monday, or move up there. "Just go ahead and move up there. You'll most likely need to do some shopping for something to eat! One thing you might do. Buy a power lawn mower on the Wells Bank account. I think the boy that I pay to do it seems to have left the country. Maybe you can get the yard mowed. We'll get something going up there soon. Rest up!"

I went to a dumpster in back of a grocery store downtown. Got a few cardboard boxes. Packed up my cooking things. A window box fan. That and the things I already had in the car was all I could get in the trunk, the back seats and passenger side front seat. It was my supper time when I got to Lufkin. I stopped at a place and had myself a club steak, baked potato and a salad.

I unloaded everything, got a shower and went to bed. My thoughts turned to Margaret. Since Dad and Mother moved, work was a relief actually from being alone like tonight. Wondering if she had found someone else, or was she alone like me. I finally got up, had myself a cold RC. I finished it sitting on a living room recliner. That's where I woke up Saturday morning.

I then went to Lufkin. Put my ice chest on the back seat of my car. I had to take it out of the trunk to get the mower in it. It was in a big box, so I knew I had to assemble it. I decided to add a wrench and a socket set to that. Fifteen assorted screw drivers. And a pair of channel lock pliers. I had few tools, and I suspected putting this mower together would be just the beginning of the need.

At the grocery store I stocked up on the necessities. Flour. Cornmeal. Sugar. That was the start of a full backseat and the front passenger side as well.

It took time organizing and putting all that stuff away in an empty kitchen. What really stood out was my short supply of tools to cook and eat with. I'll put that mower together, get it running. Then I'll go back to Lufkin, get a lot of pots, pans, dishes, plates, glasses, cups and saucers. Tools to eat with, like spoons, steak knives and forks. A bigger and a smaller skillet than the one I had. An egg turner, some big cooking spoons and ladle. A spaghetti strainer! I bought skinner's thin today! I needed one!

I must have spent about $80 bucks. I passed a seafood place that I gave a try. I ordered a seafood platter and it had fried fresh water catfish on it. It was good. Next time I'll just order catfish I decided.

Monday, I got on the mowing detail. Mr. Dobrinsky called me at noon. I talked to Mr. Wilson this morning. He seemed interested. I told him you were up at the ranch, you had plans drawn up to develop the place. He indicated he might drive up there, talk to you and look at those plans. You might be prepared for visitors this afternoon!

It took me about another hour to finish mowing on out to the road in front. I took a shower, went in the kitchen. *I'll fix supper for them. If they don't come, I won't have to cook tomorrow!*

I decided on my chicken spaghetti recipe I had invented since I started cooking for myself. For four of us, I would need to increase things.

I put five big boneless chicken breasts to boiling. Chopped up onions, bell pepper and celery. Combined, about a quart. With a little cooking oil, I flattened out a one-pound roll of hot pork sausage. Chop-chop with the egg turner until it was small pieces and browned. Added the quart of onion, bell pepper and celery. Added just a little water and stir-stir! I opened up a big can of sliced tomatoes. With a knife I diced them up. Into the skillet they went. Juice and all!

I keep stirring until it cooked down thick. In went a 15 oz. can of tomato sauce. One big can of Hunt's Original Spaghetti Sauce. Then two 10.75 oz. cans condensed tomato soup. One tablespoon of brown sugar. I stirred until mixed good. Turned the burner off. My boiled chicken breasts were done and cool now. I shredded those, got rid of anything not wanted in my pot. I dumped that shredded chicken in. I turned the burner back on. Heated it all up and added a little Cajun seasoning I liked!

I best wait until 5:30 to cook a pound of Skinner's thin spaghetti I decided. Since I never had French bread, decided on hot water cornbread. I liked green beans with spaghetti. I opened up a big can of cut green beans, put them in a pot. With a few slices of butter, a little bacon grease and a couple dashes of that Cajun seasoning. Got them boiling, they would not take long.

Set the table for four. Had a pitcher of sweet tea in the refrigerator. Emptied up three ice trays and filled four glasses. I was ready. I went out to sit on the front porch and wait. I hoped the varmints up here liked spaghetti if they never came!

I waited not long! I heard those mud grip tires he had on the back of that GMC humming. *That's them*, I thought. Shortly after, they turned in!

"Come on in," I said. "Mr. Dobrinsky called and said you might be coming! I got supper ready!"

"Aw, no need of you doing that! We could have stopped on the way back to eat."

"Not often I get to try out my cooking experiments on people! Let's eat!"

"It never took Wade long. Mom, you better get his recipe!"

"I second that," Mr. Wilson said. "This ain't no Momma Mia! This is Texas stuff!"

"I want the recipe," Mrs. Wilson said. "This fried cornbread is so good with it! I never thought of that before!"

"Well, I never thought of it either until I discovered I forgot the French bread yesterday!"

The drawings I made were on the card table in the Living Room. After looking them over, doing my best to explain things, answer questions, Mr. Wilson finally voiced his opinion.

"With the right equipment, and good help, we're probably looking at three years before cattle can be bought. And spending a lot more money than I've ever seen!"

"Mr. Dobrinsky told me to come up here, lay the place out like I would if it were mine. He's looked at these drawings and said don't worry about cost. We'll go for it!"

"Yes, he thought you did a good job. And so do I. That cow pasture you laid out. That's a cowboy's dream!"

"Well, I was laying by corn when I dreamed it!"

They all laughed! But it was time to go. He and Bessie Mae needed to talk it over. He would let Mr. Dobrinsky know what they decided tomorrow.

Mr. Dobrinsky called me the next day. Mr. Wilson has accepted. It will probably take the rest of the week to get all the paperwork, deeds and what have you done. We've agreed that his wife and son will stay on the place until he finishes this school year. And they need time to get a house built up there. He can stay there with you, I want you to help him build that house. Both of you will be paid right on as you have been. Work as many hours a day as you feel like, or think the need is.

I've been thinking about a way we need to get your paychecks lined out. And whoever else we hire. I think the solution is we'll use the punch in, punch out time card system like here. Start the week up there on Friday and end on Thursday. For the most part, Saturday and Sunday still be off days.

Everyone's first check will be for 40 hours. That week's overtime will be on next week's check. You or Mr. Wilson will need to come in Friday morning, bring that week's cards and pick up everyone's paycheck. Also bring in receipts for everything purchased on the Wells account that week. Can you think of a better way to handle it?

That sounds fine to me. I need to get a mailbox put up. I do get some mail from family. Probably Mr. Wilson will as well.

Just apply for it in your name. Probably all you'll have to do is put up a box. Ask the mail carrier to assign you a box number. I forgot to mention this, but I assigned Mr. Wilson an easement to use our driveway. No need of him having to worry about putting in a separate road culvert. He'll probably put a mailbox next to yours.

I stopped the mail carrier the next morning. Said he had been wondering why this place has no mail box. He got out a pad with carbon copy. Handed it to me with pen. Just write your name in the blank. I did and handed it back to him. He wrote in a box number, handed me the carbon copy. Just put up a box and we're in business!

The copy he gave me also included instructions for the proper height of the box. Which gave me something to do. I went in to Lufkin, bought a black mail box. A can of white paint and a small brush. Then realized I needed a two by six board and two creosote posts. Which I could not haul in my car! I went back to the ranch, painted my name and box number on the box. *It should dry well before I get it up,* I thought!

It was Monday before Mr. Wilson got up there. Driving a brand new three-quarter ton pickup with a 16-foot four-wheel trailer behind it. On the trailer was a small portable building. In the pickup bed was a new table saw, and a miter saw. A 13 HP portable generator. Along with his personal hammers, hand saws, crowbars, levels, etc. He had concrete blocks, we set the building up, put all that stuff in it out by where he meant to build.

He locked it up. Mr. Dobrinsky paid for the generator, the power saws. He said we would need all of that building barns, sheds up here. He also bought this Ford Pickup and trailer. You need to go back to Livingston with me and get yours. He said we both need a pickup and trailer up here. He told me to tell you to come by the office after you get the truck.

Never had I dreamed such. Five speed stick-shift. Radio and heater. Air conditioning. Two regular tires were in the back. They told me at the Ford Place, "He thought, you would need mud grip tires up there. Said save those that come on it. They'll fit the front!"

I went by the office. He had a box of time cards, the gadget to punch in start and stop time on the cards. He showed me how to set the time and date thing on it. Told me where to go pick up the trailer. Then asked, "You got that mailbox up yet?"

"I got the mailbox. Got my name and number the mail carrier gave me painted on it. It's not up yet. I needed posts, post hole diggers and lumber which I could not haul in my car."

"Well, go over to the hardware building and get what you need. But I want to talk to you about that car. You have it paid for. Any thoughts about trading it in on a new one?"

"Yes sir. It's starting to use a little oil."

"If another Ford suits you, bring it down one day next week. I can put you in whatever you want at whatever the Ford company charges us. It's like this. My partner and I can do that for some people. I've helped his kids and parents get cars at our cost, a number of times. Our cost is considerable less than retail! Finance for 36 months and your payments won't be much."

"I'll be back Monday," I said.

I got a new 1958 V8 Ford, with an automatic transmission. Black in color. My monthly payments with liability insurance included was $43 a month. What the heck? I was not paying rent now.

Mr. Wilson and I got lined out on building his home. To Mrs. Wilson's specifications, she drew the floor plan. He figured out the dimensions. She wanted large bedrooms and a lot of closet space. Two bathrooms with both tub and shower stall. Two bedrooms shared one bath. The master bedroom on the other end of the house had the other. There was also a two car garage.

The two of us spent a day with stakes and strings laying it out. Next, he hired a fellow with a back-hoe to dig his wall lines for a concrete tier and beam set up. He meant to use rough siding for the walls. But he had the concrete poured for later bricks if it was decided in future years. He also had the man dig holes for a septic tank and field lines.

Materials including lumber, three quarter inch rebar, nails, a septic tank and field lines were delivered from the business at Livingston. When we got the forms ready, three ready mix trucks arrived to pour concrete from the business at Livingston.

"Mr. Dobrinsky is letting me have this stuff a lot cheaper that I could get it anywhere else," Mr. Wilson said.

"Yeah, that new car with insurance is only costing me $43 bucks a month. Hard to believe!"

Mr. Wilson left Friday at noon, took our time cards. Picked up our checks. I agreed that just bring mine back Monday. He could spend the weekend with Bessie Mae and Wade. I meant to open an account at the Wells bank. Mail one check a month for deposit at the bank in Livingston. Which would cover my car payment. And save a little.

But I had the weekends to myself now. I went to Oakwood. Drove out to the cemetery. There was a fresh mound of dirt there by Sam Craig. Not a sign of ID at it, not even a funeral home marker. Who I wondered? His ex-wife? *Not likely*, I thought. It had to be family. And as far as I knew, that was no one but Martha, Margaret, Harry, Katrina and Kevin. My best guess was Martha.

I went by the service station to see if that man knew or heard anything. No, I ain't heard of anyone being buried out there since Sam. Don't think Jim Williams knew either. He was by here yesterday. Never said anything about it. Course he probably just went to check on his place and never went to the cemetery.

I was wrong, he don't live in Palestine like I told you. He lives in Long Lake. He gave me his box number. Hit's right on 294 over there. He said he would be glad to talk to you, but he don't know where Martha and those kids are either.

I never had any problem finding Jim Williams at Long Lake. I introduced myself as Robert DuPree. You must be Ben's boy. I knew him way back yonder. He and Sam cut rails for my Grand Pa.

He seemed shocked there was fresh grave in the cemetery. Like me, he thought it must be Martha or one of her kids.

I explained to him Margaret had agreed to marry me when we both were 15. Because of her Daddy, they moved and she never got a chance to tell me where. Then we moved to Livingston. She does not know where I'm at either. I need to find her.

You get that Margaret for a wife, you'll have one. I guarantee you that. You may know this, or you may not know it. Martha still owns half of that place. Her kids get her share when she's gone. And I fear that's her out there in the cemetery!

But that hussy ex-wife of Sam's tried to sell that place. Sell it to me! I took her ass to court! I testified that I knew it was a matter of record that Martha owned half of the place. And that Sam told me more than once he had willed his share to Margaret! That I supposed his will probably burned up in the place.

That Judge popped his gavel on his desk by golly! "If Martha or her kids have not been found in ten years, you may sell Sam's share. But if Margaret is found, Sam's full share is hers. Lady, I've known Jim Williams all my life, Sam as well. I know Jim Williams to be an honest and truthful man! This court is adjourned!" I thought he would break the handle out of that gavel when he hit that desk! He knew about that hussy as well as I did!

I thanked him for doing what he had done. Gave him my phone number and address. Asked him to let me know if he learned anything.

"Sam and Martha were like brother and sister to me," he said. He gave me his phone number. "Call me if you find out anything. I'll dance at yours and Margaret's wedding with a cowbell on if you do!"

I went on to Jewett. Spent the night and most of Sunday with Mom and Dad. Dad was working a good bit with his nephew Marvin DuPree. Marvin did all sorts of cement work. Well curbs, septic tanks. He even made concrete grave markers for people who could not afford expensive markers. But he also contracted brick, rock and Austin Stone jobs. He also built a lot of chimneys for people.

Dad got a black man to break his garden. From there he went with a push plow, his hoe and grass fork. And his sister had a number of peach trees. I left with tomatoes, green beans, purple hull peas, okra and sweet corn Sunday evening. Along with a half bushel of white clear seed and yellow cling seed peaches. The seed I resolved to save and plant on the Ranch.

We had the Wilson's home complete but the inside painting. Mr. Wilson had been hiring his old friend, the Rev. William Davenport to help us. Everyone called him Rev. Billy. He was a big man, quiet spoken. When I say big man, get a load of this. Putting half inch sheetrock in the ceiling, he just picked it up, and arms reaching to almost each end. Standing on the floor he slapped it into place. Then he would say "If that looks alright, y'all nail it now!" We used step ladders to nail it.

"I ain't much at painting," Mr. Wilson said. Rev. Billy is good at it. We'll let him finish that sheetrock and painting. We'll start on my fence. Mr. Dobrinsky had told us to do that as well. Get everything shaped up for the Wilson's first," he said.

"I had a high school classmate who worked for the Electric Company out of Lufkin now. Matter of fact his uncle was company manager at Lufkin. We're taking up and renewing posts in a lot of lines now. We probably got 300 of those old poles on the lot. I bet if I tell my Uncle you will give him $5 each for those poles, and deliver them out here, he'll go for it."

We got 320 good solid but used poles delivered. Which would go a long way in all the fencing we needed to do. We could cut eight-foot post for corners. Cut and split six-and-a-half foot lengths for line posts. We cut some of the smaller ends for Mr. Wilsons barn ten feet long.

Another thing I talked to Mr. Dobrinsky about. We need a tractor and attachments. For fencing, a post hole digger. Disks and a bush hog. Breaking plows. A front-end loader. Right now, the post-hole digger is the most urgent. We also need a couple of chainsaws and another air compressor.

"Your layout and game plan called for two tractors, all of that. Shop around, get the best deal you can on two tractors and equipment. Same on that other stuff. The account at Wells will handle that. You know more about tractors than I do. Have those delivered in the deal."

I shopped around, got figures on John Deere, Case, New Holland and International. I wound up getting two Fords at Lufkin. On one, I got a front- end loader, and added a box blade to the attachment list. The air compressor I got at an Industrial Supply Company place in Lufkin. I found the best deal on chain saws at a place in Wells.

Mr. Wilson thought we needed to set all the corner posts, stretching in line set up posts and gate posts first. Let it rain, settle the post in before we stretched any wire. We got a couple of rolls of heavy cotton trotline cord to stretch from point to point to make sure we got the post lined up just right.

Mr. Wilson left at noon one Friday to turn in our time and get our checks. Of course, he would stay until Sunday evening late. It would be one day the next week before I deposited my check. Which suited me fine. I meant to dig post holes with the tractor and set posts on a line we had stringed off. Mr. Dobrinsky called before I got out of the house.

"Robert, my salesman friend from down Austin way just left. Has Mr. Wilson left yet?"

"He's been gone about five minutes."

"Well, I'll talk to him when he gets here. That GI equipment auction is next Wednesday. I thought if we left early Monday morning, we might have time to look at things Monday evening and Tuesday. I've talked to one of my driver's, we hope to purchase three trucks. He's agreed to go with us. Unless Mr. Wilson tells you something different, I hope to be at the Ranch by 6 a.m., Monday. Never said so, but that salesman will meet us at the place, show us around, what the deal is."

"I'll be up and ready to go," I said.

"Might pack a few extra clothes. I'll make reservations for four of us at a motel for three nights. I know some good places to eat down there! And I'll tell Mr. Wilson. Don't eat breakfast before we leave. We'll stop in Crockett for breakfast."

"I've heard Mr. Wilson talk about some of those places down there to eat. His daughter lives there. Her husband is part owner of a TV station in Austin."

"I never knew that. I'll let him use my car one night, he can go visit her, perhaps."

Monday, he and his driver Monroe Sylestine were there at 5:45 a.m. A big Indian I had never met. Mr. Dobrinsky told me later he replaced Mr. Wilson. He knows his way around in Houston and Beaumont. He's one smart Indian, I was lucky he applied.

We got to Austin and had lunch, which we all offered to pay for our own. "No, eats are on me on this trip. By the way, I'll have them give you a card and number at the motel. Breakfast, mid night snack or whatever you might want to eat, present that card with your ticket. They'll put it on my bill, I'll pay for it when we check out."

We went to the auction sale site which was out towards Round Rock. His salesman friend that I knew met us there. He showed us around. Not supposed to be anything with a motor in it that won't start. You can get on it, start it up. But due to space, they don't want you to move it. They got all manners of things here. Boots, army clothing, coats. Army cookware and used rifles. I saw some of those boots that I had a memory of. Lace up half way, buckle up the top part. I wanted a pair, but you had to buy in bulk.

What I did see was something I wanted. For myself and others. It was stainless steel army pots and the large pans they served the troops out of. That whole display was about 30 pieces looked like to me. Provided we got a dump truck, it would hold it.

I told Mr. Dobrinsky: "Provided we secure a dump truck first, if you'll bid on that cookware and get it, I'll pay for it. But don't go over $150 bucks, that's all I'll pay for it!"

"Ok, I'll try to get it for you. Provided we get that dump truck first. I don't think it will fit in the trunk of my car."

We went to a seafood restaurant Monday night. Mr. Wilson told me he liked shrimp grilled over pecan wood, so I ordered it as well. Two sides and a house salad. I chose fried rice and fresh steamed broccoli. I ordered ranch dressing on my salad and asked for shrimp cocktail sauce.

They brought out two skewers with eight big shrimps on each. Big Monroe caught me eating my fresh broccoli. "You dip broccoli in shrimp cocktail sauce Little DuPree?"

"Only way to eat broccoli. Sounds like you've been talking to Big Jimbo Batise!"

"Yeah. He talks about you and your Dad often."

"I miss working with Big Jimbo. He taught me a lot. My best friend in high school was Andre Batise. Do you know him?"

"Yeah, I see him now and then. He's married and has two kids. He works in the woods logging."

Mr. Wilson made his first, second and third picks on a dozer, a track hoe, a truck with a low boy trailer, dump truck and an 'A' frame truck. All those trucks had eight driver tires in the rear.

Tuesday night, he told Mr. Wilson. They serve good food in the motel. Take my car and go visit your daughter if you would like.

He accepted. "Robert go with me. It's time you met the rest of my family!"

I went with him. Met his daughter and two kids. Her husband was in Dallas on a business trip. Never in my life had I been in such a mansion. She fixed supper for us, insisted we eat. I always cook more than I need anyway she said.

"Robert, you must be the one that invented that chicken spaghetti recipe?"

"I may be guilty," I said.

"Mother sent me the recipe! It's great. We love it here."

We left about nine. "That's the most mansion I ever been in! Looks like she could have someone cooking for her."

"He husband is making the bucks alright. He's offered to hire maids and cooks. She won't have no part of that. Nobody's taking care of my home and my kids but me, she says. He's a good old boy, but not much in common with me. She met him over at Sam Houston while in college. She's already told me 'Leave everything Mother and you have to Wade when you leave this world. I've got more than I'll ever need.'"

I suppose Mr. Dobrinsky meant to get everything Mr. Wilson listed as first choice. He never got out bided on the dozer, track hoe, 'A' frame truck and dump truck.

"Ok, we can bid on that cookware now!" They all laughed. We were waiting on bids to start on the truck and low boy trailer. I had to find a rest room. Quick!

When I got back Big Monroe said "Mr. Dobrinsky got your cookware while you were gone!"

"How much, I asked?"

"Twenty-five bucks," Mr. Dobrinsky said.

I hauled out my wallet and paid him.

Thursday morning, we went back to get everything ready for the trip to the ranch. One thing Mr. Wilson said we needed was a dozer blade that was more like a big rake.

"That's what we need for cleaning up those clear cuts. We can haul it on that "A" frame truck," he said.

I loaded my cookware in the dump truck. I drove the truck up beside a bulldozer. By getting up on the tracks, I could step over into the truck bed and stack it in. Mr. Dobrinsky handed it up to me, piece by piece. We passed a hardware store back there he said. I'll go get you some rope to tie it down. Which was no small project. I had to run that little rope through at least one handle on everything I bought. But I got it fixed so it would not blow out!

They took the cable down from the "A" frame pulley and winched that extra blade up on the bed. They had bid on some chain, tie down equipment and got it. They tied that thing down. Mr. Wilson had that dozer on that low boy trailer in minutes and they tied it down. He was elated about that dozer. "Look at that blade! It's a near new dozer. That blade ain't got no wear on it."

We had to leave the track hoe. Mr. Wilson would come back for it. "Robert, you might come back with him. He may need help. I'm going on back to Livingston now. I'll go through Navasota and Huntsville."

Mr. Wilson led out first. I was next in line with the dump truck. Big Monroe followed up with the 'A' frame and the spare dozer blade. I had my license, had drove a truck very little actually. Mr. Wilson hit the bottom of those hills doing 75 mph. Before the top of the next it was gear down and crawl. It was constantly gear down, then gear up! Mr. Wilson had said "You'll be a truck driver before we get to Caldwell!"

We stopped in Madisonville about 1:30 p.m. for a burger. Big Monroe said "Little DuPree I think you still got all your pots. I ain't seen none blow out!"

We got in and Mr. Wilson unloaded the dozer. I gave Big Monroe a couple of pots and pans. He went on to Livingston. Let's get cleaned up and get to bed. We'll unload that blade and pots later. We need to leave by five in the morning. It's going to be another long day!

It was a long day! But we got Mr. Wilson's fence up the next week. He got permission from the Highway Department to fence under Hurricane Creek bridge so his cattle could come up to his barn. We put up a cross fence to keep his cattle out of about 15 acres he meant to grow different things on across the creek. The whole thing was fenced hog proof.

Mr. Dobrinsky leased fuel tanks from a business in Lufkin that supplied most of the service stations in the area. Just call, they would come fill the diesel tank or the gasoline tank. We had those put up by the big field we hoped to farm. They had hand crank manual pumps which fueled things up fairly quickly. And they could be locked.

The school year ended, we moved the Wilson's into a new home. They insisted I eat with them at lunch time, no need for me eat a sandwich for lunch. I started buying meats and taking it there. Mr. Wilson had a home built barbeque, which Mrs. Wilson used frequently. I noticed she always bought groceries on Wednesday. I went Tuesday evening after work. Wednesday morning. she knew what I brought, she could plan her list.

Mr. Wilson taught me to run both the backhoe and dozer. But his experience was needed on that dozer. Like it was with Dad and the axe, I wasted his time trying to work with that dozer.

He hit the roads first. Got them graded up. A dry summer, I would use the back hoe to dig the creek bank down. Then he would put that dozer in that dry creek bed. Sometimes 200 yards in each direction he pushed that sand and gravel into a pile. I dipped it up out of the creek bed and put it into piles. We thought it urgent to get it out before it rained. We could use the dump truck and put it on the roads later.

We got the roads laid out but not graveled. He started clearing the fence line. I followed with the tractor and trailer, loaded with eight-foot big posts. I bought ten-foot brace poles. I unloaded posts and braces at corners. I figured 50 yards was long enough to stretch, so I unloaded post and braces for each 50-yard stretch set up.

I saw my Texas Forest Service friend in Wells one day. He told me he had just finished working with a crew of Mexican's setting out pine seedlings nearby.

"They live here at Wells, sometimes they work with us. These folks are here legally, their families have been here for years. My job is to keep tract of their time, the Forest service pays them $1 per hour."

"Do you think they would work for me?"

"Come go with me! I'll take you to the one that seems to be the leader."

In short, I hired eight Mexican men for $1.10 per hour. They had transportation. They would punch in the time card morning and evening. They would bring lunches. Eat on the job. By the time card, they got paid to eat lunch. Which I thought fair, I knew what it was like to dine in the woods. They also agreed to starting the work week on Friday, ending the work week on Thursday. That their first check would be for 40 hours, overtime would be held back until the next week.

I took three men with me. All said they could drive a tractor. Use an axe or a chainsaw. One tractor had the posthole digger. The other pulled a 16-foot trailer with posts, wire, staples, wire stretchers, hammers and posthole diggers. The auger bits usually let dirt fall back in the holes. Manual diggers were used to get it out. Wade might go with me one day, his Dad the next. He might stay home if his Mother was going to town!

Mr. Wilson had five under his direction. I bought two more chainsaws. With that rake like blade he was loosely assembling a pile around a rich pine stump he pushed up.

74

The Mexicans axed those stumps up some, then cut and piled what he loosely pushed up around them on the stump. When they got it all piled on, they used a little diesel fuel and set it on fire.

There were a lot of those pine stumps. He pushed them into a pile in a good size area. Later we would transfer them to a huge pile down by the big field. When we got fruit trees going, I thought we could burn them in the fruit rows to prevent frost damage.

Both crews came together early on to clean up and fence a ten-acre food plot. We meant to plant garden produce there next spring!

Mr. Wilson and I worked on his barn on Saturdays. That was on our own time, we never put that on the time cards. But we got it up.

Free on Saturdays again, I went a few times down in the Houston area. I had been told by a friend whose Dad was a Merchant Seaman to check out the offices where they went to sign up for ship duty. They had to list their qualifications, cook or whatever.

I checked an office in Channel View.

"Burkett? Let me see. Otis Ray Burkett. He's on a ship to China now. Lists his address as Pine Burr Street in Palestine Texas."

"That's him." He may have moved them here. I checked a phone book at a pay phone booth. No Burkett's listed! Then the office in middle school. I asked if there were any Burkett students in school there.

"Are you the father of a Burkett child?"

"No ma'am. I'm just a friend of the Burkett family. I hope to find out where the family lives."

"If you are not the father of a child in this school, I can't give out information to you!"

I drove around thru residential areas for four hours hoping to find some clue, perhaps one of the family in a yard—I found nothing. Maybe Baytown. I found a phone book. It listed one Elizabeth Burkett! Not a family member. There was a Houston city phone book there. About five Burkett's listed. None had a first name that was a family member.

I got a surprise call the next week from Mother. "Virginia, her husband and little boy were back home. He was discharged from the service. They'll be here this weekend. Hope you'll come over. Most of the family will be here Sunday."

I got there Saturday morning before they did. They came from his parents' home near Austin. Virginia and I sat out on the back-porch Saturday night long after everyone else had gone to bed. Virginia said they had a house in Turkey off base. Nothing was safe there. They would sneak in your house, looking mostly for food. It had been a fearful experience for the most part living there.

She knew I was working on a ranch somewhere. I explained Dad's old boss, Mr. Dobrinsky, had taught me to run his business in case his health failed. Then sent me to layout plans to develop his 3600 ranch near Wells in Cherokee County. I lived there now in his home working to develop the plans I drew up. Along with another of his employees, Mr. Justin Wilson. We had a crew of eight Mexicans working under us.

She asked if I ever found Margaret.

"No, but I'm still looking."

"Do you ever hear from Mary Ellen?"

"I have not seen or heard anything from Mary Ellen since we graduated. Only that a friend told me her family moved back to near Tyler and she's in college there."

"We've written one another regularly. She is attending a two-year college there now. Soon as we get an address somewhere, I'll let her know."

Most of the rest of the family were there the next day. That evening I drew Virginia a map of where to find me. Added my phone number and address. She and the boy would be at Jewett that week. Her husband was going to Houston to do job interviews.

We decided to hold up on the 2400 acres, cross the road and develop pasture 3. That meant barn, corral, fencing, and water well, including tractor disking and seeding grass. It was Mr. Wilson's thinking. Get about 15 head of jersey cows and a red-poll bull. Start saving heifer's, building a herd. Get rid of the red-poll, bring in a red roan bull. Red roan is fair milk stock. Your foundation herd to eventually move into other pastures will have milk producing stock in their backgrounds.

Most people think you can take just any old cow, buy a registered good bull to put with her, and bingo! You'll get great calves. That may help to some degree. But what it takes to raise a good calf is a cow that produces plenty of high fat content milk! That's why I recommend starting with Jersey cows. And I'll tell you something else, by jingos! If you want a good steak, butcher about a half breed jersey yearling.

The first thing that had to happen was clean up that clear cut over land. We cleaned up for the inside and perimeter fencing first. Then with two of the Mexicans I started fencing. Mr. Wilson with the other six started clearing up the rest of the pasture.

We all met at lunch time. The Mexicans brought their lunch. Mr. Wilson and I went together to his house to eat. We crossed the road to the 2400 acres, I got out to open the gate. We heard a dog running, then boom! Somebody shot a deer. The gate was up, posted signs as well. The fence however was not. We found where someone had cut a few bushes, drove around the gate into the place.

We just decided to block their trail in, wait until they came out. We never had to wait long. They pulled up in 20 feet of us and stopped. The man on the passenger side got out. Mr. Wilson said: "Robert's that's a big dude, you want me to handle it?"

"Not unless that other fellow gets out." I got out. "You fellows know this is posted property?"

"Yeah, we know it. What the hell you gonna do about it?"

He was big, but had a beer gut. I hit him right in his short ribs. He grunted but came down with an overhand right that would have drove me in the ground. But I was on the move. I went behind him. Before he could straighten up I hit him across his nose just below his eyes. His knees buckled. I doubled my fist, but hit with the heel of my hand. My second lick got him right across his teeth. I had his hair in my left hand now. My third got him on the chin. He was now limp as a rag. I hit him one more time below his eyes.

"What to hell you gonna do about it leaked me off!"

The other opened his pickup door, started to get out. Mr. Wilson got out, stood up. He got back in his truck! I grabbed the dude by his legs, drug him around to the back of the truck, and let the tailgate down. I drug a big old doe deer out. A poor old hound dog was tied to a spare tire. Laying there was a double barrel 12 gage shotgun. I took it, broke it down, and stuck the barrel in the dirt. Threw the 3-gun pieces back in the truck bed.

I lifted the dude's shoulders, got them on the tailgate. Grabbed his legs, got him loaded. I put the tailgate up, walked around to the driver. "That deer don't belong to yall, it belongs to us. Tell your partner back there if he gets any more stupid questions to ask, come back to see us. And you need to feed that poor old dog. Now get the hell out of here!"

"Will you move that truck so we can get out?"

"We ain't moving nothing! You are good at building roads, make you one right through there!"

76

'Right through there' had two-inch sweet gum bushes and a stump. He hit it and I stomped a valve steam on his rear tire as he left. I could hear air spewing out!

Mr. Wilson looked at the stump.

"There's a lot of oil on that stump. He busted his oil pan. They won't get far." He was laughing.

We loaded the deer and drove on. He kept laughing. Finally he stopped, put his head on the steering wheel, still laughing.

"What's so funny?'

He raised up. "Were you mad at that fellow?"

"I was madder than I ever have been in my life!"

"Then why were you smiling at him?"

I never knew I was smiling. He asked me "What the hell you gonna do about it!? I was mad!"

"Well I ain't lying. You kept smiling until you told that driver to leave."

I never saw my Dad fight. Or my great grandfather Bethel DuPree. But I've been told they smiled at people they fought with.

We skinned that deer, quartered it up and iced it down. We were late getting back to work, but the Mexicans were working when we got back. They were good men, good workers.

Mr. Dobrinsky told me who he had drill his artesian deep well. I called the man and we got one in pasture three. He installed the three-inch steel pipe. Elbowed it over with external threads on the outside end of the elbow. The man said "I've drilled wells all over this country. Stretch in here about a mile wide and five miles long. We're on the upper edge here. It runs about five miles yonder way!" He pointed south.

The way he pointed ran through our pastures two and one and across the black top FM road and beyond the Neches River.

We got a three-inch straight pipe fitting with a screw on cap. Mr. Wilson cut holes, welded in two 1-1/4 inch pipes with valves. These would point out to each side. Two 3/4 inch pipes with valves were welded into the bottom of the three inch. A water distribution manifold so to speak. What he did to the well at the house to distribute water to all points needed, when needed!

We used PVC pipe up here. We piped the water to troughs on both sides of the road in pastures three and two. The last trough overflow in pasture two was piped to a pond we built. In pasture four, we built a trough on each side of the road. From the last one in pasture four, it ran out into a small ravine, crossed the road into the 2400 acres where we planned to build a pond.

Before we finished, each 150-acre pasture would have two or more ponds in it. The ones in pasture one had to be deep small lakes. We could not get well water to that pasture without a pump.

I had to go into the office now on Friday morning. To take now ten time cards. And return to the ranch in time to give everyone their checks before they left Friday evening. I usually got the card and check business over with Mrs. Ivers before I went in to talk with Mr. Dobrinsky. I opened the door and guess who I met. Mary Ellen! It seemed to me she sort of sucked in her breath and just froze for an instant. Perhaps as shocked as I was to see her there.

Then we gave each other a brief hug and it's so good to see you jazz! Truth of the matter, I *was* glad to see her again!

Mrs. Ivers was no fool. "I see you two know each other. Robert why don't you give me those time cards and take these checks. You two go to the break room and have some coffee!"

We went out in the hall. "I was on my way to take some files into Mr. Dobrinsky. It'll only take a minute!"

It seemed like ten, but we went to the break room. "I told Mr. Dobrinsky you were here. He's invited both of us to go to lunch with him."

Mr. Dobrinsky had given her that scholarship, told her if she needed a job, come here. I know people here, it's like being back at home!

We talked a while, told her I had seen Virginia. Her husband was out of the service. Looking for a job in Houston. Virginia's over at Jewett with Mom and Dad this week. She will send her address when they get settled.

I better check in with Mr. Dobrinsky I said. I'll probably be seeing you regularly. I'm here at least once a week, sometimes more often.

I went in with Mr. Dobrinsky. Told him we had completed pasture three. It would be ready for cattle as soon as we got grass on it.

I'd like to see you get on the lake next he said.

"That's no problem," I said. "Most of the initial work will be done by Mr. Wilson on that dozer. He'll need his five Mexicans burning trees, brush there. But I could get on with the fence building with the other three. We probably won't need to work together until we start on the dam. We can't do that until he gets the earth work complete."

"That's fine. I'm going to start sending Mary Ellen up there on Friday's to bring your pay checks and pick up your time cards. Show her around the place when she comes. She can give me a progress report weekly!"

Here we go again, I thought! *I'd been here an hour, and Mrs. Ivers and he both had tried to pair us up!*

It took a month for Mr. Wilson to clear trees and brush, move earth before we started on the dam. I had to join him with the backhoe towards the end. My two Mexicans could go on with the fence building. They knew what was required. His six were still burning things at the lake.

We had not bridged the east-west road where it crossed the creek. We went to the upper side of the place, crossed over the creek at the low water crossing. Drove down the east side until we came to the place where there was only room enough for a road between the fence and creek. We got out there. The creek made a 90-degree bend west there for a hundred yards. Then turned south, 90 degrees to the east-west road about 200 yards away.

When this creek gets at flood stage, it goes right across this stretch between the bends. That being said, the east-west road on this side of the creek has got to be raised up. By using the back hoe and digging a shallow canal on each side, we can get the needed soil. I think a good sized culvert about half way to the creek will be enough.

From that bend where we parked by, dig a canal. Put the soil to build a road levy between it and the fence. We'll need to bridge the canal at the east-west road. After the canal goes under the road bridge, it can slowly become shallower.

"Let's walk on down yonder. You never have met old Woodrow Duff that lives down there, have you?"

"No, sir. I knew there was house down there. But I never met the man."

After we left where the bridge would be, he kept pointing.

"With the back hoe, we can dig out the canal, throw the dirt out here. I can level and pack it with the dozer. We can have a road down to where we can put a gate in."

We got to where he had part of the road built with the dozer. He had dug a blade wide ditch below that marshy area to let it drain into the creek.

"All we can do is cover that marsh up with water." But he pointed back up the canal. "We can run a boat up that canal, and maybe fish out in that area some. We might even stop them wild hogs from hiding out in there."

We went on and I met Mr. Woodrow Duff. He was sitting out in his back yard with a 22 rifle. I sometimes get a mess of squirrels sitting out here he said.

His back yard ended on a bluff bank. The property line between his place and ours ran right at the edge of that bluff bank.

"We'll put you a gate there when we finish fencing the place. You can open the gate, fish right in the lake. Or open a gate back yonder, put a boat in to fish."

"I see you fellows building roads. I worked for the county for years. I know where there's a good retired road grader that's pulled behind a dozer. I know the man in charge, he probably would not charge you much for it. It's just in the way anymore."

"That's what we need! A dozer is for moving earth. Not for road grading!" Mr. Wilson wanted that grader I could tell.

Mr. Wilson knows more about equipment than I do. He'll probably go with you if you'll show it to him.

We got the grader for a hundred bucks. It took a half day with the low boy trailer, but we needed it. When, was a matter of time. For now, it was back on the lake detail. But time would prove it to me. Mr. Woodrow Duff was a fine man. A neighbor you could live with!

We got back on the lake job. Mr. Wilson and I discussed it more than once. *Why was delaying everything else and building the lake so important to Mr. Dobrinsky?* We agreed on one thing! He was paying us and we were not about to ask!

Mr. Wilson found a bargain with a place that sold used metal. They were taking up a 20-inch pipe line. They cut it in 21-foot lengths. He delivered us 50 of those cheap. Never had to unload on his lot, save space, we got them for $15 bucks each. That was cheaper than buying culverts, which we needed a lot of in our roads.

Off his lot we also bought 50 used railroad rails that cost us $18 each. It took three trips with the low boy trailer to get them there. We unloaded them up by where the creek bridge would be built. With the exception of 4 at gates, we could buy metal gates a hog could not get through. A rail under the gate would keep them from rooting under. The others were for bridge building.

I ran that track hoe across a still dry lake bed and started that canal. Up that marsh edge it was as wide as that back hoe would reach. I threw that dirt out which was hard under that slush on top. Mr. Wilson leveled and packed a road with the dozer. At the east-west road, we skipped over the width the road would be. We had to get the east road raised and the culverts in place before we dug that out.

Next to the creek, the land was higher. So, the levy started 35 yards from the creek. I started there digging a four-foot-deep canal and throwing the dirt on the roadway. Did the same thing on the other side. While I was doing that Mr. Wilson cleaned out stumps and brush for the rest of the canal. Pushed dirt out to form a levy on the west side of the canal.

Then he got out in the opening, dug out two 40 feet wide shallow strips almost to the levy from the creek. He spread the dirt out between them. That he said is going to be a duck hunting paradise!

He leveled out the road levy. With the back hoe, I dug out a place for six of those 20-inch culvert pipes. We did some concrete form work on each end of the pipes up to road top level. Got a ready-mix truck out there, filled in the forms. Spread the rest out on those six pipes. With poles and rubber boots we packed it between and around those pipes.

Then we dug the rest of the canal to the bend in the creek. The dirt went to the roadway and was packed down. A spring came out of the ground just inside our property line. We boxed it in, piped it under the roadway and stuck it over the canal. Later Mr. Wilson constructed a pan like thing with multiple small holes for it to fall through like rain. Below that, was another but solid. Designed to fill up and run over. And fall six feet into the canal.

"They tell me," he said. "Spring water ain't got no oxygen in it. This should put air in it. I can't wait to fish under it!"

Then we opened up the canal through the east-west road bed. One of the things we did at our gravel pile was build a platform ready-mix truck could back under. A heavy-duty screen was put in place. With the tractor front end loader, we dumped the gravel and sand on the screen. Sticks, trash was picked out of it.

We had cement on a 16-foot trailer, bags were lifted up and poured in with the sand. The Mexicans did that, the truck driver supervised all of that. Then he took the truck to a water hose, he put the water in. The truck came from the business in Livingston.

We got the canal short bridge reinforced with railroad iron finished. The lake dam was next!

At the dam site, the creek bed was narrow and deep. With the back hoe, I dug into each bank about six feet. Then dug about four feet deep across the creek bed. We built our forms, each end level with the creek bank. Out ten feet from each end, then dropped down three feet. That would leave a 14 feet long three-foot-deep spillway. Which we would bridge over. We wanted to be able to cross that dam if the creek was at flood stage.

We used three quarter inch rebar and some rail road iron inside the forms. Mr. Wilson took the lowboy trailer to Livingston for cement this time. It took two long days, with two ready-mix trucks and all hands, but we got that dam poured!

We would let it set up for three days. We used those three days to haul big flat rocks we had got out of the creek bed to the site. Below the dam, with those rocks and cement we meant to step the spill way down. Into a three-foot-deep, 12 foot wide, 20 foot long pond so to speak. It took some hand digging to form this up, we could not get a back hoe in the creek here. We felt when the lake overflowed, we might capture baitfish. And maybe fish to put back in the lake or eat!

After we got the forms removed from the dam, we did the rock work and got our pond completed. One cement truck was enough for this. It backed up to the creek bank, its outlet shoot fairly well reached everything. The Mexicans and I got that done. Mr. Wilson was out in the lake bed, pushing dirt to the dam and packing it. He sloped it back from about two feet below the bottom of the spillway. We hoped that would keep water from working its way under the dam.

They never burned all the stumps Mr. Wilson got up out in the lake. He left scattered piles around the lake. Had the Mexicans take barb wire, staple them together. A length of high line pole was set in the center of each pile. Three more poles were set in a circle out from the center pole. Other poles were set here and there over the lake bed. All were set in concrete and designed to tie trotlines to!

The lake was complete. Now we got on the creek bridge. We dug down deep with post-hole diggers. Three of the 20-inch pipes were cut the right length, set in place. They were filled with concrete, reinforced with railroad iron rails and three-quarter inch rebar.

Forms were built bottom and top. The top required a lot of cutting and welding of railroad iron rails before concrete was poured. It would support the center of the bridge. Twenty-four inches wide, 20 inches deep and 13 feet long. It contained eight pieces of railroad iron to give it the strength needed. The bottom form only contained two pieces welded between the 20-inch pipes.

The drive through area would be 12 feet wide itself. The forms were 13 feet in width for a bridge railing on each top side.

It was a relief to get that center support for the bridge in place before it rained. The lake could fill up, we could still complete the bridge.

The Reverend Billy often came to talk to me. I liked the man. He asked me once had I been saved and baptized. I told him the truth about what had happened. That I thought I was saved. But other kids tried to drag me to the front. I decided to wait, get up, and go on my own.

He was not a push and shove preacher. It's a personal decision between anybody and God he said. You're probably right not to let yourself be dragged up there. But God is waiting on you! He would be pleased with you if you went ahead and did what he knows is in your heart!

While I was working on the bridge, he came one afternoon. We always had a glass of tea together at the kitchen table. He said he needed to work about three days a week. He was wondering if I might let him work some. I can drive a truck. I can run a tractor. And I can use an axe or a shovel! I could work Monday, Tuesday and Thursday. We have church Wednesday night and twice on Sunday. And we always got something going on Saturday.

I told him yes. The more help we had the better. I explained the retirement plan at Livingston.

Well three days a week, don't think I would save much at my age. Just hold out social security.

Mr. Wilson and I talked it over. It was decided he would need two of the Mexicans on the bridge project. He was a month ahead of the Mexicans in land clearing. They knew what to do. So do the fence builders.

Let Rev. Billy take the dump truck three days a week. He can load gravel with the tractor. Start dumping across the creek here. Go around to the gate north east gate. Then around by where the pines will be. You just supervise all of them. By then, we should have this bridge completed. All the lake project will need is rain!

Rev. Billy can keep hauling gravel. I'll use the dozer to roughly spread that gravel. Then he and I will pack it and make a smooth road with the grader we bought. Then we can all get back to our pasture land clearing and fencing after I change blades.

Mary Ellen came every Friday morning. Brought our checks, picked up our time cards. Then I had to drive her around, show her what we got done that week. Mrs. Wilson insisted she eat with them at lunch time. When Mrs. Wilson insisted, folks usually complied. Mary Ellen was driving a Volks Wagon beetle. Said Mr. Dobrinsky gave her $10 bucks a week extra to drive up here on Friday.

Later, Mrs. Wilson told me, "Mary Ellen is such a sweet girl. Seems to me you and her would be a great pair."

I told them about Margaret. Of the commitment we made at 15 to marry. That Mary Ellen was a friend. But I was doing what I could to find Margaret. They never said anything about it again.

Mr. Dobrinsky sometimes came up on Saturday. We walked down to the dam site late one evening. He sat down on the dam railing, so I did as well.

"Robert, you probably have wondered where I'm from, how I got the money to start a business, do what we're doing here. My business interests have prospered, you know. But I'm going to tell you something I've never told anyone. I trust you not to tell anyone, unless maybe you marry someone that needs to know.

"I was born on a small farm in upstate New York. My parents were both killed in a train wreck when I was six years old. My grandparents raised me, but both were dead by the time I was 18. They willed the place to a married daughter who lived in Ohio. She sold the place.

"With no money but a little change, I hitchhiked my way to New York. I ate and slept at the Salvation Army until I found a job at a wholesale grocery and produce business. It was hard work and low pay.

"But I met a girl at a bingo hall I went to. She worked in a laundry. Beautiful girl. Her name was Rebecca Ann Landry. People called her Beckey. Her Mother was dead and her father was a worthless drunk. She was on her own, trying to support herself. We married, moved into the apartment she had. It had a small kitchen, a bath and a big room that was the bedroom and living room combined.

"We were happy together. She had a magazine, with color pictures of Caddo Lake in it. She loved the lake and tree pictures. "Let's save our money and move to Texas. Near a lake and trees!" We tried to save, but were making no progress. She became pregnant. She was so happy about that. We'll raise our kid where there's a lake and trees!

"The only entertainment we could afford in 1936 was to go to a bingo hall. We went one night, she was almost eight months pregnant. After the game, we were walking two blocks to where we lived. We walked right into a cross fire shootout between two rival gangs. Which happened regularly in New York. She was hit in the chest. I got down with her, and somehow, I never got hit. The law got there, along with ambulances. There were others hit, both gang members and innocent people like we were.

"The law handcuffed me; thought I was a gang member. They would not listen to me! "That's my wife they're putting in that ambulance," I said. The paramedic did, he told me where they were taking her. They took me to jail. I talked to the officer checking me in. Explained that my wife was shot and asked him to call my boss. He could identify me as an employee. I think that officer believed me. He called. Then told me, "He's cussing like a sailor, but I suppose he's on the way."

"It was 30 minutes before he got there. Still cussing like a sailor, but he did get me released. Without saying he was sorry my wife was shot, or even offering to drive me to the hospital. I ran five blocks to that hospital. The emergency room Doctor told me my wife was dead when they got her there and that he tried to take and save the baby. It was a healthy appearing baby boy. But it was too late. His Mother had been dead too long. I went to her father, hoping for help and maybe telling me where to bury my wife and son. He just said, "She's your wife and I don't give a damn! You handle it!"

"I could not afford a funeral or a grave site. I had them cremated together. I carried them both in that urn they put them in to that apartment. Set it on the top shelf of the closet. One thought kept running through my mind. *Beckey wanted to be near a lake and trees in East Texas!* I could not bring myself to bury them in New York. Yet I could not afford to leave there.

"Lots of nights, I turned the lights out, drug my chair to the window, and just sat there, staring at the street below. One night, a man came running down the street with a big suit case. On the sidewalk, he stopped. The sidewalk was in four-foot sections. No doubt, he knew about this particular section. He lifted one side up, threw that suitcase under it, and ran!

"Three men soon followed, with pistols in their hand and running as well. I soon heard shots about two blocks away. *They killed him*, I thought.

"They soon came back. One got in the trash dumpster digging around. I could hear them. 'If we don't find that suitcase, we're gonna get it!' The one in the dumpster said, 'If you had not shot the SOB, we could have made him tell us where he hid it! It ain't in this dumpster.' They moved on and out of sight.

"I waited 30 minutes. I got the old .38 pistol my grandpa left me and sneaked down the stairs. I got that suitcase out from the hole under that sidewalk. Back up in the apartment, I opened it. I could not believe my eyes. It was full of money. I might add, I never counted it until I got to Livingston, Texas. It was over three million dollars!

"I had a duffle bag in the closet that I got for 20 cents once, at a surplus store. I layered the bottom with money. Placed that urn with my wife and son's ashes in it. Packed money around it after I taped the lid on. Covered it up with money. The smallest bills were $20's. I put $200 bucks in my wallet. The bag was over half full. I got most of the underwear, shirts and pants I owned into it. I started to put the pistol in. Thought better of that and left it. Along with everything else in that apartment.

"I put that empty suitcase back under that sidewalk and walked about eight blocks to a train station. Bought a map, and some coffee. Caught that train out of there to Jersey City, New Jersey. With the map, I had a route plotted to Shreveport Louisiana and Houston Texas. Part of it was by bus, most was by train.

"I liked what I was seeing before I got to Livingston. I liked it for Beckey, really! But as the train slowed to a stop at the depot where it is now in Livingston, I saw for sale signs on the ground my business is on now. I walked down town, got a hotel room. Not where I live now. That old hotel is long gone now.

"My map indicated it was not far to Cleveland. The next day, I caught the train to Cleveland. Bought two suitcases. Bought business suits, white shirts, ties, and dress shoes. Casual dress clothes, belts, and socks. I meant to buy that land to start a business. I knew if a man started spending the kind of cash I had, he needed to look like somebody!

"That's it Robert. I slowly but surely, worked that money into the business. Into the other interests you know I have. Don't get me wrong. Your Dad is one of the finest and as intelligent as any man I've ever known. He told me once his parents died when he was nine years old. If I had not found that money, I might still be working like he's had to all his life. I saw you as a kid that deserved a better opportunity than you had. I hope you feel I've given you one!

"I think you know now why building a lake here is so important to me. I do feel I need to warn you. Those Mobster's in New York don't forget things. If they get a clue to where that money went, they might kill somebody whether they get it back are not! They got that money from poor peoples' sweat and blood. I never knew who they were, could not return it. Mob people killed my wife and son. I don't regret taking it!"

"That answers a lot of questions I had, but thought I had no right to ask. I do appreciate you telling me. I'll keep what you've told me to myself!"

I did feel better about what he was doing for me. I thought, *I now understood the man*. He was right about Dad. But I had come up feeling like I had little opportunity to amount to anything. I now realized Dad had fought the same battle.

Mr. Wilson took two weeks' vacation to Austin. I kept the Mexican's going on land clearing and fence building. I had evenings and a Saturday to myself. This was something personal I wanted no one to know about, but hopefully one day, Margaret. I built a deer stand.

It was eight feet long, 54 inches tall, and 48 inches wide. The entrance door was in one end. I put hinged boards over shooting slots around it. The top was in two hinged pieces covered with sheet iron. Flip each side back, you could stand up. Two could crawl into the stand, sit in chairs, open up the shooting slots, and wait for a deer or hog. Or watch Wood Ducks on two different sloughs.

I took it to a place between two button willow sloughs near the creek bank which would become the edge of the lake. There grew a tall clump of myrtle bushes, probably in a 20-foot diameter circle. I cleared out some in the center, set the stand over in it with the 'A' frame truck. Got in it, decided it was perfect. Anything passing through the area, had to come between a slough and the creek bank or between the sloughs. I could see out for 200 yards in any direction.

I crawled out, bent a few limbs to cover the entrance. Walked around it. *No one,* I thought, *would ever see it in that clump of evergreen myrtle bushes.* I threw the cut bushes on the truck, drove to a place we were clearing. Threw them on a brush pile.

It was two months later. He called me one day.

"Robert, I need you to pack up and move back here to help me. I got the Wilson house ready for you. You can live there. Just turn everything over to Mr. Wilson. He can continue what needs to be done up there. Take the rest of the week to move."

"Do you want me to bring the pickup truck there, or leave it up here?"

"Just use it to move with. That's your truck anyway. I'll sign the title and give it to you when you get moved. And I'll get somebody to help you get your car down here."

I moved back to Livingston. The house had been remodeled and painted. The kitchen had a stove, dining table with chairs and a refrigerator. The living room had a matching couch and two recliners. It also had two smaller chairs. Two end tables, a coffee table and two table lamps.

All three bedrooms were furnished with beds, one chest of drawers set with a big mirror. The other was taller with no mirror. In each room, was a comfortable padded chair. I liked a chair when I put my boots on! It had a telephone in the master bedroom, living room and kitchen.

Both baths had been rebuilt, ceramic tiled. The larger one had a fully tiled shower stall. The other had the shower over the tub.

He had a two-car garage built on one side of the house. With overhead locking doors. A door opened into the dining room from the garage.

I could have family visit here. Go get Mom and Dad. They could stay a week. Maybe a month!

But I knew my mom. She loved to go places. But as soon as she got there, she wanted to go home!

I noticed right away, Mr. Dobrinsky seemed to be getting around slower and seemed sort of tired out. He came to the office, but for the most part, I was running the business. Except on Friday. He sent me to the ranch with Mary Ellen. I did get a change made to that routine. We left from Livingston at 10 a.m., stopped somewhere for lunch. Mrs. Wilson never needed to fix lunch for us. And our ranch tour was very brief.

Mary Ellen was capable of taking over for Mrs. Ivers. It was her I worked with now more than Mrs. Ivers. And she could deal with customers, salesmen, anybody. Mr. Dobrinsky referred to her as a "people person."

One day, an old man came into the lobby. "Where yall want me to unload this load of logs I got out here?"

Mary Ellen just said, "I'll show you where to go."

Mr. Dobrinsky and I watched her out there talking to that old man, pointing and giving directions. He got in his truck to leave. She came back in the office.

Mr. Dobrinsky said, "I see you got that man going!"

"That poor old man! Someone may have given him the wrong directions. He's worked all these years driving a log truck. Never paid into Social Security. His wife is in bad health, he has a lot of medical expense. He can't retire, he has to keep working."

"It would have took me all day to learn all that," Mr. Dobrinsky said. "You were only out there five minutes!"

"He talked. I listened," Mary Ellen said.

One day, Mr. Dobrinsky and I were at lunch together. He commented that Mary Ellen was such a nice girl. He wondered how serious I was about her.

I told him about Margaret. That Mary Ellen was just a friend from our high school days.

"I understand," he said. "Beckey was the only woman I ever cared about. People talk about me and my business partner at the hotel. She knows that as well as I. I asked her once if she wanted me to move. She just laughed and said "No! We give people something to dream about!"

He asked me one day: "Robert, you've seen enough of this business to run it. Give me an honest opinion. What do you think the future will be for the business? What do we need to do to stay financially stable?"

"Big chain stores are moving into town. We get very little business here locally in the grocery part of the business. People have become more mobile. The cross roads country stores are shutting down because people don't shop there anymore. No longer are mules, horses, and oxen being used in the woods logging. That's become mechanized. Really, the only thing here on the rail road that has a future is our hardware business."

"I agree," he said. "I think we need to replace the wholesale grocery business as well as the feed and hay business. Take some time, give it some thought. Let me know what your plan would be to make the necessary changes."

I got more poster board, went to work on laying it all out. We had two rail road spurs coming into the business. The track belonged to the rail road, they put it there to serve the business. Most of it would come up, they might allow us to do that and get the ties and rails for the ranch. The hardware warehouse would move to the back two warehouses where the feed and large boxed case goods were stored. The rail road switch track would end at the back door of that warehouse.

The other warehouse, attached to the office we were in now would be remodeled into a retail hardware business. Stock things that people needed. Comparable to an Ace hardware store. Connected to the back two buildings with the loading dock, the lumber, cement, wire, and other heavy things would become retail as well. The office we were in now would require a store manager, a secretary, salesmen, check out and cash register. Warehouse workers, a truck driver and delivery truck.

The current hardware building would undergo remodeling as well. Converted into a feed, fertilizer and garden supply retail store. That would include mowers. Roto tillers as well. That would also require an office, store manager, secretary, salesmen and loaders and unloaders.

The hay building warehouse had 16-foot walls. Walls and roof were heavy duty sheet iron. The floor was treated two by six lumber. This building would come down. The lumber, sheet iron would be used at the ranch to build cow sheds.

A central office building for all the business would be built here. Next to it would be a building place to sell flat bottom boats and motors. And a general outdoors store to handle guns, ammunition, rods and reels, hooks, lines and sinkers! The end of the building would be separated into an out- board motor and small engine repair shop. It would service equipment we sold in the Garden Supply Store as well.

I felt flat bottom aluminum boats were the best thing to happen to middle class American family recreation. In my younger days, people could build wooden boats. Which never lasted long, and you never went far with paddles. With the lake over near Woodville now, I thought aluminum boats and motors would really sell. There was not such a business in the county.

I presented the plan to Mr. Dobrinsky. He thought it was the way to go. We decided the new office building, boat business should be first to go up. Along with rail road track removal. We also begin shutting down the wholesale delivery business. We stopped ordering, we put sales on things in the local newspaper. Spot ads on the radio. Our wholesale delivery business came to a halt. No employee was laid off. A couple retired. The rest we found work for.

For the most part, I was put in charge of all the project. I no longer punched a time clock. I was put on salary. $500 bucks per week! That was a step up I never imagined laying by corn or sawing logs. It involved things I never dreamed possible either. It seemed you needed a permit to build a chicken coop anymore. Mr. Dobrinsky and his lawyer kept me lined out on state and local requirements. For better or worse, his wholesale business was changing to retail. I hoped for the better!

Chapter Six
From Rags to Riches

Things were going very well with the change-over. May sound like cheating, but so many things reached an expiration date. We sold a lot by advertising, but a lot of things reached a date we could not sell. Different brands were picked up by their company. We got our money back.

We contracted taking the rail road tracks out to a concern that sold used ties, rails and gravel. We kept the gravel in the deal, we could spread that on our parking lots. We decided we never needed the used cross ties and rails.

We got moved in the new office. We were stocking the boat building with two different name brand aluminum boats. One was a heavy-duty boat, the other light weight but cheaper. We wanted something affordable for just about everyone.

The boat motors were name brand also. They ranged from 2.5 to 25 HP. If someone wanted a bigger motor, we could order it for them. The motor company was training two of our younger employees to work on their motors. They were stocking us with parts as well. We would furnish the tools to work on the motors ourselves.

It came a week-long rain ever day like it does in East Texas. Mr. Wilson called. The lake is full and running over the spillway. Yall might want to drive up to see it. We'll probably go to church tonight. Yall know where it's at.

Mary Ellen wanted to go. We'll go in my car Mr. Dobrinsky said. Robert, you drive. Mary Ellen, you ride up front with Robert. I'll take the back seat. I never had driven a Lincoln Continental before. It was a powerful machine.

We got up there before dark, we could see the lake. It was full and muddy which was to be expected. The spillway was handling it fine. Probably about 12 inches deep running over. A few sticks and limbs were running over the spillway, but not that much. Like it does on foggy overcast days in East Texas, it was getting dark in a hurry.

I walked around, opened the car door for Mary Ellen. He had the back door open on the driver's side. His arms were folded, he was leaning on it. He had a look on his face like you know, he was absent from this world. He was looking up toward the cemetery. After a minute he seemed to return to this world and said: "Beckey, you have a lake now. Robert and I both know it!"

On the way to Lufkin, he asked, "Do you two like Chinese food?" We both said we had never eaten it.

"I know a small place in Lufkin I've eaten at before. I would like to go there again. I think you will like it. They serve the best egg rolls I've ever eaten, and their General George Shrimp is out of this world."

We all ordered the General George Shrimp. It came with an egg roll, but he ordered six extra. The man knew about good food, places to eat. A salesman brought me here once he said. I drive up here sometimes just to eat.

I don't blame you I said. The shrimp were cooked in a thick great tasting red looking sauce. Then shrimp and sauce were poured over a plate full of fried rice. Mary Ellen asked for a carry out box. I know what I'll have for lunch tomorrow!

One day we went to lunch together. "Robert, do you have $500 you can bring to my lawyer's office tomorrow? I promise you'll get it back. You'll find out tomorrow why you need it."

"The bank does not open until nine in the morning. I can't get it until then."

"That's fine. Just sleep late in the morning, go by the bank then come on to the lawyer's office."

I still remember the date. It was September 20, 1959. The lawyer handed me some papers. "You need to sign these so we can get started. There will be a lot more!"

Dad had always told me, don't sign anything related to business until you have read it. I started reading. It did not take me long to become alarmed. I stopped reading and said, "This sounds like Mr. Dobrinsky is selling me his business for $500?"

"That's exactly what it means," the lawyer said. "If you inherit it, you would pay a bundle of taxes. By buying, you can save a lot of money!"

"I got up. Mr. Dobrinsky I need to talk to you outside. We went out in the waiting room. Are you serious about all this?"

"I've never been more serious about anything in my life. I don't have any living relatives. I saw you as a boy like me that needed a break in this life. That's why I've trained you in the business. When we are done here this morning, you will own everything, including the ranch. I will keep one account which will reward a few other loyal employees. And take care of myself until I leave this world. If you sign these papers today, it will be a weight off my shoulders."

I believed the man, that he still had all the shingles in his roof. I started signing papers, which the lawyer explained. Most of that involved his partnership, ownership with other people. I gave Mr. Dobrinsky $500 dollars, which the notary counted, then handed back to him. We signed papers until noon, but it was official. I was worth probably ten million dollars in assets and cash!

After we got out of the office, he stuck the $500 dollars in my shirt pocket. "That's just a formality we had to show that notary. You may want to go in the bank and deposit it. I'll wait for you. Then we'll get some lunch."

The bank was next door. He waited. "Where do you want to eat?"

"It's been a while since I had a hot roast beef sandwich at the Greasy Spoon."

"I've heard about that! Let's eat there."

He said he was going out of town for a few days the next week. He never said where and I never asked. I would learn later it was the cancer center in Galveston.

He often had me go to school board meetings with him. He resigned because of health reasons, he said. Then he nominated me to fill out his unexpired term. I suppose it was a testimony to the respect the board members had for him. I became the youngest school board member ever. I would have to run for reelection, however, when his term expired.

He still came into the office daily, but seemed to be growing thinner and weaker. One morning, the woman at the hotel, who was now my partner, called. Mr. Dobrinsky had me call an ambulance to take him to the hospital cancer center in Galveston. He may have never told you, but he has cancer that has spread into his bones and lungs.

It was Friday, I had appointments I had to keep. Mary Ellen and Mrs. Ivers wanted to go with me. We all needed to go home and change, they said they would come back to my place. It was after five before we left Livingston. We stopped at a burger place in Baytown, it was near eight when we got there.

He knew us all, thanked us for coming. His doctor came in, then called me out in the hall. "Are you his son?"

"No sir. I was an employee, he recently gave me his business. He has no family or living relatives."

"Then I regret to tell you this. I don't expect him to last through the week-end."

Visiting hours were eight until nine. We had to leave. Mary Ellen and Mrs. Ivers went home. I told them both to just tell people Monday I was out of town, in case I was not there. I showered, slept awhile. With extra clothes, I was on my way to Galveston by 6 a.m. Saturday morning. I meant to be with him until the end.

He knew me when I got there. Had on an oxygen mask. He just reached out with a feeble hand and shook mine. Then he closed his eyes in sleep. The nurse told me I could just stay with him. He never opened his eyes again. He left this world on Saturday, November 15, 1959, at 5:30 p.m. My hope, along with the greatest grief I ever felt, was that he knew he was not alone when he left.

They had his instructions to call the Funeral Home in Livingston if he passed on. There was nothing I could do but go home. Thinking about it on the way home, there was one thing that brought me some degree of comfort. I got baptized and joined the Baptist Church when I moved back to Livingston.

I knew he attended that Church. I was surprised to find Mary Ellen sitting on the front row with him. She had joined also, told me the Baptist beliefs were more in line with what she believed. Her dad had not objected, he said to do what she felt was right. But I know Mr. Dobrinsky was pleased with us both for joining and being there with him.

The service was at the funeral home on Tuesday morning at ten. Most of his employees sat in the place where family usually sits. Jimbo Batiste, Mr. Wilson and I were pallbearers, along with three other men who were long term workers at Livingston. The chapel was packed with friends and business partners. I saw a good many salesmen there that he had dealt with for years.

Graveside rites were at 3 p.m. at the ranch cemetery. He was put next to his wife and son. Most of his employees were there. That included eight Mexicans and Reverend Billy. A good many of his friends were there as well.

I might add, I ordered all our business shut down Tuesday. The American and Texas Flag lowered to half-mast. Everyone would be paid for eight hours.

About a month later, Mr. Wilson called me.

"They brought Mr. Dobrinsky and wife's head stone today. You may want to come look at it."

Mary Ellen and Mrs. Ivers wanted to go with me. We left at three, were up there by five. When I read the inscription on the stone, I fell to my knees crying. I could not help it. It read like this:

John David Dobrinsky	Rebecca Ann Dobrinsky
July 8, 1905	October 10, 1906
November 15, 1959	March 24, 1936
	and infant son
Together again in	Robert Alton Dobrinsky
the Promised Land	March 24, 1936

His son had my name. Robert Alton. And my birthday. March 24, 1936. That's why he picked me to leave his business to. He never told me. But he knew I would understand when I saw this stone.

Mary Ellen was the first to understand why I was on my knees. "His son had your name. And your birthday!"

I got up. "Yes, I've asked myself a thousand times 'Why me Lord? Why did he leave everything to me?' Now I understand."

Life must go on. We stopped in Lufkin at a Chinese place Mr. Dobrinsky once took Mary Ellen and I to. He had recommended the General George Shrimp on the menu. We all ordered that and I ordered extra egg rolls, as he had. Mrs. Ivers asked for a carry out box.

"I can't eat all this. It's so good, I'll take John some."

Mary Ellen added some of hers for John as well.

About a week later, the woman at the hotel called. "You need to stop here, first chance you get. He left you a lot of guns. There may be other things you want. If not, I can get the Salvation Army to come get it." He had the top floor of that hotel, which surprised me. A closet was stacked full of guns. He once told me he went to Beaumont and Houston. Buying guns, trying to invest cash. Guns are like having money in the bank, he said.

Something that surprised me was the exercise equipment he had. A weight lifting thing to lay on, equipment to exercise ever muscle in your body. There was a stand-up punching bag thing and boxing gloves. A set of springs with handles to exercise your arms. He was always so physically fit, up until the last few months of his life. Working in the office now, I needed that. I also needed help to get it out of there.

There were a few rods and reels I wanted. There was a framed picture of him and his young wife Rebecca. He had probably had it enlarged from a small photo. On the back, he had written John & Beckey Dobrinsky. That was something I wanted to keep. The rest of the things she could give to the Salvation Army.

It took me an hour to get those guns downstairs and into my pickup. She got a chair, sat out by my pickup. "I'll watch," she said. "People can grab a gun and run with it." I told her I would bring someone the next day to help me get the exercise equipment.

I gave Mr. Wilson a model 94 Winchester Shotgun and a Remington 30.06 with a Redfield Scope. Wade got a model 94 Winchester 12 gage shotgun just like I gave his dad. Also, a Henry lever action 22, which was a very expensive gun. In time, I gave my brothers a gun, depending on what they needed. Dad hunted some with my brothers on his brother's place. I gave him a double barrel 12 gage.

Mr. Dobrinsky said it. "Guns are like money in the bank." I bought a bank for those guns. A metal fire proof lock box, actually. The thing had a shelf for ammunition. It was 36 inches wide. The sides were 18 inches. I stacked those guns in stock down and filled it. Most were still in a box.

I bought myself a wide 14-foot boat and 10 HP motor *from* myself. I could not just take things from any of the businesses. It messed up the paper work, and for a number of reasons, you best not mess up the paper work.

Mary Ellen asked me one Friday "Why don't we go up to that creek fishing tomorrow? I bought a rod and reel from the boat store." We sold all manners of things people used fishing besides boats.

"They fenced up that place up there and posted it. We can't go there. We can go to Dam B if you want to."

We got over there early. I had drinks iced down, and she brought lunch. I stopped and got three dozen shiners. I had my rod and reel, a couple of cane poles I cut down on

Long King Creek. I rigged up the poles with crappie jigs. We used a cork and minnows on our rods and reels. We let them fish in one place.

The pole with jig we could move around, which soon proved the more effective in catching crappie. By noon time, we had 15 crappie that weighed about one pound each. We caught three channel catfish on the minnows which weighed about two and a half pounds each.

We had been fishing in and around a big cypress stump which was hollow, just the edges of the tree left. That hollow must have been five feet across. We caught most of those crappies out of that stump. It was next to an island which I had camped on during my high school days with my brother Lawrence. We caught a lot of catfish trotline fishing from the island.

We ate lunch. She had fried chicken and potato salad. Fritos and cinnamon rolls. I had the Dr. Peppers, which I knew she liked.

After we had lunch, I drug out a couple of coffee cans I brought. The island had beech trees on it. The ground was littered with red beech seed. We probably spent 30 minutes crawling around picking up beech seed. Seeing Mary Ellen crawling around in those tight jeans was somewhat stimulating to my blood pressure. But we poured the cans together, had about a half can. I meant to plant those seed at the ranch.

We fished around the stump for a few minutes, caught about three more crappies. We went to the boat ramp, loaded up and went to my house. She had her car there, I told her go home and clean up if you want to.

"I'll clean these fish. Come back when you are ready. We'll have us a fish fry!"

I managed to get a shower before she got back. We fried fish, peeled potatoes, fried fries. I mixed up hot water corn bread, added a little chopped up onion and a little chili powder, salt and black pepper. Fried that. I liked fried corn bread better than any hushpuppy I ever ate.

We had a great time working together, eating together. Talking about our high school days. Laughing about that car wash, eating at the Greasy Spoon. She told her dad about that hot roast beef sandwich, they went there once after church Sunday and ate. He loved it.

Mary Ellen and I split up the left-over fish, we both liked cold fish. We would have fish Sunday. She lived in that garage apartment I lived in. I had noticed lately her VW beetle was smoking a lot. I resolved Monday to do for her what Mr. Dobrinsky had done for me. Put her in a new Ford. I felt she could afford it. One of the first things I did was put the women in the office on a comparable wage scale with men. Mary Ellen was getting $1.75 an hour now.

I talked to her about it Monday. Explained that I could put her in a new Ford at our dealer costs. Her payments would be very low. I would give her $800 bucks for her VW beetle. I wanted a VW to convert into a hunting wagon to leave at the ranch.

"I only paid $850 for it three years ago," she said.

"The body is in super good shape," I said. I was writing her a check for $850. "You need a car you can rely on driving to Tyler."

"Well yes, that's true. I've been wondering how many more trips up there it would make. I guess it would not hurt to see how much my payments might be."

I handed her the check. "Put this down on it and I think you'll be surprised at how low your payments will be."

I talked her into a V8 1960 new Ford with automatic transmission. I went with her for a test drive. Showed her how the shift worked. It was a dark blue. She was still not sure she could afford it. "I like it, but we better see what the payments will be."

I had called my partner earlier. He knew what the deal was. "With $850 down, tax, liability insurance and everything, your payments will be $38 dollars and 47 cents a month."

"How much did you say," Mary Ellen asked?

"Thirty-eight dollars and 47 cents a month!"

"I wanted to be sure I heard you right. Yes! Yes! I can afford that!"

We had more trucks and vans than we needed now. I sold two to my friend Andre Batise on a low payment plan. He was making two trips a day now, hauling wood chips from our mill to a plant in Silsbee. That was paying him quiet well. He came and paid me off for the trucks after a few months. Said he and his wife had been looking at places to buy.

I invited Andre, his wife and kids and Mary Ellen to the house one Saturday night. I made chicken and spaghetti with my recipe. I had French bread, green beans and a lettuce and tomato salad to go with it. We ate, they all seemed to like it. The two kids were soon asleep after we ate. We put them on the living room couch. The four of us sat in the kitchen laughing and talking about our days in high school until midnight!

Mary Ellen said on Monday "Robert, you seemed to really enjoy being with old friends Saturday night. Being wealthy now has not seemed to change you. I suppose we were all a little afraid it would."

"The friends I have will always be my friends. Since I've become wealthy, there's a few that would not spit on me before that act like they want to be friends now. I don't admire that much. I won't let wealth change who I am. I may make new friends, but I'll still care about my old friends. I did enjoy Saturday night and I hope we do it again soon!"

The fencing and road building was about done. My forest service friend brought out the long leaf pine seedlings. The Mexicans set those out, they were experienced at that. I just had to pay the Forest Service for the seedlings.

Mr. Wilson had pasture 4 seeded, was working on two and one. Rev. Billy was hauling gravel to the roads over there now. Dumping it about 20 yards apart in the middle of the roads. Mr. Wilson would spread it later with the dozer. It was no small chore to change blades and he had the land clearing blade on.

We had 15 head of Jersey Cattle in pasture three with a Red Poll bull now. We cut and baled hay on the part of our creek bottom field where we meant to put pecan trees. With the Mexicans, two tractors and trailers, they stacked 500 bales in the barn. I thought it would hold a thousand more. But this hay was a combination of Bermuda grass, carpet grass, Dallas grass, and a wild lespedeza plant with small leaves that cattle loved. Feed the hay over a pasture and the seed would fall off.

I got family and friends to collect acorns. The court house had live oaks around it. Many times, I had seen the janitor sweeping up live oak acorns on the sidewalk. I asked him to save me some when they fell. Saved me half a tow sack full. I gave him $20. Wade picked up pin oak, about three different kinds of Red Oak in the creek bottom.

My cousin Marvin's grand kids got me a lot of post oak, black jack, sand jack which I think is also called blue oak. Also, the old black bark red oak that produced rather small acorns, but a lot of them. I paid them $10 bucks a gallon for acorns, $5 per gallon for hillside hickory nuts and bitter pecans. Same for pig nuts. Pig nut trees looked like a hickory, but produced a small soft shelled bitter nut that looked like a hickory nut.

I drove to the Ft. Parker lake dam once. Trees there looked like a post oak. But they had oval cup acorns about the size of a quarter. My brother at Weatherford, Texas, brought me a quart of wild late summer plum seed, which makes the best jelly in the world. He said the deer in a park there ate the plum part, spit the seed out. I got permission from the land owner to go on the place I was born on at Cedar Creek. I got half a tin tub of red and yellow plums.

I planted two rows of those late summer plums across that creek bottom field. They made good size trees with care. The red and yellow plums, one row was enough. The rest of the tub I spread in a number of places around the 2400 acres. Beside the roads were some of those places. Once they started producing, those kinds of plums just kept spreading.

I got Black Walnuts beside a county road in Leon County. Dad said old Timothy Dargin Nettles planted Black Walnuts all around the perimeter of that place. Where he got them, he did not know. But those that fell in the road were the biggest Black Walnuts I ever saw.

I tried an experiment with those. I put some to the grinder in the shop. Ground that black hull down thin, but not into the seed itself. I put one I ground down, and one solid to the hill across that field. I put out a few on the place at Livingston. Every hill I planted came up the next year. One to the hill. I dug up a couple. The one I ground down came up. A few of the solid ones came up three years later!

The Wilson place had eight pecans in a row there in the field. The pecans were about as big around as my middle finger. But about an inch and a half long. The best tasting pecan I ever ate. I planted four rows of these across the field which turned out to be 100 trees. One row I meant to leave. I learned grafting in FFA. I meant to graft the other three rows with larger pecans when the trees got about an inch and a half in diameter.

My cousin Marvin gave me tame berry sets, enough for half a row across the field. The other half row I got permission to get wild blackberry sets on a spring branch on the place at Cedar Creek. These made my favorite jelly and pies.

The man knew me, he knew I grew up on the place. A lot of these things are disappearing. Someone needs to start saving it! You probably don't know this. Over yonder in that branch bottom field where your daddy grew it, there's a number of clumps of that blue stripe ribbon cane. I got all I need in my garden to chew on, I don't make syrup. Get it all if you want it! I got all I needed to put out a row.

I decided to try my grinding trick with my peach seed. I planted a row, half white clear seed and half yellow cling. I bought an assortment of different kinds at a couple of stores in Lufkin. Hale Haven, June Gold, and Elberta was what I found. I set out half a row. Next year maybe I could get enough to finish the row.

I found some trees in the creek bottom that looked like a pear tree. They had small fruits that looked like a pear, and smelled like one. Small seedlings were up around the trees. I planted 30 hills on a row. The Wilson place had four pear trees, two Bartlett and two big Asian types. I could get graft stock and graft to those 30 trees. Thirty pear trees are a lot of pears.

I went across the Trinity River to the place Melton and I once hunted on. There I found scaly bark hickory nuts and white oak acorns. Also, something I had seen in the roadside park as a kid at the Lock and Dam Park on the Trinity at highway 7. It was an oval cup acorn almost as big as a tennis ball. I found two trees and found 25 solid acorns. I also got about a half pint of chinquapins. The squirrels got there first!

I called a seed company that sold potted fruit and nut trees. "If I order 25 English Walnut Trees, how much would it cost me? I live in East Texas."

"That's sort of out of a zone they do well in."

"I know a few people that have them in their yards here and they produce."

"If we put them in one package, we could ship you 25 two-foot trees for $72 dollars. That includes shipping. We can ship COD."

"Send them on!" I gave my address. I lost one tree. I put them on the opposite side of the field from the pecans and black walnuts.

Mr. Wilson built me an acorn and nut planter. It had a three-point hitch system to put behind a tractor. It had a platform with a chair, surrounded by places to set gallon buckets filled with acorns, nuts, black gum berries, beech seed, and red haw seed. All in easy reaching distance.

Underneath was welded an opening plow, two covering plows and packing wheel off an old horse drawn Oliver planter. It had wheels which were adjustable to control the planting depth. And springs under the chair to soften the ride!

Behind the thing he attached one big wheel that came off an old horse drawn hay rake. He welded a marker on the wheel. That wheel attachment was spring loaded so it never came off the ground, but would keep turning. We had to set that marker right at my eye level at the end of the row. All right, we took off at a rather slow speed. When that wheel marker came around to eye level again. I pitched whatever I wanted in a funnel right behind that furrow breaking plow. It got covered, planted and packed.

We got Rev. Billy to run over an area with a tractor and disk. The disks were set to sort of mound it up in the center. He rowed it up in about 15 yards apart rows. He usually did this on Thursday. Saturday, I got Wade to drive the tractor. I could not put him on the pay roll until he got 16. I just paid him in cash. He could drive a tractor very well, and he wanted to earn money.

We loaded up my rig with whatever I wanted to plant in an area. I got on it. He pulled it on a row. Raised it just a little. I could reach out and set the marker on the wheel at eye level. Then holler let her rip! He let the wheel down and away we went.

I could always eyeball some mark, plant a grove of a certain kind of something on several rows. Red haw and youpon berries, I just pitched a few seed in between trees now and then. Black gum berries, and beech seeds I usually tried to get about five or six in an area. They not only produced food for wildlife and hogs, they almost always contained hollows for squirrels.

The shed was up, the hog and horse pasture were ready. Until the land clearing was all complete, Mr. Wilson I felt never had time for horses and hogs. That had to wait.

Mr. Dobrinsky had lived in that hotel for years, although he could have afforded a mansion. The Wilson house was well built, but small. It set back from the highway a hundred yards. My thoughts still centered around Margaret. That somehow, some way I would find her. We would have a life together.

I drew up my floor plans. It would be built in front of the Wilson house, which would serve as a guest house. Mom and Dad were not getting any younger. If I moved them here, I felt they would be more comfortable in a private house.

I never liked concrete slabs with plumbing in it. It would be tier and beam constructed. Three bedrooms were enough. But they needed to be big with lots of closet space. Two would share a full bathroom. A separate larger master room would have a private full bathroom. The living room would be separate from the kitchen. Homes were being built with those connected with a bar. I never liked that.

The living room would be for guests, mostly. There would be a separate family room with a fireplace. Televisions were getting better now, I would get one. The room would have brown leather couch and recliners. And a few plain old rocking chairs.

The living room, family room, bedrooms and the exercise space in the garage would be carpeted. The bedrooms, living and family rooms would have ceiling fans. And the house would have central air conditioning and heating.

The kitchen would be big. With lots of cabinet space and room for a table with six chairs. An automatic dishwasher was built into the cabinet. The floor would be a combination of brown and white rubbery tiles which were popular now. The cabinets were also brown and white.

Adjoining would be a raised dining room with a table with 12 chairs. The floor would be 12x12 ceramic tiles, which would be in the halls as well. They had a combination of brown design in a field of white. What I meant to achieve with curtains, drapes, tiles and carpet was to give the inside a Spanish Ranch look.

It would have a two-car garage, with doors you could open with a gizmo you kept inside your car. In back of the garage would be a door in the center to the outside. It would contain a room on each side of that door. On one side would be installed a lavatory, potty, and shower stall. A cabinet for towels. The other side was for an automatic washing machine and dryer, and room to hang and iron clothes. In front of that would be a five-foot-wide carpeted area for the exercise equipment and a few chairs. And further in front would be the cars. I would keep my Ford car and pickup in it. The Lincoln I would keep in the guest house garage. I seldom used it.

It would be almost 50 yards to the highway in front of the house. A circular driveway would allow access to the garage, run between the back of the house and in front of the Wilson house, then back out to the highway.

A front porch would be in front of the house. A 'T' shaped sidewalk would connect both driveways in front of the porch. Then a side walk run from the center front porch steps out to the highway. Beside each side of the sidewalk out to the highway would be flower beds; 18 inches high and four feet wide, constructed with the ranch rock.

I had my cousin Marvin come over, put up Austin Stone around the house, with one exception. The doors and windows were framed with the brown colored rocks we got out of the creek bed at the ranch. The inside of the chimney were bricks, the outside was with the rocks. Those rocks were in 6-inch-thick slabs. He could split those in any shape he wanted. He also did the flower beds.

The house got built. I got it furnished. Up at the ranch, on the west side of the creek, were two button willow sloughs that dried up. The bottom was no telling how many years of rotted vegetation, leaves and wood. With the dozer, he graded that into piles down to the hard stuff below. Rev. Billy brought three dump truck loads and put in the flower beds. There would be enough to spread over our ten-acre food plot and Mr. Wilson's 15 acre field.

I moved into the place. It was another dream I had, laying by corn and sawing logs come true.

Only one thing was missing. Margaret!

Chapter Seven
Sometimes Life Surprises

I got the 2400 acres planted in oaks and hardwoods in the fall and winter of 1960. Pasture 3 had cattle in it, calves were being born. Since pasture 4 had been seeded with grass, Mr. Wilson opened up the gates from pasture 3 into pasture 2.

Each morning one of the Mexicans helped him, they scattered hay for the cattle in pasture 2, which helped seed the place. Ten percent protein range meal, which contained a lot of salt was kept in the feed troughs under the barn sheds.

The grass in pasture 3 was good, there were few cattle for the area. That's all we fed that winter.

Mr. Wilson got the dozer work completed in pasture one. Leveled the road gravel and he was finished over there. That included a number of ponds to hold water. He left the Mexicans over there to finish burning and fencing. He moved to our field by the creek.

He let that rake blade down about eight inches, he ripped that field up. With the exception of where we had things already. He had Rev. Billy start flat breaking with a three-bottom plow.

The fence builders were finished. He put one of the Mexicans on another tractor with three bottom breaking plows. After breaking, the disks went on. It would be disked over three times before spring, which would kill most of the grass roots.

I contacted the electric company. Met a man up there to size up the way the line needed to run. It would come down the north-south road about half way. Then angle across to the produce building site. That meant some bull dozing of timber in the creek bottom, but not much. We would have to do away with some that I planted in the clear-cut later.

It only took two days to change the blade on the dozer and get it done. One of the Mexicans had climbing gear. He climbed trees and cut limbs back, which saved the tree.

Mr. Wilson assembled with two Mexicans materials to build the produce assembly, cooking, canning and shipping facility. I got the rules and regulations on doing all that. First it would have to have a concrete floor that could be washed down, drain into a septic system. We knew it needed a bathroom, so we knew we would need a septic system

Next the water used in the system would have to be tested, approved for use. I did not know that.

Hold up on building! Put the well down first, get it tested. We had an artesian well within a week. It was a month before we got the government official out there to test it. Another week before I got a letter of approval!

We thought about using the artesian water for irrigation. We did not need to irrigate the year around. The lake water would be fertile to some degree. Mr. Wilson built another manifold to screw on that three-inch pipe. One two- inch pipe with valve was welded in. On the bottom two three quarter inch, and two on each side were welded in with valves.

The two-inch would stick out over the creek, fall into aerator pans. The need for a valve in the two-inch line was to adjust pressure on what other three-quarter inch lines we might use.

The building took shape. We got a propane tank. I flew to Mississippi to view such a process in action, got an idea of what we needed, and who I needed to contact to get it. That turned out to be in Houston. I kept what I needed of the GI cookware. Minus that and what I had given away, the rest would be used there.

When the Mexicans finished the burning in pasture one, six of them never came back. They thought they were through here, so they got a tree planting job. Two of the younger ones came back, and Mr. Wilson asked them to stay on. He said they acted happy about it.

Electricity had to be run to the irrigation pump at the creek. Irrigation lines ran to the field. We used inch and a half PVC and a lot of valves. The cookers arrived, gas lines had to be run, and the things set up. The barns and sheds in pasture one needed to be completed. For now, Mr. Wilson thought he had enough help. "Too much help gets in your way," he said.

I averaged going to Jewett once a month. I usually went through Oakwood. The man at the service station, nor Mr. Jim Williams had learned nothing. It was in October that I drove through Buffalo. I subscribed to the paper, sort of kept up with what was going on. But the thought crossed my mind, perhaps Martha or Margaret had subscribed to the paper for the same reason I did.

I went in, introduced myself. Told her I was looking for a Burkett family, that left the county. I needed to locate them. I wondered if they might be on your mailing list.

"I don't think so, but I'll look." It did not take her long. "No, we don't have a Burkett on our list. Are you going to attend the homecoming reunion next week-end? The football game will be here Friday night. For five dollars, you can get lunch at the High School Cafeteria Saturday noon. Starting at 7 p.m. all the classes will meet in the auditorium for a sort of informal get-to-gather."

"I never graduated here, only went through 9th grade."

"It does not matter whether you graduated here or not. We want you to come!"

I thanked her. Said I lived at Livingston. Parents lived at Jewett. I might be back.

It takes a while for something to sort of grow on you. Know what I mean? When I walked out of that newspaper office I had no intention of coming back to that reunion. But by the next Friday, I had decided to go. I might find Margaret there. A brother or sister. Someone that knew where they were.

That Friday evening after work, Mary Ellen and I walked out to our cars together.

"You going to Tyler this weekend?"

"Yes, it's been a couple of weeks since I've been. What are you doing?"

"I'm going to a homecoming and class reunion at Buffalo. Margaret, or some of her family might be there."

"Are you going to give up if you don't find her?"

"I'm not going to give up. If I don't find her there, I am going to put spot ads on the radio. A classified ad in the Houston Post. If that does not work, I'll hire a private detective. If you love someone with all your heart, you can't give up!"

"Yes, I know!" Mary Ellen knew I meant what I said. She said goodbye and got quickly into her car. Not before I saw the hurt in her eyes.

I was not a suit and tie man. I had that alright, but that was for funerals, weddings and now occasional business meetings. I was going to Buffalo dressed like who I thought I was.

I wore jeans, a western wear shirt. My cowboy boots had the big square heel. I had an inch took off the brim of my brown Stetson hat. Turned down a little in front and back. The hat band was like a narrow leather belt, with round silver ornaments on it. My Dickies Jacket was light orange in color with a canvass like texture. The collar was brown corduroy.

I got there in time for the game. I walked up and down in front of the Buffalo side stands a number of times. Saw a few people I knew. Talked to them. Each one asked the same thing. 'Where you at now?' My answer to each was different. But honest.

'Aw, I live at Livingston. Run a boat and motor place there. Aw, I live at Livingston. Own half interest in a saw-mill there. Aw, I live in Livingston. Own half interest in the Ford dealership there. Feed and Garden Supply store. Hardware and Building supply. Aw, I'm into real estate. Finally: Aw I got a 3600 acre ranch in Cherokee County!

It was pure funny, I thought. I lied to nobody. But think what they might decide and say when a few of them compared notes on what old Dupree said he owned and did!

I had seen none of the Burkett's in the Buffalo stands. I left before the half. I knew Mom and Dad went to bed early.

I took Mom and Dad to Mexia grocery shopping Saturday morning. We went to a restaurant for lunch.

The waitress asked Dad what he wanted.

"You got a bowl of chili?"

"No, we got about everything but that. We have a great chicken fried steak."

"I'll take that then!"

We all had a chicken fried steak.

I cleaned up, told them I was going to the reunion at Buffalo, then onto the ranch.

I left about 5:30, knew I was early. Left 79, took the Cedar Creek road. Stopped at the old Church House, which looked about ready to fall. Walked out back to the spring branch. The spring I drank out of a kid was not anything but a low place in the ground now.

I saw a dead deer hanging in a fence back of where the barn was on the place where we once lived. I recalled at about nine, my brother Regan H. walked a mile there and a mile back to look at one deer track he found the day before.

The high school auditorium was also the basketball, volleyball court. People were sitting in the bleachers. Standing talking. I saw a few people I knew. Talked and moved on. I crossed over under the basketball goal. Same thing on that side, talked to a few people and moved on. At the very end of the bleachers, I passed by a young man and woman with two little children sitting there. I glanced at them, no recognition came to me.

I was on my way out of there. Then a voice stopped me. "Robert. Robert DuPree!"

It's strange. You might not recognize someone you knew who was 12 years old and saw again nine years later. My heart must have hit my throat. I recognized that voice. It was Katrina. Margaret's Sister!

I turned around. "Katrina, I'm sorry I never recognized you. But I recognized your voice!"

She laughed, "I've been watching you across over there. I told Randy I thought I knew who you were. This is Randy Johnson, my husband. This are our kids, Shelly and Richard. We run a store for Randy's father in Pasadena."

I shook hands with Randy. "This is the first time I've been here since we moved to Livingston in 1952."

"This is our first also. A classmate and I have kept in touch since we left here. We're waiting to meet her here. We also went to the cemetery to check on mother's grave."

"Your mom has passed away?"

"Yes, she had the kind of cancer that spreads quickly."

"Well, how are the others?"

"Kevin got a scholarship to play football at UT. Harry is at Baytown. He's married and trying to be a preacher. Margaret's still at Highlands. She has a nine-year-old daughter. She and another woman work at a fast food place called ZUMO's. She has a daughter a little older than Cassie. They live across the street from ZUMO's. They work different shifts, so they watch out for each other's kid."

"Then Margaret's married?"

"No, that kid was born in May 1952. She's never told anyone who Cassie's father is. I think mother knew, but she never told anyone either. We'll stop in Highlands tomorrow. Where did you say you lived?"

"Livingston." I handed her my card. Home, business, ranch numbers. While she was talking, telling me about Margaret, she was looking at me like a calculator was going on behind her eyes.

"Are you married?"

"No. I've been looking for a girl that loves me."

We said our good byes, and I got out of there. Went out and got my note pad and pencil. I wrote down months. I was no expert at such things, but it appeared that Margaret's nine-year-old daughter could be mine! God let her be! I knew where Highlands was. I even remembered seeing that ZUMO's. I drove right by Margaret and never knew it. Two years ago!

I needed gas. I stopped at a convenience store, gassed up the Lincoln. Used the restroom and got me a couple of candy bars and two Dr. Peppers. At the intersection of 79 and 75, I turned left and south on 75. I put the pedal to the metal. I was doing 80 when I went under that railroad underpass. I was on my way to Highlands, Texas. I soon came up behind a truck. So many hills. Not likely I would get around it anytime soon.

I stopped at a place in Huntsville for a hamburger. I was hungry, and I needed a break. It was just the waitress and a cook in the place. Maybe it was the Lincoln out front; the waitress was a little too friendly. And suggestive. "We're closing in a little bit. I suppose I'll have to call a taxi to take me home!"

I got up, laid $5 on the table. "I got to get going. My wife waits up for me. Keep the change!" *Three dollars should pay for a taxi ride,* I thought!

It was after midnight when I rolled into Highlands. There was a motel across the parking lot from Zumo's. I had thought I might have to sleep in the car. I never remembered the motel, but a name like Zumo's sort of sticks in your mind. If I could get a room, I had clean clothes. I could shower, shave and maybe look presentable.

I asked for and got a room with a window facing Zumo's. It was hot in the room, I finally got the air conditioner going. I showered and shaved. In just my shorts, I pulled a chair up in front of that air conditioner, put my feet on top of it. I meant to wait until the room cooled off, then lay on the bed.

The sound of giggling and laughter woke me up. Two young clean up girls were standing there watching me through that window. I had on boxer shorts. Whether they saw anything they wanted to, I knew not. I did see the lights were on in Zumo's.

It was 8:30 a.m. I got dressed, put my things in my car, went and checked out. I could see the waitress moving around in Zumo's. It was not Margaret. It was a neat little white frame house across the street. It had a one car garage door. I left my car at the motel and walked over to Zumo's.

I went in, ordered a breakfast combination and coffee. I ate my breakfast, she brought me more coffee. "I'm looking for a girl named Margaret Burkett. Her sister told me last night that she worked here. Do you know where I might find her?"

"Beats me," she said. She went in the kitchen. I could see her talking to a man with course black hair and the biggest, black and bushy eye brows I ever saw on a man. As she talked, I could see him looking at me. I knew she had probably lied to me, probably seeking his advice about whether to tell me anything.

She came out, got the coffee pot and refilled my cup, "You remind me of someone I know. What was Margaret's sister's name?"

"Katrina. I saw her at Buffalo last night."

"Margaret works here. I work early. She will come in at one to relieve me. I hope you understand, we have to be careful about strangers. I do know Katrina is her sister and I do know she went to the Buffalo High School Homecoming and Class Reunion last night."

"Yes, I saw her there last night. Met her husband Randy and their two kids."

"All right then. Margaret and I live in the house across the street. Right now, she's gone to take our girls to church. When she gets back, just go on over there and knock on the door."

The car, I thought, *is a 1951 Oldsmobile*. It was blowing smoke out the exhaust pipe. She pulled it into that garage. I really never saw her.

I paid my bill and told the waitress, "I hope I'll be seeing you again. Thank you very much!"

I knocked on the door. I could hear footsteps coming. She cracked opened the door and our eyes met. Her voice was almost inaudible. "Robert." It was like she had to hold onto the door knob with both hands as she opened it wide and leaned against the wall.

I stepped inside. "Margaret, I…"

She came out of her shock. She knocked my hat off as she came into my arms. Her arms were around my neck. She was shaking, crying.

All I could do was hold her and keep saying "I'm here now, baby. It's all right."

She finally stepped back, drying her eyes with the apron she had on. She looked at my face and said, "It's been so long…" She came into my arms, again crying.

All I could do was hold her and keep saying "I'm here now baby. It's all right."

Finally, she dried her eyes again. "Let's go in the kitchen. I'm cooking dinner. We'll have a glass of tea and talk."

"I think I smell turnip greens cooking," I said.

"Yes, they are. That's the only thing you can get here that sort of tastes right. I miss having a garden and fresh vegetables so much."

"I've been looking for you ever since I got out of high school and got a car. I drove through here once. I went to the Cemetery twice. First time I found your Uncle Sam's grave. It had a funeral home marker with his name. I went back later. There was a fresh grave there. It had no marker. Katrina told me that was your mother last night. I saw her at the Buffalo homecoming. My first cousin told me your Uncle Sam was dead. That his house burned down on him."

"Yes, Mr. and Mrs. Zumo carried us up there. There was no one to ask anything. We did not know Uncle Sam was dead or why. We had to get out to 75 to come home. I directed Mr. Zumo by where you lived. The house was gone. There was a brick house back of where it was. The name on the mail box was Hambrick. Where did you move to?"

"We moved to Livingston in February 1952." I told her all about why we did, the works.

"I kept hoping you would write me before we moved. When we moved, I knew you would not know where I was either."

She got up, went in a bedroom. I saw her kneel down by a trunk I knew had belonged to her grandmother. She came back, handed me a letter. "You better read this."

It was addressed to me and un-opened. Post marked 5-28-1952. In ink, was written, "Return to sender."

"We had moved. That sorry postman! We left a card in the box to forward mail to our Livingston address."

"You need to read it now," she said.

I opened it up and got the letter out.

Dear Robert,

I know this is going to come as a shock. You and I have a beautiful baby daughter. She was born on May 24, 1952. I named her Cassie Burkett Dupree. We tricked Daddy into thinking it was Cassie Burkett. Mother thought I should wait until you finished high school to tell you, on account of Daddy. I think you have every right to know. I love you. I swear before God, I'll keep my promise. I'll wait for you.

I love you-Margaret.

PS: Cassie is beautiful and looks like you.

I got up crying, and this time, I fell into her arms.

"Margaret, I swear to God I'll keep my promise to you. I want our marriage to become legal before God and everybody as soon as possible, if you'll have me?"

"Yes. That's what I want. As soon as possible."

"One thing is bothering me, Margaret. I wonder if I should just show up here today and tell Cassie I'm her Daddy. I wonder if it might upset her. I want to see her so much now, but perhaps you should talk to her first?"

"That's the kind of father I thought you would be. It's about time to go pick them up at church. Go with me and you can see her. You're right, I don't know how she'll handle it. Let me get you a picture Katrina made of us before we go."

"When we get back here, I'll leave. I want to come back next Friday evening. Take you to Livingston. Show you and her where I live. I have a guest house and I have a three bedroom home. You and I have so much to talk about. And plans to make. Do you think you can do that?"

"The Zumo's are fine people and they care about us. When I tell them that you found us, that we are going to marry, they'll let me off."

I gave her my card with my phone numbers. "After you talk to Cassie, call me. Let me know how she feels. I don't care if it's 2 a.m. tonight. Call me collect, we may talk forever."

The two girls got in the back seat. I knew which one my daughter when I saw them was coming. Margaret told them I was Mr. Robert Dupree, a high school classmate." She then introduced them as Linda Lyles and my daughter Cassie.

Cassie was not bashful. "You are from Buffalo?"

"Yes, I'm from Buffalo. I live in Livingston now."

"Do you know any Indians up there?"

"I have good friends that are Indians."

"My teacher told us there were Indians at Livingston."

We had pulled into the driveway. She stopped, they ran into the house.

"I love our kid," I said. I loved hearing her talk. She is a blessing."

"She is, but she sometimes can strain your patience. You'll find out!"

"Ok, I'll find out! I love you. I better get going."

"I love you too. I'll call you tonight around ten. We usually close at nine."

I walked up the street to cross over to my car. I guess I was crying. I almost stepped off the curb in front of a car. The driver hit his breaks and blasted me back to my senses with his horn. I got in the Lincoln, pulled up to the street, sat looking at that little white frame house for a minute and hit the road home.

Crosby, Dayton, Liberty, and home. Outside Liberty was a pasture with Texas Longhorn Cattle. I bet Cassie would like those Longhorns. I'll get her a camera next week.

I never had lunch and was hungry when I got home. I decided a couple of hot fried egg sandwiches was what I would have. Mayonnaise went on the bread. Sliced rainbow dill pickles. Slices of sharp cheddar cheese on that. Next the hot fried egg was put over the cheese. Dusted with salt and pepper.

Topped with a slice of bread. They went well with a can of cold RC cola out of the refrigerator.

I decided I needed to tell Mary Ellen today, not wait until tomorrow at work. I went over to her apartment. She had just finished washing her car, was sitting on a picnic table with a class of tea. I sat down on the table with her.

"How was your trip to Tyler?"

"I never went to Tyler. I was not fit to be around anybody. I cleaned house. I washed and waxed the car. For the first time Friday, I realized with your determination you were going to find that girl!"

"Mary Ellen, I did find Margaret. We plan to marry as soon as we can get things worked out. We have a nine-year-old daughter. Her name is Cassie. I'll tell everyone at work tomorrow, I just wanted you to know first."

"I never dreamed you would have a daughter. Where did you find them?"

"Highlands Texas. I saw Margaret's sister at Buffalo Saturday night. She told me where they were. I drove down there, got a motel room. I never dreamed I had a daughter either. Here's a picture of Margaret and Cassie."

She looked at the photo long and hard, then handed it back to me. "Margaret is so beautiful. So is your daughter. She does look like you a lot. You were right not to give up until you found them. But I've been a fool! I've loved you since 9th grade. Mother told me I better not come back down here. But I would not listen!"

"I'm sorry Mary Ellen. I respect you as much as anyone I've ever known. You've been my best friend. Never have I ever wanted to hurt you."

"It's not your fault! You told me you were committed to that girl. My heart just never had any common sense. It would not listen."

"I understand that, Mary Ellen. God knows I do." I pulled out my old timer pocket knife. "You have a knife like this, don't you?"

"Yes, you gave it to me when we went fishing."

"Every time I use mine, I'll pray that you are happy and well Mary Ellen. Will you do that for me?"

"I can do that. I could never wish you anything else. But I've got vacation time. I think I need to go back to Tyler. Would you mind if I took vacation next week and look for work there? If I stayed here, I would be miserable and you would be too."

"Do what you think best. I'll tell Mrs. Ivers you talked to me about it. I better get going."

As I backed out to the street, I saw Mary Ellen run up those stairs and fall across what I knew to be a lonely bed. *May God be with her,* I thought. I knew how she felt.

I was beat. Not a lot of sleep and a lot of emotion. I shaved, took a shower. I laid down on the bed by the telephone. If Margaret called, it would wake me up. I slept about two hours and woke up. 7:45 by my bedside clock.

I went in the kitchen, warmed up that pot of coffee I made earlier. Small store between me and town. He kept a big round roll of cheese with a red wax looking coating on it. He would say "how much" and move his knife around slow until I said stop. He cut off a four-inch-thick pie shaped piece and weighed it.

I got out some crackers, opened a can of pork and beans. I had cheese and crackers with my beans. When I bought pork and beans, I shook the can. If I could not hear juice, I looked for a can that I could. And I kept a can in the refrigerator. I liked them cold.

I had some coffee, washed the pot, loaded if for Monday morning. The kitchen telephone would reach the table. Got my note pad and pen. Business habit I had developed. Don't waste time looking for that. I had forgotten to get Margaret's number.

It was almost ten when she called. "Sorry I'm late! Sometimes customers just keep sitting there. We can't close until they leave. I talked to the Zumo's. I can get off next weekend."

"Great! Did you talk to Cassie?"

"I went in our room to tell her. She was standing at the window. She turned around crying. "Momma was that man my Daddy?"

I hugged her and I was crying too. "He is your Daddy. How did you know?"

"He looked like that boy on that horse. And he was crying when he left. I saw him. He nearly stepped in front of a car. Why did he not tell me he was my daddy?"

"He was afraid it might upset you. He wanted me to tell you. We want to get married. We'll move to Livingston. He's coming next weekend to take us up there. He wants to show us where we will live."

"Boy on a horse? What did she mean by that?"

"Mother made mine and your picture once. That's what she was talking about." She got excited about having a Daddy and going to Livingston and said "He must be wealthy Momma. He was driving a Lincoln Continental just like Mr. Zumo's!""

We talked forever. She said she knew I had relatives around Jewett. She planned to go there, try to find out where I might be. But that old car has just about quit. I decided it might not make it.

I told her about our move to Livingston. How upset I had been. But I got a job working were dad did. That I had quit school after Thanksgiving in '51. I started back at Livingston and graduated with Virginia.

"Mr. Dobrinsky let me work after school, helped me get a used car in 11th grade. He also started training me to run his business. He always got dad's approval in whatever he did for me. After I graduated, dad and mother went back to Jewett. When he was satisfied I could run the business, he sent me to develop 3600 acres of his property into a working ranch.

"He told me to lay out a ranch just like I would want it if it were mine. I did as he asked. Then he asked me to move up there and develop it. After a couple of years, he called me back to run the business. Not long after that, he sold me his business for $500, which he gave back to me. Said he had no relatives, he saw me as a poor kid like he was that deserved a chance. Not long after that, he died. It was after his death, I learned why he did all that for me. I'll show you why next weekend."

"You told me Uncle Sam's house burned down on him. I can't believe that! I believe daddy killed him and set the house on fire."

"Mr. Jim Williams believes the same thing. He told me Sam's ex-wife tried to sell the place to him. He knew your mother owned half. Your Uncle Sam told him he had made a will, was leaving his share to you. He took her to justice court. The judge ruled that if any of you had not come forth in ten years, she could sell Sam's part."

"Uncle Sam told me he was leaving his share to me. We'll wait until we are married and settled down. I want to go there, get a sheriff and maybe the judge that made that ruling. I don't think Uncle Sam's will, his money or my gun and saddle burned up. I've got a key to drive in there to where he lived. Mother gave it to me before she died. Along with her bible. It has the family information back to South Carolina."

"All right. We'll get on that right away. And I'll pay for headstones for your mother and Uncle Sam. And if needed, I have a lawyer on retainer. He's a good one."

We said good night. I told her I might spend a couple days at the ranch that week. She could reach me up there at night.

I took the photo of Margaret and Cassie to the office Monday. Mrs. Ivers was the only one I let read the letter. "That kid looks like you. How old were you two when that happened?"

"We were 15. We declared ourselves married that day. We hope to make it legal very soon."

"I know how long you've tried to find her. Glory be! Fifteen! You two must have set a record! We sometimes don't understand God's will. He certainly has prepared you to support a family. If there's anything I can do to get that wedding moving, let me know!"

"I told Mary Ellen about it yesterday evening. She's taking a vacation this week. I think she will be looking for a job at Tyler near her parents. I guess we will know in about a week. I doubt she'll come back to work here."

"Bless her heart. With her experience, she should not have any problem finding a job."

I got caught up enough to call mother that afternoon. She went through the normal 'glad you called' routine, then it was down to it with her: "You don't normally call during work hours. Is there something wrong?"

"No there's nothing wrong. I just called to congratulate you on being a new grandmother!"

"What! There's no one in this family expecting I know of!"

"I found Margaret, mother. We have a nine-year-old daughter near ten. Her name is Cassie. Her birthday is May 24, 1952."

"What!" She was in a state of shock and wordless, I suppose.

I explained the whole nine yards to her. That I was so proud of Margaret. She worked and took care of our kid. She lost her mother, but she kept the promise she made to me. She waited until I found her.

"Well bless her heart! She's a good girl, she comes from good people. Your daddy and I thought there was something going on between you two! When's the wedding going to be?"

"We'll have to work that out. I'll let you know. I'll bring them to see you as soon as I can. I have a call on another line. We'll see you later."

That evening I went from work to the ranch. I had told Mr. Wilson I would be there Sunday evening and today. I kept clothes up there, I just left from work.

I told the Wilson's something came up and I was sorry I failed to get back to them. Then I told them what happened, that I found Margaret. That Saturday night I went to Highlands instead of coming here. I let them read the letter, then showed them the picture of Margaret and Cassie.

"My God! What you two have been through! How beautiful they both are. That little girl looks like you. No wonder you went to Highlands after all this time. I can't wait to see them!" She got up to hug me.

"I'm going down Friday night to get them. I plan to bring them up here next Saturday."

"Great! Wade and I have been baiting trotlines in the Neches for three Friday evenings in a row now. We got a freezer full of catfish. We'll have catfish!"

"Supper's about ready. You eat with us. We're having catfish tonight!"

While eating, I told them about how my great grandparents and Margaret's came to Texas together in 1856. That my mother's family and Margaret's grandparent's family visited back and forth before she and dad married. But Margaret and I would be the first Craig and DuPree descendants to marry."

"Then by gingos, it's about time," Mr. Wilson said.

I went on to the ranch house to spend the night. I called Margaret after 9 p.m. I told her I was at the ranch. That I was going to Madisonville with Mr. Wilson to look at some horses tomorrow. We had a big Jack already, we wanted to raise mules. We wanted to plow our produce with horse drawn plows. Provided I could find horse drawn plows.

"If Uncle's Sam's barn never burned, and provided no one has stolen it, he probably had what you need."

"I hope so," I said. "Those things are antiques now and hard to find. We'll get over there as soon as we can. But to change the subject, if I got you a better car to drive, would you feel comfortable about driving back home next Sunday evening with Cassie?"

"I have my driver's license. I drive around here all the time. We even go into Houston now and then. Yes, I could handle it."

Mr. Wilson and I took the cattle trailer and went to Madisonville the next day. I bought two brown and a black mare from a horse ranch there. That I thought would produce good strong mules. I told the man I would probably be back later to let my wife and daughter pick a riding horse. Mr. Wilson and Wade already had saddle horses.

The next day we went to a cattle ranch out US 21 west of Crockett. Mr. Wilson had talked to the rancher who PO'ed a bunch of young red roan heifers at the Crockett livestock auction. We paid the man a fair price for 14 young heifers and a young bull. For those that don't know, when a rancher yells PO at an auction sale, that means the bid was not satisfactory to him. He's taking his stock back home!

I went back home Wednesday evening, paid our costs for a good used 1959 Chevrolet V8 with only 35,000 miles. It had great tires, not a blemish on it. I took the keys, put the title and paperwork in the glove compartment. I signed the title on back to release to Shirley Nell Lyles. The woman Margaret lived with.

One thing I did in talking to Margaret was getting Cassie's shoe size, clothing sizes. I went shopping, bought her a pair of boy's outdoor shoes. Alright, brogans! A pair of boy's blue overalls and a blue work shirt. Some socks as well. I felt I need not overdo it, Margaret could take care of her needs later. This would be welcome to the ranch Cassie duds!

I got Margaret an engagement and wedding ring set. Knowing Margaret, I also got her a plain gold wedding band. I never had put flowers or anything in the flower beds in front of the house. I saved that detail for her. She probably would not wear the expensive rings except on special occasions. I also bought her a nice shoulder strap leather handbag. I got a camera also, I decided Margaret might need to control that for a while.

I left early Friday evening, only taking the Camera and film. We stopped in Liberty to eat. Margaret and I had a steak. Cassie wanted a hamburger with fries and a Dr. Pepper. Outside of Liberty, I pulled over at the Longhorn ranch. I never had seen a kid so excited about anything. Get a picture Momma! Is this the kind of cows you have on the ranch Daddy?

No, we don't have this kind. Not yet anyway. But I never missed the word "Daddy."

Few things had ever meant as much to me as hearing her call me that.

We got to Livingston before dark. I drove up to the boat, hardware, feed and garden business first. These I own outright. I have a half interest here in three other business places. I'll show you those tomorrow. Let's go home now.

My God, Margaret said: "That Mr. what's-his name gave you all this?"

"John David Dobrinsky. I'll show you why he did tomorrow." I wanted to see if Margaret and Cassie would have any reaction to their future home. I just drove out by it slowly. I got rewarded!

They never missed it. "What I beautiful home! It looks sort of Spanish Ranch like. I've dreamed about a home like that!"

I drove on out across Long King Creek, turned around and went back, turned in the driveway.

"Why are we turning in here, Daddy?"

"Because your Mother is about to see her dream. Here, take this and press that button and open that garage door."

She did, and I don't think she could believe her eyes when the door started opening. I drove in.

"Now press that button again and close the door." She closed the door.

"It's sort of dark in here. Let me get out and turn the light on."

They got out, the exercise things caught their eye first. Then the bath room and shower.

"I work in the office now, don't exercise like I once did, I felt I needed this. The bathroom and shower, I don't have to go inside in an emergency. I can take a shower here, leave my work shoes and clothes out here."

I opened the door into the kitchen, let them in.

"What a kitchen and dining room! It's Spanish in style too! Who designed all this?" Margaret asked.

"I did. And I was dreaming of finding you!"

I got a hug from both then.

I showed them the rest of the house. Then took them out back to the guest house. Showed them through it. I explained it once belonged to the Wilson's up at the ranch. Mr. Dobrinsky remodeled it. I lived here until after he passed on. Dad and Mother were not getting any younger. I thought that they might move into it before many more years. I think they would be more comfortable in a house to themselves.

"They would be I'm sure. And they should not be alone at Jewett! I doubt they even got a Dr. there. I can't wait to see them!" Mother cried when she opened-up the last jar of vegetable soup they gave to us and help us put up. She loved them both.

"It's your choice Margaret. I need to unload your things. You can stay here or in the new house."

"Cassie and I sleep together. Our room is too small for two beds. Just bring our things into one of the bedrooms in the new house. There's no need in messing up both places!"

I put their things in a bedroom. The one that had Cassie's ranch wear in the closet. I got it out. "I don't know if you will like this, Cassie. But this is the kind of clothes and shoes you need on a ranch."

"I'll wear it tomorrow," she said. I left them in the bedroom to unpack. "I'll go in the kitchen, make us some tea."

Cassie came into the kitchen with her ranch wear on. "She may sleep in it tonight," Margaret said.

She wore down and Margaret got her to bed. We went into the family room. I gave her the leather handbag. Her rings were inside. She found them. Opened them up. "Robert, these must have cost a fortune. The gold band. I'll just wear that when we are at home."

"The flower beds out front are waiting on you. I thought you might want a gold band for things like that."

"Is there anything you have not thought of, Robert?"

"I've had ten years to think about it. That engagement ring is for now is it not?"

She laughed. "Well, if you still want to marry me!"

My answer was to take it, put it on her finger, and kiss her long and hard. We became passionate in a minute, but stopped before we got there. I suppose it was because of our daughter sleeping in the next room.

We got down to plans. She would check Cassie out of school this next week. I would rent a small covered U-Haul trailer and come down next Saturday in my pick-up. We would move them into the house here with me. Get Cassie in school here.

We could work out our marriage plans later. I also explained about the car I bought for her to drive back in. That I had two here, she could take her pick. Shirley Nell had helped her with our kid, I wanted to do something for her. She could just sell the old car.

When I got up the next morning, Margaret was in the kitchen fixing breakfast. "Cassie is outside looking at those squirrels you have in that cage out by the barn."

"I need to feed and water them, I'll go out there, let her do that."

I showed her where I kept the feed in the barn, which was some pecans and a sack of dog food. It was a balanced food, they ate things worse in the wild. After we fed the squirrels, she asked me why I had squirrels in a cage.

"There are not many squirrels up at the ranch. They are all over town here. They come out here to the pecan trees. I trap them, put them in this cage. We'll take them up to the ranch and release them."

"I wish we could trap those in Highlands. They get rund over all the time."

"Yes, a lot do here too. Cassie, I hope you'll be happy up here."

The kid turned and looked me right in the eye: "If Momma is happy, I will be too."

That kid never pulled punches. She let me have it with both barrels! I grabbed her and hugged her. "I'm going to do everything I can to make your mother happy!" After breakfast, we started to the ranch. It only took a few minutes to show them the saw-mill. The ready-mix cement place just north of town was on the way. The Ford business they would see when we picked up Shirley Nell's car later.

I went up US 69 to Wells, drove to the northeast gate at the ranch, explaining that the FM here was the back side of the place. From there down to the canal bridge, crossed the creek and stopped briefly to look at the produce facility. From there north to the north gate, back around by the pines which were three feet tall now.

We crossed the road into the cattle ranch, we toured that. Cassie was excited about seeing the cattle.

"You told me you laid this place out. You designed a master piece. I want one more thing from you. I want a horse. And I want to find my saddle. I can't wait to ride around in this place!"

"I've been waiting to get riding horses until you could choose what you want. I cried like a baby when I took old Dan home."

We got to the Wilson's at 10:15. Wade soon had Cassie out showing her the hogs his dad had. Margaret joined Mrs. Wilson in the kitchen frying fish and fries. She also made fried cornbread, a potato salad along with a lettuce tomato salad.

"This fish is so good," Margaret said. "I grew up fishing with my Uncle Sam and I've missed it so much!"

Margaret was not raised to be any other way. I knew she would not go out until she helped Mrs. Wilson do the dishes.

The walk to the lake, tour of the shed, the hog pasture had to be brief. I saved the cemetery for last. I took Margaret to the Dobrinsky headstone. "Read the inscription on that stone," I said.

Suddenly she turned to me. "Their son has your name and birth date! That's why he left you everything!"

Yes, that's why. He never told me that. This stone he ordered put up after his death. He knew when I saw it, I would understand."

"His wife must have died in child birth then?"

"No, not exactly. He told me once how she died. It's a long story. I'll tell you later. We better get going so you and Cassie can get on the road before dark."

We took the other route on US 103 back into Lufkin. I stopped on our used car lot. Handed Margaret the keys. "It's that '59 Bel Air Chevy there I said. I'll follow you on to the house."

She drove it around back of the house. "That thing drives like a dream. And only 35,000 miles. It's like a new car!"

The next weekend we got them moved to Livingston. Monday, Cassie got enrolled in the Livingston school. Margaret chose my Ford to drive.

"We can save the Lincoln for going to Jewett!"

I ordered her checks on my private account. Showed her how much Mrs. Ivers deposited in it once a month for my private living expenses. Turned the record book I kept on that over to her.

"Whatever checks we write, we will both enter and show a current balance at any time either of us wants to look." I also gave her $200 and told her to just write a check for cash anytime she needed more. That's what I did.

That week, we got our wedding plans lined out. Cassie was in school, we would wait until spring break to go somewhere on a honeymoon. Margaret suggested we just marry on the front porch at home. "Invite mine, your family and our friends."

"I have a good friend that works on the ranch part time that's a Preacher. He's black. How do you feel about him marrying us?"

"If he can marry us legally, I don't mind. I don't care about anything fancy. I just want to get it done and get on with our lives."

We went to Jewett the next weekend. Mom was happy to hug Margaret and her granddaughter. We had dinner and supper Saturday, spent the night. I told Mother not to fix Sunday dinner for us, we would leave Sunday morning. Margaret wanted to go by the Craig place. "Half of the place belonged to her mother. She thinks she knows where to find her Uncle Sam's will also."

We were in my pickup. I thought we might need it. Margaret told me to just drive to the Cemetery first. There, we went out to check on the graves. Margaret and Cassie both shed some tears. Cassie had seen her grandmother put there, she knew where we were.

Margaret had a key to the main gate. The old log house was about rotted down. The barn was still in fair shape. There was nothing in it. Under the shed was a middle buster, a number two Kelly turning plow and a Georgia Stock, all in good shape There was a box of assorted sweeps and shovels to go with the Georgia Stock.

"You might as well get them," Margaret said. "Somebody will just steal them if you don't. I'm surprised they are still here."

I loaded them up. "What's that barrel on that slide for?"

"It had a top you could take off, lock back on." Hanging out behind the slide was a three-quarter inch pipe with valve welded into the barrel.

"Uncle Sam put rough fish like carp, his fish cleaning waste in there. It eventually turned to a thick fish stinking liquid. He used a little for baiting his steel traps. But he opened up rows with that middle buster. Then hitched a mule to that slide. He put that fish stuff in the middles for fertilizer. He might add commercial fertilizer, but he used the middle buster to re-bed, cover it up. He planted on that. The things grown in the garden never hurt me, and it did not taste fishy,"

From the barn, the road led down to the marsh. "Someone must have stolen Uncle Sam's boat. He had two. The other he kept over by his house."

"Maybe it filed with rain water and just sunk."

"No, he always pulled it out on the bank and turned it upside down."

There was a tree about six inches in diameter about eight feet out from the bank.

"How deep is the water out by that tree?"

"It's about chin deep to me. I've been in swimming more than once here. Why?"

"His boat might not have been stolen. But we'll need a boat here to find out. Let's drive over to Uncle Sam's house now."

The road led to a gate, I got out and opened it. Drove through and closed it. "Turn left right up there," she said. "We're on Mr. Jim Williams place now."

I turned left. Drove up to a creek bank. Stopped. The banks were sloped down on each side and well graveled. The creek appeared about four inches deep, 12 feet wide and running over a flat rock creek bed. Twenty feet below, it dropped off into fishing water.

"This is Keechi Creek. It's down to normal, just drive on across." About 50 yards from the creek, she had me stop.

"You can see Uncle Sam's place from here. That chimney is where his house was. The barn is still standing, as you can see. See just over the fence there? That branch comes down through his place from some springs on the place just this side of the Flo road. It almost runs into Buffalo Creek, but turns to run into Keechi.

"See that big plastic pipe over that branch. His water pipe to the house and barn is inside that pipe, stuffed with rags to keep it from freezing. The electric line on the poles go to a spring on this side of the branch. Which you can't see from here. Below is his hog pen, which the branch runs through. Let's drive over there now."

We crossed over a cattle guard made with cut creosote highline poles into the place. "Behind us, this road goes through Mr. Wilsons place and James Baker's place to the Flo road," she said.

We crossed over the branch bridge and shortly she said, stop.

"There's Buffalo Creek. See the rock crossing there. Before my time, the Centerville and Oakwood road crossed both creeks here.

"I imagine my Mother has come through here in a wagon. Dad's been here I know."

"I know she has. My mother has told me of going to visit your mother's family at Social Grove. And where we stopped over there where Uncle Sam kept his boat, that's where Uncle Sam whipped that boy that killed grandpa's hog! Your dad was with him."

"And that boy was the worthless Sheriff that never investigated your Uncle's death. Mr. Jim Williams told me that."

We pulled up in front of where the house once stood. "I see the boat," Cassie said.

We walked down there. It was on the bank. Upside down.

"He usually kept his motor and gas tank under it," Margaret said.

I lifted the edge of the boat up. Under it was a ten-horse power Johnson motor and a gas tank. And two paddles.

We walked out to the barn. A shed walled up at both ends was built in front. In one end, was another turning plow and Georgia Stock. On the other end, was a counter like outfitted with a kitchen sink. It had water piped to it. This is where Uncle Sam cleaned fish. It had a heavy cutting board on that counter. Sticking through the bones of a dried catfish head was what looked like a screw driver. The backbone, all other bones were gone. "Is that a screw driver," I asked?

"Yes, Uncle Sam ground one down like an ice pick. He stuck it through the fish head and skinned it. He had a yellow handle pocket knife he used. I see his fish skinner's way over here by the wall. I don't see his knife anywhere."

"Don't touch it," I said. "That old fish head is ready to crumble. I want the sheriff to see it. A man finishes cleaning his fish. He gets rid of the head."

"That's right," Margaret said. "He took that out to finish dressing the fish. And I don't remember red on that wall!"

I looked at it. "If a man was stabbed in the back and in the lungs, he might have fell back against that wall. Dropped those fish skinners. The Sheriff may be able to get that red color tested, determine if it is human blood. If that other boat is where I suspect it is, if that red turns out to be human blood, common sense about that fish head, I suspect a good Sheriff would believe your Uncle was murdered, dragged into that house and burned up.

"You can tell him you know that your daddy has said he was going to kill him. Something I have not told you yet. Thinking that he signed on to a ship and perhaps left an address to where he moved the family to, I found this name and address in the records at Channelview: Otis Ray Burkett. Pine Burr Street in Palestine Texas. That's where your uncle's ex-wife lives."

"That's him alright. And I know where she lives. But I wonder if that would be enough to convict him?"

"I don't know. But I'm sure it would be enough to convince a Sheriff to arrest her, get a confession out of your uncle's ex. She knows your daddy killed him. And he probably expected to get the money for the place if she sold it."

I opened the barn and looked in. A lot of harness hanging on the wall, and saddle hanging from a rafter. In a corner was an assortment of rakes, hoes and shovels, a pick axe, and a double bit axe. A sledge hammer and three steel wedges laying on the floor.

On a shelf was a number of cans, probably containing nails, nuts and bolts. And I could see a hammer. I never went in to look closer. We decided not to take the plows, disturb anything.

"Was that your saddle in there?"

"No that's Uncle Sam's saddle." We walked down to the house.

"You see that tin that collapsed in front of that chimney. I never knew about it until he found out Mother was moving us to Buffalo. He took some floor boards up he had under a rug. Built under that fireplace hearth is a locked-up space. He put my saddle and gun in there. All his deeds, his will and most of his money he kept in there. He gave me a key and told me not to tell anyone until he died. He told me he had willed his share of the place to me."

"You don't think it got too hot to ruin it all?"

"No, you will have to see it to believe it. We may have to cut that lock to get into it. It could be rusted. He gave me a key, I still have it. I forgot to say so, but he kept Mother's deed to her half of the place in there as well."

We called Cassie to go. She was down by Buffalo Creek pitching pin oak acorns into the water.

"We better go out to the Flo road. I need to see if my keys still work. The lock into the Williams place was a little contrary."

But with a can of WD-40 I gave it a spray job and it opened. The gate out into the Flo road had two locks. One for the owner, the other for Mr. Williams and her uncle. With a little spray, it opened as well.

We stopped in Long Lake. The Williams invited us in, seemed so glad to see Margaret. "Where did you find her?"

I told them how it happened, that Cassie was our daughter. That we planned to marry next Saturday. They were invited, we planned to marry at our home in Livingston.

"We probably can't be there. I don't drive much anymore. You both got our prayers and blessings for a long life together. I got something for you Margaret." He got up, went in a room, came back with a long envelope. He handed it to her. On the front was written 'For Martha Burkett or any of her children'.

"Sam had some horses, mules, a few cattle. I fed what feed he had at the home place barn until it was gone. I took them and sold them. I never knew what else to do. The money and receipts are in that envelope. The hogs, I just turned them out the day his house burned down. I have not seen them since. No telling where they went."

"You keep this Mr. Williams! You earned it doing all you have did."

"No, it belongs to you kids, I suppose. Your Mother and Sam were like brother and sister to me. That is Martha in the cemetery, is it not?"

"Yes, the people I worked for brought us up here. There was no one at your place, so it was just us, my boss and his wife and the funeral home people there. I suppose I was just too upset, I could have carried a jar, left a note with our address in it."

"Mr. Williams, it may be a few weeks. We think we found evidence that her Uncle Sam was murdered when we were there today. I'll try to get the Sheriff there. We need to get that judge you took his ex to court with there, as well. Keep this to yourself, but Margaret thinks she knows where her uncle's will is. Do you think you could get that judge down there on a Saturday?"

"He's just the Justice of the Peace in Oakwood. I'm sure I could. I've known him for years."

I told him I would call him and let him know after I talked to the sheriff and we worked out a Saturday date. We said our goodbyes and headed for home.

Cassie being in school complicated our marriage plans somewhat. Mother and Dad agreed to come, spend a week with Cassie. She rode the school bus, so we could leave town for a honeymoon trip. Margaret's family, and most of mine, lived in a go there and back home in one day from Livingston.

With the guest house, two family members of my family could stay the weekend, provided they wanted to. They lived to far away to make it in one day. The Zumo's were shutting down the business for the day. Shirley Nell and Linda would come with them.

Rev. Billy would come with the Wilson's. He married us on the front steps of our home. The crowd was on the porch behind us, some on the sidewalk. Andre Batiste stood with me, Shirley Nell with Margaret. Afterward, the punch bowl and wedding cake were in the kitchen. A lot of pictures were made. Cassie had the camera, she probably spent a roll of film.

Katrina hugged me and laughed. "You found the girl that loves you!"

Margaret and I had decided on New Orleans for our honey moon trip. We got a motel room in Lake Charles for the night. In just a few minutes after going into that room, we were in a bed together for the first time. Afterwards Margaret laughed and said, "It may never be any better than on that cotton sack, but it sure is more comfortable."

We went out to a seafood restaurant. They had hickory grilled shrimp over rice. I had fresh steamed broccoli and shrimp cocktail sauce. Margaret ordered fried coconut shrimp, with fries. We both had a salad.

The next morning. I was up and ordered breakfast brought to our room. I ate, but noticed Margaret was only picking at her food. She looked about ready to break down and cry. I suspected I knew the reason.

"Is there something wrong? You don't look very happy."

"I've never been this far away from Cassie in her life!"

"We don't have to go to New Orleans. We could go there next summer, take her with us if we want to. What if we just went back to the ranch? We could let Dad and Mon know where we are. You could call every day. I probably need to go to the office one day anyway. We could check with Mom and Dad while Cassie's in school."

"You're sure you don't mind?"

"We'll be together, that's what matters to me. And to be honest about it, I prefer being at the ranch." We slept at the ranch that night.

Chapter Eight
Adapting to becoming a Daddy

We went back to Livingston Friday morning. I needed to go to the office, check on things. Mrs. Ivers told me our lawyer had called, requested I call him as soon as possible.

"You may recall, Mr. Dobrinsky kept a special account that he said was to reward some of his employees for their loyalty and service. I just carried out his instructions on how he wanted that done. You need to inform those people before they get a statement on their retirement fund and think it's in error."

"So that it would draw interest, this is what he had me do. Into the retirement fund of Mrs. Ivers and Mr. Justin Wilson, he had me transfer $100,000 each. To Mary Ellen Grimes, $75,000. Big Jim Batise and Monroe Sylestine each got $50,000. The rest of his employees got $2,500 each. You will probably need to inform each of them to keep what they've received confidential."

I called Mrs. Ivers into my office. "I just talked to our lawyer. Since you are in charge of records keeping, which includes retirement funds, I need to tell you this. Which you will need to keep confidential.

"The lawyer just informed me that from the special account Mr. Dobrinsky kept, he has ordered $100,000 transferred into yours and Mr. Justin Wilson's retirement fund. Mary Ellen Grimes got $75,000. Big Jim Batise and Monroe Sylestine each received $50,000. The rest of his employees got $2,500 each."

"What did you say he gave to me?"

"A hundred thousand bucks. I'll talk to Mr. Wilson, Monroe and Big Jimbo. If Mary Ellen comes in, and provided I'm not here, you need to inform her. She may want to draw it out. But she knows it's drawing interest right where it is."

"A hundred thousand dollars. If I'm late from lunch today, it will because the big steak I order will be tough. I did talk to Mr. Wilson, Big Jimbo and Monroe. Told them to keep their lips zipped on how much they received. For the rest of the employees, I put a note on the bulletin board. Check your retirement fund balance. Mr. Dobrinsky had an amount of appreciation deposited in your account after his death."

At home, Cassie followed in my footsteps. With a lot of questions about why, when and where about things. More so at the ranch. If Wade was not helping his dad, then they were always together up there.

I was at the ranch the day Mary Ellen came in and checked out. She told Mrs. Iver's she really had not looked for a job yet, but she had a friend that ran a road building Construction Company. She meant to talk to him. She said she would think about her retirement fund, she might find a place to pay more interest on it.

I suppose she did, at the end of the month bank statement, Mrs. Ivers told me Mary Ellen had withdrawn her retirement fund.

One night, about a month after our marriage, I put my pillow against the head board and sat up.

"You can't sleep? Is something bothering you?"

"Yes. I don't know where to start. Before you hear people wagging their tongues around town, I need to tell you about something."

"You must mean Mary Ellen?"

"You already know about Mary Ellen?"

"Yes, Mrs. Wilson told me. She said everyone tried to pair you two up. Even both herself and Mr. Wilson. You finally told them the truth about me. Even Mr. Dobrinsky hired her, trying to get you together."

"Mary Ellen was a friend of Virginia's. Her dad was a preacher. She dressed like a lot of women of their faith do. I suppose because I was a football player, I was able to get her involved in school activities more. I told her I was committed to you."

"I can't blame her for caring about you. Mrs. Wilson said she left town when she learned you had found me. She did the right thing."

"Yes, she did the right thing. Mr. Dobrinsky left her $75, 000. I have not heard from her. As far as I know, she's in Tyler with her folks. I wish her the best. I respected her."

Mr. Wilson had a sow with pigs. They were about three weeks old. The biggest male pig in the bunch, the sow stepped on and broke his front leg. Wade decided they could put a cast on that pig's foot. Mr. Wilson told them to do what you can, if it does not work I'll have to cut his leg off.

Wade cut four small splints from a huckleberry bush. He caught the pig, brought it outside the pen. He laid it on the ground. "Hold it Cassie. Like this!" He grabbed one ear, put his knee on his neck, and grabbed both of his rear legs. She did as he told her too.

"He's squealing out of his gourd! Wade I must be hurting him!"

"He'll get over it! Let him squeal and just hold him."

Wade got those sticks in place, pulled that broke leg in place and clamped down on them with his right hand. He was left handed. With black tape, he started taping around those sticks. At the bottom and below its foot, slightly, he put the end of the sticks in a bottle cap. He taped around it as well. He taped over everything again twice and got in the pen. Hand him to me Cassie. He set him down.

"They watched him. He's not squealing anymore. But he's not walking on that foot yet."

"He'll learn," Wade said. "What do we need to name him?"

"Let's name him 'Louie'!"

"Well, ok. That rhymes with 'sooee' I guess! I wonder how long we'll need to leave that cast on?"

"I don't know, but I'll find out!"

"Wednesday night of that week, Cassie asked if she could call Wade. I told her to go ahead."

Mr. Wilson told me what happened. He answered the phone. "Mr. Wilson, I need to talk to Wade." I handed Cassie the phone. Cassie wants to talk to you"!"

After he hung up, his mother said, "My, my. You are getting calls from girls now!"

Wade turned red, but said, "Cassie told me she got a boy in her class whose daddy was a doctor to find out how long we needed to leave that cast on that pigs leg. It's six weeks. And I'll tell you this about Cassie, if she tells you she will do something, she gets it done!" Then he went to his room.

Six weeks later, we all were there to witness the removal of Louie's cast. He was a lot bigger and stronger, but Cassie held him. Wade slit that tape with his pocket knife, put him down in the pen. There was a knot where the break was, but the pig seemed to be doing just fine on a front leg that those kids saved.

114

I called the young Sheriff of Leon County and Mr. Jim Williams and arranged a meeting at Sam Craig's burned down home site. I also talked to my lawyer about why and what we hoped to accomplish.

"I'm on retainer and I would like to be there with you. If she finds that will, I can check it out, determine if it's legal and binding in case it's contested. Few people seem to know this, but a lawyer can be hired to prosecute or assist a DA in criminal cases. You may not need or want this, but like I said, you are paying me to represent you in whatever jumps up. And beyond that I have a brother in Fairfield I need to visit."

We all met at the Flo road, Mr. Williams had brought the justice of the peace. I had my boat and motor behind my pickup. In the bed, I had a hook I made out of a piece of concrete rebar about seven feet long.

We went out to the barn first. I showed the Sheriff the fish head pined on that block. Then the fish skinners on the ground by the wall. Then pointed to the red on the wall, suggested it might be blood. He got a sample of that. He and my lawyer took pictures of everything. We looked in the barn, but we never went in there.

"We need those things, but left it until you saw everything."

He went in the barn, looked around. "I never saw anything in there to help us," he said. "I don't see any reason for you not to take those things. We have pictures of what we need here, I think. If your wife knows where the things you told me about are, we need to look at that."

"It's down there where his house burned down," Margaret said. There were some "how could that be looks" among some people, including the Sheriff. But they said nothing. We all walked down to the ashes and a lot of twisted and black tin roof.

Margaret pointed, "We need to move that tin out from the front of that fire place. Uncle Sam showed me where he kept his will, other paper work and money. He put my gun and saddle in there as well. He did that when mother moved us to Buffalo. I told Robert about it when we were here. All that is in a space under that fire place hearth."

"You don't think it burned up or got so hot it ruined?" the sheriff asked.

"No, I don't think so. You'll have to see it to believe me."

I had rubber boots on and my shovel. I waded out into the burn and threw that tin back. It only took a little shoveling of ashes so the Sheriff could get out to it with me.

It was two feet deep, three feet wide, and five feet long space under the heart. The entrance had a concrete door that slipped inside. It had heavy duty handles. I pulled it back and around on the concrete he had put there for that purpose. Inside that was a steel door he had shop made. Margaret handed me the key and I got the padlock holding it shut to open with no problem.

I handed out three wide mouth glass coffee jugs. The judge and my lawyer opened them up one at the time. The first jug held his money and a sealed envelope. It was all paper money. It was counted and found to be $1,250. The envelope was addressed to Sam Craig. So was the return address. It was post marked at Jacksonville, Texas. On it was written in ink, 'Last Will and Testament of Sam Craig.'

Written on a plain sheet of note book paper were these words;

I, Sam Craig, do declare that Margaret Burkett, my niece, shall inherit all my earthly possessions, after my death.

My lawyer got a picture of the envelope. The Justice of the Peace declared it a legal will, that Margaret Burkett, would inherit all his earthly possessions. "When I get to the office, I'll draw up paperwork that will indicate the witnesses to the opening of his sealed will," he said, "the sheriff, Mr. Williams, and I should come in and sign it." He was a notary as well.

The other jug contained his and Martha's deeds to their 160 acre share of the place. He had it surveyed, his share was on the west side of the place. The Cemetery was in the east corner of his part. The line crossed the marsh, cornered across Buffalo creek. He owned the home place and barn as well.

The third jug contained the title to his pickup truck sitting under a shed with two flat tires. Also, the title to the boat and motor, another title to the missing boat. Other paperwork that really had no value any more.

Margaret's saddle was practically new, they had used saddle oil on it before putting it in there. It was in good shape. The shotgun was a late model 16 gauge Winchester pump with a 28 inch barrel. I could not believe my eyes when Margaret put it to her shoulder, pointed it away from the crowd. Pumped it three times in rapid succession and said, "Yeah, that's my gun!"

The sheriff laughed and said, "Yeah, and I hope you never shoot at me! But where do you think that other boat is?"

"Follow me," I said. I drove across to where Margaret said her uncle kept his other boat. I put the motor in my pickup bed. We slid my boat in the water. All I needed was a paddle and the hook I made.

"My theory is this," I said. "See that tree out there about eight or ten feet. A man could tie a rope around that tree. Poke the rope down with his paddle. He could paddle into the bank here. Pull the plug in the boat, get out and shove it back out in the water. Watch until it sunk then leave. If I'm right, I should be able to find that rope with this hook."

I paddled out to the tree. It only took a minute to come up with mud stained nylon rope. I got it untied from the tree, paddled into the bank. The sheriff tied the rope to his bumper and slowly eased up. He pulled a 14 foot flat bottom boat out on the bank. The paddle was tied down inside it. The plug, connected to a chain was out, and in the bottom of the boat was a yellow handle knife. The aluminum boat was not hurt, all it needed was cleaning up.

"That's Uncle Sam's knife," Margaret said. "He must have cut the string to tie that paddle. Laid it down and forgot it."

"I've seen enough to convince me that Sam Craig was murdered. If that red on that wall tests out to be human blood, then I don't believe there remains a doubt about that. But all we've found is circumstantial evidence that he was murdered. We don't have anything that really indicates who killed him."

A grand jury would not indict anyone with the evidence that you have now," my lawyer said.

Mr. Williams spoke up, "His ex-wife tried to sell me this place and everything Sam had right after Sam's death. That hussy knows who killed Sam, I guarantee! Otis Burkett lives there with her when he's not at sea. She might spill the beans if she thought it would save her hide."

The sheriff said he would get the Anderson County sheriff to pick her up, he would send a Deputy to get her. He would tell her she was facing conspiracy charges with Otis Burkett to commit the murder of Sam Craig.

Everyone left but the three of us. We went back over to Sam's barn. I loaded up the plows, the box of assorted sweeps and shovels. We got the saddle and harness for horses and mules. He had pipe wrenches, pliers, wire cutter and staple puller, wire stretchers, handsaws, hammers and nails. That we would leave, we would be back to work and need those things.

"Are you going to get the boats and that motor?" Cassie asked.

116

"Not this time. We'll bring a 16 foot trailer over here for that. I'll have the boats steam cleaned and let our outboard mechanics see if they can get that motor running again. We may just sell those boats or put them in the lake at the ranch."

Before we left, I put that tin back over the hearth. We went out to the Flo road to be sure all the gates were locked. The sheriff, my lawyer, Mr. Jim Williams and the Justice of the Peace went out that way. We talked about it on the way home. Margaret said she suspected her brothers and sister would want to sell their share of their mother's half of the place. She needed to see them anyway. What Mr. Williams gave her in that envelope, if divided by three, would give each of them about $1,400 dollars. "I'll keep what Uncle Sam left me in that jar."

"Your mother's share would give each of you 40 acres. Provided they want to sell, let's buy their shares. We both were forced to leave this county. It would mean so much to us to have a place to come to. We could build a camp house, do a lot of fishing and duck hunting."

Cassie spoke up. "Build it big enough for the Wilson's too Daddy!"

"Well, that's a good idea Cassie! We're about to get that ranch to where we want it. I've got to find him more help as we get those pastures stocked. I need people that live close. I intend to see if I can hire Essie Mae full time to oversee the produce building production. During the summer growing season, we'll try to get part time workers out of Wells."

Margaret contacted them, they all wanted to sell their part. Katrina wanted to keep ten acres. Land in the county was going for $200 dollars an acre in the county at that time. We gave them $300 dollars an acre. We had a surveyor stake off ten acres for Katrina just past the Jim Williams place by the road. That was on Margaret's half of the place. But it was accessible, a great building site and super fertile land. They just traded each other ten acres of land. Our lawyer took care of the deed work. Margaret had 310 acres in her name, Katrina had ten acres.

The young sheriff from Leon County called in three weeks. "I had to let that woman make a phone call. Her sister drove up here from Houston, testified that Sam's ex was with her at her home in Houston at the time Sam Craig died. She also stuck to a story that when she got home, Otis Burkett was in her home. He threatened to kill her if she did not sell the place. His dead wife owned half of the place. After that, the judge ruled on the case and he left, said he was going back to sea."

"I got a Texas Ranger to check out her story. Neighbors confirmed that she was in Houston with her sister. Neighbors confirmed Otis Burkett was seen regularly coming and going from her home in Palestine. I could not get a confession out of her that she knew Otis Burkett killed Sam Craig. I had to let her go. We both know she's lying and Otis Burkett killed Sam Craig. But what we know in our guts won't convince a Grand Jury to indict either of them."

I thanked him for doing all he could. He said he would jump on the case if any leads came up.

I hired Essie Mae Duncan full time to put in charge of the produce building. We had tame berries first, then later, the wild blackberries. It took four women two days to pick over the tame berries. They started over the third day.

Essie Mae and two other women were cooking them down to juice, making some jelly. The jelly cooker held about ten gallons, was equipped with an agitator. When ready, the burner was shut off. It had two hand operated spigots which allowed two women to fill pint jars. The jars had plastic lids. They came labeled "Shady Oak Farms - Tame Blackberry Jelly" and other information. The other berries would be labeled "Wild Blackberry Jelly".

It was costly, but built connected to the produce facility was a building divided into two compartments. Half was to freeze things, the other just air conditioned to store produce at about 65 degrees.

We got plastic containers, most of that cooked down berry juice was frozen. I meant for Essie Mae to pick one of the women to work full time with her. They would work on making jelly from frozen juice. It was shipped out 12 jars to cardboard case. Which were labeled "Shady Oak Farms - East Texas Best" in big letters. Product name also.

I made a deal with a leading grocery chain to handle our line of products and produce. When ready, Essie would call, they would send a truck to pick it up.

I bought a "Super C" tractor with cultivator plows. A seed planter, fertilizer distributor and hay cutting mower. Next year, we expected to plant a lot of produce, the chain wanted it as well. Our peaches probably would produce also. We had a row of those big tame red plums that got about as big as a half dollar. Red plum preserves would join our line. Tree sets I bought were producing fruit. The peach seed I got from Dad, the red and yellow wild plums would probably produce in two more years. The late summer wild plums might take another ten years.

I bought Cassie a saddle, we put it on Wade's horse, got the stirrups adjusted. I did the same with Sam Craig's saddle, he was a lot taller man than I. It was just like Margaret's, older but in good shape. It had a high behind seat rest, which I liked. I had to buy Cassie the modern version, hardly any height to it. As a kid, I heard that called the 'candle' which may not be the correct name for that part of a saddle.

We took our saddles and went to Madisonville, to the ranch where I bought the mares. Cassie fell for a black and white paint horse. Margaret selected a brown gelding which she said looked like the horse she had at the Craig place. I decided to wait.

The horse I wanted was owned by a young man at Livingston. He worked for people with hard-to-pen wild cattle. He was at the auction sale about every Monday. I saw that horse in action a few times if something got loose. He was a cow horse that knew his business. He was big, he was black, yet on his ribs the ends of his hair had a red tint to it. He was one tough horse.

I liked the young man, I talked to him regularly. He told me he had applied for a job in Houston. "If I get it, I'll have to sell my horse and saddle."

"If you need to sell that horse, give me a call. I need a good horse like that up at my ranch."

We just about went to the ranch every weekend. We attended Church Wednesday night, and usually got back in time for services Sunday night. During the summer, sometimes Margaret and Cassie just stayed up there. Since we were now totally in the retail business, I had to have store managers, which gave me a lot more freedom to go to the ranch, take the time to visit family more often.

Truth is, I hung out in the garden supply store most of the time. People knew me, they asked advice from me often. I enjoyed talking to them, I considered them friends.

My friend got the job in Houston, I bought his horse and saddle. He called the horse "Old Buck," although he was a young horse. Mr. Wilson had a two-horse trailer. I bought a stock trailer that would handle four. I covered it with a heavy-duty tarp so the horses and saddles would not get wet. But it could be used as a cattle trailer as well.

Mrs. Wilson did not care about horse riding at all.

We all went to Margaret's place in Leon County one weekend. We rode around the place and came to a conclusion. This place was the place for year-round outdoor recreation. Fishing at any time, hunting deer, hogs, squirrels and ducks during the season.

In a couple more years, I meant to make most of the 2400 acres a free, employee hunting club. I would, however, reserve for family; ranch employees everything below the east-west road over to the north road. Which included the field, produce building, hog pasture, wooded creek bottom and the lake. And the horse pasture, which was across the north road.

Mr. Wilson worked for me, he would be on the payroll. I felt like Cassie, I wanted a camp house big enough for both families. First of all, we would bring the dozer in, dig a hole and bury all that burned down house. We would build a four bedroom camp-house and use the fireplace and chimney still standing. Then he would take the dozer back, bring back building materials.

Before we could start building, I got a pole with meter box and outside electric outlets so we could use power saws. I got the spring electrical pump line hooked up. The pump and motor had been setting to long, I had to replace those. Then, try to get the electrical company out to connect to our meter box and turn us on.

Her Uncle Sam had a wood stove, which we buried. I got a propane tank brought out and filled. We would read the electric meter and mail it in. Don't matter if it's only twice a year. To refill the propane tank, we would need to be there to unlock gates.

I aired up the tires on Uncle Sam's old pickup. Put a new battery on it. Inline six, I pulled the plugs, they looked beyond hope. I poured a little gas in each hole, went all the way to Palestine for new plugs. I poured a little more gas in as I installed each plug. That old dude started! It smoked up the neighborhood for a few minutes, but it settled down.

Mr. Wilson hauled it to our Ford place on the low boy trailer. Margaret signed the title, it sold for $500. After we got the house built, I had a company put up a metal building big enough to hold a flat bottom boat, a tractor with a bush hog, the Dodge Power Wagon, and a few other things. I could lock it up, not have to drag a boat or trailer over there every time we went. Roads were growing up on the place, that tractor was needed.

One of the other things was the VW I got in trade from Mary Ellen. I took it to a high school friend who owned a garage. He installed a rebuilt engine, ordered different rims and put wider mud grip tires on the back. He outfitted it with a trailer hitch. And repainted it with brown and gray camouflage colors.

My neighbor at the ranch, Woodrow Duff, had a VW just like it. I had the motor overhauled in the old International pickup Mr. Dobrinsky had. Had it painted a dark red. I traded it to Woodrow for his VW, which may have been in worse shape than Mary Ellen's. Woodrow was on Social Security and a small retirement check from the county. Buying another vehicle, I knew, he could not afford.

My friend did for it what he did for the one I got from Mary Ellen.

With a couple of used lightweight boat trailers we got in trade at the boat dealership, I put a light weight bed on both. With a pair of come-a-longs and 200 feet of nylon rope in that front end trunk, Cassie and Wade could go about anywhere they wanted too. We took one to the Craig place. The other we kept in the shed at the ranch.

Another thing we did on part of the Craig place was build a crossing on a swift running spring branch that ran into the marsh above what appeared to be a solid rock dam. The branch had holes, Margaret said, and were full of goggle eye and yellow war mouth perch. And polly-wog catfish.

We took over a couple of those 20 inch diameter pipes, which Mr. Wilson cut in half. We had to ditch the branch around to do it, but we put in a concrete dam to raise the branch level about two feet. Then we laid in the four pipes and poured concrete, around and over them, creating a ten and one-half foot bridge we could drive over.

I had two steel drums I used to transport shad to the lake at the ranch. I bought small pumps to pump air into each barrel. Both operated from one cheap car battery. I learned to use a cast net. Below the dam at Dam B, I sacked up a lot of shad. I made two trips, and put a lot of shad in the lake at the ranch.

Also in the National Forrest was a creek that ran into the Neches. Wade and I trapped a lot of red horse, spot tailed minnows and red perch.

In short, we let the bait fish develop before I had it stocked with crappie, blue and channel catfish. Bass, there were so many private ponds to overflow in that creek, I felt in a short time we would have those.

I wanted those goggle eye and war mouth perch in the lake. We went over to the Craig place one Saturday. I put out a couple of perch traps. It was early in the year, we took a lot of small crawfish we seined out of a pond at the ranch.

With cane poles I cut over across the Neches in Houston County, we all had a ball catching those goggle eye and war mouth yellow perch. Those that were hooked too bad, we put in ice chests. Most we put in the barrels on the back of my truck.

We also caught a number of yellow poly-wogs, or mud cat which went in the ice-chests. About mid-afternoon, my traps were loaded. I put those in the barrels. Late Saturday evening the lake at the ranch got stocked. Mr. Wilson, Wade and I cleaned fish at the shed for two hours. Sunday noon, we had a lot of fried fish and fries to eat.

In the creek bottom, I put up an automatic corn feeder. We set posts in a square about ten yards from the feeder on all sides. We stretched a cable about knee high all around it. Soaked burlap bags in used motor oil and wrapped the cable all the way around. Deer could step over it, hogs had to go under. The big hogs greased their backs. Hogs bed up together, the big hogs greased smaller ones. Used motor oil would keep lice off a hog, and sometimes cure the mange on a dog.

Mr. Wilson told me he heard a 22 shoot at that corn feeder the last three Monday's in a row. He went there, could not catch anyone. But he did find blood near that feeder. Somebody's slipping in here and taking advantage of that corn feeder.

I drove up there to see what I could find. It was a long way from the roads, the gates were locked. They had to walk a long way to that feeder. There were a number of big rock elm trees on the creek bank near the feeder. We cut those because they would seed a lot of territory. One fell across the creek not more than 30 yards from that feeder. The brushy top still had dried leaves, a regular ambush place to watch that corn feeder. I walked out on it. I found a 22-long rifle hull laying on that log. It was a Federal, we all shot Winchester.

I crossed the creek and walked out a short distance. In a place where water had dried up, I found tracks. Headed for that log. *He comes in this way, but there are no tracks here going back.*

I went back to the corn feeder. Where would I go to field dress something and hide while doing it? My eyes fell on a deep ravine coming into the creek bottom nearby. It was brush lined. I started up it, found tracks. Looked like rubber boots, same as I saw across the creek. I went on about 20 yards more. Leaning out over the ravine was a good size sapling. Big enough to hang a deer or good size hog on. There were a lot of tracks under it.

That dude may have been field dressing something here when Mr. Wilson came up here thinking he might catch him. Under the nearby roots of a big tree stump, I could see flies swarming. As I got closer, I could smell something. I leaned over and looked. A deer skin. I found a limb and raked it out. With the limb I unrolled it. A nubbin bucks head rolled out. It's neck was cut off right behind its head. Not much meat on that neck, I never saw anyone save that much of a deer's neck. This dude must be hungry.

I went back to the corn feeder, then walked up the creek bottom. I soon found a rubber boot track headed north. I went back to my truck, drove up to the low water crossing on the north side of the place. I got out, found a rubber boot track where he stepped down into the road crossing. I walked nearly to the gate in the northeast corner and found not one track.

Across the FM road from our northeast corner gate was a driveway to a neat looking white frame house which was about a hundred yards from the road. I went back to my truck. I bet that dude listens for a car right here on this rock crossing. If he can't hear one, he probably crawls over our fence, goes under that creek bridge. He waits until he hears nothing, crawls over his fence over there, and goes home. That little white house up yonder!

I drove up to the northeast gate, turned south. I went about 200 yards, stopped and got out. I soon found a rubber boot tracks headed south.

Whoever the dude was, he walked this road before day. Hid out on that log across the creek. Killed something. Less likely to be seen, he went up through the woods going home. I felt like I knew where home was now. Margaret and Cassie went back home Sunday evening. I stayed.

Monday morning, I was up by 5 a.m. Made me some coffee. Had a couple of cinnamon rolls out of a package. Filled my thermos with coffee. Wrapped the last cinnamon roll up and put it in my jacket pocket. I got my over and under double barrel 12 gauge. Five number one buckshots. With lights out, driving slow, I turned west on the east-west road. Then turned by the long leaf pines almost to the north gate. Just far enough away that the dude could not see it when he got to the low water crossing.

I put my thermos in a five gallon bucket I had in the truck, loaded my 12 gauge. Just below that rock low-water crossing was a bluff bank. It had sort of caved back in under some tree roots. I backed in under those tree roots. Took my thermos out of the bucket, turned the bucket up-side down. A five-gallon bucket is better than no chair at all I always say. I knew I had a long wait. I sat down on the bucket.

I finally heard that .22 rifle pop. No doubt in my mind, it was at that corn feeder! I looked at my watch, 7:45. I got up, stretched. My butt felt like it had a ring around it. I poured myself a cup of coffee and ate that cinnamon roll. I turned the bucket over. Sat down again. Maybe a bigger ring on my behind won't hurt as bad!

I never waited as long as I thought I might. Rubber boots make some noise walking. I heard him right over my head almost. He never looked down that creek. We had a pipe-welded together fence in that creek bed. Before crawling over, he stopped to listen. I could see a hog's hind legs sticking out of the sack he had on his shoulder. The dude centered probably a 165 pound hog belly on one shoulder and had that .22 slung on the other.

With my hand on the hammer of my gun, but holding it casually, I stepped out of my hiding place. My words were: "I expect you better lay that hog and gun down and let's have a talk!"

The man nearly jumped out of his skin. But he turned and laid the gun and hog down. He must have been about 35. Well-built and probably at least 6 ft. 4 inches tall.

"You know this place is posted?"

"Yes sir, I know it. Look he said, "I've been laid off from my job. I tried to find work. I've hitch hiked to Lufkin and found nothing. I can't let my wife and kids go hungry. That's why I'm in here."

"Well, I can understand that. I've sort of been there. Do you live up yonder in that white house?"

"Yes, sir. We got 60 acres my parents left me."

I laid my gun down.

"No sense of you toting that hog up there. Wait here and I'll go get my truck. I'll take you home."

You may think I'm crazy, but I trusted the man. He had offered no smart mouth talk, and had did as I asked him to do. I also felt he told me the truth.

We loaded the hog, he laid his single shot 22 in my truck bed. I put my gun in the rack I kept behind my pickup seat. I got my five gallon can and thermos from my hiding place.

On the way, I asked him, "Where did you work and what did you do?"

"I worked at that big sawmill up near Alto. I worked in maintenance. Try to fix whatever broke. That included log trucks as well. I did a lot of welding, some electrical work. Luther Fowler, a black man that lives in that settlement over by Forest worked there too. He's got a mule and plows, he breaks gardens for people."

About half way between the FM road and his house was a blue Plymouth car. "Something wrong with that car?" I asked.

"No, it's a good car. My wife ran out of gas there. We ain't had money to buy gas."

I helped him unload the hog where he wanted it. "You got a five gallon can, I'll go get you some gas. Family needs a way to go. You go ahead with your hog, I'll be back shortly."

I went in to Wells and got some gas. I never had a lot of money on me, I withdrew a hundred from my account there. They gave it to me in 20 dollar bills.

I stopped at the car, poured most of the gas in it. It might have to be primed, left the can there. He had a fire around a wash pot, he meant to not waste anything skinning that hog.

"I need a man to work on our ranch. I need one that lives near as well. You may know Mr. Justin Wilson. He's the man in charge up here. The work is regular farm and ranch work. Feeding cattle, cutting, baling and hauling hay. At times, you might work at our produce place. That might involve plowing, harvesting. In other words, doing whatever Mr. Wilson thinks needs being done. Do you think you would be interested in working for us?"

"Yes, sir. I've did a little of all of that! Luther Fowler told me his girlfriend Essie Mae was working for you. I remember Mr. Wilson, he was a friend of my dad."

"My business headquarters is in Livingston. I'll need to take you there tomorrow to sign you in. You'll need your Social Security Card. Does $2.50 dollars per hour, heath care insurance, a retirement plan and two weeks paid vacation sound all right to you?"

"It sounds better than what I had at that sawmill."

"Can you be ready by six in the morning? I'll get you back home."

"Yes, sir! I may not sleep any tonight!"

"There's two things I need to ask you."

"Yes, sir. What's that?"

"You are a little older than I am. No need for you to say sir to me. The other is, what is your name?"

"My name is Joe Ed Walters. My wife's name is Susan. We have two boys and a girl."

"My name is Robert DuPree. If you are willing to take a chance on working for me, here's an advancement. No strings attached. You won't have to pay it back." I handed him the five 20's I had folded in my shirt pocket. "By the way, I left a little gas in that can. You may need to prime it. I'll see you in the morning!"

Near the FM road, I looked back in my rear view mirror. His wife and three kids were with him. I imagined he was doing some explaining. I also imagined they would get that car started, she would go for some groceries. They would have more than fresh pork for dinner today.

I was reminded of something Mr. Dobrinsky once told me. "Robert, you can help some people, and some it don't do any good to try. Give some people money to get on their feet again, they'll take it and try to better themselves. Others will take it, live it up, and then come back with their hand out!" Time would tell, but I felt like with a job and income, I found a family that would better themselves.

We went right to the office the next morning. I left him with Mrs. Ivers to get his paperwork done. In my office, I called my partner at the Ford place. "I need another pickup for the ranch. Just like the one Mr. Wilson has, with the Shady Oaks Farm & Ranch sticker on the side doors. When do you expect it to be ready?"

"It'll be ready by one o'clock."

Next I called Margaret.

"Did you catch that dude sneaking into our place?"

"Yes. I hired him to work at the ranch. He's here at the office now. Do you suppose you could fix dinner for him as well? You'll be seeing him soon anyway."

"I have a pot roast cooking. No problem."

"We'll see you at dinner then. I'll tell you more later. I love you!"

He was soon finished with his paper work. We spent the morning at the boat place, the hardware and building supply store and then the Feed and Garden Supply store. I told him that often he would be driving here to pick up things needed at the ranch. Back at the office, I gave him keys to all the locks at the ranch. Went over how the work week was set up at the ranch, his family health care insurance plan, his option to participate in our retirement plan.

I took him home with me to dinner. Margaret asked him questions about his wife, kids. Where they lived. She had the ability to make people relax, comfortable, and learn more about them in a short period of time than I could all day.

After lunch, I drove to the Ford Place. The white Ford three-quarter-ton pickup with the Shady Oaks Farm & Ranch logo on the doors was shined up and ready to go. "This is your ride home, your work truck. You have a key to the fuel tanks at the ranch. Just fuel it up when needed at the ranch. Drive it back and forth from your home. Short family trips like Lufkin, Nacogdoches, and Rusk, feel free to use it. Local advertising helps. Don't think we need that in California though!"

"Just go on home. Write in eight hours today on your time card. Mr. Wilson starts at 7 a.m. at the ranch equipment shed. I'll call him, he'll be expecting you. He'll show you about punching in and out on the time card. At times, you will work overtime, sometimes even on Saturday. I'll probably see you in a week or two."

I could imagine how proud Joe Ed Walters might feel when he drove into his yard and his wife and kids ran out to see who was in a new Ford pickup truck. Honestly, I felt good about that myself!

I called Mr. Wilson that night and told him I caught the fellow hunting in our property. Who he was and what his name was. That I hired the man, he could expect him the next morning.

"I knew that family when I was young. That boy was just a kid when I went in the service. They were good people. Surprises me he was slipping in the place. Sort of shocks me that you hired him."

"He said he was out of work, out of money, and could not find a job. He had a wife and three kids and they needed to eat. I understood that, believed he was telling the truth."

"He likely was, Robert. This end of the county has little in the way of work opportunity. In the past, the county officials sort of ignored us. I'm hearing people talk about you. This ranch is providing people with jobs. A lot of money has been spent in this end of the county, developing it. And you know what your tax bill is. People are saying we are not being treated by county officials like trash anymore."

Margaret and Cassie drove up there to visit Joe Ed's wife and kids the next time we were at the ranch. "Susan is such a nice person," Margaret said. "I'm glad I know someone else up here now. Their daughter was about the same age as Cassie."

"Wade and the girl were friends in school. Any friend of Wade is a friend of mine," Cassie said.

I suppose she meant that. She talked about Jason Batise a lot. They seemed to be friends in school as well.

Margaret soon had roses, lily and all manners of flowers in the flower beds. We got white spider lily bulbs at the cemetery where Mother's side of the family was buried. I suspected my grandmother put them there. Something was blooming in those flower beds at all times.

Margaret bought herself some red coveralls when we were shopping in Houston one Saturday. She took over my wheel barrow, kept her gloves, shovel, rake, hoes and hand tools in it. Along with seed and boxes of fertilizer for different things. In those red coveralls, people would pass and blow their horn at her. She just waved and kept working.

She was having trouble accepting the fact that we had money, we never needed to be as conservative as we grew up needing to be. At lunch one day, she said, "Our water bill is getting to be sky-high. It was $28 dollars this month!"

"Maybe one of the commodes is overflowing. I'll check."

"It's not that. I've already checked."

"I'll look under the house then. Maybe we have a leak."

"It's not under the house. I looked. It's you! I timed you last night. You were in that shower 20 minutes!"

"Well, I sort of loose track of time when I'm singing in the shower. I'll try to watch it!"

Give it time, I thought. She had to support herself and our kid on a waitress salary. Every penny had to be accounted for.

Three years after our marriage, our pastures were all stocked with cattle. We were selling hogs, releasing a few into the wild. We started with a Hampshire boar and sow, two red Duroc sows. Pigs from the red Duroc's were white banded. Mr. Wilson traded me his boar Louie for one of those red banded boar shoats. I put Louie in the release part of the pasture with three gilts and three barrows. Louie had grown to be one big sized hog, I thought he could defend himself.

Joe Ed had seen him, so had Mr. Wilson. A big wild Russian boar hog. We released one good boar, Joe Ed found him dead the next day. He thought that big Russian boar killed him. Essie Mae, during the hunting season on Saturday, would take a 30-30 rifle, a fishing pole and a chair. Sit on the creek bridge and fish. And hope to shoot a buck deer or a hog.

"That's the biggest, meanest hog I ever seen. He big in de shoulders, but little in de hind part. He not like our hogs. He running across dat road. I shot at him. I must have hit his personals in his rear. He fell down on his behind. With his old front legs he just drug his self about ten feet. He got his self up an ran before I could shoot again. I seed dogs scratching his self like dat. I know I hurt that big hog! If he Russian, I don't eva won't to see no Russian!"

At our ten acre food plot, we set up four of those big highline poles. Put a five by five boxed stand on top. It had a roof, and a chair. You could sit in that chair, on a moonlight night see the gate, and maybe the field. Mr. Wilson rigged a heavy gate you could raise up, pin. Connected with a wire, sitting in that watch tower, you could pull that pin. That heavy gate would fall, trap whatever was in the field. The thing was 20 feet high. The ladder ran up to a door in the bottom of the stand. You could flip that door open, get inside. Flip it shut, you could stand on it or put your chair on it.

It needed to be a moonlight night so you could see what went in that gate. Which likely would be hogs and deer. Not only did we hope to catch that big Russian boar, but also his off spring. We might run them through the auction ring, or release them on the Craig place in Leon County.

Never heard it discussed or read about it, but deer in a certain area likely become inbred over a period of time. By building a ten acre food plot and trap at the Craig place, we could trade deer, so to speak. And perhaps improve the deer in both places.

Mr. Wilson built out of lumber and plywood a platform in the dump truck bed to hold gravel. It looked like a load of gravel, but underneath we could haul a herd of deer. The floor was filled with sand. Hopefully, they would not make a lot of noise.

It required a special loading shoot to get those deer in that dump truck. From the field, we opened a gate into a covered small corral. From that corral it was up the shoot and into a dark dump truck. There was a separate pen and shoot for loading hogs into our cattle trailer also.

I got moonlight night duty. I watched hogs and deer go through that gate. When I was satisfied I had a sizable bunch of deer in the field, I pulled that pin. Went to the house and got some sleep. Meantime, Mr. Wilson and Wade were at the Craig camp house. They set the trap, pulled the pin as well.

We left the deer and hogs in the field until late that evening. Joe Ed helped me. We loaded the deer first. Then we loaded and culled out the Russian hogs and put them in the cattle trailer. The rest we turned loose. Old Louie was one of those. Joe Ed just went on to the Craig place to release about 20 hogs with Russian in their blood.

Cassie and I waited until dark. I expect if I got stopped, no telling what the jail time and fine might be, but I felt I was doing something the Texas Wildlife People needed to be doing a lot of. I might add, for a reason I could not explain, I managed to put my dad's old ear mark on a young eight-point buck. He called it the "crop split in the right." It had to be on the right ear.

We met Joe Ed coming back home, he had released those hogs. Mr. Wilson and Wade were waiting on us.

"We got 18 ready to go. How many y all got?"

"We got 15," Cassie said. "Daddy put a mark on an eight point's ear."

I opened up the tail gate. We beat on the side, they would not come out. "I'll raise it up to dump a little," Mr. Wilson said. That did the trick. I saw 15 deer hit the ground running.

We loaded 18 and headed home. Mr. Wilson and Wade decided to get some sleep, return home in the morning. At Crockett, I gave Cassie money. She went into an all-night place and ordered us a burger and strawberry milk shake to go. I stayed in the truck, kept it running. Tried to act like I hauled a load of gravel somewhere every night. It was 4 a.m. when 18 head of deer hit the ground near the ten acre food plot on our ranch.

One thing on the ranch kept pointing to the need for something else. In four pastures, we had about 180 head of cattle, which required a lot of hay. The baler pulled behind a tractor and spit out square bales. The pecans and walnut trees were still small, we baled hay there. Mr. Wilson fenced off part of his creek bottom for a hay meadow. We used my equipment and I paid him for what was left after he filled his barn.

Feeding all that hay in racks that we built under the cow sheds and in the horse pasture created a clean-up job every spring. Hay waste and you-know-what pointed to a need for a compost bed. A big one. It required water. We thought water out of our irrigation system would speed up the process. We wound up putting it about a hundred yards from the produce processing facility.

We laid out our forms, got a ready-mix truck up there, with our sand and gravel we poured it. The floor sloped to the back. The walls were ten feet high, sides and back. It was divided into two 25-foot-long, ten-foot-wide compartments. Next to the back wall floor we built in a trough, you might say, which held five bales of hay.

Water in the system drained to the back, filtered through that hay. Then through a number of four inch PVC pipes put in the back wall. They drained into an underground concrete pit we put in back of the facility. We equipped that with a pump to load into a spray tank.

We would back the dump truck in one side and dump clean up waste. We wet it down with irrigation water. Of course, it got rained on. One side held the cleanup. About mid-summer, with the front end loader on the tractor, we transferred it to the other compartment. Then gave it another dose of irrigation water out of the lake. The bugs that break matter down into compost need oxygen. We felt by doing that, it speeded up the process.

I found a thousand gallon tank and a four wheel trailer to put it on. Mr. Wilson rigged up a pump to run off a tractor power take-off. The pump out line could be set to circulate back into the tank to mix or keep mixed. The other function was to regulate how much flow you wanted to put on a field row, or spray on a field. It had two attachments for both of those details. The quick open valves on the thing could be operated with a system he invented that could be reached by the tractor driver.

The liquid fertilizer tank might need emptying more than once during the summer. Mostly it got sprayed on pastures. The solid compost went in the produce field in the winter time.

My cousin Marvin had probably a quarter acre of pure old blue stripe ribbon cane. He meant to quit making syrup. He gave me the cane grinder Dad once had. "Just gather all that cane this fall if you want it. I ain't got time to fool with it no more."

I had a couple of rows in the produce field already. We were out of room for more cane in there.

I selected two acres I thought would produce ribbon cane well in the cow pasture by the barn. Fenced it both hog and cow proof. Downhill from the artesian well, we piped with PVC an irrigation system to it. Joe Ed and the two Mexicans gathered Marvin's crop.

We had flat broke that field, disked it until we killed the grass. Furrowed it up with a middle buster. Laid those cane stalks end to end in those furrows. We moved the cane from the produce field to finish the two acres. That included stubble. We used the middle buster to cover it all up.

The grinder Mr. Wilson set up to run with an electric motor. I got two pans built, and we built two wood burning furnaces. We got oak slabs from a nearby hardwood saw mill. They gave it to us to get rid of it.

When we got ready to make syrup, I had Dad and Mother over for a week. He taught Essie Mae, Joe Ed, Wade, Cassie and I how to cook syrup. "Don't let it get too hot! It'll have dark streaks in it if you do!" Dad enjoyed the week. "I thought I would never make syrup again," he said.

Chapter Nine
Life Moves On

In 1963, our son was born. Margaret said it was much easier this time. She did not want me in the delivery room. "You just be here when I get out." Myself, I had never felt so useless and helpless. I prayed to God to let us have a healthy child and that Margaret recover with no problems.

Margaret wanted to name him after dad, but thought Benjamin was a little long. "What about Benton?" she asked.

"What about Benton Craig? That represents a little of your family and mine as well."

We named him Benton Craig DuPree. Cassie was 11 years older. Margaret and I had been here 27 years.

Margaret was raising our son the natural way. "I had to put Cassie on a bottle because I had to work." And no, she did not want me to hire a maid to help her in the house.

Cassie was great in helping her mom care for her brother. I learned to pin diapers myself. But we just sort of stayed home for a while. No more weekends at the ranch or at the Craig place for the time being. Virginia and her husband brought Mother and Dad to see their grandson. Katrina and her husband and kids came up.

Shirley Nell's husband was from Jasper. She told Margaret "I don't want to live that close to my in-laws. Livingston is about the right distance." But they wanted to establish a fast food business like the Zumo's.

I helped them by buying a lot near the high school. I let them find a home in a subdivision they liked. I bought it, rented it to them with an option to buy. I also let them have a lot of building materials at my cost for building their restaurant

They got the place up and going. They named it "Lions Hangout." It was near the high school and when it came to sports, they were the "Livingston Lions." The high school kids sort of adopted the place to hang out. And many of them ate lunch there.

Business was good, they soon paid me for the lot. And agreed to buy the house. They got it financed, I let them have, it minus the rent they paid. Their daughter Linda was a year older, a grade ahead of Cassie in school. She often rode the bus home with Cassie. They both had two batons. Sometimes with one, sometimes with two, they practiced.

Those girls got out in the yard, run thru all sorts of strutting moves and twirling routines. Margaret said they had been doing it since they were seven and six years old.

We soon returned to the ranch weekend routine. Well Cassie did, and I for the most part. Our baby boy restricted so much of Margaret's freedom to just get out and go with us. She never seemed to mind. "You just go on and do what you want to."

I started teaching Cassie to shoot a .22 at first. Then a 16 gauge Winchester shotgun. I had a friend who ran a gun store in Livingston cut a little off the stock to fit her. I bought a couple of those things that pitch those clay pigeons. Cassie soon could knock down two with no problem.

Mr. Wilson, Wade and I took turns along with Cassie practicing our shooting. It did help, you got the feel of the gun and over the awkwardness I always felt at the beginning of each hunting season.

One day, Margaret walked out with little Benton, watching us shoot. Cassie kept after her "Momma, why don't you shoot?"

Finally she picked up my pump 12 gauge gun and said "Pull both of them at once." She knocked both down before they traveled far. Then she laid the gun down.

We were all a little more than amazed at how quickly she did that. But Cassie said "Shoot again Momma!"

"No, that's enough for me. I'd rather save my shells until I see some meat!"

Growing up, my dad or older brothers seldom bought a whole box of shotgun shells. Merchants would sell you one out of a box if that's what you asked for. They normally asked for six. Margaret and I were the same age. When people bought shells that way, you shot at meat.

I gave Cassie a 243 with scope next. She was a natural shot, she could hit what she wanted to. One day she said "Daddy, Wade told me a 243 was too small to kill a deer. He said they would just jump up and run off. Is that true?"

"Well, it's like this, Cassie. Yes, I've killed a number of deer with my 243. You got to hit a deer in the right place. Like in the neck, head, top of the shoulders, in the lobe of the shoulders, or back of the shoulders, provided you get it in his lungs. They may run some, but they'll go down."

Then as sort of joke I said "I always shoot them right in their ear hole. They won't run off if you do that."

When deer season opened, she and Wade hunted together. Wade got an 11 point the day before Thanksgiving. Their stand was on an old logging road in the creek bottom that ran through a pin oak flat. Wade shot it because it was on his side of the stand. They agreed on that before they started hunting.

Of course, it was back to school until the Christmas holidays. Wade had his deer, he wanted to work with his dad. I took Cassie a couple of times, saw a couple of eight pointers. She would not shoot. "I want one with horns bigger than Wade's."

We got a lot of rain, the ground was boggy. Then it turned to sleet and snow; everything was iced up. Saturday morning, the sleet and snow stopped, but the weather man reported 18 degrees at noon. Cassie wanted to go hunting.

"All right, we'll go up to the barn in pasture there. We can drive in there, get up on that hay." We had built in slots to see out across the pasture, hunt there. Deer crossed back and forth from the place west of us to our creek bottom. I had seen them more than once doing it.

We put on our warm clothes. I took a thermos of coffee, she had a six pack of Dr. Pepper's in the refrigerator. "You won't need an ice chest today," I said.

The road was graveled, we had no trouble in driving to the barn. I drove inside and pulled the door down. I had to move a few bales of hay to arrange it so we could sit on a bale and see out across that pasture. Inside out of the wind it was bearable.

It was mid-afternoon when we saw that buck. He stopped about a hundred yards away. "How many horns has he got, Daddy?"

"I can't tell Cassie. But that's the biggest deer I've ever seen. You have to go back to school Monday. If you want to kill a deer this year, you better shoot!"

That convinced her. I was watching that deer when that 243 popped. It was like that bullet just slung him around and he fell. He was kicking very little.

"Want me to shoot him again, Daddy?"

"No, see his tail quivering. He's had it!"

I had to start the pickup, wait for the heater to defrost the windshield. Which took about 15 minutes. But we warmed up some, had a Dr. Pepper.

I hit that pasture moving, I knew if I stopped we would walk home. I could actually see the ground shaking in places. I circled that deer and stopped with him near my pickup tail gate.

"Where you think you hit him Cassie?"

"He had his ears pointed forward. I could not see the hole in his ear. I just aimed through his ear. I must have hit the hole. He never ran off!"

I had a hard time keeping from laughing. My young daughter had turned my joke into reality. But I said "Yeah, you must have!"

I told her to just stay in the truck. I left the motor and heater going. I got out, field dressed that deer, which was a ten pointer. I could not get that deer into my pickup bed. Cassie jumped out to help me. I got his head and shoulders on, she held him there until I got the rest of him loaded.

I knew I better not use the same route we came across the pasture on. I chose another and by some miracle we made it out of there.

When we got to the shed, Mr. Wilson and Wade had just hung up a big eight-pointer. They had been putting out hay in their pasture, that deer came across chasing a doe. Mr. Wilson grabbed his 30.06 and stopped him.

We weighed Cassie's deer. It weighed 174 pounds field dressed. "That's the biggest deer I ever saw," Mr. Wilson said. "He had to weigh at least 200 pounds. What we need now is a couple of hogs to make sausage with all this deer meat."

Wade said he had been putting out corn up near the creek bridge. They been on it. "I bet they are now in this weather. We'll go see!"

He and Cassie jumped in Mr. Wilson's truck and up there they went. We started skinning the deer. About 30 minutes later, we heard two shots. The first was the 243, an instant later, the 308. I knew Wade had did for Cassie what I did for Wade when he was seven years old.

"We better go up there and help those kids," Mr. Wilson said. "Ain't no telling how big those hogs might be! A hog ain't no picnic to drag." Wade had one halfway to the truck when we got there. They had killed two barrows that weighed about 185 pounds each.

We skinned those hogs, which proved fairly easy. That fat was so cold, it made slicing through it quick. We soon sent Cassie in with pork ribs and sliced loin, as well as deer back-strap. Margaret and Mrs. Wilson had everything ready about an hour later. With hot biscuits, gravy, and mashed potatoes, it was good. Mr. Wilson said "It don't get any better than this!"

It was midnight before Mr. Wilson and I took a tin tub full of bagged sausage of two flavors out to his smoke house and hung it up. Got the hickory chips lit and smoking. Cassie and Wade, Margaret and Mrs. Wilson had been there helping us. We had a pile of meat to wrap for freezing, grind, mix and bag.

After cleaning up, I went to bed but could not fall asleep. I put my pillow against the headboard and sat up.

"What's bothering you. Why can't you sleep?"

"When I was a kid, a week or two before Thanksgiving, we killed hogs. Then hit the woods hunting. We were sort of intense about killing ducks and squirrels for Thanksgiving dinner. If we had much for Thanksgiving dinner, we had to do all that."

"Today, I had a hand in getting us all involved in all of that. It's really not necessary that we do that anymore."

"We did that also at the Craig place. It was the best time of the year, I thought. We all enjoyed it back then. We all enjoyed it today. It's who we are. It's part of our background. I hope we do it again. But not until next year!"

"I hope it's not this cold next year," I said.

I had a salesman who told me his father had a pecan grove near Madisonville. Creek bottom ran through his property. For some reason, the red squirrels were bigger than they were anywhere else. They were also a big problem for his dad. They carried off his pecans. "Strange about squirrels," he said. "Dad has watched them. They may work all one day taking those pecans to a hollow tree, or burying them. Then it might be two or three days before they did it again."

"Dad traps them. When he gets a cage full, he'll drive somewhere at night and release them to a new home."

"My ranch has mostly gray squirrels. Do you think if your father captured a bunch, he would let me have them? I would go after them, release them on our ranch."

"He would be happy to do that I'm sure. I'll tell Dad to call you when he gets his cage full again. I was there Sunday, he has a bunch already." Before he left, he drew me a map and directions to the place.

I realized I had been there once before hunting with my older brother when he lived in Madisonville. They were the biggest red squirrels I ever saw.

His dad called. Friday evening, Cassie and I loaded up the squirrel cage and went to Madisonville. Margaret took Benton and just went on to the ranch. "Don't bother with cooking supper for us, we'll eat somewhere before we get back to the ranch."

I told the man I had been there once with my older brother, Frank DuPree, to hunt when I was just a teenager.

"Oh yes, I remember you had that Long Tom Shotgun that was taller than you were! Frank helped me out, he killed a lot of squirrels."

We loaded up the squirrels, there must have been at least 50. I covered the cage with a tarp. We hit the road to the ranch.

"What do you want to eat, Cassie?"

"I like that place in Crockett. You know where we got that burger and strawberry milk shake."

Cassie went in for our burgers and shakes again. I sat in the truck on the parking lot as far away as I could get from anyone else. Had my window down. Those squirrels were not making a sound. I meant to reave up my motor if they did.

When we got to the ranch, I checked to if see the squirrels had water. We just left them on the truck. Release could wait until daylight.

The next morning, the Wilson's, Rev. Billy, Margaret with the baby, Joe Ed and Susan, their three kids, all gathered around to look when I took the tarp off the cage.

"Why did you get all these squirrels," Wade asked.

"It's the genetics," Cassie said.

For some reason everyone looked at me and laughed.

Wade wanted to be a rodeo cowboy. He wore three hats. One he wore to town, church. He kept it in his room. The second hat hung on a nail on the back porch. His work boots sat in front of the porch swing. He would come out, put on his hat, then his work boots.

That hat he might wear to an auction sale or just around the place. But if he was working, he went to the shop, took his worn to the 3rd degree hat off a nail and put it on. Hung his 2nd degree hat on the nail until quitting time. Needless to say, at quitting time, his 3rd degree hat went back on that nail in the shop. His 2nd degree hat went on the nail on the back porch. And he left his work boots in front of the porch swing.

One Saturday morning, Mr. and Mrs. Wilson went to Lufkin. I was off looking at cattle. Margaret was cooking dinner. Wade and Cassie jumped on the opportunity to be rodeo cowboys.

Mr. Wilson had a young bull yearling he meant to keep. The young bull was the perfect image of what a beef type animal should look like. He was heavy in the shoulders and in the hind quarters. He was shaped like a rectangular box.

His color was a blue-gray speckled with small black dots. He already had horns over an inch long. Mr. Wilson could walk up to him, put his arm over his neck, and rub his head between his ears. That young bull never allowed anyone else to do that.

Wade and Cassie found him in the corral by the barn. Wade shut the gate and roped him. That's when the fun began! Mr. Wilson had a pole set in the corral for what they needed to do. Snub that bull up to that post and put a short rope around him so Wade could ride him.

Wade got the rope around the pole. Cassie whipped his rear end with a stick. They got him up close to the post. But not close enough.

The bull just set back on the rope. He was too strong, Wade could not get him any closer. The bull was choking, the rope was so tight around his neck.

"You better let him go," Cassie said. "He's choking to death!"

Wade turned the rope loose, the bull fell back and down on an incline. His feet were up hill. Wade took the rope off the bull. Thrashed his rear end a few times with the rope. The bull tried but could not get up. Because his feet and legs were up hill.

"What are we going to do Wade? Your daddy and mother may be back soon."

"I'll be back in a minute. You just wait here. I think I know how to make him get up."

Mr. Wilson liked hot sauce. Like me, he preferred Tabasco sauce. But people gave him all manners of hot sauce. Homemade, store bought. Tabasco was mild compared to how hot some of it was.

Wade got a plastic drink cup. He poured some of it all in that cup. Stirred it good with a spoon. Then washed and dried the spoon. No evidence in his mother's kitchen was left.

He came back to the corral holding that cup.

"What do you have in that cup, Wade?"

"Hot sauce!" He poured some on the bulls tongue. "Open that gate and get out of here Cassie. He may be mad when he gets up!"

He poured some in his ear. Then on the end of the young bull's personal pride. Grabbed his tail and splashed the rest under the bull's tail.

It took a minute. That bull started to kick and thrash around. He moved his body to a better position. He got up and left that corral in a run. So did Cassie and Wade!

Wade's dad and mother came home. "What's my bull doing sitting down yonder in my water trough?" Mr. Wilson asked.

"I don't know," said Wade. "I guess the heel flies got after him."

It was a number of years before we learned why they named that bull

"Hot Sauce!"

The area beyond the horse pasture between the FM road and the spring branch up to the southeast corner had a stand of young mixed hardwood timber on it. About half way up, by the road was a five-acre open field. It was half-moon shaped. We fenced up the road side, around the back side of that moon shaped field, then up the road side to the SW corner.

131

I never knew why I did that really. Margaret knew what she wanted to do with it. "Let's put a circular driveway in there. Plant wild flowers of different types all over it. I know where there are Flocks and Indian Paint Brushes on the Craig place."

"There are so many types of yellow wild flowers. We would have something for people to drive through and see all year long. We could call it 'The Shady Oaks Wild Flower Garden'!"

If Margaret wanted to do it, that was enough for me. Personally, I thought it was good for our Shady Oaks Business. Margaret often took little Benton, got in the VW beetle, planted flowers along the roads in the ranch. Benton was walking and talking now, she was getting out more.

Getting Flocks and Indian Paint Brush seed presented a problem. Not likely we could be there when they shed their seed. We went over there, staked of areas when they were blooming. Later we went back after the seed fell. With a little fireplace shovel, I would scoop up a fine layer of that sand. I filled eight five gallon buckets about half full.

Back at the Wildflower Garden, I scattered that sand where she wanted me too. It worked! We got seed with that sand! We had a lot of flocks and paint brushes come up, bloom, go to seed and multiply.

Virginia brought us a lot of Blue Bonnet seed from their place near Austin. They lay there for two years before they came up. We transplanted Spiderworts. A clump had a root system that looked like curled up spaghetti. We might get a dozen sets out of one clump.

On the back fence, she wanted the little wild blue Morning Glories. There were a few big white ones growing on our creek bank. They were in the wild, but perhaps seed washed down the creek from a yard somewhere. We planted some of those on the fence. We also set out some Wisteria just over the fence to grow up trees. Yellow Jasmine were already growing there.

We went back to the cemetery in Leon County where Mother's family were put. Got a lot of those Spider Lilly snake looking egg balls they put on and shed. Over winter them under leaves or hay, then plant them they would come up.

Cassie was 13, Wade near 15. Between the oak and hardwood trees we planted needed to be bush hogged. They wanted the job. They were both competent tractor drivers. Her mother agreed to stay at the ranch that summer, providing I did not mind. I went back to making my own hot fried egg sandwiches.

"Start Monday. Check the oil, water in the radiator each morning. Friday at noon, bring the tractors to the shop. Clean up the tractor and bush hog Friday afternoon. Change the oil every three weeks. Put grease in every grease fitting. Check the transmission level. And the hydraulic fluid level. Check the oil level in the bush hog gear box.

"I'm going to pay you $70 for five eight-hour days. I'll pay you cash. If you get those tractors ready to go again in an hour or two Friday afternoon, you can go fishing."

They split the cost of some break time items, which Margaret got for them. Wade liked Cokes, Cassie Dr. Peppers. You could return those bottles, get a return deposit on them. Lance cheese and peanut butter crackers they wanted. Milky Way and Butterfinger candy bars also.

One day, about mid-afternoon, they went to a big post oak shade tree for a break. Shades were rare, this one happened to be up the east west road. Not far from the gate where you crossed the road into pasture three. They were mowing probably a quarter mile from that tree.

Cassie was sitting on the ice chest. Wade was sitting on the ground leaning against the tree. He had his rope, nothing much to rope but his foot. They heard a vehicle stop up near the gate and a door slam, but thought nothing about it. Lots of people used that road. Suddenly, Cassie whispered: "Look Wade, there's two dogs coming down the road!"

Wade looked. It was a big Walker hound dog and an almost grown Airedale pup. Wade said years later the big Walker seemed intent on probably a deer cold trail. The pup was just a nuisance to the old dog, he said. In front of him at times, trying to sniff the trail too, the pup was in the old dog's way.

The old dog was so intent, he got within ten feet of them before he raised his head and saw them. Wade's rope fell around his neck an instant later. Cassie grabbed the ice chest and retreated.

Wade dragged him snarling and growling to that tree. Tied him to that tree where snarling, growling would not, could not lead to him sinking his teeth into anything. The old dog knew that, he just resigned himself to whatever.

The old pup ran up like he knew not what to do. Wade grabbed him by the scruff of the neck and tied him with the loose end of the rope. Cassie came back to the shade, sat down on the ice chest to watch whatever Wade meant to do.

Wade went to the toolbox on his tractor. He came back with a roll of red ribbon we sometimes used to mark things with. A roll of black tape and a length of red hydraulic hose he found coiled up in the box.

He cut off a length of red ribbon. Grabbed that old dog's testicles. Quickly, he tied that red ribbon in a hard knot around that old dog's personals where it would not come off. Then he tied that red ribbon in a bow, the way folks tie shoe strings. Then he took the red hose, which was minus the end fittings, and taped it to the old dog's tail.

The old pup was laying there panting, like he really did not care what happened to the old dog. Wade worked up the spit in his mouth. The old pup was laying there with the tip of his you-know-what sticking out like all pups do.

Wade spit in the mouth of his empty coke bottle, grabbed the old pup and shoved that empty but slick mouth coke bottle on his you-know-what. The old pup acted like he was about to bite his arm, but stopped. Maybe it felt good to him. Anyway, the knot on his you-know-what was in the bottle. It could not come off.

Wade untied him first. The old pup got up moving around. He was just a near grown pup, but his legs were longer than the old dog. In the words to a popular country music song, that coke bottle was 'Just a Swinging!'

He turned the old dog loose. The old dog decided it was time to get out of Dodge. He ran about 20 yards. Then started going in circles trying to catch that thing tied to his tail. Wade ran after them with his rope yelling "Git from here! Git from here!"

The old dog lined out then. The old pup was right behind him. "Just a Swinging!" They left!

Wade turned around. Cassie had her arms folded leaning on the tree. Her head was on her arms. Her body was "Just a Shaking!"

My God, Wade said he thought. *Is she laughing or crying. Maybe I went too far doing this. Maybe she's in shock!*

Cassie finally turned around. She was laughing so hard she could hardly speak. "Wwwade wwhhy did yyou doo thhat to thhose dooggs!"

"If you turned your dogs loose in someone's property, and they came home looking like that, would you ever turn them loose in there again?"

Still laughing, she said, "No, I guess not!"

Wade in the lead, they hit the north road back to where they were working. Wade looked back. Cassie had stopped. Had her head on the steering wheel. Laughing!

Luther Fowler, Essie Mae's fiancé, let the dogs out. He knew how a deer would run when his dogs jumped. He had been hunting in that place since he was old enough to follow his daddy.

He drove out to the FM road, turned south, then north on the FM road that went into Wells. There was an old logging road that led across some property, then turned right down that ranch place fence. He knew just where a deer would jump that fence.

He killed a deer once, covered it with a ragged old tarp and pulled his plows over it. He met the man, the warden going home. He waved at him and laughed. He thought I was just another black dude going to plow a garden. He told Essie Mae he killed that deer in the Neches river bottom.

About two weeks ago, he was waiting to hear the dogs jump. A big old red hog with a white band rooted right up to him almost. He killed it. It was heavy. He had trouble getting it over that hog wire fence. He bent the wire down, pulled some staples out of posts in the process. His dogs knew the way home, he went on home with that hog.

He was about to turn down that fence when he saw a white pickup down where he killed that hog. He stopped, he could hear a hammer driving staples. "That's that man Wilson fixing that fence I tore up!"

He backed out of there, hit the road back the way he came. The old dog decided to follow the way his master's truck went. Luther met his dogs coming down the county road. "My Good Lord A'mity! What somebody don done to my dogs!"

He stopped, got out and scolded the dogs. Picked up a limb. Trashed his britches leg with it. "Git yo-self on home!" The old dog headed home. The thing behind him was driving him crazy! He would run for a short distance, go in circles trying to catch it. Then line out again. The old pup, well that coke bottle was still "Just a Swinging!"

He followed along slow. *If I lay's back a-ways, people won't know dey my dogs.* The dogs got to the place where water seeped out of the roadside banks. Both sides of the road. The county had not put in a culvert, you just drove through it. On the lower side of the road, Mr. Wilson hit it a lick with his dozer blade when he was cleaning out fence lines. Water stood in that recession all year long now.

Luther saw his dogs go off in it, lapping water like they had never had a drink. He let them cool off a few minutes. *Maybe dat cool water make dat coke bottle come offen dat long legged old pup. Who-eva dreamed of doing sech a thang to a po old pup anyway! It jist ain't right!*

He drove on down, scolded the dogs. Got them back in the road and headed home. Neither dog had lost any of their decorations. He meant to set there a minute, let them get on out front. It was a long uphill stretch of road ahead. A car came over the top of that hill, fishing poles sticking out of the rolled down passenger side window.

He knew who it was, recognized the car. Women that lived on the street he did in the settlement. *Essie Mae gon kno about dis fo sho. Ain't no way I gon hide dis from her.*

The women saw the dogs coming. Pulled over and stopped. Fishing poles hit the ground. They all got out, laughing, leaning on the car.

"Laudy mercy! What Luther don done to his dogs! They watched the dogs go over the hill top and out of sight.

Ize had it, Luther thought. He drove on. As he passed the women, he tried to act like his normal self. "How you ladies today?" he said as he passed.

One hollered back, "It's a long time till Christmas, Luther!" He saw her fall back against the car laughing.

His house was at the end of the street. Everybody had dogs. As his dogs ran down the street, all those dogs ran out barking in an attack mode. Doors came open. People came out on their porches laughing. One yelled "We didn't know you gonna have a parade today Luther! Is you running for Mayor?"

Luther tied the old dog in back of his house. It was a simple matter to cut the ribbons off of him. And the black tape that held the rubber hose on his tail.

He tried, but the coke bottle would not come off.

Old Jack, Essie Mae's older brother walked up. "What you trying to do Luther? Save dat dogs piss?"

Luther just ignored him. Jack never worked, let Essie Mae do that. Their Daddy left them the house, she let him stay. Jack walked out to the highway about once a month. Caught the bus up to Jacksonville. When he came back he had a little money.

Man across the street had a business selling white lightening by the drink or by the pint fruit jar. He also had a woman in the backroom that for ten dollars you could visit. Besides letting men roll dice, he offered them a deal on the lightening. "Buy a pint, drink half of it here in one hour. If you are still standing after an hour, you can visit the woman in the back room. At no extra charge!"

Jack never visited the women in the back room. But he did drink that white lightening and rolled those dice. When he passed out, the man had a couple of guys carry him across the street and lay him on the porch. Essie Mae just let him lay there until he crawled into the house.

When his money was gone, his mission was to antagonize Luther. He saw Luther's dogs go down the street. He knew if Luther and Essie Mae married, his free loading days might be over. He meant to make the most of a perfect opportunity.

Luther just left him standing there. He went in the house to his refrigerator. He had a couple of Lone Star beers left. He popped the cap on one, went back outside, and took a long drag on that bottle of Lone Star.

Old Jack wiped his hand across his mouth, "You ain't got anotha one of dem, haz you?"

"Diz de last one I got." And he started pouring the cold beer on the old pup's you-know-what.

"What you wasting dat good beer on dat dog fur?"

Luther never answered. He reached down and jerked that coke bottle off of the dog. The cold beer did the trick.

Luther just left old Jack standing there. He went in the house, cleaned up. Got dressed. Outside Jack had given up, went back to sit on the front porch.

Luther loaded up his dogs, took them to Alto, and sold the old dog to a man that had tried to buy him before. He gave him the old pup for good measure.

He found out accidently once, visiting a friend in Jacksonville. He saw old Jack in a neighboring house yard with three children and a woman. Jack never saw him. He told his friend Jack lived near him.

"Yeah, them chillun his'n. That women on welfare, he come about once a month when she got a little money. Den he's gone again!"

Luther knew that, but had not told Essie Mae. Today, Luther saw the light, he said. He had to change his ways and he knew it. He said whoever dat to his dogs made him knew he was in a rut he needed to get out of.

Jack was sitting on the porch when he got there. "What you doing heah? What you done done wid dem dogs?"

"Iz heah to talk to Essie Mae! And what I did with dem dogs ain't none of yo business! You need to get yo ass up outa that chair and git up to Jacksonville and take care of yo woman and yo chillun!"

Essie Mae had the door cracked open. She heard every bit of what he said. "Come on in Luther. What do you want to talk to me about?"

"I wants to marry you, and I wants it to be befo this week out! Ain't no kneed us fooling around no mo about it!"

"Well ok Luther. I been waiting for you to ask."

Rev. Billy married them the next Saturday night. Luther joined his church Sunday morning. He had seen the light.

Old Jack saw a light as well. He packed his clothes, caught the bus to Jacksonville! In time, he would come back to visit. He got a job as a chauffeur driving a wealthy business owner around. He married the woman, the welfare check stopped.

Monday morning Rev. Billy brought Luther to talk to me. Luther and Essie Mae had married. Luther needed a job.

Joe Ed had told me Luther was a good worker. That he had been laid off and was breaking gardens for people. And Rev. Billy thought all Luther needed was a job and a chance. A man that was a good worker and knew how to plow was someone we needed. I hired Luther, he got the same treatment Joe Ed did. Pickup truck, the works. It was a decision I would never regret.

My brother Regan H. and his wife went to Las Vegas. I suspect they must have won a great deal of money. If so, they never told any of us, but they bought 320 acres of land. Bought it from someone they attended church with. The house on it was down by the gate going into Jim Williams place. The driveway to the house was also a black top hard surface, wide landing strip. On each side were fairly good size live oak trees. Beyond the live oaks was a fence, to keep cows or whatever off the landing strip.

Regan H's son, Jeff, had been in South America for about eight years. He was an engineer, had worked for the Texas Highway Department. His wife flew the coup, left him with a two-year-old daughter.

Jeff took an engineering job with a company in South America that provided a house to live in, day care for his little girl and even a teacher after she was old enough. Needless to say, he was paid well.

He decided it was time to return to Texas. Where he worked in South America had become a little too politically unstable. He got his old job back working out of Palestine with the High Way Department.

He learned that the Jim Williams' place was up for sale. Jeff called me and asked if I might want to buy half of it.

"It's 1200 acres. I can't handle that much."

"Give me a couple of days to think about it. I need to talk to Margaret. I'll call you back. I know Jim Williams. Margaret has known him all her life. I may talk to him. Sort of a surprise to me he's selling the place."

Margaret may have been more excited about it than me. We both wanted the place. And to be honest about it, owning it would be somewhat of a tax write-off for me. Always take advantage of what the government will give you, Mr. Dobrinsky told me more than once.

I called Mr. Jim. "Jeff DuPree told me you were selling your place. Wanted me to buy half of it. I'm surprised you're selling it. I wanted to talk to you before I made any decision."

"Well Robert, it's like this. I have always held on to the hope that our only son would come back to Texas and live on it. He's married, owns a farm in California. Says he never expects to come back to Texas. You need to sell out, come live with me, he says.

"We're not getting any younger, we probably don't need to be here alone anymore. I'll let you DuPree's have it for $200 per acre. That's house, hook, line and sinker and all. I have already sold all my livestock."

I called Jeff back. "Margaret and I are ready to go on the deal. We need to meet Mr. Jim and his wife at the Justice of the Peace's office in Oakwood on Saturday to close the deal. Do you have any preference to which part you want?"

"I sort of want the side with his house on it. I want to fix it up and live there. My game plan is to lease most of it out for a hunting club."

"Ok Jeff. We really wanted the Buffalo Creek side. Looks like we both get the part we want. The Justice of the Peace is handling the deal for Mr. Jim. I'll bring my lawyer. You may want to bring one. My lawyer might charge you some, but he could handle your part as well if you want."

"If you will, just ask your lawyer to handle mine as well."

We got it all handled the next Saturday morning. Mr. Jim and his wife thanked us.

"We may be in California in a couple of weeks. My boy will come after us. We've either given away or sold everything. I got a fellow wants my pickup truck. We may not see you again in this life. But our headstones are in the Craig Cemetery now. We made our boy promise to send us back home when we pass on. We'll die knowing our place is in the hands of DuPree's and Martha's girl!"

Margaret was crying as she hugged them both goodbye. I felt like it.

We had lunch there in Oakwood. My lawyer advised us to get it surveyed. "With that information, I can get everything recorded in Centerville in one trip."

"Jeff, it's good to meet you. You don't owe me anything. Your uncle pays me enough to take care of everything." With that, he returned to Livingston.

Jeff and I drove out to the gate by his dad's home going into the Williams place. "Jeff, I'm not a surveyor, but I think the road to our camp house is going to fall in our 600 acres."

"I think you are right," he said.

"You said you wanted to lease yours to hunters. They will need to come in this gate. I got a dozer. This gate could stay open. Corner a fence right on this right hand gate post. Go straight ahead about 20 yards. Turn left with the fence."

"I'll put a gate in the road to our property. We'll get the surveyor to map out a road easement right down your dad's fence line to your property. I'll get the dozer over here. We'll clear out a road to anywhere you want it put on your property. Also clear out for the fence line between us."

"Sounds good to me," he said. "I can get a lot of crushed used asphalt for probably $25 a dump truck load for our roads from the High Way Department. If we had a dump truck!"

"I have a dump truck. Let's drive on down to the lower end of this place." I turned left down the road at our fence line at the Craig place. "See our camp house there, Jeff?" Then I pointed left. "The line between us is going to be somewhere about here. I would like to corner up there about a hundred yards, cross Keechi Creek. I'll drive across over there and show you why."

"All right. Mr. Jim always let the Craig's use the crossing, cross the creek. Then go back into their place on this side. If we do as I suggested, I just need enough on this side of the creek to get in that gate and back into Margaret's property."

"We can put a gate in the fence, so you can use this crossing. Also, we can bring a road all the way through your property, on out to this road we just crossed the creek on. Put a gate so you can cross the creek, go in your place on this end. Or up our road to your dad's house. I'll give you a key."

"I'll be honest with you, Jeff. I don't want a bunch of hunters near our camp house with 30:06'es. I don't want them in the road to our camp house, or anywhere near it."

"I don't blame you and I know what you mean. This all sounds fine to me. I don't intend to let them near my house. They'll have about 475 acres to hunt on. It's mostly pasture land on this side of the creek anyway. They can fish in the creek, but not cross it. I'll probably fence off what I need on this side of the creek and lease the rest for pasture."

"I might be interested in that. We've been thinking of putting cattle on Margaret's place. Call me if you do." We got it surveyed and worked out to suit us both. Easement and all. My lawyer told me, "Now this easement will be permanent from now on. Even if Jeff sells his property."

"That's fine," I said. "That easement keeps coon hunters away from our property!"

"I see what you mean," he said.

I asked Mr. Wilson and Joe Ed if they would agree to stay in our camp house until all the fencing and road work was complete. Monday, Tuesday, Wednesday, and Thursday start at 7a.m., work ten hours a days. Friday work five hours and come home for the weekend. They would get paid for 48 hours.

They would be there for almost four months that summer before completing all we needed done at the new and Craig place as well. Mr. Wilson and Joe Ed liked the hours, requested they continue to work that way at the ranch. Luther and Essie Mae were agreeable, that became the ranch 45 hour work week. It gave them a longer weekend to attend to their personal needs.

Jeff hired four men to build the fencing between us. I furnished the wire, posts and steel gates. Mr. Wilson used the lowboy trailer to haul the used poles we got from the electric company. They could cut, split as needed. Jeff furnished a tractor with a posthole digger.

Our tractor with the front end loader went over on a trailer behind the dump truck. Joe Ed used it to spread the used asphalt on roads, and the trailer to haul posts and wire to the fence builders. He also used the dump truck to go after that used crushed asphalt. It had good size lumps in it, but Mr. Wilson flattened it with the dozer.

We straightened out our road to the camp house. There were three different good holes on Buffalo Creek Margaret knew about. I had them build roads to those places to fish. And access to deer stands we meant to put up. All three roads had to cross the spring branch that came out of my brother's place.

After we were finished with the fencing between us, the fencing crew moved over to do the fencing Jeff needed done. That was what they did for a living, they did a good job.

When all the road work in Jeff's part and ours were complete to our satisfaction, Mr. Wilson and Joe Ed moved to the Craig place. Roads were built, that used asphalt spread. Three ponds were built for cattle water and crawfish ponds which I would stock from our ranch ponds. Strange thing I learned about East Texas. Crawfish were not very good catfish bait there. In Buffalo Creek, the blue channel and big flat head catfish got after them.

Two big sheds were built with hay and sack feed storage. The old Craig barn was in good shape. It would hold hay and feed. Sheds were built on both sides and the back for cattle to be fed under. A corral and loading facility was build there as well.

People may wonder why, at the ranch and at the Craig place as well, I built so many cow sheds. First, we had a lot of cattle. Second, if a cow could find protection from cold wind, rain, sleet or snow in the winter time, it conserved energy, which conserved fat. And I felt better about it sleeping in my warm bed.

Third, we fed all year a low protein, mostly salt feed under the sheds so rain would not ruin it. They only licked a little at the time. It made them graze more in the process.

We fenced off ten acres just past the cemetery. I got a well put down, they got good water at 25 feet. I bought a good used 16x80 foot 3 BR two bath trailer house. Set it up with propane tank, installed a sewer system. Set a meter pole and got electricity to it.

Before doing that, I made an agreement with my Cousin, Marvin's grandson. He married a girl at Oakwood. Had a day job in Palestine, they rented a house and lived in Oakwood. Paid their own utility bills.

They would move on the place, they would have ten acres for their personal use. No rent, they just had their utilities to pay for, which included propane.

All he had to do was look after our cattle. Feed them in the winter time. Call me if there were any problems. Beyond that, he had fishing and hunting rights on the Craig place. That I think cinched the deal.

Jeff got his place fenced the way he wanted it. He had a garden area and a place for two horses. A wooded area to hunt in and access to Keechi Creek. "Uncle Robert," he said, "I don't have time to fool with cattle. If you want to run your cattle on about 75 acres, have at it. They'll keep it from growing up, and I don't like to mow either!"

"We could use the pasture, Jeff. How much a year you want to get for it?"

"For you and Aunt Margaret, not a thing! I could not have had this place without your help."

He was living there now. He had cousin Marvin put Austin Stone around the house. He added on another big room for a living room, combined the once kitchen and living room into a more modern kitchen and dining room.

Something about having the ranch, people who wanted to sell their cattle came to Mr. Wilson. Sometimes he bought some, provided his grass was good and he could put weight on them. He never kept so many cattle, he bought lean and sold heavy. He made more money doing that, he said.

He found 25 head of young red angus heifers, and a bull. He called me. Told me what the fellow wanted for them. "It's a good deal." he said. "My pastures full up right now. I can't handle them. They would do good over yonder at the Craig place."

"Buy them out of the Well's account. Have Joe Ed and Luther take them over there. Why don't we hand pick about 12 head of red cows out of our pastures and put them over there while we're at it. Take a Santa Gertrudis bull over there as well. I sort of want to keep that bunch of cattle all red."

"That'll work," he said. "We'll get on it."

They had the FFA livestock show and sale every year at Livingston. I never tried to buy the grand champion. What I did do was try to buy each year at least two good heifers, or maybe two young bulls. I had four bulls and six Santa Gertrudis cows in my pastures already. I paid some kids a good price, but I got some good blood lines in the process. Those animals came with papers to be registered!

After we had roads and fences built, Marvin's grandson moved into the trailer. With Jeff's 75 acres, about 110 on the Craig place, we had about 185 acres pasture. Counting two bulls, we put 38 head of cattle on it. With so much carpet grass in the creek bottom, we thought it would handle that many.

It was a time for me to explore the 600 acres we bought on Buffalo creek. I took old buck over there, stayed in the camp house overnight. Let him loose in the fenced area Sam Craig kept his horse in. Plenty grass and water, he had a day ahead of him come tomorrow.

I rode up through the woods between our road and the fence that divided the 1200 acres. I rode back and forth from road to fence. Old deer rubs and tracks like I had never seen before. There were a number of myrtle head draws that wound up in Jeff's part and Keechi Creek. I rode up on both deer and hogs before I reached the north end of the place.

I took the road next to the fence to Buffalo Creek. We had it graded up and in good shape. There was a rocky bottom low water crossing on Buffalo Creek just below the fence. About 50 yards below that was about a hundred yards of good fishing water. Back away from the creek about 25 yards was a second bank you might say. It dropped straight down about eight feet. We graded a place down to get my pickup down to the creek.

Margaret and I had driven to the creek to check the road out. And she wanted to show me the fishing hole where she went with her Uncle Sam.

Back then we could not get past that spring branch. Uncle Sam drove slow, led a harnessed mule behind his pickup. We put everything in his boat and drug it with that mule to the creek. We always fished here when the dogwoods started to bloom.

Next to that embankment we found where someone had built a small fire. Two forked sticks on each side, even the stick they cooked something on. It was no telling how long it had been since someone had been there. It was not Uncle Sam Margaret said. No need for him to cook like that. And Mr. Jim never fished anywhere but in Keechi Creek.

I had dinner at the creek. A can of pork and beans, crackers and a can of Dr. Pepper. I had four cans in my saddle bag, I stuck them in the freezer when I got up this morning. They were still cold.

After I ate, I crossed the creek and headed down the creek bottom. The creek was crooked. It might be a hundred or three hundred yards out to the back fence of the place. Sloughs pushed me near it a few times. I could see a dim wagon road by it. The fence was in good shape.

But out in that creek bottom I saw what a virgin forest looked like. There were a lot of healthy oaks, some huge, some younger. Huge logs lay on the ground decaying. Other huge oaks were still standing, with broken big limbs, hollow and dead at the top. A few green limbs, but near death. Full of woodpecker holes. A haven for squirrels, coons and other wildlife.

This bottom land timber had never been cut. Some may think I'm not being truthful by saying this. I don't think I ever felt closer to God than I did in this wilderness that was just the way he created it.

I saw them before they saw me. I stopped old Buck to watch. Two Spotted Poland China sows and a big boar. About 15 good size pigs. They were rooting in a small open place for grass roots. Mr. Jim said he released them when he found Sam Craig's remains in that burned down house. These were descendants I felt sure of the hogs Dad sold to Sam.

To avoid disturbing them, I turned old Buck and rode out to the fence line. I thought I was near the old Centerville-Oakwood road. If so, I knew there was a good size button willow duck pond ahead of me anyway. I was right, I soon came to the old road.

It was July, the time for afternoon brief showers that might not be 50 yards wide or last ten minutes. Thunder and lightning indicated one was coming my way. I spurred old Buck and went to a huge Holley Tree I could see ahead. Thick leaves, it would provide some protection from the rain.

Under the shelter of the tree, I saw initials carved in the slick bark of the tree. B.D, W.B.D and B. F. D. Bethel DuPree, my great-grandfather. William Bethel DuPree, my grandfather. And Benjamin Franklin DuPree, my Dad. They were all up high, sitting on a horse like I was when they carved their initials into that tree bark.

140

I pulled out my Old Timer pocket knife to carve my initials below Dads. I thought of my promise to Mary Ellen and said, "Dear Lord, wherever Mary Ellen may be, let her be happy and well. Amen."

The words were just out of my mouth when a lightning bolt struck a sweet-gum tree not 40 yards from me. Old Buck never moved, which seemed strange. And he never seemed to be aware of that smell coming from that scorched tree.

Nobody to talk to but old Buck. "God just answered my prayer. Mary Ellen has found happiness and is well. He zapped that sweet gum tree to let me know that!"

I carved my initials below Dads. I crossed Buffalo creek to the camp house, loaded Old Buck and went home. I never told anyone about putting my initials on that tree, or the message I thought I received. I would not forget that it happened on July 23, 1965.

On the top of a hill on the 2400 acres, about five acres of big pines had been left by the timber company. Because of the nearly extinct Red Cockaded Woodpeckers nest holes in a number of those big pines. I thought the best thing to do for those woodpeckers was to fence it off. I enclosed about ten acres in the process of fencing it.

As soon as I got the employee hunting club going, it would be off limits to any hunting, going inside that enclosure for any reason. They might set up at the fence with binoculars and watch if they wanted to. The timber company of course reported it to the Parks and Wildlife. They sent someone occasionally to check on the birds. Asked me if I would be willing to let people drive in and see the rare birds.

My answer was no. This property is for my family, personal friends and employees. You people have a key. Study the birds all you want. But this is a working ranch, it's not going to become a public park!

The big place west of our cow pasture was wooded, had a big creek bottom in it. They stocked eastern wild turkeys there. I knew the owner, talked to him fairly often. He told me about the turkeys.

Some of the turkeys moved across our cattle pasture and crossed the county road. We saw them a few times. They were roosting in those tall pines where the woodpeckers were. I told the man about it. He just shrugged and said, "Looks like you got turkeys. Might be the best thing to get 'em started in both places. I'll need to tell the wild life people. They're trying to check on them, to see how they are doing."

"That should be no problem," I said. "The turkeys are roosting with those Red Cockaded Peckerwoods. They have a key, check on them very often."

It was during the May Squirrel season. Cassie and Wade were sitting very near that five acres of big pines in the creek bottom when daylight came. They heard those turkeys fly down, heard one gobble. Someone had given Wade a turkey call. He decided to see if he could call up a turkey.

After a little, they saw that gobbler come out to the edge of the pines. He would fluff up his feathers, then strut around and gobble. After ten minutes, he had not moved closer.

Once. Cousin Marvin heard Cassie mocking a rooster after he crowed. "She did that so well," Marvin said, "Go like a hoot owl." Cassie mocked a hoot owl. After that, he asked her to go like a bull frog, a cow, a donkey, a goat, and a number of other things. He finally said, "That girl can go like anything she wants to!"

Cassie, I suppose got into that turkey calling. That old gobbler up there on the hill gobbled again.

Cassie answered him. She went like a gobbler! It must have been perfect. Down the hill, that big bird came. Wade said in later years that gobbler was coming so fast, it looked like he was kicking his self in the rear end with his spurs.

He was ten yards away when Cassie blew his head off. Wade said that it looked like someone reached between that turkey's legs and flipped him on his back. Kicking!

Wade jumped up and grabbed the turkey's legs. He ran to a nearby thicket and threw the turkey out in it.

Cassie caught up with him. "Why did you throw that turkey away Wade?"

"Don't you know, it's against the law to shoot a turkey? Why did you shoot it anyway?" His voice sounded a little testy.

"Because, I thought he was going to jump on your hat! I'm going to get him. I want his tail feathers." She went out in the thicket and got the turkey.

He cut off the part the tail feathers were attached to.

"Your Daddy see's this, he may take our guns away."

"I'll tell Daddy, I killed the turkey. No need for you to worry about it!"

Wade said that he poked the turkey down into an armadillo hole, with his gun barrel. And hoped that nobody found it.

Cassie told me that she killed the turkey. She had his tail feathers. "The thing acted like it was going to jump on us. I think, it made him mad when I went like him."

"Well, he's a dead turkey and we can't bring him back. Best thing we can do is not tell anyone. Those Turkeys are on our place and sort of belong to us anyway. Just don't be calling those turkeys anymore until we get an open season to hunt turkeys."

I had the turkey tail put on a plaque and hung it on the wall in my office.

On the Craig place, near the marsh, were about two acres of the finest creek-bottom, black berries that I ever saw. They were later than the other wild berries. You could pick berries around it, but you could not get out in it.

While the dozer was there, I had Mr. Wilson run blade wide strips through it. Then leave about a blade wide strip. We could keep the open strip mowed with the bush hog. And have access to a lot of berries!

I got Essie Mae a Ford Van to seat eight people. Most of the part time workers had no transportation. She had to pick them up daily in the morning and take them home in the evening.

She could pick up the women workers and be at the Craig place in less than two hours. Luther would follow in his pickup with a 16 foot trailer and 25 five gallon buckets. They picked berries until the buckets were full, or for eight hours.

They usually made 12 hours that day, there and back. Luther brought the berries back, put them in the cooler. The next day, they were cooked down into juice, strained, and put in the freezer. Jelly making would take place as needed.

At the place where we bought used metal pipe, they had a stack of used eight inch PVC pipe. I bought 15, 20 feet long. I put them on the ground beside our cleared lanes in the berry thicket. I knew swamp rabbits would go in a hollow log, if chased by a dog. I put them there in February.

I made six inch long blocks out of a seasoned dead pine I cut, which just fit into those eight inch pipes. On each center end of each block, I screwed in a fitting with a ring on the end. Tied 12-feet of trotline cord to each end.

Joe Ed had four beagle rabbit dogs. In October, we went over there. With a length of stiff wire, I centered those blocks in those PVC pipes. With the 12 foot long cords, you could pull the block out from either end. And a swamp rabbit!

I put the blocks in, late one evening. Joe Ed was there the next morning with his beagles. That day, Cassie and Wade, Joe Ed and I put 22 swamp rabbits in a cage in the back of my pickup. Those beagles put those rabbits in those pipes!

Seldom did we see a swamp rabbit in our creek bottom at the ranch. They had been hunted too much for too many years. We scattered them out in our creek bottom and planned to do it again, the next year. I never hunted rabbits, but Joe Ed and Luther did.

The mustang grapes grew on fence rows, up trees all over Leon County. To eat many would blister your lips, they were such strong acid. I felt that would not bother a hog or a deer. And the seed that turkeys, quail, and doves would get after.

Mr. Wilson bought enough used two inch pipe to put up five besides the roads, in the 2400 acres. They would be 6 feet high and 84-feet long. Each joint of pipe was 21 feet. The post pipe that he cut, would be set in concrete.

I got the seed at the Craig place; planted those Mustang Grapes. In the produce field, we had wild post oak and muscadine grapes growing on six feet wide concrete mesh, six feet off the ground. You could stand under it and pick grapes. We made jelly from those. The mustang grapes were for wildlife only.

I told my forest service friend that I wanted about 500 cypress seedlings to put out in the shallow upper part of the lake, at the ranch. He brought me about 5000. Nobody else had ordered, I got 4500 for free!

We had a week of rain; the creek was on a rampage. The high water was the perfect opportunity to paddle up into otherwise not accessible areas of the lake to plant cypress seedlings. Mr. and Mrs. Wilson, Cassie and Wade, Margaret and I set out one Saturday morning to get it done in three flat-bottom boats.

The boys did the paddling and the girls did the planting. Benton Craig was along for the ride. The seedlings were small, four-foot pine tomato stakes were all that was needed to stick a hole in the mud, drop a seedling in and move on. We covered the area in a couple of hours.

We had sandwiches for lunch, back at the lake dam. We probably had 4200 cypress seedlings left. Wade kept pitching a few out in the lake and watched as they went over the spillway and down the creek. After a few minutes, he said, "We could go up yonder to the creek bridge, throw these seedlings in, a few at the time and plant cypress trees to the Neches River and down it!"

The creek was out in sloughs, low places on the ranch. *We would get a good many,* I thought, *to live.* Along the creek bank, sloughs; wherever they drifted to.

"That's a good idea, Wade! Who wants to help me this afternoon?"

"Count me out," Margaret said. "I have had enough of this fun already!"

"Likewise here," said Mrs. Wilson.

Mr. Wilson with Cassie. Wade and I went up to the FM road bridge. We took lawn chairs. We sat there, pitching cypress trees into the raging, swirling hurricane creek water. If you threw in too many, they became tangled up in a wad. We had to take our time about it. We got rid of the seedlings. Time would tell if we wasted our time or not.

We had four young mules to break. Two brown, one black, and one paint mule. Somehow, the Jack managed, without any help, to score with Cassie's paint mare. She was incensed about it for a while, but I asked her if she had ever seen a paint mule? I never had. Sometimes, having the one and only can change a person's disposition. She was thrilled when that paint mule colt arrived.

The paint mule and the two brown mules, Luther and I rode with no problem. The black mule was a different story. One Saturday morning, Luther and I both tried to ride him. He kept throwing us both. He beat both of us up. And every time that son-of-a-gun jumped, he farted.

I went home for lunch. My shoulder was killing me. I told Margaret that black farting mule is killing me and Luther. "We can't break him to ride!"

"Did you turn the mule out?"

"No, we left him in the corral. He's got feed and water. I'm going to meet Luther in the morning. We're going to try riding him again."

"I'll go with you in the morning. Mother never knew it, but Uncle Sam taught me how to break horses and mules. I'll ride him. He's going to kill you and Luther!"

We got the mule in the shoot. We put Margaret's saddle on him. She brought a hoe and leaned it up against the shoot. She had her leather gloves. She got on that mule. Folded a leather glove over an ear. Then bit it, long and hard. She did the same to the other ear. I could see that mule's eyes. Mad he was!

She straightened back up in the saddle and said, "Luther, take that hoe handle and lift his tail up to where I can reach it." Luther did as he was told. She grabbed that mule's tail, twisted that hair around her hand and pulled his tail over her shoulder. "Now let him out of here!"

We could not believe our eyes. She spurred that mule every time his feet hit the ground and farted. And she leaned forward and pulled hard on that tail. She wore that mule down to just standing there. She spurred him to go again. He would walk a little; no more buck to it.

"Open the gate and let him out in the road," she said.

She rode that mule a half mile down the road. She had him stopping, turning, and walking like a mule should, on the way back.

"Mr. Robert, Miz Margaret done rode dat mule till he ain't got a fart left in him!"

When she got back, she grabbed that mule's ear and whispered in his ear, before she got down.

"What you tell dat mule Miz Margaret?" Luther asked.

"I told him that if he gave you and Robert any more trouble, I'd come back and ride him again!"

Later she explained it to me. "It's one thing to ride a horse or mule for eight seconds in a rodeo. It's another to break one to ride or work. You got to show him you are meaner than he is. A horse or mule can't lift his tail but so high. If you pull it beyond that, it hurts. Biting his ear helps. They're not all that dumb, they get the message!"

The mule never bucked again. But riding behind him was risky. If he was touched with spurs, he would stop, kick as high as he could, and fart.

"I can't break him from that," Margaret said.

I had one of the brown mules at Livingston. With the turning plow and Georgia Stock, I grew produce for ourselves, but also for seed. I bought a bushel of red ripper peas once, liked them but dried most for seed. I never had seen any in Leon County. I was told they were getting hard to find in East Texas anymore. That and the pink and yellow DuPree corn were big sellers in our garden supply store.

For the first time since I became a member of the Livingston Independent District School's Board of Directors, I had an opponent. The guy was a newcomer to town, had an office job with the telephone company. He was hot-to-trot in civic affairs. My guess was that he wanted to start with the School Board, then try to advance, step by step, to a Senate seat in Washington D. C. He ran an advertisement in the local newspaper which focused on two things:

1. *We need a new High School built for our growing population and we need it now!*
2. *How could a farmer who spends most of his time behind a mule possible understand the growth needs of our Livingston Independent School District?*

I had seen the dude pass a few times, even waved at him when I was plowing in the evenings, after my work day. He never waved back. Which put him in a class of you-know-what people, as far as I was concerned. Margaret and Cassie saw the advertisement in the newspaper. It made them fighting mad. Myself, people knew me. I thought the guy was actually helping me by his comments.

Homecoming week was coming up. Friday morning there would be a parade featuring the homecoming High School Queen. Friday night the football game. Then Saturday night political speeches. A friend who organized the parade, and knew we had horses, wanted us to lead the parade with the U.S, Texas, and the High School Banner flags.

Margaret and Cassie decided, no we won't ride our horses. We'll ride our mules! I had one mule at home, the other three were at the ranch. Luther was at the ten acre food plot plowing the brown mule. We found the black and paint mule in the pasture.

"I'm not riding that windy black mule Margaret said."

Cassie had a quick answer. "I'll ride him Momma! You can ride my paint mule."

We rode the mules from the house to the north end of town where the parade would start. The organizer of the event put the convertible with the home coming queen and her escort out front. Next, I want you three flag bearers to follow. Behind you three the rest of the horseback riders. Then the High School marching band.

"John," I said, "Animals don't care where they do their business. Maybe you should put the Marching Band in front of us."

"I never thought of that," he said. "Yall follow the marching band."

I was on the left with the American Flag. Margaret was in center with the Texas Flag. Cassie was on the right with the Livingston High School Banner. The streets were lined with people. A roar of applause went up as the High School Band passed the Court House Square.

I saw my opponent before we got there. He was standing in front of the corner drug store. He had a bunch of campaign circulars that he was trying to give to people. People seemed to be sort of avoiding him; he had the corner to himself!

When we got even with him, Cassie turned the black mule sideways and stopped with the mule's rear facing the man. She hit his ribs with her spurs three times. Three high rear end kicks and three loud farts! She then turned the mule and caught up with us.

A roar of applause went up from the crowd! Margaret's neck was a little red, but she never looked back. I knew she was as proud of our daughter as I was. I did look back at the man. He looked like a mule had just farted in his face!

Saturday night, the political speakers were seated on the bed of a flat-bed truck trailer. It got down to my opponent. We were told to hold it to 15 minutes. He went over and beyond with a tirade of "We must have a new High School and we must have it now!"

It came my turn to speak: "Good evening Ladies and Gentlemen. I know most of you. For those that may not know me, I'm Robert DuPree. And I thank you all for your patience and coming out to night.

I have something in common with many of you. I have a daughter in our High School and I pay taxes. Taxes are a burden on all of us, and to build a new High School will increase that burden.

Currently, there are five more students in our 1st grade class than there are in our 12th grade class. We've did a study, and as the population increases, the number of that 1st grade class predictable may increase by five more by the time they are in 12th grade.

Must we build a new and bigger High School now? I'll leave that decision to you. I thank you again for coming out tonight, and may God Bless each of you!"

I received a roar of applause and later won by a landslide victory. The man got 11 votes out of over 650 cast.

We shut the gate on the ten acre food plot in late summer. We only meant to mark the young boar pigs and shoats. Cull out the Russian strain of hogs. We captured the big Russian boar.

I got a nylon rope behind his tusks on his snout. Hitched to a pickup, he was pulled up to the oak board fence, his snout sticking through. I got in the pen and did a complete marking job on him. Which included cutting his tail off and putting Dad's old crop-split-in the right ear. His left ear had a diamond shaped mark punched in it by someone probably when he was a pig.

We loaded him, his offspring with the Russian strain into the cattle trailer. We backed it up to a bluff bank on the Neches River which bordered our new property I bought. They had to swim the river to the other side, which was National Forest land.

The deer I decided had become too much of a risk to take to Leon County. But we had to pen them, I gave them a spray job to kill ticks and lice. In the pen, was a monster eight-point buck with guess what? He had Dad's old crop-split-in the right ear mark. As the crow flies, that deer had traveled 100 miles, crossed two rivers and came home. The only deer I put that mark on was released in Leon County.

The new property I had recently bought was 1500 acres across the FM road west of the ranch. The owner had once farmed, had cattle on it. He lived in Rusk, grew old and sold all his cattle. Leased the place out to hunters to pay the taxes. He and his wife had two daughters who indicated they had rather they left them money than land.

I personally thought owning land was better than money in the bank. I also wanted to go in the hog business. Big time. Raise the corn to fatten them. Grow field crops to turn the sows, shoats and pigs into to keep from buying much feed. Also grow hay or clay peas to bale for cow feed. I wanted more pasture for cattle. The boundary on the back side of the place was the Neches River.

The east edge of the place was next to the county road that the west edge of Justin Wilson's place was on. Mr. Wilson's place never went all the way to the river however. The county road ended going into a place below his that was owned by a man by the name of Buford Trahan. He was a good man, he allowed us to drive in to the river and fish when we wanted to. I had to have the place surveyed anyway. I had 500 acres surveyed across from the Wilson place on down by the Trahan place to the Neches River. I had plans for that, but got on with developing the remaining 1000 acres first.

I got the Mexican crew back out of Wells. I drew up a blue print of what I wanted. What I wanted was to develop the hog business first. Then the other later. We had to have a corn storage barn big enough to hold 25 acres of ear corn. We had to have a modern electric corn sheller. We had to have a hammer mill to grind cob and shucks. We had to have a bigger compost facility than we had near the produce field.

I set aside 50 acres for corn growing. We would try 25 acres the first year. If two much corn for a year, we could cut back. If not enough, we could increase the number of acres. And if necessary take in more pasture. One way or another, half of the corn land needed to rest a year. And have a lot of hog compost and liquid hog waste disked into the soil.

The fattening pen had to hold 30 to 40 head of hogs. That's about what I hoped to ship once a month. It had to have a roof over it, with four big fans blowing down on the pen in hot summer time. The feed trough was in front, they could be fed from the corn storage barn. Two 55 gallon drums were filled about half full of shelled corn daily. Then filled on up almost full with water. Soaked overnight and fed the next day.

The hogs could not get up in the barn, those barrels set on a four foot wide raised plat-form. The trough sloped slightly so it could be washed out to a door at one end into a sloping concrete ditch. Which ended up in a sloping concrete ditch in back of the pen.

Hogs went to the back of a pen to do their business. Daily that concrete ditch would be pressure washed down into an underground concrete storage tank. It would be outside of the fattening pen.

The raised platform to feed from was open to the fattening pen, but walled up into the corn storage room with a ramp to the door. Half a barrel of shelled corn could be pushed up that ramp easily with a two-wheeler. The corn storage room had a concrete floor a tractor could drive in through double doors. Or the new dump truck I bought to gather corn in. The building was designed to keep rats out.

To gather corn I bought a machine to do that, it put the ear corn in the dump truck. In the building, was a portable conveyor which piled the corn high. Two men shoveled corn in with corn scoops off the floor. It was on wheels, it could be moved across the floor as needed

The concrete storage tank bottom was fitted with four one inch perforated PVC pipes about two feet apart. Twice daily each one would receive about three minutes of compressed air to mix and keep it from settling out. And oxygen was needed to keep the bugs in the tank alive and working.

That underground tank was pumped into the top of a 30 thousand gallon steel storage tank. It was equipped with a float inside attached with wire to a weight outside. If the weight was at the top of the tank, it was empty. At the bottom, full. The tank itself was equipped with a pump to either circulate, load into the liquid spray tank we had, or spray on the hammer mill chopped cobs and shucks in the compost facility.

Mr. Wilson and Joe Ed cut holes in 20 inch pipes a hog could get his snout in to drink, but he could not get in it. Each end was welded shut with flat iron. A two inch pipe with valve was put on one end. One 20 feet long was set in the center of the pen so it could be washed down into the rear concrete drainage ditch. The fattening pen was 30 by 40 feet in size.

The floor had to be cleaned out after each shipment and put in the compost facility. It was replaced with hammer mill beat up cobs and shucks before the next bunch were put into it to fatten.

A big slough ran by the edge of the river bottom. Once, I figured it to be the old river channel. It was deep, the man said it never dried up completely. We bridged it next to the west fence and built a road to the river. Took some doing and used two inch pipe welding, we put fences across it on both sides of the hog pasture. A hog wire fence enclosed the back side of the pasture across the slough.

Between the west fence and the hog farm I planted 25 acres of live oak trees. It would be years before it needed to be fenced hog proof, but when the acorns did fall it would save a lot on the winter feed bill.

The slough was within ten acres most of the hogs not in the fattening pen could get to. Exceptions were two boars under two separate pens with sheds. We had also four farrowing pens with sheds. Sows were put in these to have their pigs. They were kept in the pen about a month before released into the hog pasture and fields.

We fenced off 80 acres into four separate 20 acre fields. A fenced in travel road was built in front of all four fields for tractor and farm equipment as well as hogs. A gate opened into each field. Across from the gate was one of those 20 inch water troughs. Also in each field we dug a good size pond.

We staggered planting times of the fields mostly with Mississippi Silver Skin Crowder Peas and a row of Watermelons occasionally. The last field for fall and winter would be the Silver Skin Crowders. Porta Rican Sweet potatoes and Purple Top Turnips. The hogs would eat vines, peas, sweet potatoes, tops and turnips.

We put down an artesian well, which supplied water for the hog farm. We put a pump on a pressure wash down system, it was free flow to everything else we needed. The excess was piped up beside the outside road fence to the four fields on into the cattle pasture. We could keep one of the four field water troughs full of water whenever needed

Beyond the hog farm, water from the well ran into a concrete water trough out in the cow pasture. From there it drained into a spring branch which crossed the place and the road into Mr. Wilson's property. A number of holes were dipped out in the branch with the back hoe for more places for cattle to get water.

I found a hog farm in Louisiana that had the newly developed long bodied hogs called Spots. I suppose they evolved from the Spotted Poland China hogs like Dad once had. I bought 16 gilts and two boar shoats that were breeding age. This I done in early January. Corn would be planted in February. By the time it was harvested that fall, I should have 30 to 40 head of hogs ready for the fattening pen.

Sows could have pigs twice a year easily. Four sows should produce 30 to 40 pigs. I got number tags to put in sets of four sows. They were bred four at the time each month to have pigs a month apart. It takes almost four months for pigs to be born.

The Mexicans we had on the payroll would run the hog farm we decided. Two would be off Sunday and Monday. The other Friday and Saturday. Corn for Sunday would be put in soak Saturday. Wade was in ninth grade in High School now, he worked in the evenings after school. I would give him four hours Sunday evening to help the one working. Luther would help him on Monday.

But Mr. Wilson, Joe Ed and Luther needed help now that the Mexicans were gone. Wade wanted to go full time when he finished his senior year. I knew Mr. Buford Trahan's son Cole worked off shore. His wife and two kids were there with Mr. Buford. His wife had passed away a couple of years ago.

I went to visit them. We went out on the back porch to talk. From there you could see to the Neches River and Hurricane Creek. All the underbrush was cleared, they kept it mowed, only a few May Haw trees were left among the big oaks and sweet gums.

His daughter-in-law brought us coffee. And sat down with us on the porch. "This is such great view from this porch," I said. "I think I would sit out here all the time!"

"I do most of the time," he said. "Strange thing has happened. We got little cypress trees growing on the creek bank all the way across this place. How that has happened I don't know."

"I regret to tell you I'm guilty. I told him what we did with all those seedlings the forest service brought us. We can come down and pull them up if you don't want them."

"Oh no, they'll be valuable timber someday! I just wondered how they got there. That creek was about as wild as I ever saw it in my 75 years."

"Mr. Trahan, I know Cole works off shore. I was wondering if he might consider working for me. We provide our help with health care, a retirement plan. A new Ford pickup to drive. Mr. Wilson and other hands like to work four ten hour days starting at 7am and five hours Friday morning. They like Friday evening and Saturday to have more time for personal business."

""I'm sure he would be interested," Mr. Trahan said. "What do you think Lucy?"

"God and I knows he would be," she said. "He so tired of driving all the way to Cameron Louisiana and being on that boat 24 hours a day. It's the only work he could find. He will be in Friday. I'll tell him you asked.

Tell him I'll be up here Saturday Morning. Have him come talk to me if he's interested. We'll go over everything. Both of y'all and the kids come with him if you want to. You can meet my wife and our kids".

Cole and his wife came Saturday morning. They left the kids with Grandpa Buford. They met Margaret, Cassie and Benton Craig. Margaret had coffee and cookies, we sat at the kitchen table and talked. I went over wage scale, retirement plan, health care and details about the pickup truck. Then explained what all the job involved.

He accepted the job. I could tell they were both happy about it.

If you'll meet me here Monday morning about 7am, we'll go to Livingston and get the paper work done. You'll get eight hours Monday. Tuesday just meet Mr. Wilson down at the shed at 7am. He'll show you how to punch the time card, show you where the fuel tanks are and around the place. I'll give you keys to everything Monday.

Monday morning we got his paperwork done. I showed him through all our business. Explained he would probably be coming here often to pick up things needed at the ranch. I took him to the house for lunch. Margaret had fried chicken, green beans, mashed potatoes, homemade biscuits and gravy for lunch.

Shortly after lunch he left in the new Ford pickup for home. It had the Shady Oaks label on the doors and he seemed happy about it all. So was I.

The hog farm used up about 130 acres. Out of the 1000 acres, that left 870 acres. About 300 acres of that was hardwood river bottom land. Which I fenced off. Cattle don't need acorns and they can swim a river.

70 acres I put into fenced farm land to raise the clay peas for hay, a ten acre bull pasture, and five acres for chinquapin trees and pigmy plum trees. Margaret knew where both grew on the Jim Williams place we bought. We got the seed there.

The chinquapin trees would be a half mile from the nearest timber. Hopefully far enough away that squirrels would not get them! But the acorn like seed they produced people liked to eat. I thought they could be bagged and sold for a good price. I also thought that would be several years after I left this earth!

The pigmy plum trees seldom got three feet tall. They were rare also. Driving down Texas highways or country roads you might see one in a fence line blooming in the springtime. There was a place out on the farm at cedar creek where we found enough to collect the plums and make jelly.

Three rows with seed planted three feet apart were put between the chinquapin trees. With luck I might see us make Shady Oaks Wild Pigmy Plum jelly before I passed on! But in my mind this five acres was a conservation effort that I hoped would spread to other areas in time.

We kept four bulls to move from pasture to pasture each month. A fifth bull followed each month to take care of anything missed. The ten acres was a rest area for the bulls, or a place to sell them after they needed to be replaced.

About a third of the remaining 55 acres was planted in the hay or clay peas each year. We had a round hay baler now. The pea vine hay we used to feed cattle only. The rest of the 55 acres got a rest and a lot of hog juice and compost fertilizer. We never ate anything fertilized with hog waste.

The remaining 500 acres was divided into two 150 acre pastures and one 200 acre pasture. Each pasture had a shed that contained a small storage barn for sack feed. The rest of that side was for round bale storage. The other side of the shed had feed troughs.

Ten acres were fenced off in the 200 acres at the edge of the Neches bottom for a hay meadow. We could not feed horses and mules pea vine hay. It balls up in their digestive tract and often kills them.

To avoid any confusion among employees, signs were painted and hung on the gate into each. Example: East Pasture One. Across the road: West Pasture One. Same thing for 2, 3, and 4. And also the east and west new 150 acre pastures 5. The new 200 acres was labeled "Hay Meadow Pasture."

This may sound ridiculous to label pastures like this. But if Mr. Wilson said take the Santa Gertrudis Bull out of West Pasture One and put him East Pasture Five, there should be no mistake made. Even by a new employee.

Next to work on was the 500 acres I had surveyed next to the county road and across from Mr. Wilsons place. I put a road through the center of it from the FM road to the Neches River. Starting at the FM road, I put 150 acre pastures on both sides of the road. Each side had a shed to feed under, also a sack feed storage barn and storage for round bales of hay.

Water was problem in these two pastures, we dug three ponds in each. If they should go dry, the cattle could be released into the 200 acre pasture where there was a spring branch and the Neches River. And soon a lake!

I put a cattle guard going into the 200 acres. A gate next to it going into a corral you could drive cattle through and out a gate into the 200 acres. The corral had loading facilities and a shed like the ones in the 150 acre pastures. Cattle could be put in the corral from any of the three pastures.

We put a dam on the spring branch in the 200 acre pasture creating about a seven acre lake. The west side fence line centered it to serve two pastures. We set two inch pipe posts in concrete, welded three quarter inch concrete rebar to fence across the lake. We put a gate in the center we could get a boat through.

In case the smaller ponds dried up, half of a seven acre pond could now water cattle in a 500 acre tract of land. The other half was in my "Hay Meadow Pasture." In the Neches bottom, I fenced off 30 acres next to the west fence. It ran up to some fertile hillside land you could farm or plant winter crops for cattle. Down in the lower part you could cut hay.

We got all that finished. The crew finished seeding with Bermuda, Dallas and Carpet grass. The carpet grass seed we got from sweeping it up in the barns after the hay was gone. I bought some of the Dallas and Bermuda seed.

Everybody had gone but Mr. Wilson and I. We were setting on the tail gate of his truck drinking a cold Dr. Pepper. "Get some rain to get this grass up, and the ponds full, you should be able to put cattle in these pastures by July of next summer."

"Well, I guess I could. Can you bring a hundred dollars and meet me at my lawyer's office in the morning at nine?

"I think I can find a hundred dollars. But why do I need it?"

"You are going to buy the 500 acres we are sitting on for a $100."

"Robert, are you serious about this? I don't feel right about doing it."

"I am serious. I could not have accomplished all that I have here and in Leon County without you and Wade. You know as well as I what I had to start with was given to me. The $100 is just a formality we have to go through. I'll give it back to you after we finish the paperwork."

"I'll have 820 acres! The size ranch I've always dreamed of! All these barns, the corral and the lake! You paid for all that knowing you were going to sell it all to me for a $100?"

"Margaret and Cassie know about it and wanted me to do it. I have only one request to ask of you. You'll need to tell Mrs. Wilson and Wade. Anybody else, well I just bought a thousand acres and you bought 500. Like I said, you and Wade have earned it. I can't do this for every employee I have."

I understand. "We'll zip our lips!"

Chapter Ten

My Life is Threatened.
Mary Ellen Comes Back and Marcella Gets Even!

Mr. Wilson and Wade took some calves to the Buffalo Auction one Saturday. Mr. Wilson did not want to miss seeing his calves come through the ring. He knew how to yell "PO" if he thought the price was not up to snuff. He sent Wade to the restaurant to get them a hamburger and drink.

He was sitting at the counter waiting on his order when a man sat down next to him. The man struck up a conversation with Wade and got around to saying "I buy cattle and hogs for a number of different businesses. I need hogs for a business in Oklahoma and I can't find any. Seems people have quit raising hogs."

"My boss is getting close to getting his hog farm ready to start selling fat hogs. He has 38 head in the fattening pen now. He expects to sell 30 to 40 head a month."

"How many a month?"

"30 to 40 head. Every how many 4 of those Spot sows will produce a month."

"Spot Sows. Likely they'll produce more than 40 a month after their first litter. He must have quiet an operation going. Where is he located and how could I reach him. I'd like to make him an offer on those hogs."

"The farm is in Cherokee County near Wells Texas. My Dad is his ranch foreman. Mr. Dupree lives in Livingston Texas. He has a number of business places there."

"I'm going to be at the Livingston Sale Monday. Any chance you could give me his phone number. Is he the owner of the DuPree Ford place there?"

"He's the one. I'll give you his office phone number. If he's not there, they'll tell you where to reach him."

The man called me early Monday morning. Said his name was Tommy Cassels. "I live near Durant Oklahoma. I go to auction sales, and buy cattle and hogs for a number of different concerns. I talked to your foreman's son at the sale in Buffalo Saturday. He said you would soon have 30 to 40 head a month of fat hogs to sell. I'd like to talk to you, make an offer to buy all you get ready each month."

"Where are you now?" I asked.

"My wife and I are at the Lively Motel. She travels with me most of the time."

"Wonder if you could come to my office? It's not but a short distance away."

"Tell me where and I'll be there shortly!"

I gave him directions. Margaret told me Tommy Cassels was the name of the man who drove the U-Haul truck to move them to Highlands. And the man said he was from Oklahoma.

He was there shortly. He introduced himself as Tommy Cassels. And got down to business. "Is it true, Mr. Dupree, you expect to sell 30 to 40 head of fat hogs a month?"

"Yes sir, it is. The long bodied 'Spots' hogs. Fattened on corn."

"I can offer you a nickel a pound above whatever the current market price is. And the company I buy for will send a truck to your place and pick them up."

"We got truck weigh scales on my property. They are tested about three times a year. Do you think that will suit the people you're buying for?"

"They weigh in heavy and after unloading light at the plant. There should be no problem unless there is a lot of difference."

"Mr. Cassels I'm willing to give that a try. To be honest about it, finding a market for those hogs has been bothering me. But there is one more question I need to ask you."

"Let me have it. I'll answer the best I know how."

"Ok then, Mr. Cassels. Did you ever drive a U-Haul truck to a few miles north of Centerville Texas, load up a family's belongings and wave at a boy sitting on the tail gate of a red pickup truck as you left out with the load? And move the family to Highlands Texas?"

"I did and I'll never forget it! I don't think I ever wanted to kill a man so bad as I did the man that hired me to do that. He treated that woman and kids horrible. But how did you know about all that?"

"I was the boy sitting on the tail gate of that red pickup truck. And my wife's name is Margaret. She told me what your name was. And that you were from Oklahoma."

"Margaret! Her mother put her in the truck with me. That crazy man was giving her such a bad time. She told me he made her leave without telling the boy she was going to marry, good bye or where they were moving to."

"We moved here shortly after they left. We had a daughter almost nine years old before I found her. Margaret would be so glad to see you and meet your wife. If you are not leaving town after the sale, we would be happy to have you come and have supper with us tonight."

"We don't like driving at night much anymore. We got the motel for tonight, so we could do that. We're going to head home in the morning. Jeffie will be so happy you two are together and doing well. She prayed for Margaret and those kids after I told her how their daddy treated them."

They came and had supper with us. With Tommy and Jeffie Cassels, it was like being with people we had always known. After returning home after finding no work in Texas, a couple of oil wells were brought in on their property. It never made them rich, but it gave them a start.

After I told him I was trying to have about 30 head of calves for sale every two months, he was interested in buying those. "Call me when you are ready to sell. If I have a buyer, I can give you a little more than the current market price. And send a truck after them. Cattle are more plentiful than hogs, I can't guarantee I'll have a buyer every month."

They were going to pass near the ranch, going home. He was interested in seeing our operation, so I gave him directions to the ranch. After they left, I called Wade and told him to expect them and give them a guided tour.

It came to us through Katrina. Their father had been staying with Harry. Harry told him Margaret and I were married. That I was the Daddy of Cassie. Where we lived, where the ranch was and that Margaret now owned the Craig place. And that we also bought half of the Jim Williams place.

It sent the old boy into a rage. "I'll find that little DuPree farm plow boy and I'll kill him! Margaret thinks she can lie to me and get away with it, she's got another thought coming! I'll kill her man! Mark my word, I'll kill him! He won't be the first I've stabbed in the back."

Dear Reverend Harry, I thought. Now that you've told the old boy where to find us, you tell Katrina to warn us!

Margaret was upset about it. He killed Uncle Sam and we know it. He means what he says. He has never wanted me to be happy, or have anything. That's the main reason he killed Uncle Sam. He could not stand to see me happy when I was with him. No telling what he would do to Cassie or Benton Craig if he snoops around and finds out what they look like.

That's my main concern. I can watch my back, but I can't be with them at school. I know the Superintendent real well, I'll talk to him about having the teachers keep an eye out for strange older men.

I talked to the Superintendent. "Robert we're already keeping a close watch on your kid and any strangers around the school. For children with wealthy parents we feel the need to do that. Kidnapping children for ransom money happens more often than you might think."

I thanked him. I suppose being wealthy enough someone might kidnap our kids for ransom had never entered my feeble gourd. Now I realized that one lunatic was not all we had to worry about. It could be someone we knew, or a complete stranger.

Margaret and I talked it over. We had our way of life, what we had to do and finding enjoyment in the process would not be stopped by fear of a lunatic or some stranger!

Back on the farm out at Cedar Creek in Leon County, Sunday evening was a get-together with neighboring friends. The Heston family lived on one side of US 79, the Bolton family lived across on the other. Tommy Heston was about my older brother Melton's age. Charles Ray, his younger brother was my age. Nancy Kaye Bolton was Regan's age. Faye and Annie were a little older than Nancy.

We all met at Dad's cane mill on Sunday evening, weather permitting. Winter time, we might have parched peanuts. Summer time a couple of water melons. Come fall of year, ribbon cane stalks to chew on for the juice. Somehow or another we always wound up on Caney Creek Bridge to do that.

Nancy Kaye's Dad, Bill Bolton grew up near Keechi on a farm that Buffalo Creek ran through. He worked for the depot manager at Keechi. The manager was transferred to Buffalo. The manager asked Mr. Bolton to move to Buffalo also, work for him there.

Ruth, Bill's wife was not in good health. He sold the farm he had inherited. Then he bought eight acres across from the Heston's and built a home there.

William "Bill" Bolton was drafted into WW11. He was killed in action in Germany. His body was returned to Leon County and put in the Bolton Family Cemetery on the place he sold.

His wife Ruth received a small pension for his service, which she and Nancy Kaye, with help from the Heston's survived. Ruth Connor Bolton died two years after her husband and was put by her husband in the Bolton Family Cemetery.

Nancy Kaye could not draw the pension on her father's military service. After going to work in a cafe in town, she was brutally raped by the woman's husband she worked for. It was raining, he offered to drive her home. Instead he turned on the Cedar Creek road. She could not open the door to jump out. He had removed the handle.

He stopped at the Caney Creek Bridge and started trying to undress her. She resisted and he hit her with his fist and knocked her out. When she came to, he was brutally raping her.

The sheriff seen them when he turned on the Cedar Creek road. He followed them and jerked the man off of her. Then laughed and said "The first time ain't as much fun as you thought it would be!"

She knew the way home, she out ran them and escaped in the dark. That was through the place we once lived on and the Heston place. She told Mrs. Heston about it the next day. They took her to a Doctor, then the District Attorney, who got a Texas Ranger who happened to be in his office to investigate.

The Ranger went with her, retraced her route through the two places home. They found one of her shoes which she lost crossing a muddy branch. The Ranger kept that and her bloody underwear as evidence, but it boiled down to her word against the man and the Sheriff. It never came to trial.

The Sheriff, the man Raymond Morehead, and Margaret's father Otis Ray Burkett had become friends as Merchant Seaman prior to and during WW11.

Nancy Kaye had the man's child, wound up in Tyler working for a small independent Office and School Supply business. It was owned by an elderly couple. They wanted to sell her the business, finance it themselves.

She called one night to my surprise, and asked if I might loan her the money to buy the business. I told her I would bring my lawyer, I felt sure I could help her on the deal.

In short, I bought the business, gave Nancy Kaye a check for $10,000. Pay me back as you can Nancy. The $10,000 is to get you started, you must have money to run the business on. Those people wanted to live off the interest in financing the deal themselves. I'm not charging you interest.

Tommy Heston married a woman with a teenage daughter. He worked in Waco, they lived there. The woman left her teen age daughter there with the Heston's to spend a week.

Charles Ray was 19, he slept on the screened in back porch in the summer time. The girl slipped into his bed naked two nights in a row and gave him an education in something he had never did before.

The woman then told the Heston's Charles Ray either marries the girl or I will file charges on him for assaulting my daughter! Which she did.

Tommy had caught the girl two months before in bed with a Mexican boy named Amundo Rios that looked to be 25 years old. He got on the phone to call the law. Amundo left and had not been seen or heard of since.

Charles Ray had been set up to be the father of a child that most likely was not his. Charles Ray flew the coup! His Mother and Dad went to Mexia to buy groceries. Charles Ray packed some essential things to cook with, a bedroll and a small tarp. He took an axe, set hooks and a single shoot 22. He hit the woods across US 79 headed for Buffalo Creek.

He left a note: "I'm leaving home until after that baby is born. I'm not going to jail or marry until we see who that kid looks like! Don't worry about me, I can take care of myself. I'll be back next spring."

Charles Ray spent the winter in Buffalo Creek Bottom. He later told me he cooked a fish where we found an old camp fire had been on the place we bought from Jim Williams. Sam Craig smelled the smoke, slipped up on him. Sam helped him eat the fish. He then took him home with him. Charles Ray had a hot shower and washed his clothes. They had a sirloin steak, baked potato, green beans and biscuits for supper. Charles slept in a bed for the first time in five months that night.

Sam Craig, Charles dad John Wesley Heston, Abraham Batson and my Dad had been friends and rode together as young boys. Sam knew Charles Ray and knew why he had left home. He offered to take Charles Ray home, or anywhere else he wanted to go.

Charles Ray would not let Sam get involved. The sheriff put a blood hound on his trail. Charles Ray shot the blood hound and got away. He felt like the sheriff was still looking for him in the area.

Sam gave him cooking oil, salt and pepper, coffee, sugar, sardines and crackers. He left Sam's place headed for my Uncle Alex DuPree's place. Uncle Alex was a lawyer. He wanted his advice on what he needed to do.

He had to hit the woods and hide in a thicket near a cemetery one night. He had waited until after dark to cross US 75. He was walking up the road to the cemetery when he saw car headlights behind him.

It was the Sheriff and Raymond Morehead. They had a young black woman with them. He had to watch as they both raped her. He heard the Sheriff tell her "We can take you back where we found you, or I'll take you to jail and charge you with disturbing the peace!" They left with a beat up crying black girl.

The next person he saw was Paula Juliene Batson. Her dad was Abraham Batson. They helped him get to Uncle Alex DuPree's, who was a near neighbor to the Batson's. He advised Charles Ray to go home, get a haircut and shave. I'll go with you. Turn yourself in to the law. I'll get you released on bond.

Uncle Alex got Charles Ray exonerated from being the child's father. The Sheriff charged him with killing his blood hound in "a hail of bullets." With a single shot 22, how can there be a hail of bullets Uncle Alex asked the jury.

Charles Ray was a free man. He and Paula Juliene married. He went into cahoots with her father farming the place. He had a big peach orchard, they took peaches, watermelons and other produce to neighboring towns and sold it to produce market places.

He also had a few cattle and a lot of hogs that mostly ran out on free range territory adjoining their place. Mr. Abraham and my cousin, Kinard DuPree were partners in the hog business.

Mr. Abraham was taking a trailer load of watermelons to Mexia. He managed to pull over and stop. But he had a heart attack and died. Paula Juliene was his only daughter. His wife had died in child birth. He raised her, never married again. The place and his assets became hers.

A section of land, 640 acres came up for sale with 50 head of white Brahman cattle joining the Batson place. Charles Ray called me to see if I might want it. I told him I would be over the next day to look at it.

I talked Charles Ray and Paula into letting me buy the 640 acres. Pay me back as they could. I would add ten thousand dollars to the loan to get them moving on the property. Charles Ray did not like Brahman cattle. I bought them and moved them to what we called the Hay Meadow Pasture.

Mr. Wilson and I traded bulls a lot. Sometimes he wanted Hot Sauce, other times I needed him. I put him with those Brahman cows and expected to get a lot of cross bred heifers to keep. Over a few years, I would phase those white Brahmans out.

Mr. Dobrinsky said it once "Give some people a boast and they'll take it and try to better themselves. Others will just live it up and come back with their hand out."

In five years, Nancy Kaye and Charles Ray had paid me back in full. They never came back with their hand out.

Spring break in school and dogwoods blooming occurred at the same time. We spent the week at the camp house on the Craig place. Margaret wanted to put away a supply of catfish in the freezer. Fish are better after being in fresh water all winter. In hot summer time, the water is not as fresh and they are not as good.

We took minnow jars up to that big hole in Buffalo Creek she wanted to go to. Below the fence at the rocky shallow water crossing, we caught big red horse minnows. We baited in the evening, went back the next morning. Flat heads up to 20 pounds, blues and channel up to about six. We averaged catching probably 35 pounds daily.

155

Cassie would stay at the Camp House with Benton Craig when Margaret went with me to put lines out. Then Cassie might go with me, and Margaret would stay at the camp house with him.

I commented I had never caught a flat head catfish over about 20 pounds. We had been too busy for me to see the marsh. I wanted to go down one creek and come back up the other.

Margaret had me rig up four throw lines 18 feet long with six big hooks on each. These will hang straight down where they will be put. Big catfish don't bite every night. We may fish a couple of days before we catch a big one. We may catch a few smaller ones however before we get Old Tom.

With live perch we trapped over in the spring branch, we headed down Buffalo Creek. I'll drive Margaret said. I know where I'm going! I always ran the boat for Uncle Sam.

It was only a couple of hundred yards down the creek that she pulled into a bank that went up at least 25 feet. See those steel rods drove in that bank. Tie the throw lines to those. Put heavy weights on each. They need to hang straight down.

Uncle Sam told me he once dived down here a number of times when he was a boy. The current has caves carved in that bank down under there. We'll catch Old Tom when he decides to swim out and feed.

It never took long to put out four throw lines. You want to see the rest of this marsh, hold on to your hat! She let that 25 HP Seahorse rip down that creek. Button willows started to make it hard for me to see the creek channel. But she knew where it was, she seldom slowed up.

We came out into about five acres of clear blue water. The creeks fork here in the lake she said. We'll get out on the lake dam, you need to see that to believe it. She pulled up to a rock that looked to be 20 feet wide and a hundred feet long. Each end seemed to extend into a high hard clay bank. Steel rods were driven into that rock to tie the boat to.

About the center of the rock was about a ten foot wide three foot deep cut in the rock the water flowed through. It spilled down about ten feet into a huge hole of water. I had seen the water hole and the water spilling over the rock before. There was a road through the pasture to get there.

We headed back up Keechi Creek. It was even harder to tell where the creek channel was because it was so crooked, and the button willows so thick. She stopped occasionally to show me openings backing out away from the creek. You can catch catfish in these. Also it's good to duck hunt in these late in the evening. They come from all over to roost.

We also saw some of the wood duck hardwood nesting boxes she helped her Uncle Sam put up. For me it was a joy ride, and a lot to look forward to. For her, well it had to be much more than that.

We turned left through the button willows headed for the camp house. About 30 yards from where he kept his boat, she shut the motor off. We have to paddle on in. Uncle Sam bought waders, dug this boat lane out before I was born. He struck rock, it's not deep enough to run the motor. But he fixed it so he could get from one creek to the other here without much trouble.

The next morning we had two flat heads that weighed in at 18 and 22 pounds. With what we caught up the creek, it was a 75 pound day. Fish dress out about like anything else, you lose almost half in the process. But we re-baited both places that evening.

The next morning we had old Tom. Margaret had me work with him for 20 minutes before he came to the surface. Grab him in the gills and stick your thumb in his eye. Then put him in the boat! That's what Uncle Sam always did!

Maybe I was not Uncle Sam. That dude pulled my chest down against the side of the boat before I stopped him. I managed to get the other hand in his gills and another thumb in his eye. Then I drug him into the boat.

"I had to stand up in the boat to weigh the fish. He weighs 58 pounds," she said. "I sat back down."

She picked up her camera. "Hold him up again and I'll get your picture." She then clicked the camera twice for good measure. "Now throw her back in," she said.

"What? Throw it back in?"

"Big fish are not fit to eat. I saw that other line move a little. It might be smaller fish fit to eat. You don't shoot old male hogs do you? Throw it back in!"

"Then why did your Uncle Sam fish for them here?"

"To sell. People don't know any better. Throw her back in!"

I threw it back in. The other line had one that weighed 16 pounds. We took the lines up.

Up the creek, we had a dozen more blues and channel catfish. We took those lines up also.

We had about all the frozen catfish fillets our ice chests would hold. Some we would put in the freezer at the ranch, the rest went home to Livingston.

We had a freezer at the camp house, but never left anything but frozen water in it. Electrical outages could be lengthy, and you might not know it happened.

Depending on the dates Thanksgiving and Christmas fell on, we managed to spend some time there during the hunting season. The kids got about a week out of school. But those days often involved being with family somewhere else.

Cassie and Wade took the beetle and went hunting one afternoon. They went to a stand at the head of one of those myrtle head draws. It was between the road in and the fence with Jeff. They saw deer, but nothing they wanted to shoot.

Late that evening they saw about ten flying squirrels go in a small hollow sassafras tree. Wade stuck his cap in the hole, then went to the beetle for his axe. Cassie came driving in, Wade was sitting on top of the beetle with the hollow sassafras on his shoulder.

I had seen a couple at the ranch. As a matter of fact, I probably had not seen ten in my life! But they said at least ten were in that little sassafras they knew for sure. By the squeaking they were making, it sounded like it.

I found a small board to nail over the hole and cut about four feet off one solid end. That shortened it to ten feet. I could tie it down over my pickup tail gate and go to the ranch with it.

We took it to a big sweet gum tree with low limbs we could climb. Lots of vine covered pin oaks around it. With eight inch nails, I nailed it to that sweet gum. Removed the board and backed off to watch. We saw 11 come out of that hole into a new world for them.

That'll improve the genetics here Cassie said!

It was on the local news. A picture of a 570 pound Russian barrow hog. The man said he killed it in a hunting club on the Neches River west of Lufkin. Said he marked his left ear and released him as a boar pig. They showed both his ears. The diamond shaped mark in the left. Somebody else neutered him and put this mark in his right ear.

Yeah, somebody did, I thought! The mark was Dad's old crop-split-in the right. The Russian hog survived my surgery and traveled 20 miles back home!

Wade graduated from High School in 1967. He was offered some basketball scholarships but preferred to work on the ranch. For reasons Cassie did not understand,

Wade changed. He always seemed to be somewhere else when she was at the ranch. Or something else he had to do if she suggested they do anything.

Someone asked her once "What's got into you and Wade. I don't see you together anymore."

Cassie's answer was very short. "I don't know, but being rude is not a one-way street!"

Margaret took Cassie and a group of girls to a summer camp meeting place the Baptist had up near Athens. Two other women went as well. She took Benton Craig along because she knew I had to work. They spent the week there, then came home. They had a great time there, but glad to be home. As for as I knew, that was that.

Two weeks later we had my family reunion at the ranch. Everyone was there, even sister Annie and her husband and kids from Arizona. We had built down near the lake dam a building for such occasions. It was complete with a gas stove, refrigerator, kitchen cabinet and sink and things to cook with. My big pots and pans I got at Austin were kept there.

We had 14 folding picnic tables about ten feet long with folding chairs set up. I was up until midnight cooking barbeque pork ribs and two rib eye roasts. I saved those from a 550 pound yearling I had butchered. That was all sliced, in the big stainless steel pans.

I covered those with foil. I had it sitting in the barbeque pit Mr. Wilson made from a new steel propane tank I bought. It was mounted on a four-wheel trailer to travel. With low heat it would keep the meat warm.

I had my two-burner fish fryer going with a small propane tank. Margaret had a dish pan half full of Buffalo Creek Catfish ready for me to fry. After each batch was ready, I put it in a big pan in the barbeque pit. That kept it warm and gave it a light hickory taste.

Sitting around watching me work and talking was Dad, Elton, Melton, Lawrence, Mr. Wilson and our cousin Marvin.

I heard Virginia yell "Robert, look who's here!"

I looked around to see what it was all about. Virginia and Margaret had Mary Ellen arm to arm between them! Following was a man I had never seen. *That must be her husband,* I thought. To be honest about it, I was in a state of shock!

But I laid my fish turner down, we gave each other a brief hug. Then she introduced the man. This is John Rains. My husband! Then she picked up a piece of catfish out of the pan. I'm not waiting until dinner to try this!

Virginia and Margaret went inside the building to get things ready in there. The men went with her husband out on the lake dam to look it over. Suddenly Mary Ellen and I were alone at the fish fryer.

John owns a highway construction business. He and I were class mates before we moved to Livingston. He hired me as his office manager when I went back to Tyler. We worked together a year before he asked me to go out to dinner with him. It was one night after we worked late. The girl he was engaged to married someone else while he was away at college. He just had not felt like dating anyone until he realized he could trust me.

His place joins my parents. One evening we were out there fishing at the lake he built. It started to rain. We ran to a hay barn to get out of it. He asked me to marry him in that hay barn.

Was that about mid-afternoon on July 23, 1965?

As a matter of fact, it was! How did you know?

I was sitting on a horse under a holly tree trying to keep from getting wet. It was on property Margaret owns in Leon County. I took out my old timer knife to carve my initials in that tree. I kept my promise to you by praying that you were happy and well.

When I said "Amen" a lightning bolt struck a tree near me. I believed God did that to tell me he had answered my prayer.

Well it seems he did. I'm glad you have the kind of faith to know when God answers your prayers. I believe it, but I doubt many people would. How else could you have known that date!

God knows you and Margaret belong together. She's such a wonderful person. We talked a lot when we met at the camp meeting. I'm so glad she invited us to come here today. It's been so great seeing Virginia again.

The men came back. Mary Ellen went in the building to help Margaret and the other women. Her husband was interested in seeing how the ranch was laid out. I invited them to come back, we would show it to them both. In the following years, we visited back and forth a good bit.

I changed my mind about making the ranch an employee hunting lease. One reason was the distance they would need to drive. The other was the Lake Livingston Dam on the Trinity River was nearing completion. I decided on the land across the Trinity River Melton and I once hunted on.

A highway was re-routed to cross the proposed lake and made the property probably 20 miles closer to Livingston. Also, I only had a half mile of county road to get to it now. I sold 110 acres which would be under water when the lake filled. Which meant my employees would have access to the lake. And 2450 acres of land to hunt on left out of the original four sections.

I had a deep well drilled, pump installed. Had electricity run to the site. A meter pole was set by the pump. I would pay for running that pump. And electricity to a shower and restroom separate facility for men and women. Each had hot water heaters and septic tank systems.

I then had lots surveyed off 100 feet wide and 150 feet deep. I put a road or street between 20 lots. Ten on each side facing each other. I ran a water line to each lot. Beyond that, electricity and septic system was the responsibility of whoever wanted a camp house on a lot. Those that pitched a tent could use the shower and restroom facility.

It was necessary to have rules about camp houses. Number one, I owned the lot.

Number two, if an employee quit, he could sell his camp house to another employee, or move it within one year. If not sold or moved within one year, it would become my property.

Provided you retired as an employee, you and your family had access to the property as long as you lived. Your family had a year after your death to remove or sell to another employee your camp house. I secured and paid for insurance covering any liability for accidents that possible could occur on the lease.

I hired two young men to supervise and check on a number of other tracts of timber land I owned. I bought out my partner in the saw-mill, which included a lot of land. I wanted each tract of land I owned fenced. I would then turn it into private hunting clubs or leases. *Lease money,* I thought *would pay the taxes on each tract.*

I furnished the two men with Ford pickups to drive. Gave them keys to get gas out of the tank at the saw-mill. Built a small office and a storage building for them to work out of at the mill. The storage building had double garage doors. A 16 foot trailer, a 14 foot flat bottom boat and motor and fence repair tools were kept there.

I hired five men who were professional fence builders. They furnished a tractor with post hole-digger and other equipment needed to build fence. I furnished the wire, posts and staples. The man who headed up the business, charged by the yard. I paid him, he paid his four helpers.

I ordered posts, wire and everything delivered to our building supply business. The two men I hired delivered it to the job site. I got a good price on steel posts by buying 500 at a time. Creosote posts with a three inch top cost a little more. The fence line would be two steel, one creosote, two steel, one creosote. I thought the creosote posts gave the fence more stability.

The saw-mill had a road building crew, so the places for the most part had roads. If needed, we could get the crew and dozer on it. Water and electricity were what we had to get on the property before we could lease it to hunters. I found insurance that would cover any risks for accidents that might occur on each property leased. That cost would be added to each members lease fee.

After everything was fenced, water and electricity provided, we leased it out to hunters. The two men I hired then became pasture riders. Which meant members of the lease were checked on to abide by the lease rules and the State game laws. A game warden could be called in if State law violated.

If lease rules were broken, they would report it to me. I might warn the person about doing it again or kick him out. Their duty also would be to check on fences and roads. Well pumps, the shower house at the employee lease. Fix if you can, or contact me to get it done. Main thing to do, is make an appearance at no set time in all the leases on a regular basis.

I also sold a lot of property south of Lufkin, at Crockett and down at Cleveland. Loops were being put around towns, residential areas developed. Mr. Dobrinsky had invested in land knowing the time would come to cash in. I felt that time had arrived. I cashed in.

My partner at the Ford place wanted to retire, he sold his half interest to me. I moved it out on the loop which came across the edge of the Wilson place I now owned. I had a lot of offers to buy more lots next to the loop. I sold some lots, but kept about half of my property there. The time might come when we needed it.

The old Ford place became our used car business place. What we took in on trade we sold there. My manager also bought a few clean cars and pickups at auctions to sell there as well.

Marvin's grandson called me. My wife has seen him three days in a row. A man has been coming out here and going down towards that corn feeder you have down next to the marsh. I tracked him, found where he's been hiding to watch that feeder. Strange thing is, she has not heard him shoot. There's plenty to shoot coming to that feeder. And outlaw hunters don't care what they shoot.

Could she see if he had a gun or not?

Yes, she said he had a rifle. And was driving an old black Chevrolet car. She never got the license plate number.

I never told Margaret that he had called. After work, I went home, loaded up some corn, an ice chest with some drinks. And my 243 rifle with scope. I ate supper and told Margaret I was going to the Craig place to check on things and fill up the corn feeders.

I stopped at a grocery store in Rusk for some cinnamon rolls, some lance crackers. We had coffee, sugar, pork & beans, Vienna sausage at the camp house. With luck I felt like I would be on the way home by noon tomorrow anyway.

At Corrigan, I took US 287 to Palestine. I had been deliberate about waiting until after dark to get there. I drove by Sam Craig's old ex-wife's place. I was not surprised. A beat up old 1955 black Chevrolet was sitting in the driveway. I was the reason the lunatic had not shot at anything. I had not been there to fill up the corn feeder!

I was up early, fixed a pot of coffee, and had a couple of cinnamon rolls. Took a thermos of coffee and stuck a RC cola in my hip pocket. Loaded my 243 and put my duck call by the string it hung from around my neck. I waited until daylight to go to my ambush hiding place.

I managed not to get my feet wet at the rocky crossing on Keechi Creek. We placed rocks in the four inch water to walk across on. I went directly to a clump of myrtle bushes out in the open pasture. It was about 65 yards to the edge of the woods across the open pasture. Those woods extended from the marsh all the way up to Craig place barn.

He was sneaking down through fairly open woods to watch that corn feeder. I took my pocket knife, trimmed a few limbs to shoot through. Even found a limb just right to rest my rifle on. I tried to get comfortable in the thick bushes and settled down to wait.

It was about midmorning when I heard the old car up by the cemetery. I saw him coming. I put my rifle on that limb rest, clicked the safety off. I waited until he got in an open place and gave that duck call one long blast.

He never knew where it came from, or what it was. He quickly moved to a big black jack tree and squatted down by it. The gun was under his right arm, the stock sticking out behind him. I put the cross hairs on that gun stock and pulled the trigger. It shattered that gunstock and the bullet hit that black jack tree. I figure he may have got splinters in his back. And bark from that tree hit him on the neck and side of his face.

He left the gun laying there. The old boy could run and he was trying to keep behind trees as he did. I put the cross hairs on the next one he would come to. I blew bark off about butt high on him as he went around it. And gave the duck call another blast! I soon heard that old car door slam and he roared out of there!

I went back to the cabin, got my truck and drove back over to the feeder. I filled it up with corn and found his gun. It was a 7-mm surplus gun probably taken from the Japanese in WW2. I then filled the other feeders and ate a late lunch at the camp house.

I decided to drive by Sam's ex-wife's place on the way home. I saw him come out the door into the yard. I was even with him when he stooped over to pick up a rolled up newspaper. I hit that duck call a long blast. He left the paper and hit the door running! I got out of there in a hurry in case he had a gun handy inside!

I called Marvin's grandson that night and told him what happened. "If your wife sees him out there again, call the sheriff. He can be charged with trespassing and hunting out of season. But don't either of you go near him."

I had a gun smith put a new stock on the gun and re-blue it to look brand new. I put it in a cheap canvass zip up case and sent it by Katrina to leave with Harry. "Give the gun to his daddy and tell him it was a birthday gift from Margaret's husband."

I thought I knew what I was doing by trying to enrage the old boy. I wanted to get it over with as soon as possible. And I suspected if he became angry enough, he would throw caution to the wind and come after me.

Cassie decided to try out for back strut with the Livingston High School band her senior year. Shirley Nell's daughter had that position for three years and she did not want to compete against her. Cassie won over four others that tried out.

We started staying at home on Friday nights to go to the ball games and watch her perform. After the football season ended, the Livingston band won in competition against bands in the area and advanced to state wide competition at Austin. The Livingston band lost to a class 4A school in the finals.

But there was a separate contest for individual girls that marched with the bands as majorettes and back struts twirling those batons. Cassie won over ever girl in the state that competed. She was offered some scholarships when she graduated, but she wanted to stay home, drive back and forth to the college in Huntsville.

College bands travel all over the country performing she said. I'd never be home. I just don't care about doing that for four years. I told her I wanted to get her a car for her High School graduation.

What kind of car Daddy?

I can get a Jaguar at cost.

What do they cost Daddy?

I could probably get it for $25,000.

You want to spend that much on my graduation?

Yes. You need a car and I'm proud of you!

What about giving me a Ford Station Wagon like Mother's and the difference in cash. I could invest the money!

I gave her a Ford Station Wagon and $18,000. A high school teacher told her how he was making money by buying and selling stock. She saved her allowance, was already into that. She bought a Sunday Houston paper every weekend to check on when to buy and when to sell. And she kept a weekly chart on the stocks she was watching.

It's sort of like what you do Daddy. You buy those poor cows, fatten them up and then sell them. My Teacher gave me a list of companies to watch. Their stock rises and falls. When it falls buy it. When it rises to a high point sell it. Keep your profit and buy back into it when it falls again.

She seldom went to the ranch anymore. Lots of weekends she stayed at home with Benton Craig. He was playing little league baseball and she took him to the games. In college with boys, no doubt she had the opportunity to date. She never dated any one. Margaret and I never said anything to her about it. We knew her heart was with Wade at the ranch.

During the summer, she worked in my office. She was taking business administration in college and often pointed out things I needed to do differently. I was teaching her the way Mr. Dobrinsky taught me, one aspect of the business at a time. *She, I thought, might be the one to take over the business after I departed.*

Wade never dated either according to Mr. Wilson. He'll go up yonder and sit in that tower by the ten acre food plot. On Saturday night, he'll set there until 2 a.m. eating peanuts. He works like a Turk, but he seldom leaves this ranch.

I left one evening early to go to the ranch. Mr. Wilson and Wade cut blown over or dead trees in the creek bottom. They drug them with dozer out by the hog pen fence across from the equipment shed. There we sawed them up and split for fire wood as needed.

It was cold, I needed to cut up some wood for the winter. I left for the ranch after lunch. Margaret would come later after Benton Craig got out of school. As I drove by the county road that went to the Trahan place, a 1963 Ford car was parked there. Standing by it was a red headed woman, like she was waiting on someone. She was nicely dressed and looked to be about 30 years old. *Who could she be,* I wondered. *Not anyone I knew for sure. Why was she standing there? If she is waiting on someone, where were they? And who might they be?*

Call it sixth sense, or whatever. My alarm went off! That car had Harris County tags on it. It was Friday. Everyone went home at dinner time on Friday. Mr. and Mrs. Wilson usually went to Lufkin to buy groceries Friday evening. I never saw Wade's truck, he was gone.

I had to turn in the gate past the cemetery to get to the equipment shed. On the left of the road, was about 200 yards of woods before getting to the horse pasture. Old Buck was standing looking up towards those woods like he knew something. That convinced me. Along with Harris County on those plates. That woman was waiting for Margaret's lunatic Daddy to kill me and go home! If he meant to shoot me, he could have done that already. And that gun I had rebuilt and sent to him was minus the firing pin I took out! He might have to send to Japan to get another.

Keep your cool, I thought, *and your eyes peeled. Stay close to that double bit axe and start cutting firewood.*

I got the axe and chain saw out of the shed. I made four cuts on a 20 inch log and laid the chain saw down. It needed to be sharpened. I turned a block on end and stuck my axe into it. If he was in those woods like I thought, he would have to cross the road, climb over the cemetery fence and out the gate into our front yard to sneak up on me.

I got that block split and started on another. The sun was still high in the west. I saw a bird's shadow cross the road behind me and slightly to my left before the Blue Jay got there. If he came like I thought he would, his shadow would warn me. I finished that block and started on the third.

I saw his shadow cross that road before he did! I guess he was too intent on his sneak to notice his shadow was out in front of him. I put the axe down to the ground like I was leaning on the handle resting.

I waited until he was right behind me before I turned and said, "How you doing, Mr. Burkett? I been expecting you!" His hand was almost out of his old coat pocket with that switch blade, when I brought that axe up. The flat side caught his elbow, and that switch blade went sailing up and away. He stumbled back and around with the end of that that big log behind him. He was trying to get his left hand in his coat pocket. I hit his left elbow with the flat side of that axe hard.

He sat down on the log. I then brought the axe flat side against his jaw. Not as hard as I could have, but I heard his jaw bone pop. He fell back on the log, his old hand clutching at the end of the log, trying to get up. I hit that knife holding hand as hard as I could with the flat side of the axe. I think he passed out with that lick.

I brought the axe down hard on his right knee, then stuck it into the log between his legs. I must have got some skin because I saw blood on his pants. I found the switch blade knife and carved on each of his cheeks the letters AH. That could be read as AH or HA. I labeled the man with what I hoped would be permanent scars.

I went through his pockets, came out with some keys, change, a wallet, and a small pistol. I kept the pistol and the switch blade knife, put the other things back in his pockets.

I backed my truck up and loaded him. I took him down to the waiting woman. "If you are waiting on this man, here he is!"

"He has my car keys and my pistol. He forced me to drive him up here. He said he was going to kill a man he called Robert DuPree."

"I'm Robert DuPree. He never killed me!"

"My name is Marcella. He was in my apartment when I got home last night. He found where I keep my money. He's got it on him in a money belt. Give me my money, pistol, and car keys and I'll take him away from here. You don't want the law involved in this do you?"

"A lot of people know he's threatened my life. I think I could survive dealing with the law. But if you haul him away I would just as soon not go through with that. Are you sure you will not be afraid of him? Don't you realize that if he killed me, he would kill you?"

"Yes, but I never had a lot of choices. He does not look like he's able to hurt anyone now. Give me my pistol, and I won't be afraid of him. I'll put him out some where he can get medical attention. But I want to see my money before I leave here."

I took off his money belt, handed it to her with the keys, his wallet, and the pistol.

She took a quick look in the money belt. Then said to me, "Help me get him in the car and I'll get the hell out of here!"

I drug him out of my pickup and between us we got him in her car. He groaned some, but offered no resistance. She put a vodka bottle in his left hand. "He was saving the vodka to celebrate your death," she said. Then Marcella kept her word. She got the hell out of there!

Marcella pushed him out in an alley in Cleveland Texas. She felt a crunch as she was leaving. "Dam," she said. "I must have run over his foot!"

At her apartment, she packed her things. Got some warm water and soap and washed the blood out of her car seat. She fixed some sandwiches, loaded her car. Left a note in her landlord's mailbox that she was moving to Dallas.

He next stop was at the bus station. She recognized a key the old boy had. It was a locker key at the bus station. She once had rented one there. The night clerk was sleeping at his desk when she went in. The number on the key she matched with the number on the locker.

She opened up the locker. Inside was a duffel bag. On top of everything, was a money belt which contained over $5000 bucks. She took that and left his wallet which contained almost a hundred dollars and his ID papers for going to sea. The locker key she put on the desk as she left. The clerk never knew she was there.

The next morning, she found a motel in Seguin Texas. She slept about three hours, cleaned up, and checked out. She went to a Ford dealership, traded in her car and paid cash for a new one. She told the salesman she was going to Dallas.

A friend recently told her about a man who ran a book store in Sacramento, California. He took care of his aging mother until she passed away. He had never been married but clearly wanted to. The thought of working in a book store appealed to her. She would check him out! She was near the age it never paid to be in her profession.

They found Burkett in the alley, beat up. No ID, he became a ward of the county. He pretended he did not know his name, or remember anything. He was patched up in a hospital by a Doctor who worked for the county on cases like him. A nurse asked the Doctor what the letters AH might stand for on his cheeks.

The Doctor laughed. "Somebody thinks he is an Ass Hole or a Horses Ass! And I agree. He knows who he is and he knows who did this to him. He'll be out of here and gone as soon as he's able. And all of you nurses better be careful around him. He might need a chauffeur when he goes!"

They put an elderly old man in the room next to him. His wife put his clothing and shoes in a closet. She left her purse and went to the nurse's stand for some reason. He took part of her money, and left some, thinking she would not miss it very soon or look in the closet. The old man's clothes and shoes fit. In minutes, he was out of there. He had been in that hospital for three months.

There was enough money that he rode the bus to Humble. He had a number one burger combination at a fast food place then hitch hiked to Highlands. At the bus station, he told the desk clerk he lost his key to his locker. The desk clerk opened it for him.

That woman! She took most of his money, left him almost a hundred dollars and his ID. He would sign on a ship as a cook. With his broken hand, crushed ankle, and busted knee cap, he could not do anything else. He had to leave this country.

An FBI agent had questioned him last week, trying to determine who he was. If that hussy up at Palestine ever squealed on him, he would be charged with killing Sam Craig. The FBI was on his trail and he knew it!

That DuPree boy was a step ahead of him, both times he tried to kill him. *Shot the stock of the gun he paid $11.95 for at a war surplus store. Sent it back to me looking brand new minus the firing pin. He did that to taunt me into coming after him!*

How he knew I was there at his ranch I don't know. That woman Marcella never told him. I watched him drive by her. He was waiting on me with that axe. And he was smiling at me when he beat me to near death with it!

That woman Marcella was gone. The landlord had a "For Rent" sign on the place she lived in. No chance to get his money back. The only thing to do was sign on a ship to China. He had a woman there and three kids. She hated him but was honor bound to take care of him. He would go there and not come back to this country again.

Emanuel Newhouse was a neighbor across Buffalo Creek from the Bolton's place. Emanuel, was somewhat different from other men. He was small, awkward, his clothes always seemed to be two sizes too big for him. He and his wife Sadie grew up with my parents, Martha and Sam Craig, the Hestons, Boltons, and Abraham Batson.

Sadie was one of the most beautiful and gracious young women in the country it was said. She could have married a number of young men. Yet she chose Emanuel to marry. Mother heard someone ask her on her wedding day "Why did you choose Emanuel over so many others?"

Her answer was "Emanuel needs me."

Emanuel was sitting with Charles Ray Heston at the Buffalo Auction Sale. Emanuel got up and went to the restroom. A young man came and sat down by Charles. I'm looking for a man by the name of Raymond Morehead. I was told he might be here today. I wonder if you might know him.

Yeah, I know who he is. Charles took a quick look around. That's him headed for the rest room now.

The man thanked Charles Ray, got up and followed the man into the rest room. In about five minutes, he came out and left.

Shortly Emanuel came and sat back down. He kept laughing. He would stop, then start laughing again.

What's so funny Mr. Emanuel Charles Ray asked?

Raymond Morehead was standing at the latrine. Young fellow came in. Said to Raymond "Do you remember Nancy Kaye Bolton?"

Raymond turned around and said: "Who the hell wants to know?"

That young fellow hit him between the eyes. Old Raymond fell back and sat down in the latrine. That young fellow kicked him in the ribs. Then three times in his crotch. Then he shoved old Raymond's head back and flushed that latrine. He then turned to me and said "You best get out of here before you get involved. I don't know you and you don't know me. Understand? Nancy Kaye Bolton owed that bastard and I paid him!"

He left without saying another word. After a few minutes someone found Raymond. An ambulance was called and he was taken to a hospital in Fairfield. Emanuel and Charles Ray never knew anything about what happened to Raymond when a Sheriff's Deputy got there.

Raymond's wife at the restaurant told someone later that his testicles became infected and Doctors removed them. She sold the restaurant and her home, then left the county.

John Wesley Heston, Charles Ray's dad had a few months earlier caught the ex-one term sheriff at the sale. The sheriff never went to the rest room, he was inside an empty stock pen taking a leak when Big John caught up to him. Big John said "This is for Nancy Kaye Bolton." Then he knocked him out cold with one punch. He fell on his back into a pen full of fresh cow patties. He kicked him in both sides of his ribs, then in his crotch. Then left him there.

One of the young workers at the sale helped him up, told him he best get out of there. They were about to put cattle in that pen! The one term sheriff made it to his truck and left, cow stuff and all! He never wanted the law involved, because it could renew interest in the Nancy Kaye Bolton case.

We did find out the name of the young man who beat up Raymond Morehead. His name was Riley Long. He ran a yard care and landscape business in Tyler. He owned and lived on property west of Tyler on the Neches River.

Nancy Kaye hired him to do yard work at a home she bought. He recognized Nancy Kaye from a picture her wounded Dad gave him in Germany. Bill Bolton's last words were "Find my wife and daughter at Buffalo Texas and tell them I loved them."

Riley had a little girl from a broken marriage the same age as Nancy's boy. We were invited to their wedding. So was Mary Ellen and John. Mary Ellen and Nancy Kaye both attended the same Baptist church, became friends. It was Mary Ellen who gave Nancy Kaye my phone number to call me about helping her buy into the office supply business.

Riley served as a private under her Dad who was a sergeant. Bill Bolton was called the "Old Man" by the young troops he led out on patrol. More than once he used the skills he learned in Buffalo Creek bottom hunting to save his troops.

The night he was killed, he stayed behind to draw the fire of German troops that had the patrol pinned down in trenches. He told Riley and the young boys "Get out of here, I'll catch up to you." He kept firing his BAR to draw the Germans attention while they escaped.

They jumped out of the last trench into a ravine that led back towards the base. Riley and Bill were from Texas, they became friends. He knew that Bill came from Buffalo. The other troops kept running, Riley waited for Bill to jump into the ravine.

Bill made it into the ravine, but had been hit. He gave Riley the picture of his Wife and Nancy Kaye out of his shirt pocket. Tell my wife and daughter I love them. Then he died. Riley put him on his shoulders and carried his body back to base.

With the help of a State Senator in Tyler, Riley Long succeeded in getting William "Bill" Bolton the Distinguished Service Cross. There were over 300 of us at the Bolton Family cemetery when the Commanding General of the division Bill was in awarded the Cross to Nancy Kaye posthumously.

The Senator spoke to the crowd and said "Look around you folks at what surrounds this cemetery. It is from places like this that so many young men came to serve and die for our country in WW11. Let the Distinguished Service Cross always be a reminder to you Nancy Kaye that your father went beyond the call of duty to serve his country. And let this monument put here at the foot of his grave by the United States Army remind us that all men who served our country in WW11 deserve our respect."

Nancy Kaye became you might say "The Darling of Tyler" because of the award she received for her father. She was someone the people could identify with, most had family and friends who served in the war. "Buy it from Nancy Kaye" was a form of patriotism in their minds.

She kept the store she bought, branched out with two other Nancy Kaye Office Supply stores in conjunction with "Riley's Yard Care and Landscaping." She also became owner of a women's wear store in Tyler. They built a new home at his property on the Neches River.

The man and woman who owned the Bolton place on Buffalo Creek wanted to sell the place. Their daughter lived in Tyler, they were getting up in years and wanted to be near her. Nancy Kaye traded her home in Tyler to them as part of the deal. Riley put up the rest of the money and they owned the Bolton place. Which was near our place on Buffalo Creek.

Each year now, we let the sixth grade class at Livingston and Wells come to see our operation at the produce facility. The teachers thought syrup making would be the more interesting for the kids, so we set it up for early October. We provided drinks, the kids brought a lunch.

One problem we solved by renting four facilities from A-1 Johnny for the day! Two for girls and two for boys. And a number of trash cans. The teachers had them get back on the bus to eat their lunch. Which was another problem solved.

The kids seemed to enjoy seeing that ribbon cane crushed in that grinder. We gave each a small paper cup of juice to see how it tasted. And to each we gave a stalk of ribbon cane to take home. And a pint of ribbon cane syrup with the Shady Oaks Label. The bus drivers and teachers also got what the kids did.

They were lined up and passed by the complete operation. I think the kids enjoyed the day. And it seemed to form a lasting bond between the students of the two schools. The teacher at Livingston told me the kids talked about the trip and being with those kids at Wells the rest of the year.

In 1971, Mrs. Wilson passed away. She was out raking leaves in the yard when something snapped in her shoulder. Cancer spread quickly and she was gone in two months. She was only 55 years old. Mr. Wilson was eight years older at 63. Wade was 21.

It hit us hard to lose her. She was truly a remarkable woman. She never asked "What can you do for me?" It was always "What can I do for you?" She had treated me like I was a family member since I was a teenage boy.

It had only been a year before. She and Margaret went shopping together in Houston. Margaret found her standing looking at a mannequin all dressed out in a woman's suit complete with blouse, shoes and small hat. This is perfect for Cassie she said, "If you don't buy it for her, I'm going to!"

Margaret agreed. She bought it for Cassie. She wore it to church once with Mrs. Wilson at Wells so she could see her in it. Cassie put it away after that, saying I feel a little over dressed in this. I've never worn a hat before except in the outdoors! She wore it again to Bessie Mae's funeral.

The pastor at Wells conducted her service. The woman's choir at Wells and Reverend Billy's Church came together to sing some songs. It was an impressive service in more ways than one. Following was a procession to the Cemetery. Mrs. Wilson was put to the left of the Dobrinsky's.

It was the custom in our part of Texas, maybe all over as far as I knew. The women in the Church at Wells brought food to the Wilson Home. After the cemetery service, people came there, ate food together. They spent a couple of hours there then went home.

Wade was standing in the Living room. Cassie walked up to him crying. "Wade I loved your mother!" He took her in his arms and said "I know you did Cassie." They were standing there in each other's arms crying when a well-meaning old lady walked up, grabbed Wade's arm. Come on into the kitchen, there is plenty of food for everyone!

That broke them up and apart. Wade followed the old Lady into the kitchen. Had she not intervened, I think they would have cried it out and got back together.

That night I put my pillow against the headboard and sat up.

You can't sleep? What's on your mind Margaret asked?

When I die, I don't want people bringing food to our house. After the service, I think it's time for the family to be left alone. Not enduring two or three hours of being surrounded by people. I know they are well meaning, but I just don't want you and my kids to go through that.

It surprises me sometimes how much we share the same thoughts. I agree that the time comes when grief should be left alone. I don't want you and the kids to go through that either. I'll tell Cassie how we feel. She'll take care of that situation I'm sure.

Chapter Eleven
We Lose Some Old and Gain Some New

Mr. Wilson had been working at a supervisor status only for the last five years. Joe Ed, Cole and Luther kept up with the ranch work very well. Joe Ed could run the dozer and back hoe if needed. The Mexicans were doing a good job at the hog farm, as Essie Mae was at the produce facility.

He had worked long and hard enough developing everything we had, I thought. He remained the foreman over it all, he kept a check on everything and still did purchasing through the Wells Bank account.

He stayed on the job until he was 64 after Bessie Mae's death and then told me he was ready to retire. He would draw Social Security, and interest on his retirement fund. He wanted to spend more time on his own place, and that was a source of income as well.

I talked to Joe Ed, Cole, Luther and Essie Mae individually about the foreman's job. They all said they had their own interests to go to after work hours. Give the job to Wade. We know we can work with him and he knows more about the responsibilities of the job than we do.

So at almost the age of 22 years, I gave the job to Wade. That included purchasing power on the Wells Bank Account. He had his Dad to advise him if he needed it. I trusted the boy completely and he was doing a good job. And the other employees seemed happy under his leadership.

I told him when he needed help on their place, use our crew to get it done. Sometimes an hour's help is enough to load cattle. But baling and hauling hay could take a week.

Mother's health reached the point that Dad let us move them into our guest house. The rest of the family thought it was right thing for them to do. Dad did not drive, and they had to get someone to take Mother to the Doctor.

Margaret clearly loved them both. They seemed to fill the empty spot in her heart at the loss of her Mother and the Daddy she never had. She took them to the Doctor, helped them grocery shop. And insisted they come to the ranch with us on weekends.

Mother only lived a year after moving into our guest house. She was the first in my family to go. She had nine of us kids and it was tough losing her for a long time. It took some time, but I realized you don't actually lose someone you love, and know loved you. They are always with you in your heart and mind. My accountant, book keeper and tax expert advised me I needed to donate to some charity or church at least $150,000 to avoid paying so much tax. Give it to someone that needs it or give it to Uncle Sam. It's your choice!

I could not decide what cause I wanted to donate that amount of money to. I left the ranch headed home one day. As I passed Rev. Billy's Church, he was up on a scaffold painting the building. I waved at him and went on. I was a half mile down the road when I had the thought: *Charity should begin at everyone's front yard gate!*

I hit the brakes, turned that pickup around and went back to the Church. I got out, Reverend Billy got down off the scaffold. We shook hands and he said "Let's get over there in the shade of that tree. It's hot out here this morning. What's you got on your mind mister Robert?"

"I saw you painting and got to wondering Brother Billy. What would you do to this church building if you had the money to do it?"

Reverend Billy was an elegant speaker in the pulpit, or when he wanted to. I suppose my question was something he wanted to be clear about when he answered.

"Well Mr. Robert, the building is getting too small for the crowds we are having. But it's in good shape. I've dreamed about adding about 25 feet on to the back of it. You can see the roof is straight, it would be easy to do. We could add more seats and in back a place to be baptized. No more going to the Neches River for that."

"It does not cost anything to dream. But we need a building separate from the church we could get together and eat. Maybe play games and have Sunday School classes for bible study. Part of it would be a regular kitchen, we would need folding tables and chairs."

"Rev. Billy, your dreams I can help make come true. I got money I can give to Uncle Sam in taxes, or give to this church. I think we can do what you want and more. I'll send a builder up here as soon as possible. He'll draw up plans the way you want it. Then we'll get it done!"

"God has answered my prayers! I wonder how he chose you, Mister Robert?"

"He told me that Charity should begin at everyone's front gate. You and the people in this Church are my friends and neighbors. Your Church is near my front gate. God has blessed me by being able to help you."

The Church building was enlarged the way he wanted it. The floor was carpeted. The area for the pulpit, and the choir was raised. Then it was raised again three feet higher for the glass fronted baptismal tank. The pews were ordered custom made 12 feet long. There were two rows with an aisle between them and down each side. Then the building was bricked up and aluminum framed windows put in. The roof was completely recovered with new composition shingles.

The building in back of the church was put on a concrete slab and walled up with tongue and grove pine siding. It was painted white and the roof was the same as the church. It was complete with a kitchen and rest rooms for men and women. There were enough folding tables and chairs to handle about 60 people.

Mr. Wilson bought used pipe and put up swings for the kids and things for climbing on. He also put up basketball goals at the ends of the basketball court we poured with concrete. He completed his work by building a steel barbeque pit big enough to cook a 550 pound yearling calf in!

My records indicated I had spent $135,000 on the project. I gave Rev. Billy two checks for $7, 500 each. Deposit one in the church fund. The other in your private account Reverend Billy. I know you and Josie Mae have bills to pay like everybody else.

Margaret and I, Mr. Wilson, Joe Ed and Susan, Cole and Lucy, and Cassie were invited to their grand opening celebration of the new church. I thought Reverend Billy preached one of the best sermons I ever heard. He called it "Let charity begin at your front yard gate!"

It was later that year during the deer season. Wade said his Dad told him at lunch time he was going down to the stand where he and I once hunted. It was after dark when Wade got in. It got dark so quickly this time of year, he heated up some supper. His Dad had not come in, he went to check on him.

He found his Dad sitting there in that stand. Like he went to sleep and never woke up. He had to go back to the house to call an ambulance and the sheriff's department. He called Joe Ed and asked him to come direct those people to where his Dad was. He went back to stay with his Dad until they got there. Which took about an hour. But his death was determined to be a heart attack.

They held his service at the church in Wells. At his request, Rev. Billy preached his last rites. It was an honor he said for him to preach in a white church. Brother Justin did one last thing for me, after he did so much for me since we were kids growing up together. He wanted me to be here in this church today with him and all of you.

He talked about their life together. We played together as kids, we have fished and we have hunted together, and we have worked together, and we have laughed and we have cried together, and we have prayed together. We have always helped one another when we could.

Miss Patricia, and you Mr. Wade. You miss him like a father you loved that loved you. I miss him like a brother I loved that loved me. But this I know. Mr. Justin is up yonder with your Mother and I know they are happy. Your memories, my memories of him are a precious thing. They will sustain us through the grief we feel now. They will sustain us until we have a joyous reunion with him and those we love up yonder.

Patricia stayed with Wade about a week. She wanted a few things like pictures, patchwork quilts her mother made, her old sewing machine. The house, land, cattle, money and everything else was Wades. She never needed any of it.

The Federal Government located Harry Burkett at Baytown. His father had been found in front of The United States Embassy in China. Dead, he had been beat to death with a cane. No one knew who did it, or left him there during the night. What did the family wish for them to do with his body?

Harry got out voted. He wanted his body brought back and buried in the Craig Cemetery by their Mother. Margaret, Katrina and Kevin told them to cremate his body, dump his ashes in the middle of the Atlantic Ocean.

The agent from the Government said their wishes would be carried out. "In China," he said, "a form of punishment is to be caned. Struck on the back the number of times as the persons estimated age or until death. Whichever came first. Otis Ray Burkett died after 35 licks with the cane."

We would never know why he was beat to death. Margaret, Katrina, Kevin, and I shared the same feeling. Justice caught up with the man! For him the Atlantic Ocean had been an escape route. That's where his ashes belonged!

When Cassie went to the ranch, she rode around with me very often. I went to the barn, loaded up about six bags of 20% protein cattle cubes and a couple of square bales of hay. We had round bales under the shed the cows could get to.

I let Cassie drive, told her to head out across pasture four where the bunch of cattle were. When we were near, I had her stop. I got out, filled a five gallon bucket about half full. Standing in the pickup bed, I shook it few times to rattle those hard cubes. When the cows heard that, they came on the run.

"When they get here, Cassie, start easing the truck back towards the gate." I scattered a 50 pound sack helter-skelter behind that pickup then told her to stop.

"Why do you drive out here in the pasture and do this, Daddy? They have hay under the shed."

"To a cow, Cassie, these cubes are like ice cream to a kid. I can rattle cubes in that bucket and they'll follow me into the corral. But you need to give them a taste every now and then to make it work. I count 39 grown cows and a bull, Cassie. How many did you get?"

"I got the same, Daddy. That old cherry red cow with the horn sticking down is not here." She was right. We had to saw that horn off so she could eat without turning her head sideways. The other horn stood straight up. We sawed some of it off to match the other.

"She's probably got a calf up there in those pines somewhere. Drive up there and maybe we can find her." She drove down by the edge of those long leaf pines and we found the cow. She was trying to have a calf.

"She looks like she's been here a long time Daddy. Is that it's front feet sticking out?"

"Yes, that's the calf's front feet sticking out. It may have its head back over its shoulder. We'll go check on the bunch in pasture three, then come back to see if she's had her calf yet."

"You hope you are not going to have to do anything." An hour later the cow had made no progress.

"What are we going to do, Daddy?"

"I'll have to try to push the calf back some, then try to get hold of its ear and pull its head out. I can take you to the house. I'll come back and do it."

For the first time, I saw a little anger in her eyes at me. "Just because I am a girl and I am your daughter, do you think we need to let this cow suffer another hour?"

"Well since sometimes you act like your mother, I guess we better get on with it!"

I knew this cow had three calves already without any trouble. I put on a shoulder length plastic glove. The cow had been at it so long she offered no resistance. I pushed the calf's shoulder back, and found an ear. In a matter of minutes, we had a bull calf on the ground.

"That's one of Hot Sauces calves, Daddy!"

"Yeah, it is. And one of these days, maybe you and Wade will tell me why you named that bull, Hot Sauce!"

She pretended she never heard me. She held out a sack for me to put the plastic glove in.

"The last time I talked to Mr. Wilson he had said, "I wonder why those kids named that bull, Hot Sauce"."

"I don't know. But I bet you and I never find out!"

"Well they named him right. He can work a cow over like no other bull I ever saw!"

Cassie only liked a few weeks before she graduated from college. For some reason she never had to go that Friday. I took off work at noon, we went to the ranch. Dad was with Virginia and had been spending time with the rest of the family.

Benton Craig was glued to the TV. Margaret and I were reading. We would not get out until the next day. We felt more like just relaxing and resting. Cassie walked outside looking at her Mother's flowers.

She saw Wade come in, get out of his truck and walk out to the road to get his mail. It can be said love has no common sense and it seldom listens to reason. Cassie forgot her resolve to ignore him. She met him walking back to the house.

"Hi Wade! I was wondering if you might like to go fishing tomorrow."

"I can't go. I got to work on some of my fence tomorrow."

"Well, why don't we go to Nacogdoches and eat tomorrow night. You can buy me a steak!"

"I don't imagine I will get through with the fence in time."

"Well, since you don't have time for your friends, at least your old friends anymore, I'm sorry I asked." She turned and ran for the house crying.

Wade went in, threw the mail on the couch. Cassie was smiling when she said that. He had seen her mad before. She was like her Daddy in that respect. But she turned and ran. He knew she was crying when she went around the back corner of their house. He also knew her bedroom was in the back corner of the house.

Dam it to hell! She knows I'm lying to her and making excuses. I ain't doing it again. I'm going to tell her the truth about the way I feel. She may hate me after she hears it. But I'm not lying to her anymore. After I finish feeding the cows, I'll get cleaned up and ask her to go somewhere and talk.

I went to the kitchen to get a cup of coffee. I suppose Cassie was so upset she forgot to close the door. She was lying across the bed, crying. I went in and softly shut the door. She never knew I was there until I sat down on the bed and said, "What's wrong baby?"

She came up crying on my shoulder. "It's Wade. He won't have anything to do with me anymore. If he's got a girlfriend, he could just tell me."

"I don't think Wade has a girlfriend, Cassie."

"Then where does he go every Friday and Saturday night? He stays out until three in the morning. Sometimes he leaves here Friday and is not back when we leave late Sunday evening."

"Wade goes up to the ten acre food plot. He climbs up in that observation tower and eats peanuts. He got sick eating peanuts. He took pecans the next time. He ate so many pecans they made him sick."

"How do you know all that Daddy?"

"He tells Luther. Luther tells me. Wade never had drank any beer. He took a six pack up there. He drank one really quick. He started on number two and passed out. Thunder and lightning woke him up. He started climbing down out of that tower in the rain. He dropped his ice chest. Hogs and deer came out of that gate running. He ran with them through the rain to his truck."

She laughed. "That sounds like him. But where does he go and stay all weekend?"

"He goes to Austin to visit Patricia. She comes up here one month, he goes there the next. They agreed to do that after their Daddy died."

"I'm glad they are doing that. But it does not explain why he does not want to have anything to do with me."

"Cassie, he's the only one that can explain that to you. But I suspect I understand why he acts like he does. It has not been that long since I was a young man myself."

"Then why do you think he avoids me, Daddy?"

"When I was 14, I met your mother. I knew right away that I loved her. We lived 12 miles from town. I never had a dime in my pocket and I could not take her anywhere. I never felt I had the right to tell her I loved her. I imagined she wanted a boy that had money and a car to take her places."

"I can't see how Wade would feel that way. He has money and he has a way to go."

"Perhaps that's because you are not looking at it from his perspective. In his mind, he has little compared to us. He's one of our employees, just a ranch hand. You are going to college, he is not. He may think you will marry a Doctor, or someone well off."

"I never have thought about that. But what happened to get you and mother together?"

"I give your mother credit for that. She did it with only three precious words. She said "I Love You!" Cassie, I want you to answer a question. You don't have to tell me the answer. Just answer it honestly for yourself."

"What's the question, Daddy?"

"Do you love Wade?"

Suddenly she was on my shoulder, crying again. "Yes, I love Wade. I've known that since I was a teenager. I won't ever love anyone else."

"Cassie, when I found out where your mother and you were, I drove almost all night because I wanted to tell you both I loved you."

"I know, Daddy."

"Someone has to say it first, Cassie. Don't you think it's silly not to tell Wade you love him and be miserable the rest of your life because you never told him?"

"He does not seem to want to talk to me, Daddy."

"Just maybe he has not heard the words he wants to hear. Wade's a creature of habit. Do you know where he'll be at five o'clock this afternoon?"

"He'll go to the barn in pasture three. He'll load eight bales of hay then drive out in the pasture to feed the cows. Yes, that's where he'll be. But you know Wade as well as I do. If you look him in the eye and ask for the truth, you'll get the truth."

"That's the way it was between us for a long time. Don't tell Mother about this. I don't want her to worry."

"Your Mother has been worried about it Cassie. But I won't say anything to her, I'll leave that up to you." I went to get my coffee, left her sitting there on her bed.

Cassie probably broke a record getting a shower, into jeans, and tennis shoes. A blue work shirt topped that off. She went to the shed, backed the beetle out to where fishing poles were leaning against the end of it. She got out, felt of two or three, found one that suited her. She stuck it in the passenger side window.

She was sure Wade saw her, he came out on the back porch. Good, he thinks I'm going up to the creek bridge to fish with Essie Mae!

She never turned right to the creek bridge, she turned left to the county road. By opening two gates, she crossed the county road into pasture three. She drove around behind the barn and corral. She left the beetle crawled over the corral fence and went in a back door of the barn.

She pulled down a bale of hay to sit on. After a minute that became a little uncomfortable. She found a couple of empty paper feed sacks to lay on it. That's better! She looked at her watch. Wade should be here in ten more minutes.

It was closer to 20 minutes. He pushed up the big garage type overhead door. Got back in his truck. He backed the trailer in to the stack of hay. He got out and started to the stack. For the first time he saw her.

"Cassie, what are you doing here?"

"I came to talk to you. I want to know what I've said or done to offend you."

He sat down on the other end of the bale of hay. "You have not done anything Cassie."

"Then why do you avoid me? Why can't we do things together like we once did?"

"We grew up, Cassie. My feelings for you became more than friendship. You were going away to college. I felt you would meet someone that amounts to more than a ranch hand. With your looks, Cassie, you could marry a Doctor or someone wealthy. I stay away from you because I know I can't control my feelings for you."

"Wade, I went to college because I did not know what else to do. I don't care about being some wealthy Doctor's wife. Here at this ranch is where I want to be. Truth is I've loved you since you fixed that pig's broken leg. I won't ever love anyone else."

Wade had heard enough. He pulled her to him and buried his face in her hair. "I love you too Cassie. I could never love anyone else but you."

Their lips found one another's and passion held back for much too long, then on a trip they had both dreamed about. Wade was trying to unbutton her blue work shirt when she pushed herself apart and said, "We have to stop, Wade."

"I don't want to stop!"

"What!"

"I said I don't want to stop!"

"We have to, Wade!" She was laughing about it now, pleased at his reaction.

Wade was beginning to get his senses back. "Why must we stop?"

"Because I was nearly ten years old before Mother had a husband and I had a father."

He realized she was talking about a goal she had set for herself a long time ago.

"Ok, I'll stop. Just as long as you realize I don't want to."

"I know how you feel. I don't want to stop either! I promised Mother I would wait until I was married."

"Does all this mean we will be married and you will be my wife?"

"Yes, Wade. I will marry you and I will be your wife!"

He took her in his arms and they started to kiss again. Passion was going up like a rocket when Wade pushed back.

"Since you are going to marry me, there are a couple of things I need to tell you."

She put her arms around his neck and whispered, "What's that, darling?"

"The wedding can be anyway and anywhere you want it to be. Second, I want it to be as soon as possible. I don't want to wait a minute longer than we have too!"

"I don't want to wait either. I've always wanted to marry you in our Church at Livingston. I graduate college the last of this month. Daddy has paid my tuition. I suppose we should wait until I get my degree."

"Then we can marry the first of June?"

"Yes, sometimes the first of June. I'll have to work it out with our preacher."

"That's settled then. I better load some hay and feed those cows. They're wondering where I'm at. They've already started bawling." He reached down and picked up the bale they had been sitting on. He climbed up the stack with it to the top. He turned it sideways and stuck it between the rafters.

"Why did you put that bale of hay up there?"

"That bale is special. We'll save it for a special occasion!"

He loaded the hay and she drove out into the pasture. They had done this so many times before. She stopped, and he got out and walked around to the back of the trailer.

When he put his foot on the trailer, she gassed the truck.

He jumped off and yelled, "Cassie!"

He heard her laughter ring out like a bell in the evening air. It was a great sound to hear again. He had known she would do that. And he knew she would not do it again.

When the hay was unloaded, she drove back to the VW where she had hid it. He let the ramps down on the trailer, she drove it on the trailer. They would ride home together.

"Do you still want to go to Nacogdoches tomorrow night and eat?"

"Since you have to fix fence tomorrow, and can't go fishing I suppose we can!"

He laughed. "I do need to fix fence tomorrow. We can't have our cows getting out and going to the Neches River. But we'll go to Nacogdoches!"

It was dark and Cassie had not come in. Margaret had already suggested I go look for her.

"She and Essie Mae probably got to gabbing. Let's give her a few more minutes, she'll be in."

Margaret was sitting with her back to the front door. Cassie came in, closed the door behind her. She stood there with both hands behind her on the door knob. Then she smiled at me, gave me a thumb's up sign and headed for her room.

I gave her a thumb's up and went back to reading the paper.

"What was that all about?"

"What?"

"I saw you give Cassie a thumb's up sign as she went by!"

"Well, why don't you go in her room, get her down off the ceiling, and find out!"

Margaret got up and gave me a kiss. "Do you really think I should?"

"Yes, I do. I can't wait to find out myself!"

Cassie had about four dresses on her bed when Margaret got there.

"Why are you dragging out all your dresses for Cassie?"

"Wades taking me to Nacogdoches tomorrow night."

"What got into him?"

She suddenly grabbed her Mother and started crying.

"It was not him Mother. I've been such a dummy. I should have told him I loved him a long time ago."

"You told him you loved him. What made you decide to do that?"

"Daddy did! He said someone had to say it first. I'm not as smart as you were Mother."

"Your Daddy's not all that slow himself. But what does Wade think about it?"

"Wade's not that slow either. He wants us to get married as soon as I get my degree."

Wade went through his pasture, through our new one and went to Jacksonville the next morning. A few months ago, he had been walking in a mall there. He passed a jewelry store, and he stopped to look at rings in a show case. He found himself staring at a set of engagement and wedding rings he liked.

The beautiful girl behind the counter walked over and said, "Do you think she would like these?"

Wade looked up a little startled. "I don't know. But if she ever says yes, these are the ones I'm getting."

"I'm sure she would. Any girl would appreciate these."

The rings were still there when he arrived. The same girl was there behind the counter to wait on him.

"I want those rings. She said 'yes' last night."

"They are marked $4200. They've been here for three years. Let me see if the manager will give you a discount."

She went to the Manager and came back. "He said you could have them for $3800."

"Ok then. I'll take them."

"Wait. I'll tell him you offered $3600."

She went to the manager again. "He said you could have them for $3600. But that is as low as he will go."

"Fine, I'll take them. But why did you do that for me?"

"Let's just say, I admire a man that knows what he wants. My best wishes to both of you."

Wade paid for the rings with cash. He started putting money in a coffee can he kept in his closet the summer he and Cassie had the mowing job. He added to it occasionally as the years passed. This was the purpose he saved for.

Wade went back the way he came. The fence was down between him and the Trahan place. Cole was there working when he got there. Between the two of them, they soon had it re-stretched and back up. A dead pine had fell on it.

Wade wanted to give her the rings as soon as they left the house, Saturday night. But he knew they would become passionate, and he would mess up her lipstick.

At Nacogdoches, he had the 12 oz. rib-eye. She had the 10 oz. New York strip. She gave him half of hers. Cassie never ate that much, but she never missed meals either. He was so thin, she needed to start building him up. Living by himself, he probably never ate right.

After eating, he drove to the northeast ranch gate, went to the creek bridge and stopped. He reached up and turned the dome light on. He opened up the glove compartment and took out the rings. He handed the open box to her.

"Wade these are so beautiful! You should not have spent so much."

"I started saving for those rings in a coffee can the summer we mowed. I've been adding to it over the years. I knew I wanted to buy you rings back then."

"You knew you wanted to marry me back then?"

"Yes, I did. When did you decide you loved me?"

"It started when you put that cast on that pig's foot. But I was sure of it the day we threw those cypress seedlings in the creek. It was cold. You gave me your coat!"

"I'm not going to let you get cold anymore! Which one of those rings are you supposed to put on now?"

"This one," and held out her finger.

He slipped the ring on and turned out the dome light. Then he started to mess up her lipstick. Passion took possession of them again. All of her resolutions were forgotten. She wanted this man and she wanted him now! She was at the point of no return and she knew it.

He stopped it this time. "We better go. It's getting late."

"Why must we go?"

"Because you were almost ten years old before I ever saw you!"

"Yes I was! We better go."

He backed the truck up and turned around. At the northeast gate, He turned right on the FM road the way they came in on.

"Why are we going back this way for?"

"I get to keep you out longer. And what do you suppose your folks would think if we came home through the woods?"

She laughed at that. "It's going to be nice to have a man that thinks of everything!"

"You are going to have all of my attention from now on. I promise you that!"

"I bought your ring today too, mister! But you are not getting yours until you say 'I do!'."

"I can't wait," he said.

They came in for Cassie to show us her rings. No doubt about it, they were happy together.

Margaret laughed about it when we went to bed. "I think Wade had on more of Cassie's lipstick than she did. Did you notice?"

"Yeah and ain't love grand!"

"Yes it is!" And she gave me a taste of hers. We still thought we had ten years to make up for. We did our best too!

Afterwards there was so much to think about. Margaret for instance. She could be sleeping minutes after she decided to. I never could do that. Like a hundred times before, I reached the conclusion I always did. It must be the purity of her conscience.

These two kids of ours was something to think about. Benton Craig was now just a year older than Cassie was when I brought her to the ranch.

For her, it was all an adventure, all enthusiasm, never ending questions. She could not wait to plant the next acorn or see what was around the next bend in the creek.

I knew June would not come too soon for her. Wade was here at this ranch. She loved both. I had no doubts she would be happy here with him.

Benton Craig was different. Today he wanted to go to town with his Mother and Cassie. Margaret knew this was a Mother-Daughter day that likely would not happen but once. She just simply told him no, you stay and help your Daddy.

I was planting black haw seed between some of the oaks we planted. Some of which were 12 feet tall now. He put three seed in each hole I dug with the hoe like I told him too. But truth of the matter was, he had rather put all the seed in one hole. Then go to the house and watch TV!

People were different. Cassie was about to get a degree in business administration. She had the education to handle the business in town. But this ranch was where she wanted to be.

Benton Craig's interests were more on the business in town. That's what he asked questions about. That's where he wanted to spend time with me. That seemed to be what he would be happy doing. Working in the business. I loved both of our kids and maybe God planned it that way. One for the ranch and one for the business. Time would tell. I would just have to wait and see!

We had to stay home the next weekend. Virginia was bringing Daddy back from his visit. Wade had come to Livingston three nights and had supper with us. He also asked for our permission to take Cassie to Austin with him to visit Patricia.

Margaret thought it nice of him to ask. But a little funny too. Cassie is 22 years old. I guess she can go if she wants too!

Wade was there early Saturday morning. They left by 7:30 in the new station wagon Cassie wanted. The trips to college had got the best of the old one.

Cassie meant to pay for it herself. She had been steady banking money on her stock investments. But Margaret and I decided it could be hers and Wades wedding gift. Since it would be Wades too, she took it.

I talked to her about building an office at the ranch. She could take over as the office manager with a salary. The ranch employee retirement would be transferred to the Wells bank. No longer would their time cards come to Livingston, she would handle that and write their paychecks on the Wells bank.

All cattle and hog sales as well as the produce receipts would be handled through her office and deposited in the Wells bank. That included the farm in Leon County as well.

Wade and Cassie had been on the road about 15 minutes when she asked how long it would take to get there.

"If we don't fool around, we can get there in time for dinner!"

"Wade, I'm not going there at dinner time. We can stop somewhere and fool around while we're eating!"

He laughed. "I knew you would say that. I told Patricia it would probably be after two before we get there."

They drove on in silence for a few minutes. A thought suddenly occurred to Cassie. "Wade, did you tell Patricia it was me?"

"Nope! I want it to be a surprise. She asked me, but I would not tell her."

"Wade! You beat all. What did she think of you getting married?"

"She said that this seems sort of sudden."

"What did you tell her?"

"Not for me it ain't. Seems like it took forever."

"Do you really mean Patricia is waiting on us not knowing who you are bringing?"

"Yes, it serves her right!"

"Why?"

"She's been pestering me to marry you ever since Daddy died."

"Pestering you?"

"Some things a man has to work out on his own."

"Then you think she'll be happy it's me?"

"I know she will. She says we belong together."

Patricia had been on pins and needles all morning. They had sandwiches for lunch. She had the house immaculate, she was not messing up the kitchen. They would go out tonight to eat. Tomorrow she would fix Sunday dinner.

Her husband was amused. "What's wrong honey? She's just going to be your sister-in-law!"

"That's what's wrong! I don't know who it's going to be. I hope he never fell for some bar room fluzzy!"

She was at the front door when they arrived. When Cassie got out, she left the door open and ran to her. She threw her arms around her and she was crying. Thank God it's you! Mother and Daddy would have been so happy. They loved you so much! We all love you!

Cassie's tears blended with Patricia's. Her words meant so much to her. I loved them too. We miss them so much when we go to the ranch.

That night they all went out to a rather elegant place to eat. It featured rabbit. Wade studied the menu and asked: "Which one is fried?"

I'll have that too Cassie said.

They toured the State Capitol. Cassie found a group picture with her great grandfather DuPree in it. She made pictures of the picture.

The next day she helped Patricia cook dinner. She noticed something about Patricia she had never noticed before. She was so much like her mother. She had always liked her. She would leave loving her.

May and June were busy months for us. Most of our family was there to see Cassie get her degree. My brother Regan perhaps said it for all of us. "Anytime someone in this family gets a college degree, it's worth the trip to see!"

Wade biggest concern was about where they would go on their honeymoon. Las Vegas, New Orleans, Padre Island, or where ever. You name it Cassie and we'll go.

Do you really want to know what I would like for us to do?

Yes I do.

I want to move most of my things into your house before the wedding. Then go there after the wedding. We'll pull the garage door down and we won't come out until we are ready. We'll tell mother and daddy that's where we'll be. They'll stay away.

Do you really mean that? You just want to go home?

Yes, unless you had rather go somewhere else.

That suits me fine. I'll admit I've thought of that. I just did not want to act like El Cheepo!

Wade we have the rest of our lives to go someplace we want to. Right now, I just want us to go home.

Margaret helped Cassie move her things up there. Wade mostly lived in his bedroom and the kitchen. Margaret discovered that Mr. and Mrs. Wilson's clothing was still hanging in their closet.

Cassie, you better come in here!

It upset Cassie to see those things. Margaret was upset at herself. I should have thought of this. I could have taken those things to the Salvation Army.

We could do that. But I'm not touching it until I talk to Wade about it.

Patricia got everything she wanted Wade said. She told me to give their things away. I just have not been able to make myself do it.

I called Rev. Billy about it. Bring those things up to the fellowship hall. I'm sure we got folks that can use it. If not, I'll take it to the Salvation Army.

The night of the wedding arrived. Cassie was getting dressed in an upstairs room at the church. Margaret, her bridesmaids, some of Cassie's friends and the minister's wife were there as well.

Wade arrived and parked in the appointed place so his truck would not be blocked when they left. He had it shined to perfection. He got out and walked down the driveway to the back of the church. He would go in the back door as he had been instructed to do.

He made some concessions to the occasion. He had on a rented black tuxedo. A white shirt and black string bow tie. That was it for the concessions. He wore black Tony Lama boots, a black felt Stetson hat and the big silver belt buckle Cassie had given him for Christmas years ago.

One of Cassie's friends saw Wade walking down the driveway from the upstairs window. She nudged the other girl and said, "Who is that hunk? He looks like the Marlboro man!"

"Cassie, Sylvia thinks Wade looks like the Marlboro man!"

Sylvia turned a little red. "That's Wade?"

Cassie laughed. "If he looks like the Marlboro man, that's Wade. You can look, but don't touch!"

Cassie looked beautiful coming down that aisle. I don't know how she drug all that extra cloth trailing behind her, but she did it.

Jason Batiste and Benton Craig stood by Wade. Jason's wife Maria, and Patricia's daughter stood by Cassie.

It all went fine until the minister said, "You may now kiss the bride!"

We saw the amusement in the minister's eyes as Wade put on his hat. No one saw him kiss the bride. His hat blocked the view!

They turned to march down the aisle and out the front door. At the front door, Cassie looked up at Wade and said, "You can put your hat on now!"

Wade's hand went up to his hat. He turned red. "Did I have this on the whole time?"

Jason Batiste was standing there. "Yeah, Wade! You are the only dude I ever saw walk into a church and marry with his hat on!"

Margaret appointed me to make the punch for the reception. She liked the way I made it at Christmas time.

I emptied a 46 oz. can of Welch's grape juice and a 46 oz. can of peach juice into separate pans. I froze both overnight. I put two 10 oz. cans of apricot nectar and two of peach nectar in the refrigerator, and a big bottle of Dr. Pepper as well.

The next day, I chopped up the frozen grape and peach juice with the ice pick. Dumped it in the punch bowl. Then added the four cans of nectar. I finished filling the bowl with the Dr. Pepper and gave it a brief stirring.

I had to make up two punch bowls for this crowd. I splashed grape juice on my white shirt and probably ruined it. But I got the punch ready to go. I got the job done!

Then like everyone else, I stood around and sipped punch. Went through the picture taking session. And wondered, why newly married couples have to endure two hours of this. Everybody knew they would rather just say "I do" and go!

They left the recession with "Just Married" soaped in big letters on the truck rear window. They were dragging tin cans and cars were following them blowing horns! Cassie had Wade take the New Willard loop off highway 59 to lose them. Wade got out and cut the cans off.

They never came out of the house Sunday. Monday Wade took her to the Wells Bank to get his account changed to "Mr. & Mrs. Wade Wilson" so she could write checks. She transferred $125,000 from her account in Livingston. That ended her Livingston account but she had $25,000 invested in stocks.

Tuesday, they went fishing in the lake. They found the crappie biting on jigs and caught 25. They had done this many times before in their growing up years. It seemed so good to be doing it again.

Wade had been planning on remodeling the house. He wanted Cassie's input before they did that. Wednesday they came to Livingston for supper with us. They had plans they drew up to discuss with me. They thought I could find them a contractor to do the work.

Wade wanted a garage like we had at Livingston. And he wanted an underground storm cellar you could enter from that garage. Cassie wanted a small office attached to the house she could get into from the kitchen. And she wanted Austin Stone around the house like we had with ranch rock trim.

Daddy, I don't think we need a big ranch headquarters building like you suggested. I've seen what the future of business will be like in college. I suggest we deposit ranch receipts like you said in the Wells Bank. Soon we'll be able to computer link the ranch with the office in Livingston. That's something we were taught in college.

I don't know anything about computers!

We'll all have to learn. Our records on everything can be viewed in seconds. No more digging through paper work trying to find something. Believe me, in less than five years we'll be able to convert to the system. That's why I only need a small office.

All right Cassie. We'll go with a small office next to your kitchen. I'll pay for that. I'll try to get the contractor who remodeled Rev. Billy's Church up there. Show him what you want, he'll draw up a blue print from your drawing. I suggest that you purchase the material for the job and let him do the construction. Most of what you'll need I can get for you at my cost.

Wade, looks like the garage floor is going to be concrete. "Your Dad had a foundation poured for the Austin Stone when we built the house. But the underground storm shelter will require concrete. I can send a ready-mix truck up to handle your concrete needs."

"I'll get Cousin Marvin over to give a cost estimate on putting the Austin Stone up. On my house, he put in the order for the stone. I sent a check to pay for it. That's probably how he'll want you to do it."

Things went well with the remodeling job, and by Thanksgiving it was complete. Cassie wanted the doors and windows trimmed with the rock like I had ours done. I had the Austin Stone sprayed about every two years to keep it white. Cassie wanted hers to turn a little light tan in places like it does without the spray. She thought that would give it more of a ranch house look.

Cole often talked of fishing with hoop nets and peddling fish. Buffalo for the most part. I asked him how long it would take to fill four barrels about three quarters full with buffalo and carp. Skinned and minus the head.

"If you are going to use carp, not long. Catch the river up and out. Put two hoop nets in that slough above your hog pasture. Put half a sack of 20/80 in each. Run them about three times, that that will probably do it. But what do you want with all that buffalo and carp?"

"To make fertilizer to add to that liquid hog fertilizer tank. Margaret's uncle made it to fertilize his crops with. He also used it to bait his steel traps."

I gave Cole the money to get four hoop nets made. One he could keep, the other three we would use. He and Wade put the nets out on Wednesday evening. Margaret wanted it did that way, so the wives and children could help her. She wanted to show the women that buffalo was good fish if prepared right.

Cole had his boat and motor. Joe Ed was with him. Wade was with me in mine. We towed a flat bottom boat behind each of us. We loaded them up with buffalo and carp.

I had a table set up, hooks to hang fish on to be skinned. Margaret had us start on the big buffalo first. The ribs were cut out to go in one ice chest. The rest of the fish with the small bones went into another. With Luther, Joe Ed, Wade, the three Mexicans and myself working Margaret soon said that's enough.

Wade you better go help these women with the heavy ice chests. And with the fish fryers. They're going to be cooking outside. Wade I knew liked to be where ever Cassie was!

The rest of us got down to skinning fish. Everything but the head, skinned off scales, fins and tail went into the barrels for fertilizer. The guts and fish eggs went into the fertilizer barrels along with the fish. We filled two barrels almost full.

They were taken to the tank that held the liquid hog fertilizer. The fish was covered in water. The lid was put on and sealed tight. Each barrel was vented to a PVC pipe that went into the vent pipe at the top of the storage tank. Margaret said in about six months it would be in a thick liquid state that could be pumped into the liquid hog fertilizer tank. Half a barrel would be enough to add to a full storage tank.

The women were frying the buffalo ribs. The ribs were big bones, they did not contain the small bones like the fillets did. Those were in pressure cookers out in front of the equipment shed. Don't ever pressure cook fish in the house if you want to continue living there!

We all got cleaned up and went to dinner. The fried buffalo ribs were good tasting fish. And Cole said these tuna sandwiches are sho-nuff good as well!

His wife laughed! Cole that's not tuna. It's buffalo cooked in a pressure cooker. Margaret taught us how to use the rest of that bony fish. You can keep it in the freezer until you want sandwiches! It's just as good as tuna!

They also had fried fish patties made out of the pressure cooked buffalo. Chopped up onion and bell pepper were added. Then corn meal and flour, salt and black pepper were added to make the patties. Deep fried it was about the same as fried patties made from salmon.

Luther loved it all. Miss Margaret, you beat all I ever see. People been wasting fish like dis and it's good to eat! Jo Ed, after we get those other two barrels full, You, Luther and I may keep the nets out longer Cole said.

Yall just keep the buffalo out like we did today. That carp will do in the barrels. I don't think Margaret could make it fit to eat!

The three Mexicans had brought their lunch, said they needed to get back to their work at the hog farm. Maybe they never liked fish for all I knew. But we put some of all of it in an ice chest. I had Luther take it over to them along with a loaf of bread, a jar of mayonnaise and a few plastic spoons.

Growing crops on fields depleted the soil quickly. The game plan was to add back to it during the winter. By adding a half barrel of that fish emulsion to 30,000 gallons of liquid hog fertilizer, and circulating the tank about four hours to mix, it would get the land ready to plant another crop come spring.

We normally sprayed on our fields 60,000 gallons or two tanks full during the winter. Four barrels would last us four years. During the summer months, the liquid hog fertilizer was sprayed on pastures without the fish emulsion.

Mr. Wilson had rigged it when we put the tank in. He used an old crank telephone to operate a spark plug he put into the vent pipe on top of the 30,000 gallon tank. Stand on the ground, crank that telephone and ignite the methane gas coming out of that vent pipe.

182

A few flying saucer tales got out, but we got the word out we were burning methane gas at the hog farm. After we vented those barrels with the fish in them to the top of the tank, that flame became a little more blue!

The other thing he did was rig two 1500 gallon tanks to pull behind a tractor. The pump operated with the power take-off on the tractor. Quick open valves were linked in reach of the operator. You could circulate the tank until you reached the field or pasture to be sprayed. Then it was pumped out through a ten foot perforated pipe behind the tank.

In the fields that we grew crops in, tractors with discs followed the spray tanks. In the pastures, we never ran the discs. We did need to wait until it rained to turn the cattle in.

When I was a kid, people had an ornamental plant in their yard they called fern. I don't suppose they knew it was asparagus. I never heard of anyone eating any of it when the shoots emerged in the spring.

I called a nursery and got a special deal on 500 sets. We had a row prepared for it with the cow barn compost. With irrigation water out of the creek we got it going. We never put the Shady Oaks label on those asparagus bundles. I knew from way back, if you were successful with a crop, and getting a good price for it, then every farmer in the vicinity would jump on it. Then the price would go down!

Margaret and I were horseback riding in the sand flat country between the road into our camp house and Jeff's fence. We rode up on a patch of bull nettles. The stinging skin had dried and peeled off the seed balls. Margaret and I dismounted, tied our horses and started picking bull nettle balls. Margaret and I were experienced at this game. We knew how to deliberately touch bull nettles without being stung.

To accidentally touch one was another story. They would sting us. We must have gathered about a gallon in a paper sack I got out of my saddle bag. That included the white outer covering that enclosed the seed.

Back at the camp house, Margaret and I were eating the things. "First pull off the white seed covering. Then pull off the rubber like tip on the end of the seed. Then crack the thin but brittle seed covering with your teeth. Then peel it. Then eat the seed!"

Cassie was first. "Daddy what's that you and Mother are eating?"

"Bull nettle seed. They are good. Try one!" I handed her about four seed.

"What's this rubber like tip on the end for?"

"I don't know, Cassie, why it's on there. You don't eat that. You eat the white seed inside after you peel it."

"These things are good! Try one, Wade. How did you and Mother get started eating these things?"

"Well there was no radio. There was no TV. There was no automobile. There was no air conditioner. By the time we were five years old, we followed the older members of our family on their favorite hot summer time pastime. That was to go bull nettle ball hunting!

"By the time I was ten, Mother had me take the hoe, cut some bull nettles down. Then drag them to put in her flower beds. That kept the dogs from digging holes in her flower beds. I deserved hazardous duty pay, but that was a word that had not been invented yet!"

In September, we had a little cool norther. Wade and Cassie went up to pasture 3 late one evening to feed the cattle. Wade opened the barn door a little, and Cassie walked in. Wade followed her in and closed the door behind him.

"Wade, why did you close the barn door?"

"We can't save that bale of hay forever!"

Her eyes flew to the rafters. The bale of hay was gone. It was there yesterday!

"There it was on the floor with a folded blanket on top." Wade's intentions were clear. No doubt about it!

Cassie soon had all the symptoms of being pregnant. She compared notes with Essie Mae. Essie Mae summed it up. "It sure looks like you is. Looks like Mr. Wade done hit a home run already!"

She met Wade at the door when he came in for lunch. She held on to him a little longer than usual. Then said, "I think you hit a home run on that bale of hay, Wade!"

"You mean…?"

"Yes. I think you are going to be a daddy!"

Wade held her close for a while. Words did not come quickly. Finally they did. "Sounds like you been talking to Essie Mae!"

"Why?"

"That home run business. That sounds like something Essie Mae would say."

"Yes, I talked to her. She knows about such things, and Mother is not here."

"You told her we did it on that bale of hay?"

"No silly! I told her my symptoms. I think it happened on that bale of hay!"

"Oh!"

"I have an appointment with Mother's Doctor at Livingston, tomorrow at 11 a.m. I'll probably have lunch with Mother and Daddy, afterwards. I'll be home in time for supper. Do you think you can find something for lunch?"

"I'll manage. But call me at lunch time. I want to know what the Doctor thinks."

Margaret had an appointment at 9 a.m. They missed one another. But Margaret went with the same symptoms that Cassie did. The Doctor confirmed that she was pregnant.

After the Doctor told Cassie it was almost certain she was pregnant, he asked Cassie if she had seen her Mother lately.

"Not since last weekend. But I'm going by there, after I leave here and will tell her."

"I'm sure you two will have a lot to talk about he said."

Cassie told Margaret what she had found out at the Doctors office. Then she called Wade.

"How did Wade take the news Margaret asked?"

"He's excited about it. Everyone at the ranch will know by the time I get home!"

"Did Dr. Carter tell you I was there this morning?"

"No, he asked me if I had seen you lately. Strange, he never told me you were there."

"Is there something wrong, Mother?"

"There's nothing wrong. It looks like you and I might have a baby on the same day!"

"You're going to have another, Mother? I thought…what happened?"

"Your father woke up in one of his moods! I think I forgot something I was supposed to do."

"You mean Daddy does that too! I've told Wade he was worse than Hot Sauce!"

"I've told your father that, a few times. It's terrible, don't you think!"

"Oh, it's awful!"

"I wondered what they were laughing about when I came in for lunch."

"It never happened the same day. Our son, William Bethel, came a day earlier than his niece, Cathy Wilson. That might make him feel better about being called 'Uncle' a few years later."

"Margaret insisted we name him William Bethel. This is the last grandchild Daddy DuPree is likely to have. There won't be a William Bethel in this generation of DuPree's if we don't name him that. I think it would make your father happy."

"Well, ok. Just as long as you and Daddy are happy. But we ain't calling him 'William'. And we ain't calling him 'Billy'. We will call him 'Bethel'!"

Jason Batise's wife, Maria, had a little girl the day after Cathy was born. They named her Cynthia Ann. They had a boy, two years older. His name was Austin Earl Batise.

Some of the oak trees I planted were now 19-year-old. Some were producing acorns. I could see squirrel nests out in some. But they were years away from being any hollow trees among them. Red squirrels needed hollows to survive it seemed to me.

I had some selective post oaks brought to the mill. I wanted ten inch wide and one inch thick rough cut lumber to build squirrel boxes out of. For box bottoms and tops I wanted a few cut 14 inches wide.

There would be a lot of 4, 6, and 8 inch lumber in the process of course. We would sell that.

I set up a table saw in the equipment shed for the project. Built a work table to be able to stand up and put the things together. The boxes would be three feet tall and divided into three compartments. Each compartment had an entrance hole.

The back of the box was cut four feet long. The extra 12 inches hung below the box to nail to the four by six penta-treated post I ordered to put them on. The posts were of fir lumber 12 feet long. They were the cheapest post I could find, and were easier to nail to than a round post.

They were loaded on a 16 foot trailer pulled by a tractor. Another tractor had a six inch post-hole digger on it. We dug the hole, nailed the box to the post. We positioned it so the box was up among the limbs of the tree. We spaced them about 100 yards apart in our hillside young oak timber.

The older man I got the squirrels from in Madisonville had passed on. His son still trapped the squirrels. He called me about twice a year, and I went after them. I released the big red squirrels three times near Buffalo Creek in Leon County. Also in our Neches River Bottom where the Mexicans hunted.

Now that we had the boxes up, I wanted to release more in our young oak timber. Cassie had little Bethel with her at the ranch. He and Cathy were like brother and sister. They loved to play together. Margaret, Benton Craig and I were on our way to Madisonville to pick up squirrels.

Benton Craig had his little radio in his lap. His ear phones on his head. He was laid back with his eyes closed. It made no difference to him where we were going.

Son, what kind of music are you listening too?

He did not hear me. Margaret lifted one earphone and said "Your father wants to know what kind of music you are listening too"

He handed the earphones to me. I put my hat on his head and put them on. Some guys were singing about Winslow Arizona. I was enjoying the song. But I handed the earphones back to him. "Who are those guys, singing? They are good!"

"The Eagles. They are the best!"

"There is getting to be a lot of good music. I like that young girl Tanya Tucker. She's got a sound and style that's all her own. If I could play music, I would want to hook it up and get it on like she does!"

"She's from Seminole, Texas, Daddy. And her sister sings too."

Cassie had sat on the edge of her seat coming over here after squirrels. It was a great adventure to her. Benton Craig had his interest strapped to his head.

There was one thing about the trip he was interested in. A restaurant there cooked a pile of meat as big as a washtub. How they put it all together in one ball I don't know. But they would cut off a slug of it to put on your order. Benton Craig would lay down his earphones for that. Margaret and I liked it as well.

Bethel and Cathy were four years old when I decided we needed to go on vacation. I mean a go yonder vacation. Not just a few days at the Craig place or the ranch. Cassie and Wade wanted to take off and go. And Benton Craig had to be out of school for the summer.

I bought a travel trailer big enough for all of us to sleep in. And a Ford diesel truck to pull it. We needed another truck at the ranch anyway to pull cattle trailers and the low boy trailer.

Instead of a bed in the sleeper, I had them put in three comfortable chairs for adults. Side windows to see out of. The seats were higher than the driver and passenger seats, seeing over was no problem. There was room in the floor board for Cathy and Bethel to play. Sit in a couple of small chairs or sleep some on a pallet.

I had the Shady Oaks, Bar D Ranch logo painted on the doors. And a list of all of our products. All this was inside an outline of the map of Texas. A star was placed and labeled Wells Texas. And below it all, the ranch phone number.

We went through Denver, across into Wyoming, turned east into South Dakota, then north into Canada one day. We ate at a restaurant in Brandon Manitoba, then back to Bismarck North Dakota. We did that so we could say we had been to Canada.

From there we crossed Montana, Idaho into the Pacific Northwest. There at a camp ground, we were invited to eat with a family who caught some salmon. They were nice folks, we accepted their invitation.

The man cooked that salmon on a grill. The trick he said is not to overcook it. I thought it barely warm when he took it up. But these people were natives to this country. We were guests and I never had cooked salmon. I hoped he knew what he was doing.

We ate outside. They had plenty to go with the salmon. We were guests. We ate salmon and tried our best to act like it was great. Later we privately agreed that maybe you had to acquire a taste for it.

Little Cathy had her way to deal with it. I saw her put it in her mouth. Her napkin went to her mouth next. Napkin and salmon went in the pocket of her jeans. That went in the can in the kitchen when we got back to the trailer.

The next day we stopped at an observation post to watch grizzly bears catch salmon in the river down below. They would splash out into the river, catch one then come on the bank to eat it.

Little Cathy watched it awhile. Then she had a question. Why does them bears dist bite the head off and then dist throw the rest away?

I answered that. The head is mostly bone. It don't taste like the rest of it!

We stopped in Redding California. My sister and family had once lived there. Their teenage son had been killed in an automobile accident. He was buried there. We found his grave and left flowers. My sister and family now lived in Tucson Arizona.

I should have already explained it I guess. We could get out from under the travel trailer on a camp ground. Then we could take the truck to sight-see. We might stay two or three days in one area. Getting groceries, finding a place to do laundry was another reason to free the truck from the trailer.

We found a camp ground just outside Reno Nevada. We left the truck hitched to the trailer. We only expected to stay one night. It was fueled up and ready to go the next morning. Truth is, we were getting in a "Let's go home mood!"

The fitting was broken where we needed to hook our sewer hose. Wade and I walked down to the office to see if they had another. If not, they would need to let us move to another spot to park.

The woman said she never knew it was broken. Just look in the box outside. "You should be able to find what you need. If not, I'll sign you in at another spot."

Wade had the lid up, looking for the fitting in the box. A pink painted VW van drove up. It had all sorts of weird designs on it. Two guys got out. One had orange hair and ragged cut-off jeans. The other had on ragged long jeans, no shirt, and his long hair looked like it might have cuckel burrs in it.

I suppose it was our hats and boots. They walked by and the one with the orange hair said, "Are you fellows looking for your horse?" Maybe it was the mood I was in. Or the way 'it' said, "you fellows!"

I answered 'its' question. "No we are not looking for a horse. And we never thought we would find a grinning jack ass either!"

Wade stood up to all of his six feet four inches. He had a fitting in his hand. I don't think they liked the look on his face. They got back in their painted weirdo wagon.

Wade was in the same mood I was. I guess those "fellows" decided they were barking up the wrong tree. This fitting will work. We won't have to move.

We started back across the lot. They made a circle and headed right at us in the VW van. We had to stop to let them pass. The one with the orange hair on the passenger side shot the bird at us.

Wade was carrying that three inch double female quick coupling fitting with the ring on one handle around his finger. They were that close. He swatted that window class with the quick coupling fitting. The glass turned white, and fell out as they hooked it out of there.

We put the fitting on. We let the canopy down and got some chairs out. I sat down. Wade had other ideas. I better tell them we are hooked up. And maybe I can get Cassie to make us some iced tea.

I could hear them laughing inside. Wade was telling them about orange hair and long hair I knew. I'd probably hear about this stop for years!

Wade came back out and sat down. In a little time, Margaret came out with iced tea. Do you "fellows" want your tea, or do you want me to give it to your horses?

I don't want to talk about it I said. She went back in laughing!

In a little while, we saw a police officer drive in. He looked us over as he drove by. He went on down to the office and went in.

They must have turned us in. I guess we've had it Wade said.

They probably did. But it may not amount to much. Did you notice the shape of that officer's hat?

The brim was not straight like officers up here wear their hats. His was rolled up.

That may be a good sign. We'll wait and see. Here he comes now.

He got out and got on with it. Couple of fellows down at the station in a VW van says you broke their window out.

I did it Wade said. They made some cute remarks to us down at the office. They nearly run over us as we were walking up here. The one with the orange hair showed us his middle finger. I swatted that glass with a fitting I had in my hand. I should have hit his orange head!

He looked around at the truck. "You folks from East Texas I see."

"Yes," I said. "We are from East Texas. Never been anywhere before. We've took vacation and are seeing part of the rest of the world. If those "fellows" had not said anything to us, we would not have bothered them."

"Let me talk to the dispatcher. I may be able to get this all squared away." He went to his patrol car and got in. We could see he was talking on his radio, but we could not hear him. It was a rather lengthy discussion.

He came back laughing. "The dispatcher told them we would have to lock them up with the two of you in the same cell until Monday. They decided to leave and forget any charges. That works every time!"

"Well I'm glad that's settled. How about having a glass of tea with us?"

187

"Don't mind if I do," he said. "It's been a long time since I talked to anyone from home."

Wade got up to get his tea. "So you are from Texas?"

"I grew up in Van Horn. Dad worked for an oil company. He got transferred there. He and Mother both are from San Augustine. We still have folks there. My wife and I go to Van Horn on vacation ever year. I married her here while I was in the service. Dad has a travel trailer and this next year we plan on going to visit folks at San Augustine. And maybe fish some in that Sam Rayburn Lake."

I got up and gave him some ribbon cane syrup and a few jars of jelly with our label on it. "Stop by our ranch at Wells. We got a lake you can fish in. And we'll be making syrup the first week in October. Anybody in Wells can direct you out to our place."

"We might just do that. Dad has always talked of making syrup when he was a boy. It's been nice talking to you folks." He shook hands and left.

"You were right about that hat!"

"Yeah! And Thank God we can get out of here in the morning!"

We stopped at Las Vegas Nevada that evening late. We booked into a camp ground for the night. Margaret and I, Benton Craig stayed with the kids. Wade and Cassie said they were going into the city to invest in the slot machines. I think they just rented a motel room for the night to have a little privacy. But they were back at the camp ground early the next morning.

We left there and moved on to Tucson Arizona. We booked into a camp ground for two nights. We spent most of the next day with my sister and family. She seemed pleased we had stopped in Redding and left flowers. We left for the camp ground and told her we would be headed home the next morning.

We voted that night in Tucson. From here we would head home. We had a listing of KOA camp grounds in cities across the United States. The next morning we got the office at the camp ground to book us into one in Odessa Texas that night.

It was after 7 p.m. when we made it to Odessa. Wade, Cassie and I all took turns driving. We had a hamburger supper at a fast food place and sacked out. We had breakfast in the trailer the next morning and were out of Odessa by 8 a.m.

I drove to Abilene, Cassie on to Weatherford. We had lunch there and fueled up. Wade took us on home. We rolled into the ranch about 4 p.m. We raised some windows in our houses to let them air out. We had been on the road almost two months. It was great to be back home.

It may not be at the top of the list. But getting home to sleep in the bed you are accustomed to is one of life's greatest pleasures. Here at the ranch, no sirens or flashing lights, no traffic sounds. A Katy-Did singing rocked me to sleep that night.

One thing I learned about the people in this country. We had been in places it got so cold I would be afraid to live there. Places that got so hot I would not want to live there. But people adapted to where ever they landed.

Those people up in the Northwest though that Salmon was something special. They adapted to liking it. Here in East Texas, we adapted to eating Polk Sally and Catfish. I think it's something special! But the people in the Northeast probably would not agree.

The next day I gave the Travel Trailer and Truck a cleaning inside and out. After I pressure washed both, I backed them under the shed. The truck would see duty on the ranch. The travel trailer would get a rest. It would probably go to the Craig place whenever we had a family reunion there.

Dad had been with Virginia while we were gone. I called to tell her we would be home at Livingston by the week end. She said she would bring him home.

Not long after we returned home, Rev. Billy passed away. His wife had been gone for three years. As we sat in the Church, he preached in so long at his last rites, my mind went back to a conversation we once had.

It was when Mr. Dobrinsky had me move up to the ranch to start developing the place. We had drug some trees blown over out to the road to cut up for firewood. It was Saturday, I was there cutting firewood for the coming winter.

Rev. Billy drove up and got out. We shook hands and sat down on a log to talk.

"I just drove up here to take a walk in the creek bottom. Sometimes I do that when I'm troubled about what message I'm going to bring Sunday morning. You may understand that. You once told me that sometimes you felt closer to the Lord up here in the woods than you did anywhere else."

"Yes, I remember telling you that. And I still do sometimes. But I remember you told me I needed to get back to going to church Sunday morning. You gave me the shove I needed!"

"I'm glad you were willing to listen. A lot of white folks would have thought I was being an "uppity nigger." Mr. Justin and I have always been able to talk. I'm glad we can too."

"Rev. Billy, I think all races are the same. There are good and bad among all of us. I know some white people I would not invite into my house to eat dinner. It's the same with any other race. God gave us all life, he made us the color we are. I think God expects us to be proud of whoever we are."

"I wish all people could see it that way Mr. Robert. But it's hard to get people to understand that. They seem blinded by resentment. Like a mule with a blind bridle on. They just want to plow straight ahead without thinking."

"I'll be honest with you. There is something I resent about Black People. Not all black people, but a good many."

"What's that Mr. Robert?"

"I can't help what my Great Grandfather did 150 years ago. I can be sorry about it, even ashamed of it. All I can do is treat people right and with respect now. That being said, I find some in all races, including mine that won't allow you to do that. I believe we all have been blessed to live in this country together now, regardless of what happened years ago."

"We are all blessed Mr. Robert. I thank the Good Lord for it every day. He stood up to shake hands again. I best be getting on back to the house."

"I guess I should not have talked so much! I'm sorry I've kept you from your walk in the woods."

He laughed. "It's not that Mr. Robert. I still have plenty of time for a walk. The Lord has blessed me today. I never had to go far today to find a message for tomorrow!"

He was put by his wife out in the cemetery at the ranch. Their headstone were already up. Luther and Essie Mae had marked off a plot where they wanted to be as well. I could walk out on the front porch and see the headstone where Rev. Billy was put. And be reminded that he was a man like God meant for a man to be.

Daddy remained remarkable healthy after mother's death. He took over the garden work there at Livingston. Growing things was what he liked to do. He seemed to enjoy hitching up that mule, plowing again. William Bethel was usually two steps behind him when he did it.

Growing things was an interest Margaret shared with him. They worked together in the garden and the flower beds regularly.

I think they looked forward to grocery buying day. He bought what he needed, she got what we needed. She had him saving coupon stamps. When he got a book full, he gave it to her. "Get something for the kids, I don't need anything!"

Dad liked to talk to people when they went shopping. Margaret was always laughing about the time it took to get him in and out of a store because he had stopped to talk to people so much.

William Bethel called him "Pappy". Dad fixed his own breakfast and lunch, but ate supper with us. Margaret put us on a fat free diet. We only ate eggs and bacon on Saturday morning. She said that Dad fried his eggs so hard you could stick a fork in one and it would stand straight up.

She took William Bethel over one morning early. Dad was frying two eggs to eat with a can of biscuits.

Daddy DuPree, they say eggs are not good for us. They have a lot of cholesterol in them!

Oh Yes! It's all over TV and in the Newspapers. I've been eating two eggs every morning for over 80 years, and they are killing me! He laughed and went on frying his eggs.

Margaret was laughing about it when I came in for lunch. "You and Daddy DuPree are just alike. I can't teach either of you anything!"

"Well I guess he made his point! I still never had eggs until Saturday morning!"

Two years later, he had to have his prostrate removed. That seemed to set him back. He quit eating much of anything. He kept getting thinner and thinner. Daddy did not die, he just faded away. His mind had left before he did.

In his mental state, we had to put him in a rest home. Two weeks later, they called at 5 a.m. in the morning. He appeared to have left this world in his sleep. It was December 7, 1984. Dad was 86.

We took him back to Leon County and put him by mother. He was there by his parents. We all knew that's where he wanted to be.

The nine of us were an independent lot. But we could come together when we needed to. We agreed that day, at least once a year we would have a family reunion. They agreed with me on something else. In the red clay and white sand of Leon County, was where our roots were.

We would meet between the forks of Buffalo and Keechi Creek in Leon County.

Chapter Twelve
1980–1990. A Decade of Change

We settled on the second weekend in June for the family reunion at the Craig place. Margaret and I usually spent the week prior to that anyway fishing and putting fish in the freezer. School was out and it was a good time to fish.

Margaret and I talked it over. We were in agreement that we should make the place between the creeks comfortable for family to come to. Not just the reunion, anytime they felt like spending time there. As a matter of fact, come spend the week prior to the reunion with us.

We screened the sand and gravel we still had a lot of at the ranch into both dump trucks. Joe Ed and Cole made three trips each over there and dumped it. That would go into a concrete slab for the building the family reunions would be held in. We also meant to build a bridge to cross Keechi Creek on.

Wade, Cole and Joe Ed would spend their work week over there working on the projects. I spent a lot of time delivering needed materials to the site.

Rather than haul our big dozer over there, I hired a man at Oakwood to do our needed dirt work. I would have needed to get a permit to put ours on the road. And it was really risking an accident to put that big thing on the road.

He graded a road to where we wanted to put the bridge across the creek. And did the work for our building foundation in one day.

The building would have a men's and woman's shower and rest room in one end. That would be a shower stall, lavatory, commode and mirror. Between them was an electric hot water heater and an automatic washing machine and dryer.

On the other end, would be a well equipped kitchen with two gas stoves, refrigerator and a big freezer, and automatic dishwasher. An electric hot water heater was put in a closet in one corner. Just outside the kitchen in the big room were gas fittings to hook up three two burner fish fryers or other cooking needs.

We put the building on a separate electrical meter from the camp house. We also had to have another propane tank for the building. And a complete separate sewer system from the camp house. We laid that out so six RV trailers could park and hook up to it, the water and electricity.

The building was 22 feet wide and 80 feet long. The big room was 60 feet in length. We had folding tables and chairs for 80 people. It had a ceiling with three attic fans installed. Open up the windows, turn the fans on it was cool in the room even in the summer. The building was well shaded by big oaks with Spanish moss hanging all over.

I might add we put steel bars over those aluminum framed windows. To enter the building, a key was needed to open one door. It had two doors on each side, but three had locking bolts on the inside.

Outside, we built a shed to cook barbeque under. It was big enough to back our big pit on the trailer under. And I bought a couple of smaller family size pits to keep there in case it was just a family or two there. I piped propane gas there for fish fryers or whatever the need might be. A shut off valve was inside the building.

I gave keys to all my brother and sisters, Cousin Marvin and Joe DuPree. Charles and Paula Heston. Nancy Kaye and Husband had places across the Flo road on Buffalo Creek. We just traded gate keys so we could visit back and forth. They never needed a place to camp, hunt and fish.

Cassie and Wade and their kids would bring our travel trailer. We would stay in the camp house and probably a couple of families could sleep there as well. Regan H. lived just up the road. Some could stay with them. And there were RV hook-ups for those that had them. Beyond that, someone might want to bring a tent!

If the creeks were up some, you could not use the rocky crossings. We could live with that on Buffalo Creek, but on Keechi, it was another story. We needed to cross there often, and if the creek was up, it was a 20 mile drive to get to a destination a half mile away.

I had a bridge in mind when Jeff and I bought the Jim Williams place. Above the rocky crossing on Keechi, the creek narrowed down into a deep and straight up bank stretch. It never got out of banks through that stretch of creek. But it was shallow when down normal, flowing over rock.

The center support was with three of the 20 inch pipes like we did at the ranch. On each bank, we poured concrete support. Then built forms 12 feet long, 20 inches wide and ten inches deep. With three rail road iron rails in each, and three-quarter inch rebar, it was filled with concrete. Seven forms were poured on each side of the creek. Two of each of the seven would have stand up pipes to weld two inch pipe side railings to.

We put the old "A" frame GI truck on the low boy trailer and took it over there. It was in good running condition, I just never registered it to put on the highway. With it we put those 12 foot sections of concrete in place. The bridge was 12 feet wide with a small crack between each section of concrete.

There was enough gravel and sand left to put on the roads we had graded up to it. There would be no need to put heavy loads on the bridge, but cars, pickups, and tractors would be no problem. It solved a problem the Craig family had lived with since 1856!

I was under the shed, cooking up barbeque for the last Sunday of the first family reunion. Margaret and I, with William Bethel had been there a week with Cassie and her two kids, Kathy and Justin Robert. Justin Robert was named after both of his grandpa's. Bethel and Cathy were ten years old, Justin Robert was only six.

It was after 10 p.m., the kids had been allowed to stay up with me. It was Kathy who asked the question: "Grandpa, how do you think that big rock dam that formed this marsh and lake between the two creeks happened?"

All I can do is guess Kathy. I don't claim to know for sure. But I believe millions of years ago, a huge meteorite struck here. I've showed you that big hole in the ground they call the 'old basin" near where your Grandmother and I once lived.

That thing I believe was shaped somewhat like a plane. It may have not been a meteorite, it could have been a small planet. No telling how big it was before entering the earth's atmosphere at faster than the speed of sound, and started to burn up. As it neared the earth, it was so hot trees just exploded into tooth picks and burned up.

The right wing burned off and I believe it fell where the "Old Basin" we call it now is. I showed you the big rocks they had to blast with dynamite to put a pipe line across it. I believe those rocks were part of that wing.

With the loss of that wing, it turned to the left somewhat. You can find red rocks laying here and there out in the sand flat country. That's what the fireplace chimney there at the house is made from. They were most likely big as a car when they fell, but burned down to those small rocks you see now.

Ok, the nose of that thing hit down right where the edge of the marsh is now. It plowed up dirt ahead and on top of it. It finally stopped where the rock dam is now. But that wall of mud and dirt on top of it formed a dam. It backed up both creeks and formed a lake all over this country.

After a few years that earth dam broke. A wall of water hit the Trinity River and swept down it. That's why on the East side of the Trinity River bottom, we have those high banks now. That raging water swept away high places and cut into the hills.

But the lake finally drained down to the Marsh we have now. It took years, but squirrels and birds replanted the now dry lake bed in trees like we have today. This is what I think happened. Most likely you can find some teacher that will not agree with me. Truth is, none of us really know.

Margaret came out and sent the kids off to bed. I was left alone with my barbeque for the time being. Did they believe the theory that probable existed in my mind only? Well maybe not. But one thing I was sure of. The kids knew I had given it some thought!

Frank, Lawrence and Elton soon joined me. They had been here with us for three days. Running trotlines down Buffalo Creek, they were fishing with chicken blood and live perch. Their live box was full of catfish. Tomorrow they would fry up a lot of catfish.

All nine of our bunch was present. Even the sister and her family who lived in Arizona. Somewhere spending the night with Regan H. We had a couple of families in the camp house with us. Five of the six hook-ups for travel trailers were being used.

The next day, old friends of the family showed up. John Wesley Heston and his wife Ruth. Charles Ray Heston and his wife Paula. Riley and Nancy Kaye "Bolton" Long and their two kids. They brought Emanuel Newhouse and his wife Sadie with them. Mary Ellen, her husband and two girls were there also. Duncan "Cat" Williams and is wife came.

After dinner, the tables were folded and the musical instruments brought out. Melton had the fiddle, Franklin and Franklin Jr. had rhythm guitars. Regan H. played a Galloping Gibson lead guitar. Our Cousin Douglas DuPree was on the bass guitar. Benton Craig was on the drum set he loved. I was trying to play rhythm guitar.

Nancy Kaye and Mary Ellen did most of the singing. Those two could have been in Nashville! They did a recording at a place in Tyler of gospel songs to raise money for their church. It raised over $500,000 locally.

Franklin did a few Bob Wills songs. Douglas got down on the "Milk Cow Blues." Then I shocked myself and the crowd I think. I got down on singing "Love Me like You Used to Love Me" recorded by Tanya Tucker. Those that felt up to it, danced.

It had cost a lot to prepare for this. It was worth it!

Benton Craig started working in the business at 15. During his four years of High School, I started him in the feed store first. When he graduated High School, he had worked in most of the business and was learning the ropes in the office.

I felt he would one day be the one to run the business. He was trained like Mr. Dobrinsky trained me. I personally had another reason for letting him work and sweat some. I thought it should be against the law for a man to employee people to work if he had never worked himself!

Athletics was something Benton excelled in. He lettered four years in football, basketball, baseball and track. He made all district defensive end his junior and senior year. He played offensive end as well, but the coach he had never designed plays to throw to offensive ends.

Wade and Cassie attended most of his football games. And Wade taught him a lot of moves in the yard up at the ranch. Wade never got to play football, but Benton learned more from him than he did his coaches.

The game had changed since I played. Back then, you could not use your hands blocking. A good block was to put somebody on the ground. Now it was rooster fight with your hands and try to get in some one's way. Don't try to coach your son was the advice I gave myself!

Benton graduated from college in 1983. He took Business Administration along with Computer training as well. For four years, he stayed with my brother Lawrence and his wife. Their kids were grown and gone. Benton had a car, he could come and go as he pleased.

They would take no pay for letting him stay there. I did manage to put a calf in their freezer a couple of times. And they often went to the place in Leon County to hunt and fish.

No, we don't need to be paid! You're giving us a free hunting and fishing lease.

Such was the attitude of my family!

We went up to the ranch on a Friday evening. Margaret and Cassie had their heads together as usual. Margaret brought everything to make burgers down by the Lake. Mid October, it was pleasant outside.

Benton Craig and I went on down to the lake and I got the charcoal going in a small grill. It would be dark by the time Wade got in, but I could turn on the lights. I sat down to wait and read the paper. Benton Craig was skipping rocks across the lake.

Reading the paper, I was thinking about him. Most boys would have brought his car up here. He rode up here with us to save gas. And if you stood him on his head, you probably could not shake five dollars out of his pockets, He kept his change in the bank!

About that time we heard a .22 rifle pop across the lake. You could not see his house from where we were, but I knew it was Woodrow Duff. Woodrow would sit over there and fish. And if a squirrel got near, he popped it with that .22 rifle. He would kill two, that's all he and his granddaughter needed.

Benton turned around to face me. I think that's someone shooting on our land Daddy.

No, I think it's over our fence. He went back to skipping rocks and I went back to the paper.

How long had it been since Benton was over there? Margaret and I took him there a number of times when he was baby. Cassie and Wade liked to go over there and set with Woodrow when they were growing up. But not Benton Craig. He never did things like that. Woodrow's wife had died about three years ago. Margaret and I came up to her funeral. Benton was away in college. It was just Woodrow and his granddaughter Kristy over there now.

Woodrow and his wife had one son. He married and moved off to Houston. They had one child, Kristy. The woman would leave him and go off with some other man. He would bring Kristy up to stay with Woodrow and his wife.

The woman would come back to him. They would come get Kristy. The woman would leave again. Then come back to him. It was over and over. Kristy spent more time with her grandparents than she did her parents.

When Kristy was nine years old she said no more of this for me. I'm staying here with Grandma and Grandpa!

The girl was the top student in her graduating class at Wells. She grew up to be a beautiful young lady. Her skin was as white as Mary Ellen's. Her hair was long and black. Her eyes were what surprised you. They were dark blue, not brown or black like you would expect from a girl with black hair.

We heard that .22 splat again. Woodrow probably had two. I doubted he would shoot again.

Daddy that sounds like it's on our land!

"Yes, it may be. Why don't you go over there and see who it is? And tell them this is private property!"

"I guess I'll have to paddle the canoe over there."

"No, just go straight across the pond dam. Follow the road to the fence. Turn left down that fence. It won't be far to where that shooting is being done." He headed across that pond dam like he was on a mission. I could not believe it. The boy had never been over there since he was old enough to remember.

Margaret came with the hamburger patties, and the buns. "Cassie and Wade will bring the rest down. She's got a potato salad and some baked beans to go with it. Where's Benton going across the lake dam?"

"We heard some shooting across the lake. He's going to investigate."

"That's just Mr. Duff shooting. You know that!"

"Yeah, I know that. But Benton Craig does not. It just dawned on me he's never met Kristy Ann."

"I can't believe that!"

"I don't think he's been over there since he was a baby."

"Come to think of it, I guess you are right. You think he needs to meet Kristy Ann?"

"If I was his age, and had not met you, I think I would want to meet Kristy Ann."

"Why, because she's so pretty, or because she's so intelligent and nice?"

"All three reasons!"

Woodrow was at the spring cleaning fish and squirrels when Benton got there. He figured out the shooting was not on our property when he had to crawl under the fence to avoid falling in the lake.

"Hello, I'm Benton DuPree. I was out walking. I've never been on this side of the lake before."

"I'm Woodrow Duff. You must be Robert's boy."

"Yes, sir."

"Well, you've been over here all right. But I expect you were too small to remember." Then he started giving Benton a history lesson. "Your Daddy dug that canal and fixed that gate so I could fish. Cassie and Wade were just over here a few days ago. Any of Robert's kids are always welcome over here."

Dark was almost there before Benton got a chance to say "I better get back while I can still see!"

"I'll get Kristy Ann to run you over there. It's getting too dark to be out in the woods. Come on up to the house."

He called her out. "Kristy, this is Robert's boy, Benton Craig. It's done got dark and he needs a ride home. Why don't you run him over there?"

The blue overalls and the white T-shirt she had on might have did it. But when she turned those blue eyes on Benton, that's when he flipped!

"Let me turn the stove off. I'll get the keys and I'll be right back."

He noticed she had put on a shirt over the T-shirt. When they got in the truck it was Kristy Ann who started the conversation. "Cassie has mentioned you a few times, but I don't think we have met."

"No, I don't remember seeing you either. I never knew there was anyone my age in the neighborhood. This is really a cool truck. It looks brand new."

"I love this truck. Poppa traded that VW Cassie and Wade has for it. Your father had this truck restored and the motor rebuilt for Poppa. Then he had the VW overhauled. Cassie says it still runs good."

By the time she let him out, they discovered they liked one another. They had a date Saturday night. To eat out at a restaurant in Nacogdoches.

He started in the house. Then it hit him. He never had his car up here. And no money for a restaurant either. He turned and headed for where he always went in troubled times.

Cassie let him in. "Was that Kristy that brought you home? I never knew the two of you had been seeing one another."

"I never have seen her before today. We just met."

"Oh, how did that happen?"

"Daddy sent me over there to check out the shooting we heard. I thought it was on our property."

Cassie was smiling now. "Daddy sent you over there?"

"Yes, he told me to go over there and check it out. I met Mr. Duff and Kristy. She's the most beautiful girl I ever met. And we have a date tomorrow night to go to a restaurant in Nacogdoches. I just realized I don't have my car up here and I'm nearly broke. I was wondering if I could borrow your station wagon and some money."

"Yes, you can use my station wagon." She took 50 dollars out of her purse and handed it to him. "Take this and we'll just call it a happy birthday!"

Cassie suspected Benton had been around the block a few times. This was not the first girl he had dated.

"Benton, I just want to tell you. Kristy is a nice girl. And the Duff's have been very good friends of mother and Daddy for a long time."

"She seems so different from any other girl I've met. She does not act like she knows she's so beautiful. And she seems so honest about everything."

"She's a good girl, Benton. I don't think she's ever dated anyone before. I hope the two of you have a good time."

"Well, thanks for the birthday gift. I'll take good care of your station wagon. And I'll bring my car next time."

"Remember, we're all eating at the lake tonight."

"Oh yes! I had forgotten that."

Wade and Cassie had planned on going to the place in Nacogdoches Saturday night.

"We can't go to Nacogdoches tomorrow night, Wade. We'll have to go somewhere else and use your truck."

"Why not?

"Benton Craig is taking Kristy Ann there. And he's using my station wagon."

"Kristy Ann! Well I'll be dog gone. I bet you had to loan him some money too!" He was laughing. He knew how conservative Benton was.

"Yes, he wanted to borrow money. I gave him 50 dollars for his birthday."

"Good! They can eat the steaks we meant to. How did he meet Kristy Ann?"

"Benton heard Mr. Woodrow shoot over there. He thought it was someone on the ranch land. Daddy sent him over there to check it out!"

"We better get ready for a wedding!"

"I hope so. You better get showered. Daddy's cooking burgers at the lake tonight."

"That man is always cooking up something! He headed for the shower."

Kristy was an outdoors person. Benton became interested in doing things like hunting and fishing. And he had the money for gas to drive up there during the week!

They wanted to be married right away. I told Benton they could live in our guest house. But Kristy said she could not leave her grandfather alone up there. He was getting to be very feeble. They decided to ask him if he would consider coming to live with them.

Yes, he knew he was not able to stay by himself. He would sell his livestock and the chickens. Lock up the house and move in with them.

They were married in the Church at Wells. Mr. Woodrow told me privately it was a load off his mind. He wanted to see that girl married to a good boy before he left here. He could die in peace now knowing she had.

They took him up there to his home place every week end for almost a year. Then he left this world to be with his wife. It seemed he just hung on to life until he knew Kristy's life was secure.

He left Kristy everything he had. He told me before he died he was going to do that. That boy of mine would just sell the place and let that woman piss it all off.

Wade and Cassie bought 500 acres across the county road to Houston County from my new place. It had a good year-round creek on it and he dug some ponds.

He meant to take six good size yearlings to the auction sale the next day. Late that evening, he shut them up in his corral. The next morning they were gone. Someone had used bolt cutters on his locked gate during the night and took them. Tire tracks indicated they came from and left for Houston County.

Wade and I both belonged to the Cattleman's association. Wade called them in on the case. Wade went with their investigator to the sale in Crockett. He identified five of his yearlings when they came through the ring.

The thief was arrested when he came to pick up his check. And squealed on his partner. The sixth calf they had put in a locker plant to be processed. They meant to eat some beef.

The investigator had the locker plant manager call the man and tell him his meat was ready. He was arrested when he arrived. Wade got a calf to put in his freezer. And the auction barn rewrote the check for five yearlings to him.

He and Cassie decided to build a house on the property. Rent it out so there would be someone on the place.

I had a different idea to suggest. Survey off ten acres, sell it hopefully to the person I mean to hire as ranch foreman. I meant to promote Wade to ranch manager. The ranch foreman would work with and oversee the ranch hands. Wade would essentially take over most of what I did. Which involved what, where and when.

Wade and Cassie had to come to Livingston one day. She had some paperwork to turn in, he had some banking business to take care off. South of Diboll, they picked up Jason Batise thumbing a ride home.

"Jason, I thought you had wheels. What are you doing up here thumbing a ride? Maria kick you out already?"

"No, Maria knows I don't wear my hat at weddings! They laid some of us off at the telephone company. The battery is dead on my truck. I caught a ride up here to put in an application at that plant in Diboll."

Wade looked at Cassie. One of those "Are you thinking what I'm thinking looks." He got the answer he wanted.

Wade was not one to drive and talk. He pulled over into a roadside park. He opened up his wallet, took out 300 dollars and handed it to Jason. This can be a loan, you need to get that truck going. But I think I can offer you a job and you won't have to pay it back.

Wade explained to him about the ranch foreman's job. About buying the house and ten acres provided that suited Maria and him. "But you will need to talk to Mr. DuPree about salary, retirement and insurance. You will be working for him."

Jason laughed. "How fast will this truck run?"

Wade brought Jason in to talk to me. I knew Jason, knew he was the man for the job. I explained the work hours, insurance and salary. That he would receive a new Ford work pickup truck. And I set his salary a little less than what Wade had been getting, with an increase in 90 days.

"I'm for taking the job. But I better talk to Maria about it. It's closer to her folks. Her grandfather once owned a place in that vicinity somewhere. I think she'll be happy about it."

They picked up a battery and put it on Jason's truck. He and Wade went on to the ranch. Cassie and Maria would come after their boy got home from school. He was two years older than Cathy.

Cassie and Wade let Jason and Maria go in alone to look at the house. People deserved to be alone to make decisions. They could rent it with an option to buy if they preferred doing it that way.

Maria came out and said she loved the house. And pointed to the property that joined Wades. "That was where my grandfather lived, I've been there lots of times."

They hooked Jason's truck up to a 16 foot trailer. It was Thursday. I can move with this. I'll be ready to go to work Monday.

We also had another part time employee. Rev. Billy's son Joseph had been selected to take over as pastor of the Church after he passed on. He wanted to work part time like his Dad did for us. Joe Ed and Cole I knew were near retirement age. I felt lucky to have both Jason and Joseph hire on with us.

I knew Benton Craig could run the business. We had undeveloped land on the loop. I gave him two weeks to formulate a game plan for moving to the loop, what new business we should get into, and what part of the old did we needed to keep, or get out of.

First he said that we need to get out of the boat business. It has been a good business, but it's on a decline. These aluminum boats are too durable. If someone wants one, they can buy a good one out of someone's backyard for a hundred dollars.

"Since the lake was built, boat places are a dime a dozen here now. Big rigs cost more than a car. Banks here don't like to finance them. I don't think we need to step up into the big boat league.

"The boat building would be easy to convert into a Steak, Catfish and Seafood restaurant. Shirley Nell is interested in managing the place. She thinks her husband and daughter can carry on their business at the fast food place. She thinks the Catfish and Seafood should be a buffet. The Steak House menu would be by order only.

"We need to move the hardware business out on the loop. Let's put in a bigger store, expand the electrical supply part of it. We got weekend lake front builders up here now. Most don't know where our old store is. We can probably double our business, and it's not bad now!

"The old hardware building and lumber sheds can be torn down to create a parking area for the restaurant. The materials can likely be used in the new hardware building and sheds, or up at the ranch.

"The feed business is doing well where it's at. Local people know where the store is. The lake dweller's are not into cattle, horses or hogs. They don't even keep chickens! Local people support that business.

"Let's move the Garden Supply business to the loop. Let's increase the size for garden tractors, mowers, to include four wheelers, deer stands and feeders.

"Everything for the garden, or the outdoors. Everything but boats! We can move our mechanics into this building to work on small engines as well as boat motors. We do have an obligation to service boat motor's we've sold.

"We need to build a store to get into the computer business. Along with television, radio, record players, telephones, clocks, you name it. And I suggest we move our office into this building as well. All our business stores, the ranch will be computer linked to this office.

"We've got to go for it. I've been through a transition like this once before. It takes a lot of work and planning. I'm glad you can help me with it this time. But seems to me we will have to send some people for training.

"We'll need to send some people for computer training. The company we decide to select our computers from will most likely provide that training. Kristy Ann wants to go with me. As a matter of fact, she hopes to manage the store."

"I got a feeling she could handle it. She's a smart girl!"

"You knew that when you sent me across that Lake Dam!"

"Yes son, I guess maybe I did. But here's something I've been meaning to mention to you. I don't know how Kristy might feel about living in the guest house a few more years. Your Mother and I hope to retire and move to the ranch. We want you and Kristy Ann to have our place. William Bethel will be grown by then. Hopefully we can work him into the business."

"We were ready to start harvesting long leaf pines for highline poles. They needed thinning, and they were in demand. This income would help us get through our business transition period."

The cattle market took a nose dive, and it lasted longer than anyone expected. We never actually lost money, we were not making any. Cassie and Wade were naturally worried.

"Cassie, if this were stocks, and you thought they would eventually bounce back, what would you do?"

"I would buy a lot of cheap stock!"

"That's what I'm going to do. I'm going to stuff my pastures with cheap cattle. We've got the grass. We have the hay. And we'll plant 25 more acres of corn. Run it through the hammer mill and add salt to it. We'll make our own feed."

It meant more work growing and making our own feed. But we cleaned house on cow and calf pairs when the market rebounded. We trimmed our pastures back to normal, and went back to buying year round range feed. We did not want to tax our farm land more than we had too.

Benton Craig and Kristy bought 320 acres next to the Duff place. He stocked it with Black Angus Cattle. He sold his calves to a meat packer that would supply our restaurant with choice cut steaks and ground meat. We could advertise serving Black Angus meat.

I was insistent that we have a menu most people could afford. You could order a rib eye steak if you wanted it. But you could also get a chicken fried or hamburger steak. The old "Greasy Spoon" Hot Roast Beef Sandwich was added to the menu. It and my Chicken Spaghetti Recipe became Wednesday night specials which really brought in a mid-week crowd.

The old "Greasy Spoon" restaurant had long been shut down. Margaret and Shirley Nell experimented until they got that "Hot Roast Beef Sandwich" the way I described it. It also brought in a lot of working people at lunch time.

We advertised on billboards coming into town from all directions. With directions. People coming to the lake, or passing through could find the place.

Margaret and I sold our horses and replaced them with young ones. You hate to let a good horse, dog or cow go. But they get old and die. Cassie however kept her paint mare until it died. Wade had to take the back hoe to bury it. She had a granite marker put at her grave.

Wade felt the same way about old Hot Sauce. Nobody's making chili out of him. He was born on our place, he'll die up here.

I could not disagree. That old bull would walk up and put his neck under Wade's arm. Cassie could stand and rub his head between his horns. But he allowed no one else to touch him. Not even me.

The old bull was losing weight, Wade put him in a small area I fenced off to keep the cows away from acorns. There was enough grass and water to support him and a couple of cows he put with him.

They went up there one evening a month later to feed. The cows normally came running to meet the truck. They were standing bunched up down by the pasture gate where Hot Sauce was.

What's wrong with the cows Wade? They normally run to meet us.

Hot Sauce must be dead.

You think those cows know?

Most people think a cow is just a dumb animal. They know more than some people think. He stopped the truck, got out and headed for the gate.

Hot Sauce had died under a big red oak tree there by the gate. Cassie got out to follow Wade. She found him leaning up against the tree crying. She had never seen him break down like this. Not even at the death of his Mother and Father.

She put her arms around him and let him cry until he got it out of his system. Then she got him back to the tail gate of the truck. I'm sorry Wade. That bull meant so much to all of us.

I knew he had to go sooner or later. I've never told anyone this. The night I found Daddy. Hot Sauce was standing there behind Daddy with his head over his shoulder. He stayed with Daddy until I got back. He followed that stretcher all the way out to that ambulance on the road.

When I got to the house, I heard him blowing and running up the hill. He ran all the way across that pasture. He was trying to follow that ambulance.

I went out there. That's the first time he let me touch him. I think he knew it was him and me from then on. I think he forgave us.

You think he forgave me too Wade?

Yes, you and I were the only two that could touch him. I better go get the back hoe and bury him.

I can get Cole to do that Wade.

No, I'll do it. Hot Sauce picked his place under that big tree. It's the least I can do now.

I took care of having a marker made for Hot Sauce's burial place. Cassie had a picture of him coming up the hill behind the house. Cows were strung out behind him all the way to the creek bridge.

They treated that picture and placed it inside an oval glass cut into that stone. It was not supposed to ever fade or deteriorate. Underneath in the blue granite stone I had this engraved:

HOT SAUCE

Foundation Herd Bull
Bar DW Ranch
Nov. 15, 1960
Oct. 14, 1983
His name fit owner Justin Wilson

Wade built forms and put a 12-by-12 foot concrete border around it. Margaret and I filled it with barn yard compost. In November, we dug up Spiderwort wild flowers and filled the plot solid with them.

Hot Sauce almost made it to be 23 years old. Wade had changed his brand to Bar DW {--DW} since he and Cassie married. One day, it would all be Bar DW. I had my mind made up about that already.

It was in early March, two years later. Wade said the Spiderworts were in full bloom. Margaret and I, He and Cassie drove up there one Sunday evening to look. Most of the time the flowers are spread out individually. Growing thick, when they are blooming, they are a spectacular sight that is rarely seen.

I remarked that the last time I talked to Mr. Wilson, he asked me if we would ever find out why you two named that bull Hot Sauce. He said you named him right, that was for sure.

I regret never telling Daddy before he died Wade said. Cassie and I were going to ride that bull again. I roped him, and he fell with his feet up hill. He could not get up. I mixed up some of all of Daddy's hot sauce that Mother kept on the table. I poured it everywhere on that bull it might burn! He got up!

Margaret could not believe what she was hearing. "Wade, you mean to tell me Cassie rode that bull?"

She rode him. "He threw me both times I got on him!"

"Cassie, I thought, I could go to town and trust you to not to be out riding bulls!"

"Mother after seeing you ride that windy mule, I guess maybe I just inherited it!"

I was laughing so hard I could hardly stand. "Your Daddy's hot sauce! That beats all! That's about as funny as what you did to Luther's dogs!"

I saw the quick look they gave one another. They never knew I knew about that! Let them wonder how I found out. And blame one another for telling me!

At Livingston, we had made our business changes and moved to the loop complete, by 1990. Another thing I did was buy out and secure the dealership of a small car and truck business in Lufkin. William Bethel was staying at the Ranch, working at the dealership part time and going to a two-year college there as well.

He was different from Benton Craig in a number of ways. He liked to hunt and fish. He took up bow hunting and became good at that. But his real interest was in rock work. From an early age on, he spent a lot of time at the ranch where we had the rock and gravel piled. With red clay mud, he built all manners of things with rocks.

His other interest from early on was Cynthia Ann Batise. They planned to marry, but it was not affordable yet he thought. Jason and Maria had bought the place her grandparents once owned. Bethel and Cynthia were building a rock home on ten acres her parents gave her as time and money were available.

Bethel did two years of college and said that's it. No more College for me. I decided to put him in the business he loved. On a two acre lot I had on the loop at Lufkin, I put him in the rock business. He designed the office, the warehouse and chain link fenced the rest of the two acres. I paid for it.

Any kind of rock, flagstone, Austin Stone or even brick he could get it done. Rock was shaped and chipped there in the warehouse, which saved a lot of clean up on the job site. Wade would send a dump truck, we would use that on our ranch roads as needed.

His office was a work of art for people to walk in and see. It even had a fireplace! But he no longer did the work himself, he had people to do that. He managed the place, did the bidding and design on jobs.

The manager I had at the small car and truck dealership took a job at Conroe Texas. I put Bethel in charge of managing that as well. At a good salary, I might add. He was paying me back for the building at the rock business.

He and Cynthia Ann finished their rock home. Thick rock walls, it required little expense in cooling and heating. He and Cynthia Ann married and moved into it.

Kathy, Cassie and Wade's daughter got a CPA {Certified Public Accountant} degree in college. Austin Earl Batise got a basketball scholarship. He studied law, became a corporation lawyer. They married and wanted to be in a building together in Lufkin.

I built them a building on the last acre I had next to Bethel's rock business there on the loop. The front was a waiting room with access to Cathy Batise, CPA or Austin E. Batise, Corporation Lawyer. One secretary handled appointments for both.

My accountant and lawyer at Livingston had retired and moved on. I was not happy with the people who took over for them. I was glad I had not needed a lawyer. And the accountant got me into hot water about my taxes. I gave my business to Kathy and Austin. They deducted their fee from paying back the building cost.

It's a good thing I added extra space to that building. Cathy soon had four other CPA's in offices on her side of the building. Austin had two assistant lawyers working with him.

I wanted to see Austin Earl perform in court. A case come up, he was defending a local business against the corporation headquarters up North. Two big time lawyers from up North walked in like they owned the court house. Austin Earl walked in, laid his Stetson hat on the table. And sat down to wait. Both of the two from up north rambled for ever before they finally finished.

Austin Earl got up, and with only a few words and quotes from a law book, rested his case.

The Judge ruled in favor of Austin's client. Those big time lawyers got their butts beat so bad and quickly, they left looking like their world had ended. I left knowing I had a lawyer for myself.

We were nearing the end of the 20th century. Margaret and I wanted to retire and move to the ranch. To divide up everything we owned between three kids equally was not an easy conclusion to reach. I suppose it was our granddaughter Kathy and Austin that presented the solution to the problem.

Form a corporation. Each would continue to manage the part they liked, but the expense and profits would go through the corporation. Kathy and Austin brought their business into it with Cassie and Wade, Benton and Kristy, Bethel and Cynthia. Benton Craig was the CEO or manager of it all. I was paid a salary as an advisor to the board as long as I lived. Money Margaret and I had in personal accounts was not to be included in the corporation.

Margaret and I put the ranch and property in Leon County into the corporation. Cassie and Wade would manage that. Each manager would draw an equal salary. Benton of course received more, he had the responsibility of all of it.

Every aspect of the business was computer linked to the office building we now had on the loop at Livingston. I was no expert on the computers, but I did learn to get in and out, find what I needed. And I now wondered how we ever made it without cell phones!

Wade however made a decision I agreed with him on. He would not bring the land and cattle he privately owned into the corporation. It had belonged to his parents, he meant to keep it for his descendants.

Chapter Thirteen
Life Winds Down to Memories

Now that the corporation was formed, Margaret and I went to the Craig place and stayed for weeks at a time. She would take her Ford Expedition, I would follow with our horses in the trailer behind my pickup. Not that we were completely alone there anymore.

Katrina and her husband had sold their stores, built on the land she reserved. Kevin and his wife bought 320 acres joining us across Buffalo Creek. They were there almost every weekend. Kevin used his lawyer experience to change his last name. He was now Kevin Craig. His wife married him knowing he did that, and why. They had a son and named him Sam Craig. Margaret and Katrina were pleased about it.

Margaret was only 12 years old when they left the Craig place. But she liked for us to saddle up our horses, go to places she had went to with her Uncle Sam. Those places were on the property we bought from Mr. Williams mostly.

Fishing was something we had time to enjoy. We caught and froze a lot of catfish. Sometimes we liked to take cane-poles, go catch the big yellow war mouth and goggle eye perch out of the spring branches.

We caught yellow pollywog or mud cat out of those branches as well.

I kept a dozen eight inches to a foot long.

What are you going to do with those Margaret asked? Uncle Sam used them for bait!

I'm going to fry them for supper. They are good fish if they come out of fresh water like these did. If it were not for poke-sally and pollywog catfish I might not be here! We put fish traps in Caney Branch and trapped them.

I cut the belly off and skinned them. I gave them the red pepper and salt dusting, rolled in corn meal as we did other fish. Then fried the whole fish.

Margaret agreed they were good. Different but good. When I was a kid here, we ate fish three or four times a week. I never grew tired of it. I still love to eat fish.

In the big hole below the rock dam, we caught the spring crappie and white bass run. They came up out of the Trinity River and the rock dam was as far as they could get. We never kept any of the white bass, we never liked those.

The big crappie we caught and kept. The smaller ones we caught we released into the lake above. There may have been a few there already, but not many. Marvin's grandson did the same. We got the lake and marsh stocked with crappie over a period of time.

In the fall of the year, we combined duck hunting with trotline fishing on the Keechi Creek side of the marsh. Margaret knew where the open areas out in that button willow jungle were. We caught the catfish in those places. And late in the evening the ducks came in to roost.

Our home base was at the ranch now. We gave the place at Livingston to Benton Craig and Kristy. We went there occasionally. I might attend a board meeting, Margaret would spend time with Kristy. I liked to hang around the feed store or garden store. Spend time with old employees and customers as well.

Cassie got something done she had been working on since she was a little girl. It was in the third printing and the publisher said they would keep it in book stores for years. It was called "The Shady Oaks Farm and Ranch Cook Book." It contained recipes from members of our family and ranch employee's as well. Pictures went with the recipes.

It even had my chicken spaghetti and deer chili recipe! A section was devoted to Margaret teaching us how to fry buffalo fish ribs, pressure cook the rest of it to use like tuna or salmon croquettes. That created a lot of interest from people who had never thought of doing it.

Wade's passion was working our old GI trucks over. He rebuilt those engines in his spare time. Painted the trucks to look like new again. "No need to buy new trucks, these old dudes get the job done," he said.

He took the low boy trailer to the Craig Place and loaded up the old Dodge Power Wagon. He and Cassie stopped in Crockett to eat on the way home. When they came out, a crowd of men and boys were gathered around it looking it over.

"I'll give you $35,000 for it," one man said.

"We don't plan on selling it."

"What would you take for it if you did?"

"It's not for sale." Wade got in the truck and drove off.

He rebuilt the motor and the front wheel drive system. He gave it a good sand blasting, then painted it black. Looking and acting like a new Dodge Power Wagon, he took it back to the Craig Place.

Cole and Luther had retired. We hunted and fished some together, but mostly spent time together in the break room at the equipment shed. We had a coffee pot on, we ate a lot of peanuts, pecans and English walnuts. And played dominoes a lot. Luther was serious when he was working. But he could turn into a laugh a minute when he was not.

Cole had a black finger nail. "What you done to yo finger Mr. Cole?"

"I was driving a staple in a fence post the other day. I missed the staple and hit my finger with the hammer. Seems like I can't do anything as well as I once could."

"I know what you mean," I said. "Since I've turned 60, the only thing I can do better now is fart!"

Luther almost rolled on the floor laughing. "That's sho-nuff the truth Mr. Robert. Essie Mae say I'm worse than that black mule that near killed us. And I ain't got no control. It don't matter where I be at either!"

"The other night, we went to bed. I rolled over and cut one. I neva mean for it to happen. It sounded like I was sitting on a sheet iron roof! Essie Mae rize up from dar fanning de cova. She ain't said nothing yet. I knew I wuz in sho-nuff trouble. She got up and went out in the hall. I could hear her banging things around out there. Then I heard the attic fan come on. Then she come on back to bed. She still ain't said nothing!

"What you turn dat fan on fur! Hit's cold in heah!"

"You knows why I turnt dat fan on! And I put the cot up under it. The next time you rips one unda my cova, that's where's youse gonna be sleeping!"

About once a year, I cooked a wash pot full of lye soap. We saved the grease we fried fish in. To make the soap harder, I cooked down beef fat I kept when I had a calf butchered.

I had some two by fours nailed to a piece of plywood. We poured the hot lye soap out on that. After it cooled down, I sliced it into small blocks.

Luther, Cole and I would ride around and fill up the corn feeders. We would scatter those hard lye soap blocks around the area. The hogs loved to chew on those hard blocks. If it got to burning bad enough, they might go to water. I had watched hogs in a pasture. Most of the time they came back to the soap. A little of that soap would worm a hog.

We also poured used motor oil on the burlap bags we had wrapped around cables surrounding the corn feeders. Hogs had to crawl under it, greasing their backs. Since hogs bunch up together to sleep, they all got a grease job. Which got rid of the lice.

I scattered the soap around feeders we had the burlap oil soaked bags around in Leon county. I made my two pasture riders a full wash pot full and told them to disperse it on the land we leased out for hunting.

If a hog's tail hangs straight, has long rough hair, he has stomach worms and probably lice. The lye soap and used motor oil we put out made a difference. The wild hogs on our place had kinks in their tail, and slick short hair.

The nine of us came to grips with the realities of life. Our parents, aunts and uncles were all gone. In short, the old bunch was not here anymore. We took their place. We were now the old bunch.

I was 65 in the year 2001. My older brother Lawrence was the first of our nine to go. It was sudden, he developed brain cancer which was the fast-growing kind. I was at the hospital with him one day, he knew me. The next day, he knew no one. He left us the next day.

Regan H. was four years older than I. After his first wife passed away, he gave his daughter the home in Palestine. He moved out on the place they bought joining me and his son Jeff. You might say he became somewhat of a recluse. It seemed to me he just lost interest in living.

Then Maria came into his life. At the time, she was 22 years old. Thirty years younger than he was. She lived with her grandfather across the black top highway from his front gate. The old man held a record for a big yellow catfish he caught. He told people it came out of Buffalo Creek. Maria said he caught it in Keechi Creek on Regan's place.

Maria came to ask his permission for the old man to fish again in that hole on Keechi Creek. He thought he might break his own record. Regan did what he could to help the old man, and in the process he and Maria wound up married!

They soon had cattle on the place. And Maria started a farm project. She could run a Super C Tractor herself. She sold some green peas and watermelons at Palestine. But mostly she grew the red Spanish Peanuts. She hired women friends to pick off those peanuts, bag them with our Shady Oaks label. We bought the peanuts, sold them with our produce line of products. The vines were fed to their cattle.

Regan was 70 years old when he was diagnosed with prostate cancer. It was in his lymph nodes already. He declined chemo therapy, he thought that was worse than cancer.

Margaret and I stayed at the Craig Place to try to be of some help to Maria. We knew she was totally devoted to him, that she had given him a reason to live after he seemed to give up.

Regan liked to sit out on his back porch. He could see down his fence line all the way to the creek. With the 270 rifle and scope I had given him, he killed deer, hogs, and coyotes from that back porch. In his condition now, he just liked to be there. I spent time there with him almost every day.

He brought up a subject I had almost forgotten. Not really forgotten, I just seldom thought of it anymore. Four years older, he liked to play tricks on me. It was easy for him to do, because I had a tendency to believe whatever anyone told me. Even him! The time came when I resolved to get even.

"Let's see who can run around the house the most times," he said. He took off around the house. I followed. Older, he ran faster and I lost sight of him. After five trips around the house, I decided something is wrong here. I stopped where we started.

He came out from behind the smokehouse, laughing! He ran one lap, hid, and watched me keep running around that house. That's when I decided that I would find an opportunity to trick him!

That opportunity soon presented itself. The school bus came out of town. We were the first to get on in the morning. And the first to get off in the evening. It made a loop out in the country; came out on US 79 and back to town. Kids living on US 79, near the edge of town lived less than half a mile from the backside of the place we lived on.

Regan was sitting with a girl on the bus that lived over on 79. She was next to the window, her books were in her lap. He had his hand under those books! Before he got off the bus, he whispered something to her. I could not hear, but would soon figure it out.

Regan was cool about it. He went in the kitchen, got a chunk of cornbread, and some long white radishes. He had his after-school snack, then went to the barn, saddled old Buck, and headed, I suspected, to the backside of our place. It would take that girl an hour to get home. He was going to meet her, in the woods behind her house!

It took Mother about 30 minutes to miss him. "Where is Regan H. at?"

"He saddled old Buck and rode off into the pasture."

"He's been told not to ride that fool horse. It's going to kill him! You go find him and tell him that I said, get back to this house!"

His trail was not hard to follow. I knew where he was going. I found old Buck tied to a swinging limb near our backside fence. Regan was not in sight. He had met that girl in the woods behind her house, I knew. I untied old Buck, led him about 40 yards back away from the fence and tied him to another swinging limb. Then I hooked it back home!

Daddy had his way of dealing with us when he found out, we broke the rules. He might not jump our case about it, right away. But in one way or another, he would say or do something to let us know he knew! Then let us sweat it out, wondering when he was going to come down on our case.

That's why I moved the horse. Regan would think Dad did it. All I had to do was keep my lips zipped and watch Regan H. sweat!

When I got to the house, Mother asked me if I found him.

"He's over there in the pasture. He said he would be back soon." I leaned a straight back chair against the porch wall and sat back to wait. I wanted to see his face when he came in.

He looked gloomy alright. That night at supper, Daddy put the icing on the cake. "What are you so quiet about tonight, Regan? You have not said a word since we sat down to eat!"

Regan just shrugged in answer to the question. But I could see it in his eyes. He knew Dad moved that horse.

"You know how Daddy was," he said. "He seldom said anything to us when he learned we had done something wrong. He just let us know he knew. I once slipped off to meet a girl that lived over on the highway. He found where I left old Buck tied and moved him about 40 yards away. I was afraid to be around him until he died. I was afraid he would jump my case about it!"

"Daddy never moved that horse," I said.

"What! How do you know?"

"Because I did!"

He started laughing. "You did! Why?"

"I owed you. I got tired of running around the house. I did it to get even for your tricks!"

He started laughing again. "You got even alright! After Daddy never said anything, I was afraid to go to town! I figured he told that girl's Daddy about it." He took it all well. Even said that he was glad Daddy never knew. When he got to heaven, he would not be waiting there to jump his case about it!

Regan H. knew he never had long left here. I was glad he found it something to laugh about. I also felt glad that he felt certain he was headed for heaven.

Jeff and Maria married a year after his death. Jeff talked to me about it. There had been nothing but respect between him and Maria before his Dad's death. He had never trusted women, after his first wife deserted him and their little girl. Maria had been completely faithful to his Dad. She stayed with him until the end. He knew he could trust her.

I told Jeff that I thought his Dad planed it that way. They had to see one another every day. And they had to work together in mutual business interests. His Dad left Maria the place They had to work together on the settlement of that. Something had to happen and his Dad knew it. His Dad also knew Jeff was just three years older than Maria.

I think Jeff and Maria appreciated the way I felt about it.

Margaret was having trouble with her heart racing and her blood pressure shooting up. Her Doctor sent her to a specialist in Lufkin. He put her on medication and was trying to treat the condition, which seemed to get it under control.

It gave us all a scare. The kids thought we should not go to the Craig Place alone anymore. I agreed with that. But we did go over there with family. And we kept the annual family reunion going.

My brother, Lawrence, was the beginning of the end for the nine of us. After Regan H., it was my oldest brother, Frank. After that, it seemed we were going to funerals for family and friends constantly.

You don't cease to feel grief at the loss of someone that is close to you. A numbness settles over you. You just accept the loss and go on. Margaret said it best, I think. "We've cried until we can't cry anymore!"

But we still had our kids and grandkids. I think they liked to get me wound up and going on some subject. It was two years after all those logs fell at Texas A & M. and killed those kids. The TV News was on. They were discussing ways to make that bon fire safe with all those logs.

Cassie asked the question, "Daddy, what do you think could be done to make that log fire safe?"

I doubt there is a completely safe way. This reminds me of something Mother and Dad would say after some devastating event happened. "It is not always meant that we understand God's will. What we must do is accept it and go on."

I've learned to do that. I can go on. But I will admit that I don't always stop wondering what God's will might have been."

We all just saw that pile of logs on TV. They said there were 7,400 logs in that pile. To tell it like it is, that's 7,400 trees being wasted by going up in smoke.

I grew up in that part of the country. You've seen the trees in the sand flat at our place in Leon County. I can show you trees I saw as a small boy that still look the same now. No telling how old they are. That type of hardwood timber provides a living for a lot of wildlife.

7,400 of those old trees in that pile to be burned. How much wild life would they have supported? And considering the time it takes to produce a tree like that, it's not likely they will ever be replaced. It's not inconceivable that Travis and Crockett may have killed a squirrel out of one of those trees on their way to defend the Alamo.

Perhaps, this is the message God wants us to understand. There is no safe way to waste so much of a valuable natural resource.

So much was on the TV about how to fix Medicare and Social Security. *Wade,* I thought, *had the right answer for that.* "Put all the people in Washington on the same system that we are. They have private insurance and retirement for themselves. Kick it out from under them! Then they'll fix Social Security and Medicare!"

"Next," he said, "we have people elected to do a job. If they want to run for a higher or different position, they need to resign from the position that they hold. Not spend four years on the campaign trail and not working at the job they are being paid to do. Beyond that, no foreign lobbyist in this country should be allowed. Lobbyist are not to be allowed in Washington DC, period."

Kristy Ann had a question for me. "Mr. DuPree, how do you feel about abortion?"

"In my humble opinion, abortion requires the finest or the worst of human instincts. Only God is qualified to decide which category they belong in. I do believe more men will experience the fires of hell over abortion than women do."

Kathy spoke up. "Why do you feel that way, granddaddy?"

"Women in the final analysis must make the decision. It is men that force women to make that choice. Well, sometimes men and women. I'm talking about parents. Very often, a young girl gets pregnant by a young man and she is afraid to tell her parents. They may not approve because of social, economic, and ethnic background reasons."

"I understand," Kathy said, "that women are not totally responsible. But it's hard for me to understand how a woman could give up her child."

"Like I said, God will be the judge. But there are medical reasons. And there are a multitude of young women that does not have family support. They are working and struggling to just support themselves. The married man, who got her pregnant, decides he must go back to the wife and five kids he never told her about. It's a humiliating and devastating experience for her. In her mental state, she does what she thinks she must do."

"The bible says that God is fair and he is just. I believe he considers all things. He knows that young woman must support herself. He knows her mental state. I would not want to be in the shoes of the man involved."

"In short, this is how I feel about abortion. Those of us that have not been forced into making one of those tough decisions, should just shut up about it and let the people that have alone. Leave the judgement decision making up to God."

William Bethel spoke up, which was rare for him. "I think you are right about that, Daddy. People have a tendency to believe the worst about people. But what do you think about gun control? People are going into schools and public places shooting people."

"I think, it is unfortunate that so many people are talking about this, yet no one comes up with a plan the average citizen can support. The NRA is fighting for our right to own guns to hunt with and protect our homes. I have to be grateful to them that we can still own guns."

"They passed laws limiting people to three shots, duck hunting. They did that to keep ducks from eating so many lead pellets, which kills them. Three shots is enough to hunt any game animal in America or protect your home. But to suggest all guns be limited to three shots only, is as unrealistic as people trying to get laws passed to take all our guns away. There are too many guns out there. No way they can all be collected or fixed to shoot only three times."

"A gun does not have a mind. People do. We need to pay more attention to people with mental disorders and stop releasing habitual criminals. Controlling people like that could be more effective than any manner of gun control. Beyond that, we need to go to war with public enemy number one!"

"What is public enemy number one?"

"Fire Ants! There is no way to calculate all the damage they do. They destroy crops and damage machinery. They zero in on electrical components. They love to shut down air conditioners. And make no mistake about it, they have a commander-in-chief. They get all over everywhere, then he gives the order. They all hit you at the same time!

"I get literature inviting me to join Quails Unlimited. It's been 15 years since I've seen a quail. They are extinct in East Texas. And I can take you in the woods, show you the bleached bones of little fawn deer. All laying there like it died. Predator's scatter bones. Fire ants don't. Covered with fire ants, buzzards, or nothing else will touch those young deer.

"Deer population is on the decline in East Texas. For three reasons. Too many does have been killed. Pine plantations have crowded out the food supply. And fire ants are killing the young fawns when they are born.

"We can't grow red potatoes like we once did in this country. The fire ants go in the ground and eat those small taters as soon as they put on. We get our potatoes from Idaho now. The people up there may not believe fire ants are a problem.

"They are wrong! Fire ants are adaptable. They are moving north at a steady rate. They will get to Idaho. I shudder to think about what poor people in America will do without potatoes!"

"You'll have to eat rice, Daddy! But it's not safe to put a small child out in the yard to play here in East Texas anymore."

Cassie knew I was not much of a rice fan in the past. But we were learning from some of the restaurants, how to prepare it. The kids had succeeded in getting me wound up. I don't know how much of my beliefs they bought. But I enjoyed it. I guess they did too. Perhaps I was a change from TV!"

Kathy and Austin Earl made great grandparents of us. They named her Patricia Ruth. I told Margaret she was the youngest, best looking great grandmother I ever saw.

She smiled and said I was not too bad looking for a great grandpa. But our kids are ten years apart. Bethel and Cynthia are expecting their first. These kids are going to have trouble telling which generation they belong to.

It should turn out good for the corporation. There should be three generations running it in a few years.

I doubt I'll be here to see that.

The way she said it gave me a chill. It sounded like she knew something beyond me.

She got up and went into the kitchen. I knew she did not want to discuss it anymore.

In 2008, Margaret had a couple more rounds with her blood pressure. We got her to the emergency hospital room in Lufkin, and they got it down. Her Doctor seemed to think they had it under control again.

She seemed to be fine for two months. Then she had another attack. This time she blanked out before we got to Wells. Cassie called for an ambulance to meet us there. On the way in to Lufkin, the paramedic got her heart to beating again.

The Doctor thought she had been without oxygen too long. They kept her on life support system for a week. The Doctor told us her brain showed no activity at all. He recommended we sign the paperwork and let her go.

It was something she and I had agreed on. If it came down to this, sign the papers and let us go. I realized it was coming to this and I guess the kids did too.

Cassie was the strong one among us. None of us wanted to do this and give her up. But it's selfish to keep her here in the condition she's in. She signed the paper.

Benton and Bethel both signed it then. Our children did that for me. I did not have to sign it first. But I knew I had too. Margaret had told me to do it if it came down to this.

We put her out in the Cemetery next to Mr. Dobrinsky. I had asked her about it a number of times. It would suit me to be put in the Craig Cemetery where your Mother is.

No, that's their place. This is ours. Through the Grace of God and Mr. Dobrinsky. I never met that man, but I think we owe him that much respect. And here at the ranch is where our children are. I'll be with Mother, Uncle Sam, and my grandparents, when I get to heaven.

We had the service at the Church in Livingston. Margaret loved the town, she had found a lot of friends there. Through her Church Work, she had contributed a lot to the town and county.

Our old Pastor and Reverend Joseph conducted the service. She told me that's what she wanted. She said Reverend Billy would know his son was there. The service was at the Church in the morning. That evening she was put to rest in the Cemetery.

Cassie was the oldest and I think, she thought she had to be the strongest. She never broke down, at least not in my presence like the rest of us did. Wade loved Margaret, he took it about as hard as any of us.

In the days to come, my Daddy's words kept coming back to me. "Memories are such a Precious Thing." Then Rev. Billy's words." You don't ever lose someone you love and know loved you. They will always be with you in your heart and mind."

Six months had gone by since Margaret left me. I was till just putting one foot in front of the other. I was going through the motions of life. And I did not sleep much at night.

I went to bed one night. I lay there for two hours twisting and turning. With my selfish thoughts. I always thought I would go first. Why could I have not gone first? Why did I have to be left here alone?

I suddenly remembered I had not taken my gout medication. I put one foot on the floor, threw back the cover. I raised up to get up. I saw Margaret standing at the foot of my bed. There was a glow that surrounded her. She was dressed in a white gown. She looked as young and beautiful as the day we married.

Our eyes met and she gave me that beautiful smile. I started to speak to her and she vanished right before my eyes.

Two months later I was laying there in bed. I could not sleep. My mind was going over every little detail of our time together. I decided to get up, get myself a glass of tea and go sit on the front porch swing. I often did this because the bed became an enemy to my aches and pains after a couple of hours. The clock in the kitchen said it was 2:45 a.m.

I took a seat on the porch swing. I took a drink of tea, then leaned over to set the glass on the floor. Not likely would I drink any more, I never really wanted it anyway.

When I raised up, I looked down the driveway. There she stood by the flower beds. She had that same glow about her. And that same white gown on. But when she turned towards me, she vanished again.

I did not tell the kids I had seen her. They were worried about me, I knew that. But I knew I had seen Margaret. She came and checked on us. And it was so like her to stop and look at the flowers.

I concluded she was not allowed to speak to us. Maybe I had seen her because she came at night and I slept so little. If the kids saw her, perhaps they never mentioned it because few would believe it.

There had been so many times Margaret had spoken about it so positively. The people that have gone on know what we do down here. Had she seen her Mother, her Uncle Sam or her Grandparents? I now believed she had.

211

I lived with my memories. Margaret's and my memories. Our years together. The hardships of our teenage years. Of plowing in the field or on one end of a cross cut saw and dreaming about how I would develop a farm and ranch if I had the wealth to do so. And something else that was clear to me now. God directed my footsteps to the wealth given to me to finance my teenage dreams.

I had been able to help some people. I met others that would not allow you to help them. Perhaps my own brothers and sisters flustered me the most. They were so independent they would not accept help. But they helped me! They all drove Fords out of my place!

I gave my manager a list of their names. Sell it to them at my cost if they come in. I don't think they realized Fords cost a lot more somewhere else! I always wound up laughing about it when I thought of it. Had the situation been reversed, I would probably have done the same thing they did.

I had reason to be proud of all of them. With the exception of Regan H., I was the only one to have it given to me. He won a pot gambling at Las Vegas. But you never flew to Vegas, stayed a week to gamble and party if you were broke. Virginia worked hard in their stores, but she and her husband were worth millions. The rest just worked hard and drug their selves up out of the poverty we were born into.

I got to thinking about it. God was not finished with me. I knew Margaret would not want me to give up. She was in heaven with no pain. I prayed to God to forgive me for being selfish about being alone. I was not alone, our kids and grandchildren were here with me. They never wanted me to give up and quit either.

God left me here for some reason. Why I might not ever know. I was not worth much out in the hay fields or tending to cattle. But I still had my mind and I could write down my memories. By dam, I was not through yet! I'll write a book.

I told Cassie I needed to go to town with her the next time she went. I thought it a little strange she went the next morning. She normally went on Friday.

I told her I needed to go to Walmart's. She never said a word when I put 12, 100 page spiral notebooks in my cart. And three packages of Paper Mate ball point pens.

We went on to a grocery store, I got what I needed and she did the same. I had everything I came for. We talked a little about this and that as we headed home. We were going under the underpass at Pollack when she finally asked "Daddy, what are you going to do with all those notebooks and ball point pens?"

"I never could type worth a hoot. I'm going to write a book. The old fashioned way!"

"Good! What are you going to write about?"

"God has blessed me with a lot of memories. I plan to write about those. And I may work on politicians, a little. I hope to stir people up! People need to realize they need to quit taking and start putting something back into this country. I may even get fire ants stamped out!"

"Somebody needs to do that! How long will it take to finish the book?"

"It won't be finished until 1 a.m. If it gets published, you will probably need to finish it."

"That's fine Daddy. I know you'll write like no one before has. You just write it! I'll get it typed."

I started to write. But there was always something happening to interrupt my progress.

Funerals to go to. The annual family reunion between the creeks. Then the yearly barbeque and fish fry at the lake here on the ranch for all the employees. Younger members of the family and Corporation were keeping traditions started alive.

Sometimes just our family got together between the forks of Buffalo and Keechi Creek. I loved to go there and the kids knew it. So many memories were there.

I could still ride with Wade or drive about the ranch. Mostly I would just putter off in the old VW. The oaks planted were a joy to behold. They were a solid forest now. We had given the Forest Service permission to collect seed acorns. A lot of oak timber was being planted now. Oak timber was worth more now than pine.

I might stop and watch wildlife cross the road down toward the creek bridge. And get to wondering "How in the hell did we build that creek bridge?" To look at things again brought back memories.

I still had my pickup truck, but I never put it out on the highway. I could not hear it thunder, and my eyesight had faded.

Wade was still running the place a lot like we always had. He trapped those wild hogs, and he marked them. Nothing was left of the once wild strain of hogs. Everything was of good blood. To keep the hog population in the bounds of reason, a number were released on the employee hunting lease on the west side of Lake Livingston. And other hunting leases suitable for hogs.

Eventually, Virginia and I were the only two left out of the nine of us. Her husband was gone, so were all of our brothers and sisters wives and husbands.

Virginia was put by her husband in the Cemetery in Leon County next to Mother and Dad. I had been with all nine at the end. I was the last of the old bunch.

I told Cassie on the way home from her funeral that Virginia had outsmarted me again.

"Why do you think that Daddy?"

"She did not have to watch all of us leave. She was younger than I am. I thought I would go before she did."

"God just knew his plans for her were complete. She had a good life. God may have plans for you to do other things."

"Yes, maybe so. He may want me to finish that book!"

John, Mary Ellen's husband passed away. We all went to his funeral. Our kids all loved Mary Ellen, John and their kids. Mary Ellen seemed pleased that we came. I had not seen Mary Ellen since Virginia's funeral. John had not been able to be with her then.

A month later, Mary Ellen called me one night. She wanted to come down and see the place again. The oaks in particular. Her daughter would bring her down the next day. If that's ok with you?

"Yes, by all means come on down. I can drive you around, show you the oaks. You had a major part in developing this place. And we have so many memories to talk about."

Mary Ellen's daughter brought her down the next morning. She would spend the morning with Cassie. Cassie would fix dinner and we would all eat together. Mary Ellen and I could go tour the place.

Wade had been standing around. "Yall want me to drive for you."

"No, you can go ahead with whatever you meant to do."

I took the old VW. I circled the oaks, made the whole tour. I stopped to show her a grove of beech trees by the road. "There's more on the place. These you can see from the road. Do you remember we picked up the seed at Dam B."

"Yes I still remember that. I still think of it as Dam B. Everyone else calls it something else now. But it's wonderful to have had a part in something that will be here years after we are gone."

She wanted to see the place, but mostly I knew she came because she wanted to talk. I shut the VW down at the top of the hill looking down towards the creek bridge. The oak limbs now stretched out, forming a canopy over the road. It was a good place to watch a diversity of wildlife cross the road, "Let's just sit here and watch for a while. I come here a lot to watch wildlife cross the road. We may see about anything we have on the place." I no sooner had said it when two does with four fawns crossed the road.

"Oh, they still have their spots. I sit and watch the deer at home. It's so quiet around there since John is gone. But the deer don't seem to be afraid of me."

"I don't wonder, Mary Ellen. The worst thing you ever did was take a hook out of a fish's mouth! Deer and wildlife sense when they are safe. I can sit here and watch them now. But when the hunting season starts, I'm not likely to see anything."

"Robert, I hope you know I loved Margaret. She was such a good and remarkable person."

2Yes, I know you did, Mary Ellen. Margaret said the same thing about you. She loved you."

"I still wonder why she thought there was anything remarkable about me."

"Margaret admired you. She said you did the right thing after we had a child. We were both glad we could all be friends. We both thought a lot of John."

"I guess this is foolish of me after all these years. But I need to know. What would you have done if you had found Margaret married to someone else?"

"You want the truth?"

"Yes, I do."

"I loved Margaret Mary Ellen. And you know why I was so committed to her. The truth is I realized I loved you as well. Enough that I could not hurt you. I had to find her before I could tell you that I loved you. If she had been married, I would have run to you. I would have told you that I loved you."

She started to cry and I took her in my arms and held her.

"God just did not mean for us to be together. John was a good man and I did love him. But I never stopped loving you. I hope God will forgive me. I don't think I would have survived if you had not given me that knife to pray with when I used it."

"Mary Ellen, I think God has forgiven us. He forgave Margaret and I, and brought us back together again. We all did the right thing. We still have the knives. We can go on praying for one another."

"Yes, we do have the knives. What should we do when one of us is gone?"

"If I go first, Mary Ellen, I'll have my knife placed by my right hand in my casket. You can place yours there with it. If you go first, I'll put mine by yours. That way part of what we shared here on this earth will be together."

That seemed to perk her up. "Yes we can do that. Knowing they will be together is something I'll be happy about."

"We'll all be together in Heaven, Mary Ellen."

"Yes, Thank God. We still have that to look forward to."

It was near lunch time. We drove back to have dinner with Cassie, Wade and her daughter. About mid-afternoon they went home. It was the last time on this earth I would see Mary Ellen. I think she found peace in our talk. We both knew we were beyond anything else. Understanding was the best we could hope for.

After that, I started to do like Daddy did. I had little interest in eating and I was losing weight. I was fading away, and I knew it.

But Thank God, I could still do things for myself a little. I could still get around some with my walking stick. *I had a lot to be thankful for,* I thought.

I had my teeth pulled before I retired and learned to live with the false ones. That's as close as I ever came to any kind of surgery. I only took half of my blood pressure pill daily. I would stand on my head if I took it all.

Then there was the pill for gout. Another for what they called tendonitus in my left shoulder. I blamed that on the black windy mule that near killed me and Luther. Then there was another to help me leak. I had a contingency problem.

I took a seat on the back porch one morning. I could see all the way to the lake. Deer sometimes came out. Squirrel were running everywhere. Sometimes I saw the Bald Eagles. A pair was nesting in top of a cypress tree about the center upper portion of the lake. Cassie was proud of that, she planted the tree there.

I had been observing what I think was called a pileated woodpecker for years. It was near as big as a crow, had a red crest on its head. Its body was black with some white on its neck. It came through about every two weeks.

It had a set route it followed. I would see it at a dead tree down yonder. It left there to one with a hollow place on one side. Then it came to the bottom of the hollow tree on the hog pasture fence. Then it left there to a tree I could see out in the woods. It left there to cross the lake in the same direction it did every two weeks.

That thing had a definite route it followed. I knew where it was going next as I sat and watched. It created a question in my mind I could not answer. For the next two weeks what would its route be? Did it return to a home base in East Texas each day? Run a different route in East Texas every day? Or maybe just one route that perhaps went into Arkansas, Mississippi and Louisiana and came by here every two weeks?

I suspected my time was not far away. I was watching that big woodpecker when it hit me. It was really more like they confused my mind. Confused may not be the right term to describe it either. My mind seemed in reverse, like rewinding a cassette tape on the record player. They were reviewing my life and I knew it.

When they got to the part about Mary Ellen, I heard a voice say, "Stop it there. I want to re-run that part again. They ran it back again. That's commendable on both of those two the voice said."

"It's was commendable on all three of those people. They all passed the test we put them through!"

"They stopped it when I was about 11 years old. They just left my mind there. I suppose they reviewed all they thought I was accountable far. I never knew who they were. Only that they were angels chosen by God to review my case before I departed this earth."

Cassie caught me at the backyard gate leaning on my walking stick and trying to open it.

"Where are you going Daddy?"

"I've got to go over in the pasture and look for Regan H. Mother thinks that fool horse is going to kill him!"

Cassie got me in her Ford Expedition and headed for Lufkin. My awareness returned and I realized she was taking me to a hospital. I even marveled at her driving ability. Eighty-five miles per hour and a cell phone in one hand! She had the flashers on and she got Benton Craig and William Bethel on the phone.

I was 86 and she was only 15 years younger. What a driving feat for a 71-year-old woman! Her age bothered me a lot. According to the law of averages, she was not that far away from joining her Mother and I. If it ever bothered her, she said nothing about it.

Evidently she got in touch with the hospital. They must have notified the DPS to give us an escort from Wells to the hospital. That little black and white mustang came around us with his lights flashing. He pulled in front of us and slowed to 80.

I saw that look come into Cassie's eyes. And the speedometer climb to ninety. And her lips form the words. "You better move it buster!"

Buster moved it. We settled back down to 85.

"I'm glad he's in that little car and we're in this one."

"Why's that Daddy?"

"I would not like to be going this fast with my butt that close to the pavement!"

She laughed but I saw tears too. "You better close your eyes and rest Daddy. We'll be there soon."

They must have blacked me out completely when we got to the hospital. I did not know anything.

Then the voices came back. "We're going to put you back on normal for a short time. You'll get to see your children again. But this will be the last time. We'll start you on a journey soon."

I knew not to ask questions or argue with the voices. They were the voices of authority and I knew it.

When I opened my eyes, Cassie was standing there holding my hand. The rest of the family was there as well. "I'm glad you woke up Daddy. You've been asleep since I brought you here."

The grandchildren all gave me a hug. I think I managed to say something to everyone there.

Probably no one understood me better than Cassie. She had hold of my hand again.

"What time is it Cassie?"

"It's a little after six Daddy. Why do you ask?"

Our eyes met and I squeezed her hand. "Why don't you all go out somewhere to eat? I'll be alright."

Her eyes never wavered from mine. But she knew what I wanted. I also knew she did not want to leave me. The pain was there in her eyes. She knew I was leaving and did not want the grandkids to see me go.

She leaned over, gave me a hug and said: "I love you Daddy." Then she turned around. "You heard Daddy. Let's all go eat!"

It was hugging time again. Luther and Essie Mae were there as well. I shook Luther's hand. "Don't forget the old times Luther."

"No sir, Mr. Robert. I sho won't forget the old times we had together."

As soon as they were gone, they started me on my journey. I was so glad I had got to see everyone. But I was also thankful that they would not see me go. I had stood and watched so many go. I wanted to spare them that. God and Cassie knew that.

I was walking up through a long tunnel surrounded by white swirling clouds. Whiter than any I had ever seen. Everything seemed to glow with a silvery light.

I had on a long white gown. I was walking, yet it never felt like my feet was touching anything. My hair was down to my shoulders. The teeth in my mouth were mine. I could feel no pain anywhere. I realized I was young again. I felt better than I ever had before.

I don't know how long I walked. It required no effort and time did not matter. I could see a golden glow ahead of me now.

It turned out to be the frame work for a gate. Even the threshold looked golden. It was made of some material I knew was more precious than gold. I understood that this was the golden gate to heaven.

Margaret was here. Mother and Daddy. My brothers and sisters. My grandparents I never knew. So many people I wanted to see and be with again.

As I neared the gate, I could hear singing. They were singing "Amazing Grace." It sounded like the voice and the other voice. Vern Gosden and Tanya Tucker. But I thought she was still down there. *Maybe that's just the way angels singing sounds up here,* I thought.

The singing stopped when I got to the gate. Should I just walk on in? I never thought so. Someone would surely meet me here.

The singing had come from the left. I looked in that direction. The white tunnel continued on to a huge golden glow. *This must be the Golden City of Heaven,* I thought.

I turned my eyes to the right. Margaret was sitting there. Not in a chair. It was more like a throne! She had her elbow on one arm, her chin in her other hand. Just like years ago, when I stuck my tongue out at her in the class room.

I realized she had been allowed to wait for me here. But she was looking to the left in the direction the singing came from. Perhaps she could see them.

Then it sounded like a hundred trumpets rang out. Then a voice loud and clear announced.

"Robert Alton DuPree has arrived!"

The voice sounded like George Jones. That good East Texas woman must have performed a miracle on that old Texas Big Thicket boy!

When they announced my name, Margaret stood up, smiled, and stretched out her hand towards me. I don't think I ever saw her look more beautiful. I felt like I did the day I walked across the street from Zumo's restaurant and saw her for the first time in ten years.

I lifted one foot to step over that golden threshold, and that's the last...

Chapter Fourteen
Wade and Cassie Finish the Book

Cassie and I both read Mr. DuPree's handwritten account of his memories. Naturally, we were a little shocked at how explicit he had been about some things. Our love life for instance. I asked Cassie if she had told him all those things.

"No, not much of it. I guess if we did not want him to know, I should not have said anything to mother or Essie Mae. And you should not have told Joe Ed, Cole, or Luther anything!"

I turned a little red. "Yes, I guess you are right. But we could edit some things out perhaps?"

"Wade, I thought about that. But I understand why he did it. He wants young people to have a better understanding of themselves and feel normal. That they are not alone in the way they feel. It will go to the publisher like it is, or not at all. I'm not going to rewrite it."

"Well ok then. I see your point. But it's a good thing Joe Ed's already out there in the cemetery. He's the only one I ever told about that bale of hay!"

She laughed about that. "But you can write whatever you want to put in the last chapter of the book. You can deny ever skinning your legs up on a bale of hay if you want to!"

I had to laugh at that. "I do want to add my thoughts to his book. But I'm not denying anything!" I was worried about Cassie since her father's death. It had been nine months now. She had never broke down and shed a tear. She had been the same way after her mother's death. She thought she had to be strong for all of us I think.

I understood the way she felt. I tried to do that after the death of mother and daddy. A person just can't carry that kind of grief around and get over the loss.

I found that out when Hot Sauce died. I broke down and shared my grief with Cassie. *That's what Cassie needed to do,* I thought. *Give into her tears and share her grief with someone.* We were going to have the whole family for Thanksgiving. Cassie was not about to weaken and not do that. She told me she needed a couple of Mallard Ducks to make her cornbread dressing.

I had my gun, was sitting on the porch swing putting on my rubber boots. I had been down to the lake earlier that morning to drain the water out of the boats and turn them over. I heard some Mallards quacking in a slough not far away.

Those ducks would not leave until someone disturbed them. They could wait a little longer. I leaned back to think.

The woman from the local newspaper had been here about a month ago. Well that's where she worked when Mr. DuPree started work on this ranch project. Now she was the editor-in-chief of a large magazine published in New York.

She came here every five years to interview Mr. DuPree, get pictures, and just generally do a five year progress report since he planted the first acorn. She was, I suppose, impressed with what he was trying to accomplish.

This time she flew down from New York. She had not heard of his death. Cassie and I gave her a tour of the place and did our best to make her feel welcome. She got her pictures, her notes for a story, and returned to New York.

We had been getting the magazine for over ten years. Subscribing to it seemed the thing to do, since she put us on the map nationally. But it was about living on farms and ranches. We enjoyed reading it.

We just received it this week. She had pictures of back then and now. It covered six pages of the magazine. She said Mr. DuPree was a conservationist, a man of vision, and foresight. He was gone now, but his work lived on.

That was all true enough. And we appreciated that he got national recognition for what he accomplished. But the truth of the matter was, the woman never knew half of what the man did for so many.

Over the years, I had talked to all of his employees. All had some personal story to tell me. The roof might have blown off a house. A car wreck and the loss of a family member. You name it, and I heard it. He came to help them, and helped them out financially.

If an employee's kid graduated high school and wanted to go to college, he paid for their tuition. The books they needed, he paid for those as well. The top student in each Livingston graduating class received a $10,000 check to attend the college of their choice.

The corporation did those things now. We were only continuing what he started.

Cassie asked him once why he did those things.

"Cassie, your mother and I went through school knowing we had no chance to attend college. College was just something other kids talked about. I can't do it for all the kids, but I want our employees' kids to start high school knowing they can attend college if they want to."

I noticed at the annual employee barbeque and fish fry up here, he knew the first names of every kid they had. I asked Cassie how he did that.

"In the top left-hand drawer of his desk at the office, he kept a list of each employee, names of their wife or husband and their kids. If a baby was born, they were added. Don't ask me how he memorized all that, but he did. He told me once he thought it meant something to an employee to know their kid's name."

"Look at it this way, Cassie. I go back to talk to Fred Baxter about something. And I ask him how Billy Joe and Bobby Sue are doing, don't you think that gives Fred the notion I believe he cares about his kids as much as I do mine?"

Cassie came to the door. "Wade, I thought you were going hunting. You've been sitting there for 30 minutes!"

"Has it been that long? I guess I'm getting slow about putting my boots on!"

I got up and changed my hats. I picked up the old 12 gage pump shotgun Mr. DuPree had given me years ago. I loved the old gun, and it was something else he had been right about.

"A good gun is like a good woman. If you find a good one, keep it!"

Let me back up to what I was talking about. Dad said this to me once. "Wade, if it had not been for Robert, I would have retired driving a truck and kissing a poor man's ass at Livingston! He and I were friends. He knew I wanted to live up here on my place. He made that possible for us."

"We both worked hard up here. But what he was trying to accomplish was exactly what I dreamed about doing. When I die, I'll leave you with assets worth over a million dollars. You can thank Robert for a bundle of that. He gave us a lot more than he had too."

219

I walked up to the lake bank. A bunch of ducks came up right under me. The gun came to my shoulder, safety off.

Blue Wing Teals. I did not come after teals. Cassie wanted Mallard Ducks. If I shot these, the Mallard's would have been gone. I lowered the gun and clicked the safety on.

Mr. DuPree helped me kill my first duck at the place I was going. Later, I helped Cassie get her first three. She could work a pump gun like no one else I ever saw. Except her mother.

I picked up a dead tree limb about 20 yards before I got to the place I was going. There was a big old pin oak tree growing at the edge of a five foot bluff bank. About half way down, a big root stuck out of the bank. Like a man's elbow, it turned back into the dirt bank. I stepped up on the root, and leaned the gun against the tree.

The end of the slough ended about 20 yards away. The end was covered with button willows. It was surrounded with pin oak trees, the water was full of acorns. It was a green head duck paradise.

Years ago, Mr. DuPree put me up by that tree. "I'm going to throw this stick out into those button willows. The ducks will come right out in front of you. Be ready to shoot!"

He was right. I got my first mallard duck. It was a drake, it had a green head.

I remember helping Cassie up that bank the first time. She was so tiny, still is for that matter. It was quite a stretch for her to get up. Standing on that root, I started to put my hand on her behind and give her a shove. Then I realized I better not do that!

She looked down and saw me with my hand almost there. She smiled at my indecision and got up that bank on her own.

Today, it was all up to me. Not that I had not did it before. Trouble was, I was not as young as I once was.

I backed up ten feet and threw that piece of broken tree limb out into those button willows. I hit that root with my left foot, and picked up my gun. I downed one as they cleared the edge of the water. The second one fell in a big clump of myrtle bushes.

I let the third go. I was certain I could have got it. But it would have fell in the lake. Cassie only needed two. I did not want to go to the lake dam for a boat and paddle all the way up here.

I put two shells in my gun and leaned back against the tree. I don't know why ducks do it, but sometimes they circle back. It was worth investing a few minutes to see if these did.

Just last week, I had Cassie take me up to the creek bridge and let me out. Mr. DuPree never hunted squirrels until November. Let them shed that summer hair and get fat. I felt the same way about it.

I told Cassie it would probably be dark when I got in. I wanted to hunt in a place Mr. DuPree put me in when we first moved up here. It was not far up the bottom from where I was now.

We eased up through a thicket to a pin oak flat. "Wade, do you see that post oak tree there with all those punk knots sticking out like a mules bo-hunk?"

I could see the tree alright. It was surrounded with pin oaks. Acorns galore! "Yes Sir, I see it."

"Every one of those knots has a hole in it. It's a squirrel den. Just sit down right here. Just before dark, squirrels will be all over these pin oaks." He handed me a flash light.

"Don't move to pick up a squirrel until it gets too dark to shoot. Wait for me here. I'm going on up the bottom. I'll be back."

I had given him money and asked me him to bring me a box of shells. "Wade, I stopped in Lufkin to get your shells. They had the Blue Peters shells. I got me a box too. They are good shells."

The squirrels covered up those pin oaks just before dark like he said. I noticed every time I shot, I saw fire come out the end of the barrel. I decided those Blue Peter's shells were something special alright! I picked up six and set back against the tree with the light on to wait until he got there.

I never knew he was there until he spoke right behind me. "How many did you get Wade?"

"I got six. How many did you get?"

"I got four. We got us a mess of squirrels!"

"I ain't shooting nothing but Blue Peter's from now on," I said. "Fire comes out the barrel when you shoot them!"

"Blue Peters will burn their butts," he said.

A few years later, I would figure out fire could be seen coming out the barrel of any gun you fired in the dark!

I realized he put me in the best place in that creek bottom. And something else. Most people would have said "Dummy, when you shoot any shell after it gets dark, you will see fire come out the end of the barrel." He was not most people, he was content to just let you and time figure things out. He was not going to embarrass you about being ignorant about anything.

Last week, I had six squirrels when I got to that same old post oak. It still looked the same. I got six more before dark. I know that's two more than I was supposed to get. But I was hunting for Thanksgiving dinner. I probably would not hunt again this year.

These ducks were not going to circle back. I might as well pick up what I had and go. I walked over and picked up the one I could see. The one in the Myrtle Bushes might be a little harder to get.

I walked completely around that clump of bushes. I could not see the duck. I leaned my gun up against a nearby tree. Those limbs broke fairly easy. I would just break my way in there. I killed that duck and I was going to get it!

I started back to do that. Then my eyes caught something. Some crooked limbs in the edge that looked like they had been bent. My mind suddenly flashed back more than 60 years.

We were building the hog pasture fence. The top barbwire we were trying to stretch, hung up on one of those myrtle bushes. I picked up the axe. "I'll go get it loose Mr. DuPree."

"I'll get it Wade." He never took the axe. I watched him take limbs in both hands and bend them back out of the way. I wondered why he never just broke them off.

Cassie's Mother told her she was conceived in a Myrtle Bush hideaway he made for them to go to. Cassie and I had looked for their deer stand they said they went to. We never did find it.

I got down on my knees and pulled back a bent limb and turned it loose. It sprung right back to where it was. I pulled it back again, bent over so I could see better.

There it was! Cassie and I had walked by it hundreds of times. Sometimes looking for it!

Everyone else in the family had been by here countless times. No one had found it.

I crawled in and stood up. The whole thing looked to be about four by eight feet. He must have built the floor with a four by eight piece of plywood. My duck was laying on top of the thing.

I opened the end door and crawled in. Side by side were two folding chairs. I took a seat in one. The floor had carpet on it. I knew that carpet. It was a piece left over when he and dad built our house. I could see little tunnels through the bushes. Just big enough to shoot through. Outside, those little holes would not be noticed by anyone just walking by.

The slot in the walls to shoot through was covered with hinged six inch boards. They folded up and were secured open with screen door hooks like people once used. The top was in two hinged sections. I unlatched them and opened them up. I stood up. Ducks flying over or squirrels in the trees. You could shoot it. Deer and hogs were forced to come between a slough and the lake, or between the end of two sloughs.

This was the most perfectly positioned and best hidden deer stand I ever saw in my life.

They often took their guns and walked up this way. Yet I never heard them shoot. They never brought anything back. They just came here to be alone and watch the wildlife. They had a thing about Wood Ducks. A bunch jumped up in front of him and I once. "Don't shoot," he said. "Those are Wood Ducks."

I took the gun down from my shoulder and turned to look at him. He was standing there looking after those ducks with a look in his eyes that was hard to describe. Like he was suddenly somewhere else, in another world.

"Why can't we shoot Wood Ducks, Mr. DuPree?"

My question brought him back. "They've been on the endangered species list. And they are not as good to eat as other ducks."

When did he build this thing? It could not have been before we moved up here. He never had tools to work with. And that carpet, it was a left-over piece that was used in building our house. We never had the "A" frame truck yet either. He had to have it to drop this thing down in the center of these bushes.

We took vacation one summer and spent a week in Austin with Patricia. He was here by himself. That's the only time he could have did it without anyone knowing about it.

Should I tell Cassie about it? And bring her here to see it? I had to do it, I had no right not to. She might break down if I did, I knew. But that might be what she needed to do.

I closed the place up, got my gun and ducks and started home. It might be the wrong thing to tell her today. The weather had been so cold and wet. She might want to go right then. Maybe one day next week we would have a warm day and I'd bring her here to see it.

The next Tuesday, the sun came out, and by lunch time things had dried out. It was a little cool, but a nice day to be in the woods.

I got her 16 gage Winchester pump shotgun off the rack and a box of shells. "I want you to go with me for a walk in the woods. There is something I want to show you. And you might kill me a couple of ducks to make my gumbo for Thanksgiving."

"It's a nice day for a walk. Let me get my jacket and get some more shoes on." We often walked down to the lake. She probably though that was as far as we were going today.

When we got to the lake, I turned up the bottom.

"Why are we going this way?"

"I thought there might be some ducks on the slough. And there's something I want you to see. It's not very far to walk."

When we got to the bluff bank, I set her gun up by the tree. She knew the system, but it was still hard for her to get up there. I put my hand on her behind and gave her a shove. She looked down and gave me a smile. She picked up the gun and gave me a thumbs up. She was ready to shoot.

I threw the stick. It sounded like a whole wad of ducks came up. I went up the bank behind her. I saw the second and third ducks fall. I was looking over her shoulder and she clicked on an empty cylinder.

I had little doubt she could have got four. "Is two all you got? I need three to make that gumbo."

"I got three buster! And if you and Daddy had not put that plug in my gun I could have got four." She was busy shoving shells in her gun. She knew the system here.

We waited a few minutes. "I don't think they are coming back." I picked up the ducks and laid them by the tree.

"I told you I got three!"

"Yes, you can outshoot any grandma I ever saw. And the most pretty!"

She gave me a smile. "I'm just glad you finally made up your mind to help me up that bank!"

"It was my pleasure!" {She had just told me she remembered something that happened sixty years ago as vividly as I did.}

"What kind of ducks are these? They have a funny looking beak."

"These are Shovelers. They are good little ducks for gumbo."

"How much further do we need to go?"

I took the gun and leaned it against the tree. "We're there now." I led her to the myrtle bushes. I pulled the limbs back. "Kneel down here and look in."

She looked in. "Wade, is this what I think it is?"

"It's your mother and daddy's deer stand. Follow me in. I'll open the door."

She sat down in a chair and I sat down beside her. Her eyes missed nothing. I opened side slots and she found the look-out holes in the bushes. I opened the top, she stood up and looked out.

She sat back down. "This is not a deer stand Wade. They came here to watch the Wood Ducks. Mother loved to watch Wood Ducks. How long do you think this has been here?"

"Daddy took some vacation and we spent the week in Austin. That was the only time he could have built it and put it here without me knowing. That was about a year before he found you and your mother."

"He built this not knowing where Mother was? He never even knew about me. I..."

She could not say anymore. I pulled her into my arms. The dam broke. The tears were falling. I knew there was nothing I could say or do now but hold her and let her cry it out. She was shedding tears she had held back since her mother died.

After a few minutes, she pulled some tissue out of her jacket pocket and began to dry her eyes. "I'm sorry, this..."

She began to cry again.

"It's alright to cry, baby. Don't be sorry about it. We all need to cry sometimes. I was near it myself."

After a little while, she straightened up and dried her eyes. "When did you find this? And how did you find it? You and I have walked past it hundreds of times."

"I found it last week. One of the ducks I killed fell in these bushes. I found the opening looking for a way to get that duck. I did not know how best to tell you. I decided it best to wait for a good day and bring you here."

"You did what you thought was best. I'm so glad you brought me here." She was looking down, rubbing her foot on the carpet. Suddenly she looked up at me. "Do you think they ever...?"

"Probably at least once. It might have been about as uncomfortable as a bale of hay!"

"Do you remember the time we came down from the creek bridge looking for them? We sat down over there by that tree. You said you never believed they had a stand that they just sat on the ground somewhere."

"Yes, and after we got back to the house, they came walking in. I bet they were sitting here watching us and laughing about it!"

"I bet they were too, Wade! Somehow, I believe they know we're here now. I don't think we should tell the others. God led you here. They come up here around it. If God wants them to find it, they'll find it!"

"I think you are right. That's your decision. We better get to the house. I've got to clean these ducks then go feed some cattle."

"I'll go with you. I can still drive!"

She had not done that in years. She did go and drive. I think finding that stand and letting go of her grief did her a lot of good.

-----O-----

Wade and Jason were taking the children on a hayride tonight. We always did that the night before Thanksgiving. Perhaps we should have did that at Halloween, but it was so hard to get all those children out here.

Wade would ride on the trailer with the kids. Jason would drive the tractor and focus the big light on wildlife for them to see. Our grandkids, Benton and Bethel's, Jason's, Luther and Essie Mae's, Rev. Billy's, and some kids from our church were on the trailer.

Essie Mae and Luther, Rev. Joseph and his wife were at the produce packing shed. They were getting things ready to make hot dogs and serve soft drinks. And Luther had the sticks ready for the kids to roast wieners or melt marshmallows over the fire.

Luther and Essie Mae, I thought, *would live to be a hundred.* They were about the same age dad and mother were. There was no way they would miss being up there with those kids.

I was trying to get everything ready for Thanksgiving dinner. The pecan and sweet potato pies were ready. I had boiled the ducks, got the meat sliced and ready for Wade's gumbo, and my cornbread dressing. I had the broth ready for the dressing. But mother thought grandma DuPree was right, bake the cornbread the day you make the dressing.

Wade called it duck gumbo. It was more or less a red tomato soup, with lots of onion, celery and bell pepper in it. To that he added just a little rice, the sliced duck breast, and used seafood seasoning made in Louisiana.

We would have to fix those squirrels tomorrow. Wade was just like daddy. He never thought it was Thanksgiving unless you had squirrel.

Uncle Kevin and family, Wade's sister and family were coming. Uncle Harry would not come, he never had. I called Mary Ellen, but she said her kids and grandchildren were fixing dinner there at her place. She sounded so weak and feeble.

Luther came to Wade before dad's funeral. He never wanted to bother me he said. But Mr. Robert had handed him his Old Timer pocket knife. Luther said he told him to put it by his right hand in his casket when he died. He wanted to know if he should.

Wade told Luther if dad said put it there, then do it. He would tell me about it.

Luther put the knife there when he walked by. Mary Ellen was crying when she walked by to look at daddy. Then I saw her smile. She took a knife just like dad's out of her purse and laid it besides the one Luther left.

I had done all I could to get ready for tomorrow tonight. They were probably eating their hot dogs by now. I got the bottle of Tums out of the cabinet and set them on the bar. Wade would eat hotdogs and he would come in looking for them.

I had been putting something off since mother died. When Wade took me to the deer stand last week, I realized putting things off was not always the best thing to do. I think Wade knew that. He lost his mother and daddy a long time before I did.

After mother died, dad brought me the old trunk she had that belonged to her grandmother. And the old pedal type sewing machine her mother had. It was not a "Singer" but bore the "White" label. I had more room in my office, so I had Wade put them in there.

People that came in always noticed. Some offered to buy them, other just wanted to talk about them. They called them antiques. Although Wade kept the old sewing machine oiled up and it would sew, I had an electric one and I never used it. The trunk, well, I had never looked inside it.

I got the key to the trunk and went into the office. I turned the light on and rolled my chair over to it. For the first time in my life, I opened it up. I took out a big tin can and set it aside. It was one of those old tin cans popcorn once came in. It was full of pictures, I knew. Mother sometimes took that out and let me look at the old pictures.

I opened up a shoe box. It contained three pairs of baby shoes. I remembered two of the pairs as Benton's and Bethel's. The third black patent leather pair must have been mine. Tears came into my eyes when I looked at those shoes. Mother had so little when I was born. Yet she found a way to put shoes on my baby feet.

I picked up a stack of embroidery things. Some mother did, some maybe her grandmother did. Here was one I tried to do. Mother tried to teach me. But I was not a very good student. There was so much outside I was more interested in.

I picked up a cigar box that seemed to contain things her Uncle Sam had given her. Inside was a faded post card. It was post marked London, England. I could not make out the rest of the date, only 1943.

Dear Margaret

I've made it across the big pond to London in England. I would not trade the Marsh at home for the Atlantic Ocean. It's rumored here we'll be leaving for North Africa soon. I remembered your birthday is coming up. I just wanted to wish you a happy one. Tell everyone I'm doing fine and will write as soon as I get time.

I love you all
Uncle Sam

1943. Mother was born in 1936. She must have been seven when she got this card. There were some patches with stripes. Mother said he was a sergeant. The square one with three blue stripes must have represented the third division. Mother said he served under General Patton.

The heavy medal shaped like a star. This must be the Bronze Star mother said he received. All the other things to pen on his shirt, I never knew what they meant.

I took out another larger box. It contained a family bible going back to mother's great grandparents who came to Texas in 1856. Inside the box were mother's and dad's marriage license. My birth certificate, and those of Benton and Bethel. And the picture of her standing with Daddy on that horse. She had that enlarged after we moved to Livingston and we all had a copy.

I was about to put everything back in the box. I saw one more thing laying in the bottom. It was neatly folded and inside a plastic bag. I picked it up, looked at it and begin to cry again.

I knew what this was. I also knew I was the only living human that would know. Mother told me about it the day we went into town to shop before Wade and I had our first date.

Mother was trying to prepare me for my wedding night. She told me that I had been conceived in a myrtle bush hideaway dad had built in the woods. After they had did it, she was bleeding a little. Daddy cut the tail off his old blue-gray shirt and gave it to her.

That night, when she took her bath in the tin wash tub in the kitchen, she washed it out. It never got the red stains out, but she hung it on the bedsprings under her bed to dry. She had kept that piece of blue gray cloth all these years.

I put the plastic bag with that blue gray shirt tail into my house coat pocket. Then I put everything back in the trunk and locked it. Wade and the children should be coming in soon.

The kids were excited when they came in. They had seen lots of deer. A big hog with baby pigs. One bob cat and a bunch of coons. Then a pole cat came right down the road. "Mr. Batise turned the light out until it left."

"Were you afraid when he turned the light out?"

"No, I had hold of grandpa's hand!"

"Did grandpa eat any hot dogs?"

"He told me not to tell you!"

"You kids come go with me." I put the girls in one room and the boys in another. They had brought sleeping bags, they would sleep in them.

Wade was fumbling around in the cabinet looking for the Tums when I came back to the kitchen.

"The Tums are on the bar, Wade."

"I'll be dog! If they had been a snake they would have bit me!"

"How many did you eat?"

"Eat what?"

"Hot dogs. How many did you eat?"

"Oh, hotdogs. I ate two."

"I would have probably had a couple myself. They are better burned and with ashes on them it once seemed to me!"

"Did you get all your cooking done?"

"Everything I could. I have your duck ready for you to make your gumbo. We can finish in the morning. We better get to bed. It's getting late."

I got up at my regular time and put the coffee on. Wade would get up when he smelled that.

I went out in the garage, slipped out of my house shoes and put on a pair of rubber boots I kept there. Wade got them at a feed store in Lufkin. They were made for women and looked a lot better than the ones he kept on the back porch. I got my little hand trowel I used in the flower beds and headed out to the cemetery.

The grass was covered in a white frost and the sun was just beginning to show in the East. My feet would get cold, but I was not going to be out here long.

The smell of hickory was heavy in the air. Wade had been smoking that bagged sausage for almost a month now. He said it would be ready by Thanksgiving. It was like him to wait until the last minute, let it smoke as long as he could. We needed it for breakfast, and he put about a half pound of both kinds in his gumbo.

The cemetery gate was cold in my hands. As I turned to close it, I saw Wade going across the yard to the smoke house. I saw him glance my way, but he went on to the smoke house.

He had not even buckled his belt. I could see the big silver buckle I gave him years ago sticking out. His shirt was not tucked in, and he had on his rubber boots and his old hat.

Yet he still had that look I loved about him. Like the Marlboro man! I don't know why we all thought that. We both smoked a Winston when we were kids and his made him sick! As far as I knew, he had never smoked another cigarette.

I turned and started to mother and dad's grave. A Wood Thrush almost flew into me. It was still that early and yet not completely light. I think it scared the bird more than it did me. It looked like it did a back flip leaving me.

I got down on my knees between their footstones and started digging a hole with the trowel. I started to cry again. Cold tears were running down my face and I was talking to them both.

"I hope you like what I had engraved on your headstones. The Acorn Man and the Flower Woman. That's what a lot of people called you."

The sand was soft and I soon had a hole dug about a foot deep. I took the plastic bag out of my house coat pocket and dropped it into the hole. In it, was the old blue-gray piece of cloth that had once been dad's shirt tail.

I wiped my face with my arm and felt the sand and tears mix together. The tears began flowing again.

"The two of you were nothing but kids yourself when I was conceived. This piece of cloth belongs with you two. Not me or anyone else! Wade and I are not that far behind you. We'll be joining you in a few years."

The hole was filled with sand now. I began to pat it down with the gardening trowel. "The two of you were just kids when you fell in love. But nobody ever had a better father and mother than I did. Rest in peace. I love you!"

I got up and started to the gate. An owl hooted in the distance. I stopped to listen. That owl was in that big oak tree where Wade decorated Luther's dogs that time. I think William Bethel named that tree. He called it the Grandfather Oak. Because it stood so much taller than all the other trees.

Another owl answered. I knew one would. It was in one of those black walnut trees up at the orchard and produce field.

I started on to the gate. I had been so blessed to live in a place where I knew ever sight and sound. Not long ago I remarked to Wade that everyone we knew up here had a good marriage that lasted.

"Yeah, I've thought about that," he said. "There's something about living here in the shade of these oaks that causes people to love and be faithful to one another."

I put my hand out to open the gate and it opened for me. Wade was standing there. I could see his concern for me in his eyes. He put that concern into words.

"Is everything alright now, baby?"

I could not answer just yet. I put my arms around him, turned my head to the side and laid it against his chest. He put his arms around my shoulders and his chin in my hair. He was doing the best he could, I knew. He had a bag of sausage in each hand. We had held one another like this thousands of times.

We never counted. But it was a form of communication. Our way of saying, "I'm here for you, I need you, and I love you."

After a moment I pushed myself back. And did my best to look up at him with the smile he said captured his heart more than sixty years ago.

"Yes, everything is fine now. I think I finally found the right place to end daddy's book."